The Pagan House

Also by David Flusfeder

Man Kills Woman
Like Plastic
Morocco
The Gift

DAVID FLUSFEDER

The Pagan House

FOURTH ESTATE · London

First published in Great Britain in 2007 by
Fourth Estate
An imprint of HarperCollins*Publishers*
77–85 Fulham Palace Road
London W6 8JB
www.4thestate.co.uk

Visit our author blog: www.fifthestate.co.uk

1

A catalogue record for this book is
available from the British Library

ISBN-13 978-0-00-724962-6

Typeset in Palatino by Palimpsest Book Production Limited,
Grangemouth, Stirlingshire

Printed in Great Britain by Clays Ltd, St Ives plc

All Fourth Estate books are printed on Lettura Recycled paper with Blue
Angel environmental accreditation from the Hainsberg Mill in Germany

Blue Angel is one of the world's first and most respected
environmental accreditation programmes. This high-quality
recycled paper, made from 100% post-consumer waste, has
been manufactured according to stringent controls.
For more information visit www.blauer-engel.de

It was really quite disturbing. Was his personality changing? Was he losing his edge, his point, his identity? Was he losing the vices that were so much part of his ruthless, cruel, fundamentally tough character? Who was he in the process of becoming?

Ian Fleming, *Thunderball*

I met 'Edgar' at a creative-writing workshop I run each summer at a working-men's college in London. It's a week-long course, which attracts the usual, predominantly female, mix of hobbyists, memoirists and needy, bored neurotics. The few men who attend usually have a high-concept idea for a thriller that they are convinced can be developed into a multi-million-dollar money-spinner, but which they won't talk about at first because they are anxious that their idea might be stolen—and then, of course, when their reserve has melted away, they'll talk about it in stultifyingly intricate detail. There's probably one student each year who shows some genuine talent. Last year, it was a Bengali community worker from the East End, who was very beautiful and poised. In a private tutorial she wanted to discuss whether the *Kama Sutra* strand in her novel should be eliminated, kept in or expanded, a discussion that maybe blinded me a little to the overall strengths and weaknesses of her project. She was the youngest member of the class. It's invariably the youngest and the oldest students who are the most inter-esting, and this year the youngest was 'Edgar'.

Edgar was an unlikely-looking writer of historical fiction. He was very pale with a strong jaw, short, reddish hair and startling blue eyes. He wore modish skin piercings and studs, heavy boots and an antique black suit with a long frock-coat. He was initially resistant to me, even quietly aggressive. He always spoke quietly, which made the people around him listen harder. Something I said in a workshop, I can't

1

remember exactly what it was, it might have been about the difficulty or impossibility of writing about the past—we are not they, their world is different from ours so how can we presume to know what was in their minds and hearts?— won him over to my side and, on the third day, he found me in the pub around the corner from the college where it was my habit to look through the students' work that would be discussed in the following day's seminar.

He sat with me and didn't interrupt my reading and when I was done we drank beer and exchanged a few pleasantly rude remarks about some of the other members of the class. And then, predictably, he asked me what I thought of his stuff.

– You don't like it do you? he said.

– That's not true, I said. It's a bit mannered and there are a few things I don't quite get, but actually I do quite like it. All the same, I'd have expected Marjorie or Gwyneth to be writing historical fiction, not you.

– But it's not.

– Not what?

– It isn't historical fiction, he said, very earnestly and unironically. It's the story of how I came to be me.

And then he gave a little self-mocking laugh and went to the bar to buy us each another Guinness. He came quickly back to the table to ask if I could spare some money as he didn't have enough. I gave the few pounds to him willingly because the manner he had when asking for money made it seem like a kind of favour he was bestowing on the giver.

We drank more beer and he asked me some slightly flattering questions, which I answered more honestly than I usually do, and in return, but not because I was being polite, I asked him about himself. He talked for a long time, the pub went through several generations of drinkers around us, until he said he should be getting home, his friend would be worried about him. I was surprised by his use of the word *friend*— it was spoken in the way people use when they're being discreet about the sex of their boy- or girlfriend, and he had been entirely, sometimes unsettlingly, candid with me up till then.

He asked me if I would read more of his stuff, as he called it; he had some with him. This is something I'm often asked when I'm teaching and which I always turn down, claiming lack of time, the need to be fair to other students, but which in Edgar's case I was interested to accept. My heart sank only a little when I felt the weight of the brown padded envelope he pulled out of his bicycle bag.

Most of what we had talked about related to a particular period of his early adolescence, which he had spent in a place he had revisited the previous year, and I wondered if what he had just given me was more overtly about himself than I had read in his work before, and that made him laugh in his careful way that seemed to identify humour with truth, and say,

– No, that'll be your job.

ONE

Edgar in Creek and Vail, 1995

1

Edgar, taking precautions, left his bedroom. He walked light-footed to the kitchenette, squeezed past the suitcases in the hall, shut his eyes, pushed open the door, strengthened himself with a whisper of his new name to himself, and stepped in. Instead of the hoped-for bachelorish solitude, the leisurely pleasures of a weekend breakfast, his fastidious senses were greeted, confronted—affronted—by the sight, sound and faintly sour smell of Jeffrey.

'Geezer,' said Jeffrey.

'Jeffrey,' said Edgar.

Jeffrey often used the word 'geezer'. He used it in a matey way. It was one of his newer affectations, picked up from an approved-of hipster student, Edgar suspected.

'I'm going to make some toast,' Edgar said, speaking slowly, concentrating on keeping the pitch of his voice level and squeak-free.

'Go for it,' Jeffrey said.

It had been meant as an invitation. Edgar liked to be courteous, especially to people he disliked. He made some toast for himself and some for his mother, who had yet to emerge from her bedroom. If Jeffrey were not here, Edgar would take Mon's toast in to her. But Jeffrey was here, and that made his mother's bedroom foreign territory. Edgar compromised by preparing the toast as Mon liked it, un-buttered, with freshly cut peach slices laid neatly across, and left it on a plate by the kettle. He ate his own toast, which he had thickly spread with butter and marmalade

7

both, and contemplated the shape of his day, which, unlike most, was filled with possibility.

He tried not to look at Jeffrey. Sometimes it was impossible: his attention would be drawn to the loathsome fascination that was his mother's boyfriend. Jeffrey was wearing a baseball cap. He wore it ironically.

Jeffrey was in baggy blue jeans and black polo-neck jumper, heavy black-rimmed glasses that he often pushed to the top of his insubstantial nose; his head was shaved, but when he removed his cap the pattern of his baldness was still evident, like a join-the-dots puzzle of something horrible. His feet were bare and hairy and there was a dull metallic ring around the little toe of his left foot. Edgar had a particular distaste for the hair on Jeffrey's body. One day, thought Edgar, mouthing the shape of the word 'Edgar' to the shiny creased top of Jeffrey's bare head, this man and my mother will have an argument and I will never have to see him again. Edgar examined his heart for the possibility of any future good feeling or sentimental regret towards Jeffrey and failed to find any. He wondered what the terminal argument might be, perhaps a lapse of taste on Mon's part that Jeffrey would find unforgivable; perhaps—and this was the least likely—she would, with the help of Edgar's insights, finally see Jeffrey as he really was. Edgar concentrated on making the picture of Mon's face in the aftermath of discovery, but the face kept melting away because the sounds that were coming from the CD player were particularly annoying, even for one of Jeffrey's choices.

Jeffrey smiled his ironic smile at Edgar, who nodded, curtly, and Jeffrey stretched and his jumper rode up, so Edgar was shown the line of hair that poked up out of the waist-band of his trousers.

Today Edgar was going to America, and that event was

a big one, and not just because Jeffrey wouldn't be there, and Edgar wished there was more to do to prepare for it— vaccinations, or some kind of training programme, or at least a stab at the learning of a foreign language. He had argued that a new suitcase was needed, but Mon had demonstrated to him that it wasn't. And anyway, he now realized that Jeffrey would probably have muscled in on the expedition, because Jeffrey had very strong opinions about most things, including, no doubt, luggage.

Jeffrey had perfect taste. He knew the right music to listen to, the right book to be carrying, the right bobble hat to wear, the right toilet paper to put in the bathroom (Edgar had once heard Jeffrey in instruction of Mon: *'But never put the roll of paper on a holder'*). Jeffrey was always adamant, and ruthlessly correct, about his opinions and tastes, especially so as he changed them often. He loved them so much he wanted to keep them new.

Edgar went to the fridge and daringly drank some orange juice out of the carton and inadvertently caught Jeffrey's eye.

'Geeeezaah!' said Jeffrey.

Edgar nodded. 'Excuse me,' he said, and went to the bathroom, which had a door with a lock on it, and which he had come to think of as a kind of adjunct to his own bedroom, a sort of windowless conservatory. In the bathroom he may relax.

Edgar didn't like to be taken advantage of. Nor did he like to be surprised by things. Recently he had been alarmed by the reddening of the skin beneath his arms. He lifted an arm to inspect beneath and fancied he spied the pinprick crowns of the first crop of underarm hair. He would hate to be polluted like Jeffrey, the naked swirls of hair that surrounded pink nipples, the womanish rise of his breast. Edgar squeezed his chin to his shoulder the better to investigate the site and caught his reflection in the mirror. He twisted his face to make it look even more deformed and stuck out his tongue and gurgled.

'Eddie? What are you doing in there? I need to use the loo.'

'Nearly finished,' he said to his mother, after a dignified silence.

He lowered his shoulders, flashed an urbane smile into the mirror and sprinkled some water on to his hair, which he finger-combed into spiky tufts. His face often disappointed him: it was too revealing, too boyish. Its onset of freckles had appalled him. He wanted the kind of face that hides mysteries.

'Eddie!'

'Coming, Mother.'

Now Monica was annoyed and so was Edgar. Jeffrey had the knack of making everyone annoyed around him. Edgar had often argued that when the loathsome urge to spend time with Jeffrey overcame her she should do whatever she had to do at Jeffrey's flat rather than theirs. For one thing, Jeffrey's flat was larger. Edgar's mother had said that would mean leaving Edgar by himself, as if this was something bad, a curse rather than a blessing. What did Mon see in Jeffrey? Or was the answer to that to be found in one of those areas which it would be wise not to look into too deeply? Or did Jeffrey have some secret hold over her, a hypnotist's snaky lure, mind control?—and Edgar, just through an excess of distaste for some of the acts that adults were compelled to perform with one another, had been doing nothing at all to protect his poor mother.

Edgar sat on the closed toilet seat. He instructed his face to be friendly. If there were dark secrets to uncover it was Edgar's task, no, stronger than that: it was Edgar's *duty* to do the digging. He was, as he was sometimes reminded, the man of the house. His father would tell him so, a routine pleasantry on one of their occasional telephone conversations. His mother would tell him so too, but never without some degree of wonder and humour. Edgar narrowed his eyes to shrink his field of vision to a movie frame. Then he quickly returned his face to a smile again.

What information did he require? The secrets of dark Jeffrey's heart. The dark secrets of dark Jeffrey's heart. The dark secrets of dark Jeffrey's dark heart—the wailing madwoman beating on the locked attic door; the money swindled from the academy that had been intended for the needy purses of African students hungry for Jeffrey's lectures on the secret signs of westerns, the critical theory of motorway service stations; the art treasures he had smuggled out of Russia; the heartbreaking sex-slave victims he had traded out of eastern Europe on one of his supposed 'conferences'; or maybe it was the corrupt circle of friends he should find, Jeffrey's intimates, the pin-striped politician, the loathsome friar, the toothless woman who flounces her skirts, whom Edgar had shipped over from an adjacent part of his imagination and whose image now caused the beginnings of a process that he couldn't allow to continue towards its inevitably disappointing consummation because his mother was shouting his discarded name and beating on the bathroom door. Edgar buckled his shorts over his rebellious groin. He had been subject to much rising and lowering recently, an embarrassed boy popping up half bridges. It wouldn't be so bad, but there was nothing that this led to. He was aware, at least in a textbook sort of way, of the stages of the process, and he knew that the climax should coincide with a release of fluid. But he released no fluid. And experienced no climax. Just a blind gasping at the head of his (roughened, rawed) penis of what he had not been able to decide should be designated an eye or a mouth.

11

'ED-DIE!'

'Just finishing up.'

Perhaps there was a void within him, an emptiness that corresponded to where others contained sluicing reservoirs of stuff, of fluid, life-force. While he, the pipe within him tapped down merely to some absence, not even an empty chamber, this was a void that was empty even of itself.

'And about time too,' his mother said, when he opened the door.

Carrying his fixed smile, he returned to the kitchen, where he aimed it at the wall, at Jeffrey, at the two narrow windows, at the deflated football that was a legacy of a failed Jeffrey attempt to *bond*, at a standard lamp, and quickly to his toast. He did not want to alert Jeffrey to his vigilance. The trick, he was sure, was to convince his enemies to underestimate him.

'What's up, geezer?'

'Nothing,' he quickly said but then realized he had spoken defensive-aggressively, his customary tone, Shut-Out-Jeffrey, and anyway he could afford to be expansive today, because today he was flying to America, and his mother would be with him and his father was waiting for him and Jeffrey would be left three thousand miles away.

Edgar looked at the itinerary, which his mother had remembered to print out on her office computer. *Friday: fly to New York. Change planes. Syracuse airport. Saturday & Sunday: time with grandmother Fay. Monday: Mon to New York; Edgar and father on the road. Tuesday—*

'Oh,' said his mother. 'Toast.'

'I made it, actually,' said Edgar, who wrote himself a mental note not to speak always so precipitously, better to allow loathsome Jeffrey to take the credit for his mother's breakfast and then watch it rebound or be snatched away afterwards. Silence and cunning would be his watchwords.

'Thank you, darling,' said Mon, who was sitting at the counter in her ironic pink 1950s housecoat that she never bothered to wear unless Jeffrey was staying over. She chewed complacently on a triangle of toast and reached over to the refrigerator to pour herself a glass of orange juice and unwary Edgar failed to avoid the complicit wink that Jeffrey sent his way. Mon ate her toast and flicked through a magazine, one that Jeffrey had brought into the flat and which Edgar, when he was sure he was alone, did not find it beneath him to inspect.

'Here's a piece about that Japanese photographer you like so much.'

Jeffrey sniffed. He did not like that Japanese photographer any more. Mention of that Japanese photographer would elicit only scorn from Jeffrey. This had happened before, it would happen again; Jeffrey was slippery and quick to change in all his enthusiasms. When Mon naively said, 'Oh there's a piece here about that Japanese photographer/Australian performance masochist/Canadian poet/ American lesbian you like so much,' Jeffrey would already have, contemptuously and self-congratulatingly, moved on.

Edgar smiled to outface the world. Defiantly he mouthed the shape of his new name. Edgar was twelve, soon to be thirteen, and his name was not in fact Edgar, but Edward. Edgar was a preferment he had recently awarded himself, so far secretly. Edward and all its variants and diminutives (Ed, Eddie, Steady Eddie, The Edster) had long been unsatisfactory or loathed by him. Edgar he took as a graceful-sounding name, gently archaic, hinting at past glories, shadowy marble buildings behind vines. The creator of Tarzan was called Edgar; so was the writer of *The Tell-Tale Heart*.

'The private-eye genre,' said Jeffrey, 'what is it about?'

They were sitting in the living room. Soon the minicab

would be arriving to take mother and son to Heathrow. Edgar's earphones were on his head and he drummed along to the music on the coffee-table even though both adults had asked him not to. Surreptitiously he lowered the volume. Here, in this temporary victory, he did not want to lose any advantage by relaxing his vigilance. He continued to drum as if he were still listening to his music but instead he listened to Jeffrey rehearse tomorrow night's lecture. Mon, once his student, wanted to please her teacher. She offered suggestions. 'It's about truth,' she said, 'it's about justice, the American Way; the private eye is a bruised Galahad in disguise, Christian myth transubstantiated, the good man in a godless world.'

Jeffrey looked bored throughout. He examined his hands and picked away dirt from beneath his thumbnails. The only time Jeffrey was interested sufficiently to look at his audience was when she said *bruised*.

'Bruised? More than that,' said Jeffrey. 'Damaged. *Impotence* is what it's about. Who's the precursor of the private eye? Of course the cowboy heroes of the western, but mixed in with some Hemingway. *Fiesta*, the narrator who's been damaged in the war, who can't get it up, who will never be able to consummate anything.'

'Jeffrey!' warned Mon, who could get oddly prudish sometimes in the company of her son.

'Please,' said Jeffrey with pained expression.

'Sorry,' said Mon.

She pushed back her hair, which was red. She was wearing a leather jacket that creaked and which Edgar had suggested would be uncomfortable and hot to wear on the airplane, a black T-shirt and a long black skirt. Edgar was wearing what, after some very long time, and for which he had even consulted Jeffrey, he had settled on as his appropriate American outfit of long shorts, stripy

14

short-sleeved shirt, sneakers and baseball cap worn backwards. He winced at his mother's determination to please Jeffrey and Jeffrey caught the expression so Edgar turned it into the music-lover's appreciation and drummed harder.

'Hemingway,' prompted Mon. 'The narrator who's been damaged in the war.'

Jeffrey glanced at his notes and consented to continue. 'He can't get it up. He'll never be able to consummate anything. That's where the private eye comes from. The mood of melancholy, yearning, frustration. He can't please a woman, can't satisfy any of them, not the blowsy blonde overripe tramps, not the rich men's daughters who are driven by his disregard into lesbianism. So he's got to walk in shadows. He's got to drink to quieten some of the self-pity inside of him. Being beaten on the head by the buttside of a revolver brings him some kind of temporary release. But he's lost, finding a dark path to get revenge on some of the *whole* men in his pathetic universe. If he can restore some of the order in the universe, maybe he can repair some of the disorder inside himself. But of course not, it's a doomed quest. Some men have died, some women have suffered. The law is temporarily satisfied, but not our damaged hero. He's alone, because he has to be, drinking himself stupid in his melancholy office.'

. . . But not Edgar. Edgar was the very antithesis of the generic private eye. He was neither hard-bitten nor hard-boiled. He hadn't seen too much—he'd hardly seen anything at all—and he was bursting, overflowing, with inaccessible juvenile potency.

Some conventional techniques of the traditional private eye were denied to him: he could not, for example, sit at a bar drinking whiskey. But he did have certain advantages all his own. He could blend into any crowd, particularly one of schoolchildren. No one would suspect him of a dangerous agenda. But he could not drive a car. And he still needed permission to stay out past supper-time.

2

Edgar liked airports. He liked airports and flying and pretty much everything connected with flight except birds, which brought out his squeamish side in some primitive way. He liked airplanes and he even liked the word 'airplane', with its airplaney shape, the *a* of the cockpit, the *p* and *l* of transverse wings. Mon didn't mind airports in themselves, just what they represented. They contained shops and Mon liked shops, but these ones were signs of imminent flight and Mon did not like airplanes or flight. She was, as she told the weirdly cosmeticized woman at the check-in desk, a nervous flyer.

'Don't worry, Mrs . . .' at which point the cosmeticized woman sneaked a look at the passports.

'Ms,' corrected Mon.

'Excuse me. You're in very capable hands. Would the young man like a window seat?'

The young man in question was blushing because he could see down the shirt-front of the check-in woman, her cleavage, the rise of her breasts, freckled and tanned, and his immediate response—or, even, quicker than immediate; as if the response might have preceded the stimulus, might, in some magical way, have induced it—was a stiffening of his penis followed by a necessary cupping of hands over his groin to hide the tell-tale bulge. Pressing himself against the desk was no good, because, in these difficult times, he had discovered that any contact, even for purposes of concealment, and with a material as uninflected with erotic value as veneered chipboard, would only exacerbate his aroused state.

'The young man takes what he gets,' said Mon, severely but playfully, as if she was enjoying the possibility of being a different kind of mother. 'We'd like to sit next to an exit door.'

'I'll see what I can find,' said the check-in woman, whose search could only fail because she had already, Edgar noticed, printed out their boarding passes. Her search ended, predictably, in briskly acted disappointment and Edgar, who did indeed want a window seat, was allocated one.

Waiting to board, they played their favourite game.

'You know, I've been thinking about the hall,' Edgar said, quietly drumming with pen and pencil on holiday puzzle book.

Mon shook her head. There was probably a Valium inside her to take the edge off her fear, slow it down to a sluggish thing, but still enormous and impossible to evade.

'You know, the fireplace?' Edgar asked.

She tapped her chin lightly with a lipstick case, smiled bravely, and was ready to join in.

'What colour *are* Dutch tiles? Blue, or blue and white?'

'Blue and white,' she said. 'But we don't have to have them.'

She had failed to interest him in tiles before, which was why he had brought them up now.

'No it's fine,' he grandly said.

The departure lounge was full. There were families here and couples, and babies that screamed, and a boy with a computer game whom Mon had tried to get Edgar to introduce himself to.

'Inlaid into the floor and around the fireplace itself. They're very expensive, though, so we might have to leave that kind of thing to last. I'd like to get the library in order first. What's the matter?'

She had caught him frowning. Edgar was not sure about the library. He had alternative plans, a snooker room, where he and his father, in matching black waistcoats, should solemnly apply chalk to the tips of their cues and with all the emphatic restraint of beloved comrades congratulate each other on their shots.

'I thought we might have a snooker room.'

'We've got a games room already.'

'Yes but it needs to be separate. You can't have pinball machines and noise and things in a snooker room. It's not, you know . . .'

'Appropriate?'

'Yes.'

Even if she was laughing at him he didn't care. He had lifted her mind away from their flight and he enjoyed this sort of conversation hardly less than she did, their When-We-Move-To-A-Big-House game.

'I've decided to wood-panel my bedroom,' she said. 'You can have your bedroom panelled if you like.'

'No thank you.'

'Too proud?'

It has never been discussed where his father might sleep—start him off discreetly perhaps in one of the guest rooms, let things develop from there. Edgar's father could watch his sports through the night on the Sensurround TV set. He was, no doubt, not above playing computer games. He could make his telephone calls, to Nice and Los Angeles and New York and Las Vegas and Accra and Nairobi and Casablanca. Swim by moonlight in the pool. Edgar had wanted to telephone his father before they left the flat but the understanding was that he waited for his father to call. If Edgar ever did try to telephone his father, it was to numbers that no longer existed, or else a woman answered, who would call Edgar by the wrong name and tell him that his father was on the road.

'The pool.'

'What about the pool?'

'Can it be P-shaped?'

She smiled with indulgence and permitted it to be so. He wanted to be able to see it from the sky, the initial of his surname, a blue suburban monogram.

'I need a proper garden,' she said.

'I know.'

'A walled garden, with places to sit, stone benches, maybe a fountain, and a vegetable garden and a herb garden, and you'll need somewhere to play football.'

This was one of Mon's fantasies that sometimes he benevolently allowed her, that Edgar was a typical boy who enjoyed the usual pleasures. He pictured the garden, its straggly long grass that would be his responsibility to cut, where he would go and lounge with his friends, if he had any. Edgar wondered when he would take up smoking. Soon, perhaps. That was the sort of activity that takes place in long grass. He sometimes saw Jeffrey smoking, standing on a chair, blowing smoke out of the top frame of Mon's bedroom window.

He had to learn how to hide his thoughts better. He must have been wearing a Jeffrey face, because Mon was inspecting him and saying, 'You're going to have to let Jeffrey in.'

'In? Where? I thought he had a key.'

'You know what I mean.'

'Do I?'

'You know how much he likes you.'

She often said this, as if it were both true and argument enough. He did not believe it to be true. Even if Jeffrey was on record as saying this (which Edgar doubted) it would only have been to curry favour with Mon.

20

'He always says such nice things about you, he really likes you, he does, it's like a brotherly thing, but while we're on the subject it might be just as well if.'

She looked away, squinted nervously at a suavely tanned, gold-braided pilot pulling his hand-luggage through the departure hall on shiny wheels. Edgar was fascinated. There was no coyness or played intrigue in Mon's manner. She was actually finding it difficult to finish her sentence and Edgar was curious to know where it would resolve.

'Might be just as well if what?'

'If. If you don't talk about Jeffrey, there. When you're in America. At your grandma's. Or with your father.'

'Why?'

'It just wouldn't be appropriate.'

'Appropriate?'

'Please Eddie. Just indulge me. Trust me on this. It would be better if, people, over there, didn't know about Jeffrey. That's all.'

'That's all?'

'I really would appreciate it if you'd stop repeating everything I say.'

'Everything I say.'

'Eddie!'

There were times when Edgar knew not to push his mother, even in fun. He relented. 'Okay,' he said. 'Sorry.'

'And about this Jeffrey thing.'

'You want me to lie for you.'

'It's not lying. No one's going to ask you if there's someone I know called Jeffrey. I'm just asking you not to bring the subject up, that's all.'

'O-kay,' Edgar said, more warily than he felt. He was happy to put Jeffrey behind them. He liked the idea of being on a continent where Jeffrey did not exist, where the fact of Jeffrey was strictly to be denied, where the very condition

21

of Jeffreyness, of *being* Jeffrey, of *knowing* a Jeffrey, were causes for secrecy and shame. He admired America all the better for it.

'And I promise you a P-shaped pool, and there'll be lots of trees,' she said, reaching for him in an old familiar way, cradling him so his head rested on her shoulder. 'You used to love to climb trees when you were little.'

'Did I?' Edgar had no memory of tree-climbing and was sceptical.

'An apple orchard. I'll make you apple sauce every week and I won't forget the cinnamon.'

'You always forget the cinnamon.'

'I won't forget the cinnamon. What's the matter?'

'It's fine. I'm fine, Mummy,' he said, reverting at this moment when he felt at his most adult to an honorific long abandoned. The woman from the check-in desk, who was, frankly, hideous, had just gone by and the merry wave she gave him had lifted his penis hard. He closed his eyes, primly averted his head from his mother's shoulder as he tried to find an unerotic image to hide her behind, and cupped his hands over his groin.

'I know something's going to go wrong with the arrangements. You can never depend on him,' Mon said.

'I'm going to listen to some music now,' Edgar said. He put on his earphones and, with his Walkman protecting his lap, pretended to slumber.

'What,' Edgar asked his mother, 'did you think you were going to be?'

The airplane was taxiing across the runway, delighting Edgar with the prospect of its speed. His mother gripped the armrest and asked him to keep still. Perhaps brutally, he had passed on the first of his two most interesting airplane facts: that for the first thirty-two seconds after take-off the pilot had no control over the plane and if anything should go wrong . . .—and here, Edgar maybe oversold the idea by crossing his eyes and cutting his index finger across his throat. But now he felt contrite and had decided to spare her the other of his interesting airplane facts and was trying to take his mother's mind off things in a way that would be satisfactory to them both.

'Or maybe what you wanted to be. When you were young, a child I mean.'

Mon made an attempt at a smile that showed the newish lines at the corners of her eyes that Edgar thought of as her Jeffrey lines. She had kicked off her shoes. Her toes wriggled in discomfort. Their cracked nail polish was a lighter shade of red than her hair.

'I don't know, Ed. A fashion model, a doctor, the usual kinds of things. I don't know.'

She closed her eyes, the better to remember or invent herself as young, or just to hide, from Edgar's questioning, from the impending fact of flight.

'You know that if anything's wrong you can call me at Hen's.'

Edgar was flicking through the channels. He felt himself to be too old for the children's TV and the children's films. He didn't care for action movies.

'Nothing to go wrong,' said Edgar, who believed this.

'I'll be with her a couple of days. They're bringing the lunch trays around.'

Edgar turned his head to look at the stewardesses. Edgar liked the stewardesses. In fact, he liked everything about this flight. He liked the metal clasp of the seat-belt, the flaps that opened and closed on the wing, the heavy thrum of the engines, the blue tartan of the carpet, the overhead lockers, especially the one across the aisle that had been poorly secured and had emptied itself after take-off on to the head of a burly man in a business suit. And he liked the food they brought. He inspected it upon arrival partly in appreciation and partly because he knew that otherwise he would stare too much at the shape the stewardess made when she retrieved the meal trays from the lower shelves of her trolley, her legs together, her spine perfectly straight. And the touch on his arm from the back of her skirt when she bent to ask the burly man whether he would prefer chicken or beef ranked as number four in the most erotic moments of Edgar's life.

'Imagine,' he said to his mother, after he had finished his lunch and eaten some of hers and was waiting for the film cycle to begin again, 'if the plane caught fire, or the engines fell off. How long do you think it would take until we hit the sea?'

'I don't know,' Mon said, looking away into the perfect blueness of sky.

'You could guess. It wouldn't happen straight away would it? Do you think it would be A, two minutes, B, four minutes, C, eight minutes, or D, none of the above?'

'I really don't know Eddie.'

'Then your answer must be D, none of the above.'

She didn't answer. She was looking queasy. It would be good for her to be away from Jeffrey, if only for a few days. The horrific idea that she might already be *missing* him was too grotesque to consider.

'Which is in fact the right answer by definition because we're over the ocean, not the sea. It was a trick question,' he added apologetically. 'But I think the real answer's eight minutes, actually. Do you think they would know?'

His mother was performing her foot and ankle exercises. She extended her toes and revolved each ankle in turn and ignored him. Edgar leaned his chair back more abruptly than he should have, because it cracked against something, the knees he thought, of the divinity student sitting behind him, who yelled out a curse, and Edgar quickly said, 'Sorry', and pulled his seat forward and climbed over his mother and into the aisle.

He would have liked to go into a toilet to further test the void inside him, but the toilets were all full and he didn't want to queue just to prove, again, his incapacity, and anyway the plane had started to bounce and dip, which he enjoyed, standing by the emergency-exit door, a surfer on the waves of turbulence, until a woman's voice came over the intercom asking all passengers to return to their seats. He walked backwards along the aisle up to his row, past passengers who had blue blankets pulled up to cover their faces, as if when they slept all air passengers aspired to be female Muslims.

'Old people get into a routine,' his mother said to him on his return as if he had never been away and they had been having this conversation throughout, and Edgar wondered if maybe they had, if, thoughtfully or deceitfully, he had learned to leave part of himself, his boyish unsexual part, in this seat while the rest, the future part of him, had gone into the world to explore.

'*Older* people I should say, because your grandmother, I don't know, has always seemed so very much alive. She does a lot of volunteer work and charity and things like that. She always had very enlightened political views, which is rare in that part of America. Your father was a big disappointment to her.'

Edgar frowned. He did not like to hear either of his parents being criticized by the other, especially not his father by his mother because she found it so easy to do and because she was so obviously right. It seemed to Edgar that the easier and more obvious it was to do something, the better it was not to succumb to the pleasure of doing it.

'But what I mean to say—you *are* listening to me aren't you? What I mean to say is that you're going to have to be thoughtful, considerate. Staying in someone else's house requires adjustments. And the younger you are the more considerate you have to be. We have responsibilities as guests.'

Edgar supposed his mother was right, but he resented it all the same. She took for granted all the *adjustments* that he was required to make, and did make, without announcing the whole fuss of it. He would not allude to any of that now, because he didn't wish to compromise his own nobility of nature, but the gruesome sights of Jeffrey stretching on the sofa and the hair on Jeffrey's feet and his silver toe ring were all in his head now and he didn't know how to get rid of them.

'Stop shaking your head like that. I'm right. And close your mouth. It makes you look stupid.'

Tears of outrage were not far away now. Thankfully, his mother responded to the heightening of his mood with a softening of hers.

'Oh Eddie, I'm sorry. Let's not be bad friends. I'm a nervous flyer at the best of times and going there, you know, when I used to, your *father*.'

She opened her arms for him to wriggle through and even though he was bigger now than when they used to perform this kind of manoeuvre, and both of them were wearing seat-belts, they managed it, and the smell of her reminded him of Sunday mornings before Jeffrey.

'I wish I still smoked,' she said, and before Edgar could point out that even if she did she still wouldn't be able to do so on board the plane, she had yawned, promised him a snooker room, stretched, and announced her intention to sleep.

Edgar, *whee*! He was loving it, in this plane, sipping a Virgin Mary, chewing peanuts, looking out of the porthole to see his own reflection bounced back with clouds. The noise that had been surrounding them throughout abruptly cut out—and the effect of the silence on Mon was to wake her up, startled: she gripped the armrest and Edgar watched with what he would call an investigator's dispassion the tightening of her fingers, the whitening of her knuckles, the wrinkling of her skin.

'It's okay,' she said, hoping to reassure him and therefore herself.

'I know,' he said.

He knew too that she wanted him to hold on to her hand, to give her the power to protect him, and usually he would allow her this, but not this time, even if it caused him a pang of pity and self-reproach: he was not above punishing her for her transgressions.

The cabin lights flickered off and weakly on and off and on again, and each movement from light to dark to light was accompanied by a collective cabin-gasp of all the passengers, *ahhh!* and *O!*, and Mon gripped the armrest tighter and merciful Edgar relented: he held on to her hand and settled into the contact as she pulled his fingers tight. Her eyes were closed and her head was back and a vein pulsed in her eyelid and blue lines stood out in her throat, and the plane dipped and lurched and Edgar was enjoying himself. People all around them made rearrangements with blankets and head-rests, and the stewardess reminded them again that the captain had requested that all seats should be in the upright position and infants strapped to a parent or caregiver, and now there was rising the sound of babies crying, nothing too startling, just the discontent of children baffled at being woken from sleep and fussed over, and the burly man from across the way loudly shouted, '*Miss? Miss?! What IS going on?!*' and it took a while for Edgar to realize that the high keening note in the theological student's voice behind him signified anguish, and that the ache in his ears meant that the plane was no longer bouncing but had been losing height, perhaps drastically, and that was why everything was tilted, and glasses and miniature bottles of wine were rolling down the slope towards business class; the mood in the cabin was changed and something very bad seemed to be happening.

'*Miss! Miss!!!! MISS!!!!*'

The stewardess was sitting below them braced in her chair, talking into a mouthpiece, her hands stroking each other.

'Would everyone please return to their seats.'

Edgar straining heard her pleasant voice. Mon hadn't moved or opened her eyes. Her hand gripped his more tightly. He tried to pull his hand away because it was hurting, but she had it and was not letting go. He tugged harder and all he achieved was a tiny choking moan from his mother. The ache in his ears was hardening into pain. The lights were lost again, and in the dark Edgar heard incompetently stowed tables clatter open, the thuds of surprised flesh, petulance now in the sobbing group-noise around him.

The lights came on just as an overhead locker opened, spewing out ribbons of clothes, bottles of duty-free liquor in corrugated-cardboard jackets that clattered off seat-backs and rolled clumsily down the aisle. The divinity student started to pray but lost the thread of his words until all he was saying was, '*Oh oh oh oh, oh God, oh God, God, oh God, oh oh oh, oh God, oh God, oh . . .*'

Edgar viciously pushed his chair back against the student's knees but the litany continued unaffected. '*Oh God oh God oh God oh God, oh oh . . .*'

'Oh my God,' Mon said. 'The plane's going down.'

It was as if she had just realized it, and maybe she had. Edgar had been imagining the moment of impact: would the airplane bisect the water?—cutting through to the depths, past startled schools of fish, coral reefs, sunken galleons, mermaids' treasure, dead men's bones, down into darkness, bumping blind to a final stop on the ocean bed, the port-holes bend with the enormous pressure and then burst, an insane hydraulic gush, the divinity student's dull features washed away with the power of the water that somehow, miraculously, a benevolent corkscrew, picks up Edgar and twirls him up, pops him out into the air, the climax of a foun-tain—or would the plane somehow glide to the surface, bob along there on the waves—why else would they have been talking about life-jackets and life-boats and whistles and take your shoes off before you get on the slide? Was there an allowable moment of escape before the 747's weight took it slurping beneath the water, the frightened pilot saluting behind the glass because, nobly, he has stayed at his controls till the last . . . ?

Mon's eyes were open. She stared at the awfulness of her end and his, *their* end, he supposed; he had heard her say it often enough, that a mother mayn't think of herself any more as a free agent separate from her son, and the fat-legged stewardess was fixed to her seat and to her smile, despite the pleading of an Arab woman who was inexplicably showing the stewardess the naked chest of her infant; and several generations of orthodox Jews had taken a place up high at the rear of the cabin where the seat-backs held them in position, angled swaying with eyes closed, chanting through their beards, and Edgar wondered whether they were pleading with God to intercede here or just smoothing their own paths to Paradise; and the burly man across the way was busy removing his clothes—his business suit was off now and his shirt and his underpants, and he sat there in his tie as if he needed to meet his end almost as naked as when he had experienced his beginning; and others were making their own accommodations and most of these involved screaming or tears, but Edgar, entirely calm, knew exactly what he had to do and what he now might be able to do but he couldn't do it with his mother beside him.

'I need to go to the toilet,' he said.

Mon nodded, plaintively hopeful eyes—this will save us, yes? This toilet, this going-to-the-toilet of yours? But she clearly didn't understand what the words meant: she was waiting for his or anyone's magic trick of slipping the future back into their lives.

'I have to go to the toilet,' he said.

He clambered over his mother, clasped her shoulder as he went past, and climbed up the slope to the toilet.

Oxygen masks swung in the air. Supper trays slid past, slapping chicken and beef curry against the sides of seats. The burly man was reading the in-flight magazine, resting it on the hairy rise of his belly. The couple who had kept banging into Edgar at the duty-free shop, pushing bulky hand luggage into his shins, swinging plastic baskets against his ribs, were kissing, breathing heavily, her legs folded beneath her; Edgar could trace the blue lines of veins below her khaki shorts, the red blood-holes left behind by shaving. The ginger-haired man who had kept going to the galley for more cans of beer was sobbing. An elderly couple demurely held hands. The game-playing boy from the departures lounge was watching a horror film on his screen. Edgar briefly watched beside him—wolfman transformations, cracks of lightning, high-breasted girls running up and down stairs—until the boy, annoyed at his privacy being invaded or maybe his technology being shared, curtly leaned in front of the screen, blocking Edgar's view.

These were the last moments and it was surprising to Edgar that so many chose to spend them weeping. It surprised him too, as he continued to labour up towards the toilet—if anything, the angle had got steeper, each step harder to make—that he was so bent on privacy. He did not want to intrude on anyone else's end, but neither should an unnecessary, outmoded now, sense of propriety keep him from what he needed to do. The rise of panic all around him transferred somehow to a feeling of well-being close to exhilaration and the minutes left to him were few and he did not want to spend the rest of his life climbing.

Edgar ducked into a bank of seats that was tenanted only by a woman sleeping, untouched by the clamour, her knees drawn up under a blanket, her mouth lightly open, her eyes hidden beneath a sleeping mask.

'*Purr*-fect,' Edgar said, in his best whispery movie-villain voice, just as a trolley broke free of its moorings and lurched rattling past down the aisle. He heard a thud, a cry, and that would have been him, but he'd made it, he unzipped his trousers and settled down to his task.

There was no reason for modesty. Privacy was finished here. In the last moments there can be no rules. Edgar, masturbating, felt finally free.

He shut his eyes. High-breasted girls rush up and down stairs. The check-in woman lasciviously unbuttons her shirt, but that image was replaced by an imperishable one from his first trip to this country: a woman at a motel door, who sleepily pushes hair away from her face. She's wearing a man's shirt, his father's, unbuttoned. Quickly he pulled in an image from a magazine of Jeffrey's: two Japanese women naked below the waist, one in a white T-shirt, the other in black, sit on a hospital floor, boxes of medical supplies behind them.

Edgar became reconciled to death—oblivion, obliteration, extinction—with each back-flick of his knuckles, each pull of his fist. In death there is life and, he supposed, vice versa. The plane was going down and his pleasure was rising and something was new. It announced itself with a roar, wild, mannish, beyond images real or imagined; the void was filled and he was ferocious, bursting, overflowing; the sound grew from deep in his throat and rolled out into the lamenting world of this doomed airplane; he squeezed tighter, and, despite all the tears and furies and beseechings of God and wretched inconsolation, it was the sound that he was making that stirred the sleeping woman beside him. She shifted in her seat. She lifted her sleeping mask. His eyes met hers, which were blue, and blank at first, sleepily unfocused, then surprise registered in them, climaxing in horror at his state.

'It really doesn't matter,' he said, to reassure her. 'We're all going to die.'

He kept rubbing, long, quickening strokes leading to something inexorable, but he managed to smile sociably at her at the same time. He tightened his fist against the hardness inside, and yelp, something new, something novel, something glorious was happening, and it was happening right now.

His eyes were open but they couldn't quite focus, because what was taking place was too grand for vision: his penis was the centre of it and it was almost too sensitive to touch but he couldn't not touch it, couldn't stop touching it, grabbing it, brutally rushing his hand up and down it, and he didn't know if he could bear this any more but if he was going to disintegrate then so be it, and up and out it came, jerking, pulsing out of him, milking jerky fluid, spattering the seat in front of him, and this was a better feeling than anything. In his last act he has truly accomplished something. He has proved himself. He has discovered his capacity.

When the plane pulled out of its dive Edgar was still smiling, sitting legs apart, his trousers and underpants around his ankles, his elbows on the armrests. In front of him globs of jism slid down the TV screen, and the passenger beside him was holding her throat, which must have been hoarse by now as she continued to scream for cabin staff.

At the baggage carousel at Kennedy Airport he aimed to keep his mother between him and the screaming lady, who had been treated with the remaining sedatives and subsequently firmly and politely ignored.

'What *did* you *do* to her Eddie?' Mon asked, and Edgar looked innocent and said a shocked *'Nothin'!'* and smiled, hoping to imply something of the infinite weirdness of the world, the bottomless peculiarity of other people. He tried to find a view out of the baggage hall but the only windows were mirrored, and he knew that there would be further to go before they were allowed into the arrivals hall, and he knew too that his father was unlikely to be there, arrangements and handovers were seldom straightforward where his father was involved, but that didn't matter so much, the world has been changed—and when the screaming lady realized that or when the wreckage of her throat finally gave out, he might be able to hear his name being announced on an airport Tannoy or, maybe, through the next door or the next, he would see his name on a white card being held up by a benevolent chauffeur in uniform.

'Eddie?'

'Nuthin'!'

He felt a suspicion lingering in his mother's mind and perhaps others' that the fat-legged stewardess might have been a little too quick to push accusations away; but when the engines had come back into life and the plane lifted into cruising height again, there had been so much pressing upon her, reluctant doctors to gather to make repairs to bruises and breaks, tears to soothe, complimentary champagne to distribute along with a printed list of airline-approved stress counsellors through the crush of insistent lawyers intoning, *'Compensation.'*

Anyway, a compact had been silently made. Passengers who had been bandaged and patched leaned on trolleys, chewed gum noisily, laughed to show that they were ready for re-entry into their changed world. Something extraordinary had been shared and it was over and certain things were private and didn't need to be talked about, and he was respectful of that and his mother ought to honour it too. The burly man was wearing his clothes again.

The conveyor-belt stuttered into motion, and Edgar, jaunty in his freedom, in his maleness, hiccuped the unpleasant sip of champagne back into his mouth and lifted one foot to rest on the metal lip of the carousel until a blue-uniformed airport woman shook her head and said, 'Sir! Could you step back?' And Edgar was so pleased to be called 'sir' that he did as he was told.

3

By the time that Edgar, the aficionado of flight, announced
that the small, jittery plane that they had taken from New
York to Syracuse was coming in to land, Mon's skin had
turned yellowish white with the exertions of the day, with
the effort of keeping airplanes in the sky with the power of
her will.

'It would be nice if someone was there to meet us,' Edgar
said.

'Fay won't be up to that kind of thing. And your father
always leaves everything to the last minute. We'll have to
make our own way.'

But they were met, by a self-possessed man in pressed
white jeans and blue T-shirt, who was scanning the faces of
the arriving passengers. To Edgar's great pleasure and silent
promise of friendship he held up their names, correctly
spelled in neat capital letters on a white card.

'I'm Warren,' he said. Warren had short dark hair and a
lightly tanned skin and the manner of someone who did
things well. He shook their hands and steered their airport
trolley out towards the car-park, while others from their
flight stood hapless in the arrivals hall, opening and closing
their fists; and Edgar, enjoying how important he and perhaps
his mother must be seeming, endeavoured to look sternly
businesslike.

Warren drove them out of Syracuse in a wood-panelled
station-wagon. He was friendly and polite and informative,
speaking in a not-quite-American accent. He neither ignored

nor talked down to Edgar, who was allowed the privilege of the front passenger seat while Mon half dozed in the back. It was all very easy and adult and civilized, and Edgar turned to look at his mother from time to time just in case she had not noticed the disparity between this man and Jeffrey.

Edgar, more tired than he would choose to be—but after all, he had experienced much and accomplished something truly grand this day—drifted in and out of Warren's commentary. The heat made wavery lines out of everything, the financial towers and bridges and billboards and roads, the fields of corn, the toll-booths, distant blue hills, and it all looked bigger than he was used to, which was what he had expected, but he hadn't expected to feel smaller too.

Warren smelled of pine and lemon and cream. He looked straight ahead while he drove, both hands on the steering-wheel, the air-conditioning vent blowing the dark hairs on his arm to stand soldierly straight. Edgar cleared his throat. Warren glanced his way. Edgar had said nothing so far on this journey, just nodded every so often to show he was listening. He had to say something now, no matter how banal; he had to speak, push his voice into America.

'We thought we were going to die,' Edgar said.

Warren's eyebrows rose. 'Oh?'

'The plane went into a dive and kept going and it looked like we were going to crash and everyone thought we were going to die. The big plane. Jumbo jet. The one we came from London on.'

'Wow. A near-death experience. That's the sort of thing that changes a person,' said Warren.

'Yes. I think so too,' said Edgar.

Warren had kind eyes. He was very well shaved and his skin was smooth. He drove carefully, without show. 'We're coming off the thruway now,' he said. 'That was the interstate. We're on three sixty-five now. Not far to go.'

'What's that?'

Edgar pointed to what looked like an artwork from one of Jeffrey's magazines. By the side of the road, surrounding a dark wooden shack, four large men in shorts and T-shirts sat impassively on garden chairs with guns on their laps.

'That's the bingo hall. It's run by the Onyatakas, the local Indian tribe. It's pretty small-potatoes stuff, cleaners going there to gamble their money, welfare checks. It's a sad state of affairs. They want to build a casino but no one thinks the Governor will let them.'

'Does my dad know about that?'

'I don't know, Eddie. I couldn't say.'

'Is he at the house?'

'Uh, not yet, I think he might have been delayed a couple of days, but I'm sure you'll enjoy your time with us.'

Monica stirred and yawned and stretched. Her leather jacket that she had been using as a pillow creaked. 'God, I needed that sleep. Where are we?'

'We've just come off the interstate.'

'There's a bingo hall. It's run by Indians. They carry guns,' Edgar said.

'You're not meant to call them Indians. Isn't it First Nation or Native Americans or something?' said his mother.

'This tribe calls itself Indians so it's okay,' Warren said, and winked to Edgar. 'We're on the road to Onyataka.'

They drove through small towns, past fire stations and sports fields and boxy suburbs where everything was green and white and red, as if people here lived in a perpetual Christmas.

'Where are you from, Warren?' asked Mon.

'I'm from Ireland, more or less Dublin but not quite. But people out here, I might as well be from South Africa or Australia or the moon.'

'We weren't actually expecting to be met by anyone.' In

her habitual arrogance she had awarded herself the right to speak for Edgar. How could someone so supposedly close to him not see the change in him? 'Are you a neighbour of Fay's?'

'No actually, I live there. With her. In the house.'

'Oh?' said Mon in her suspicious tone, her voice going thin and accusing. Edgar hoped Warren hadn't noticed the rudeness.

'Has she not said? I've been there some time. Help out a bit you know. Muck in. She's a lovely lady.'

'Yes. She is.'

'And I know how fond she is of you. Of *both* of you,' he added.

Mon did not like to be flattered. Edgar knew this, Warren clearly did not. They drove on in silence, into the town of Onyataka (*Onyataka welcomes careful drivers!*), and Edgar started to pay attention. This was a bigger place than he had been expecting, there were theaters here and a cinema, the expected fire station, the unexpected sex shop; a drunk stumbled into a boarded-up store window but kept his beer can steady throughout in its brown-paper bag, and a pet shop, a video store, and—*Onyataka hopes you come back soon!*—they were out of town again.

'I thought . . .' Edgar said.

'What's that, Eddie?'

'That we were, that my grandmother, lived in Onyataka.'

'It's the nearest town, for postal purposes that's where we are, but actually we live a few miles along, in Vail. The towns of Creek and Vail. You'll see in a few minutes.'

Creek, which announced itself to be the smallest city in New York State, welcomed careful drivers no less than Onyataka. It was met by Edgar through half-closed eyes. This was not how he had intended to arrive, sleepily unalert; he forced himself to notice things—a restaurant, a factory, a pizza parlour, a gas station, an office-supplies store, white wooden houses whose front gardens, or *yards*, he supposed, were open to the pavement where bicycles lay down—

'There's a farmer's market out back there on Thursdays,' said Warren.

'That's good,' said Mon.

—a video store was neighbour to a doctor's office and a bookshop, none of which looked open; an impeccably healthy gang of teenagers in jeans and grey sweatshirts lounged in a corner of a baseball field.

'You'll like it here, Eddie. There's lots of life. Kids and trees and parks and so forth. Do you play soccer?'

'Not really.'

'Of course he does,' Mon said. 'God, it's so long since I've been here and the place hasn't changed a bit. Time just stands still, doesn't it? Isn't that the Company headquarters? That's where your grandfather worked.'

They passed an ornate, low-slung stone building topped by turrets, which looked as if the architect hadn't been able to decide whether to build a castle or a bungalow so had invented some unworkable compromise between the two.

'Did my dad work there as well?'

Mon didn't say anything. She scoffed silently, as she usually did when her ex-husband was mentioned in the same sentence as money or work.

'I don't know, Eddie. He might have had a holiday job there when he was young. Most everybody here has worked for the company at some time. It's a company town.'

'Company town,' Mon repeated, in a sort of wistful voice, and Edgar could tell she had been smitten with the same sour nostalgia or sentimentality that connected to those moments in London when she stayed up late looking at old photographs, playing records and drinking bourbon.

'It's got a very interesting history, the company. Creek was where the workers lived, the managers lived in Vail. It all grew out of the Onyataka Association. Nineteenth century. But you must know all about it, Monica, through Mike, Perfectionism, free love, Utopia.'

'Mike didn't go in for history tours. And I don't think Perfectionism would ever have been one of his interests.'

Warren laughed politely to indicate that he had noticed a joke had been made.

'And here we are. Here's the house now.'

'I've always liked it. Look, Edward.'

Edgar looked. He too liked the house, very much. It could be drawn very simply, as two intersecting triangles with a horizontal line at the top for the roof. Blue-painted wood with white shutters and weird little carved heads whenever a pipe went into or popped out of the wall, weathervane and TV aerial and a chimney behind each of the gables, it accorded to his idea of what a house should look like. It was the house he had tried to draw when he was a young child. It was the house he furnished when they played their game.

Warren opened the screen door for them. The front door had been left hospitably ajar. They walked along the hallway, past a curving staircase, black and white photographs on green-papered walls, to the kitchen, where an old lady was in the unsteady process of rising from a chair.

'Fay!'

His grandmother, whom Mon confused with a kiss on both her cheeks, was grandmotherly small and white-haired, in a blue print dress.

'If I remember you, Monica, you'd like a cup of tea after your trip.'

Her voice was clear and youthful, her face a rivery marvel of lines, which shifted and twisted and showed new tributaries when Mon said how well Fay was looking. Her eyes were blue, like Edgar's.

Edgar made up for the confusion his mother had wrought with a candid smile and an English gentleman's firm hand-shake.

'And Edward. You look *so* much like your father, you know. Would you like a chocolate milk, or are you too grown-up for that sort of thing?'

Delighted at being identified as looking like his father, Edgar replied that, yes, he would love a chocolate milk and, no, a straw would not be unwelcome, and after Warren had brought in their bags, he made the tea and poured Edgar a glass of chocolate milk, which Warren suggested and Edgar agreed was the perfect thing after long plane and car rides in the height of summer.

Fay took them on a tour of the house, which passed slowly, because she needed to sit and rest at least once in every room, and Edgar, unconsciously, until Mon pointed out what he was doing and made him too embarrassed to continue, would position himself behind his grandmother's shoulder, like a servant or a guard.

Edgar had been given the sleeping porch whose ceiling and outer walls were made of glass. It jutted from the house at the back, looking over the rose garden.

'We thought it might be fun for you to sleep here,' Warren said.

'Warren has moved out into Frank's room.'

'We're so sorry to have put you to all this trouble.'

'It wasn't much of a move,' Warren said.

'He cleans up after himself. He's very tidy,' Fay said, and Mon looked meaningfully at Edgar to remind him of his house-guest responsibilities.

In the corridor, Fay sat on a chair after failing to make it quite to the picture window.

'On a clear day you can see all the way to Onyataka Depot.'

'Oh,' said Mon.

'Good,' said Edgar.

'You can see the Company building from the corner of the window. The Administration building, not the factory. That's in Creek, of course. And across the way is the Mansion House. They have regular tours. I'm sure you'd find it interesting.'

'I'm sure I would,' said Edgar, politely unconvinced.

'But tell me, what would you fancy doing in your time with us?'

The wording of the question intrigued Edgar in its imputation that he might operate in a world of fancy rather than necessity. It supposed an alternative Edgar, foppish, with a butterfly mind, who went where things took him, who carried a battered brown-leather suitcase covered with faded stickers of faraway countries and who might even own a unicycle that he had disciplined himself to ride. The real Edgar was driven by imperatives. Imperative number one was to further investigate his capacity the first chance he got. This was not a subject to share, except he was looking forward to a moment of companionship with his father when he might somehow imply his new state, maybe eating burgers at a lunch counter, men of the world together, two guys.

'I'm not sure,' said Edgar.

'You only have to say. Supper will be in the kitchen. Warren has put out towels in your rooms. I'm so glad you're here.'

Edgar, in the bathroom, splashing water on his hair and pulling it casually into spikes, listened to his mother and grandmother in the corridor.

'Who *is* Warren?' his mother asked. 'How long has he been here?'

'I don't know where I'd be without him,' said Fay.

When Edgar went downstairs—after lying on his bed and

flirting with his capacity, which he abandoned and zipped away when he heard footsteps going past into Fay's room next door; and after gazing out of the window and wondering what Onyataka Depot might be and whether he would be here long enough to make the acquaintance of the blonde girls strolling past, who looked so unapproachably healthy and complete; and after sneaking into his father's old room to run a finger along the spines of the science-fiction paper-backs in the bookcase; and after looking into the Music Room to examine some of the record albums, the glowering 1970s faces—Mon and Fay and Warren were already in the kitchen. His mother was wearing a black T-shirt with red Asian script printed on it that Edgar hadn't seen before. Her hair was hidden beneath the turban of a bath towel. A large ginger cat snored in a basket by the stove.

'What do you think of the house?' Warren asked.

'It's really nice,' Edgar said, somewhat gruffly, because he preferred his voice to err towards brusque manliness rather than the shrill castrato it sometimes became.

'You must be exhausted,' said Warren. To which Mon was about to protest but stopped when she realized that he was talking to Fay, who performed her astonishing smile again.

4

Edgar awoke in light. Foreign dusty smells, his penis gripped hard in his hand, the taste of night and linen in his mouth. He encouraged this moment of utter unfamiliarity to stretch, with him growing inside it—and that first, good, moment was succeeded by one even better, when he remembered where he was, a new-found place.

At home, he would hear traffic in the main road, the groaning of water-pipes, the drone of his mother's radio on those days that Jeffrey wasn't staying over, all the rumble of a London morning. Here, in Vail, there was birdsong outside and frogs croaking, and a rustle of leaves, all of which were delightful at first and then unnerving. The dawn light pouring through the glass walls and ceiling of the sleeping porch made the room seem shipboard, the sky turned to sea. He stayed in bed, stretching, yawning, waiting for the voices and clatters of a usual day or the reassuring sound of his mother, until hunger drove him out in search of food.

Edgar, starving for carbohydrates and fruit juice, in his new chinos and T-shirt, stepped out on to the landing. He had expected the business of the morning to be transacted all around him but he seemed to be the only one up. There had been voices; now he heard only the creak of the corridor floor under his feet, the squeak of the stairs. On the ground floor he could walk more freely and soon was joined by an imaginary companion, a mincing European, maybe Italian or French, could even be Spanish, who wore flamboyantly long white sleeves with lace ruffs and carried a clipboard and assiduously noted down all of Edgar's instructions.

'I think we'll need to move the kitchen from here to here,' Edgar said commandingly. 'And the bathroom, of course.' He felt a slight pang for both rooms, which had done him no harm, but he must be ruthless, make his stamp of ownership plain. 'And I think we'll lower that ceiling and raise that one, and maybe that floor ought to become that wall, and do you think two indoor swimming-pools are too much . . . ?'

He paused, tilted his head, cocked his ear, allowed space for his flouncy architect-designer to offer his highly cultivated, overpaid, artistically considered response, which lordly Edgar merely brushed aside—

'. . . or not enough at all?! I want four swimming-pools thank you very much. Ha! And I want a snooker room *they-ah*, and a games room *they-ah*, and my father will be in his study, there . . .' and here Edgar lowered his voice, squeezed his chin flat to his chest and waddled as if he were the fattest man in the world into his grandmother's living room, narrowly avoiding the early-morning boy-trap of a wire magazine rack, '. . . and here, and *here-ah*, what are we going to do? Hmn? What are we going to do with you? What in the world are we going to do with you? What in the whole—' Edgar shot a nervous look around before continuing '— fucking world are we going to do with you? What do you think, Alfonso? What's your *considered opinion* now, my friend? Answer me Alfonso. Answer me, right now! Oh God, I'm so bored with your ideas, is that what they teach you at the Sorbonne? You're fired. That's right. Fired. I shall draw up the plans myself. Goodbye.'

The rejected architect-cum-designer threw himself on his ex-employer's mercy. He was losing all dignity: he cajoled, threatened, pleaded, he wept. He poured down curses on

Edgar, then repented, blessed him, his family, his mother, who reminded him of his own, after which ensued a long impossible-to-follow story set in a hillside village, involving a donkey, two gypsies and the winter wind, and Edgar had had quite enough. This display, quite frankly, sickened him.

'Enough! Alfonso! Please. Remember you are a man.'

Edgar made his heart hard and turned his face away and went back to the kitchen, and the broken Alfonso crawled after him, still weeping, his suede jeans smeared with dirt from the floor, his black curls tumbling, his white bullfighter's shirt ripped.

Edgar poured himself a glass of chocolate milk from the refrigerator and downed it in one thirsty morning gulp and poured himself a second, which he measured against his fingers and sipped slowly from, contemplating his day.

'Edward.'

'Good morning, Mother.'

Mon looked at him sharply; she mistrusted Edgar at his most formal. She opened the refrigerator, withdrew from it an apple and a bowl of pineapple chunks, which she assembled on top of two slices of white bread in an approximation of the breakfast she ate at home. After a couple of mouthfuls, and an expression of dismay at how much sugar had been added to the pineapple, she was ready for conversation.

'Who were you speaking to?'

'Nobody,' Edgar said, quickly and surprised, before guiltily remembering the corpse of Alfonso that lay in the hallway, his clothes grubby and bloodied, his unbeating heart clutched forlorn in his hand, an unwanted offering that he had held out as his last dying hope.

'Why are you looking so shifty then?'

'I'm not looking shifty.'

'You're looking shifty. Do you know what time it is?'

This was a familiar technique of his mother's, to follow

one question quickly with another, unrelated, one. It kept people on the back foot.

'No. What time is it?'

'It's a quarter to six.'

'Oh really? It's a nice day isn't it? Did you sleep well?' Edgar asked, nimbly using his mother's devices against her.

'Jetlag,' his mother grimly said.

They breakfasted to the rumble of Tom the cat snoring in his basket. Edgar ate toasted English muffins with butter and ham. He drank orange juice. His mother drank tea. They briefly speculated as to why English muffins were thought to be English, and Mon said English usually meant something sneaky in this country, and she broadened the topic to include the very unFrench phenomenon of so-called French toast and then they returned to silence. The day could turn out to be a long one but he didn't care; this was the leisurely part of his American trip, here in this fine house, submerged by the agreeable fog of jetlag, waiting for his father to come.

At lunchtime Mon had been after him to show some enthusiasm as a visitor when the telephone rang. 'I think we'll take a walk around the neighbourhood after lunch. Explore things. I'll show Ed the Mansion House.'

'You wouldn't mind getting that, would you?' Warren was at the sink, his hands full with a colander of cooked spaghetti that he was splashing with olive oil. He was looking at Edgar when he said that, who stared blankly back, because Edgar didn't like to use the telephone, and Mon took the call before Fay could finish making her preparations to leave her chair.

'Yes,' Mon said to the telephone, and as the conversation went on Edgar watched her expression change from patient to pleased.

Warren brought over the food. 'Would you like a Kool-Aid?'

'Yes please,' said Edgar, wondering what it was he had said yes to. He hoped it wasn't a piece of sports equipment. But Edgar felt expansive; he would take whatever the world offered him.

'I might be going to New York a little early,' Mon said.

'Oh?'

'That was Hen. It's all very boring but it would be more convenient if I went there a little earlier than planned.'

His mother looked both stoical and frenzied. She pushed the salt cellar between her hands and stared at it in surprise when it fell over.

'I can't do it. Your father's not even here yet. And your birthday . . .'

'He'll be all right with us, won't you, Ed?' said Warren.

For something to do, Edgar brushed at sleeping Tom's fur until he became aware that ginger clumps of the stuff were coming away in his hands.

'Ed?'

'Yes. Of course I will.'

Nonetheless Edgar was alerted. Being here motherless was not unattractive, but Mon's mood was both wilder and more discomfiting than he was used to. Perhaps it was torture for her to stay in this house, everything here a reminder of her failures as a woman and a wife, but that was a betrayal of him, who would never have been born without this place.

Edgar tried to pat the cat fur back into place. Tom's only signs of life were the shallow rises of his chest to accompany each noisy breath, and the little rivulets of effluvia that leaked out of his face.

'That's so sweet of you to try to groom him,' Fay said. 'A lot of people would see him as a lost cause and they'd be missing the point completely.'

'I've put her numbers on the pinboard. That's her work number and that's her home, and I'll call you after I get there.'

'When are you going?'

'Well. If you're sure. I could go in the morning. It's a real bore,' Mon said.

She sighed, hoping to indicate some of the boredom she purported to feel, but Edgar knew better. A small overspill of the curious excitement that was going through her seeped over to him.

Warren delivered a glass of some watery red liquid, which Edgar sipped at and found delicious.

'Your father will be here tomorrow,' Mon said—which was, Edgar observed, the first time she had given this up as an undisputed fact.

'Yes, *he* will,' Edgar said, pursuing his advantage.

'You can call me if anything goes wrong.'

She moved over to hug him and rub his hair. He accepted the hug, stiffly, and pulled his hair back into its proper spiky shape, adding a few stray hairs of Tom's to his own.

'Oh Eddie.'

She might have been about to weep. Fay reached a hand to her. 'You mustn't worry about a thing,' Fay said.

'I'll run you to the airport in the morning,' Warren said.

'That's so nice of you. I don't want to be any trouble.'

'It's no trouble.'

The rhythms of the Pagan House were based around meal-times, and Edgar was required at supper that night.

'I think it'll be amusing for both of you. Some of the local personalities will be here,' Fay said.

'Company Bob and so forth,' Warren said.

'I'm sure,' Mon said.

Edgar followed his mother up to her room and watched her pack. He tried to get out of supper but Mon was at her most ruthless: 'This is my last night here. It'll be horrible if you're not around.'

'I'll be around. I'll be upstairs.'

'You absolutely won't be upstairs. You'll be at the dinner table. It's far too rude otherwise.'

'What would be just rude enough?'

She clicked her tongue and jerked her chin, she gave him her exasperated 'Oh, Eddie!' look and checked again that her passport was in the side-pocket of her handbag. 'Please get ready. Change your trousers. Wear your good ones.'

Edgar lies on the bed and Edgar scratches. From the wall by his bed he lifts away the damp flap of wallpaper—navy blue, golden stars—and finds another layer of wallpaper beneath. It might once have been cream or white but now is aged urinous yellow, with washed-green cartoon stencils of amiable little rocketmen in large transparent helmets hardly smaller than the dinky little spaceships they ride in. This might have been his father's childhood wallpaper, glimpses of a happy boundless future, where cheerful little astronauts enjoyed the freedom of infinite flight. This patch of wall is Edgar's own time-machine. Now he sits here, in 1995, damp blue walls, faded golden stars; now he pulls himself into the early 1960s, and there's paper beneath that one, and beneath that one; brave Edgar in wartime touches *trompe l'oeil* pillars; Edgar in the Great Depression wonderingly touches something sickly yellow. And beneath that one is paint, dull brown, which Edgar scratches at with his well-practised right hand, rubbing himself into a further past, white paint, go further, bare pine wood, the original wall, on which a man, the builder, or the architect, or Old Uncle Pagan himself, had pencilled in measurements in a high, confident, sloping hand.

5

Christ charged his disciples not to publish all the truths he had committed to them, in the injunction, 'Cast not your pearls before swine', and on the other hand he forbore to tell them many things which were in his heart, because they were 'not able to bear them'. In his conversation with Nicodemus, he signified that there was a class of interior truths, which he called 'heavenly things', more incredible and unintelligible to the sensual understanding by far than the doctrine of regeneration that Nicodemus made so great a mystery of; that he classed among earthly things.

Paul refers to heavenly things when he says, 'We speak wisdom among them that are perfect.' The Corinthians to whom he was writing, 'were yet carnal'; he could not speak unto them as unto spiritual; but he stirred up their ambition to become spiritual, that they might know the deep things of God. When he was caught up into paradise, he heard 'unspeakable words' that it was 'not lawful for a man to utter'. (I Cor. 2:6. II Cor. 12:4. John 16:12, 13. Rev. 11: 15–19)

Bible Communism, John Prindle Stone, 1844

The stones are hard against the plough. Abram Carter has warned him of the damage that stones can do to the blade of the plough. George Pagan has to keep stopping the horse so he can pick the stones away from their path, digging them out half buried from the soil, his futile harvest, breaking his skin, his fingernails, his heart. Blind Jess at least is docile. She stands, tail swishing, the only part of her that shows any vitality.

Jess waits for George to nudge her back into movement.

The sunlight is fading, sun going down over the blue hills towards Turkey Street. Here, in this pre-Edenic grove, where wild roses grow and cardinals and goldfinches chirp and cheep, mocking his pretensions as a farmhand, George Pagan pushes the frame of the plough and Jess walks on. George steers, trying to make straight furrows; he has to fight to keep the blade at the correct angle. He had not thought this would be so hard: he had imagined himself into a picture of farming, the light fading on the ploughman's noble calling, the soil made ready for the vegetables that would sustain two families and whoever joined them for sustenance of spirit and flesh, man and nature united in creation. It is not the picture he had imagined when he had tired of indoor work, city work and therefore fallen work, no matter how virtuous in intent and execution, the composing and printing and distributing of Moral Reform tracts. He had longed to be in a place like this and had never conceived how brutal it would be to submit to the turning of the earth, the passage of the seasons, God's heartbeat. Here there is no joy, the plough blade turns, scrapes against this dismal earth, the shallow misbegotten furrows; he stops, wipes his forehead with his hand, merely redistributing the sweat and cutting in the sharp grains of earth that have somehow gathered to his skin. In the parlour of the old stone house, the lantern shines more brightly, lighting the scene within. Mary Pagan, George's wife, sits at the table, her black hair falling in front of her face as Abram Carter instructs her in the ways of Perfectionism. George hopes her path is less rocky than his.

He has been told to plough until called upon to stop and he will. Even though he mistrusts Captain Carter's manner— delivery obtrudes its substance: he lacks humility, takes too much pride in the sound of the words in his mouth, the orator's performance, the actor's pleasures—Mary has confidence in the teaching of Abram Carter, and Mary has an instinct for purity, and truth, that George trusts far better than his own. A hand, his wife's, reaches out to the window, and George's heart lifts—here it comes now, the call to finish his labour of the day; he will tether the horse, return the plough to its shed, move back inside to the care and, he hopes, the caresses of his wife. His wife's arm, illuminated, falls across the window like a clock hand; it is a moment of translucence and hope that, he is forced to admit, would not cut into him nor uplift him quite so directly, so purely, had he not exerted himself so greatly through this ordeal of a day. But the arm does not beckon, the window does not open, he does not hear his wife's musical voice calling him in from his toil. Instead, the curtain is drawn, pulled between him and the light and the inhabitants of the parlour.

George Pagan trudges on. Blind Jess trudges on. They have no light to steer by. The plough cuts blindly into the soil; and George Pagan devises an analogy. He is not good at devising analogies—he does not possess an associative or synthetic mind: to him things are as they are, form is form, even if dimly he apprehends the possibility of its transformation—but this is as good an analogy as he has ever framed, this the path of the believer in the fallen world finding his way to sinlessness: the way is dark, the day is endless, the horse is blind, the path is stony; his faith sustains him. George Pagan reaches the end of one furrow. Cumbersomely, he turns to begin another.

George, proud in the aftermath of his labour, and a little vain of his analogy, reports it to his companions after he has walked Jess back to her field and scrubbed some of the earth away from his skin. He sips at the hot, sweet tea that Mary has prepared for him.

Abram Carter, the appointed under-teacher of John Prindle Stone's Perfectionism, slides a finger across the short beard on his chin in the manner he has copied from his master. He

55

nods. 'Yes,' he says, 'this is the teaching that must be lived before it can be learned. The way is hard. But we too are making progress.'

Mary frowns. Something foreign passes across her face. 'Oh, George,' she says. 'You must be tired.'

He is. He hasn't realized just how tired. If it weren't for Mary removing his boots he would have fallen into bed dressed for the plough.

And so pass their days, Mrs Pagan and Captain Carter in reading and doctrinal discussion, closeted indoors, Mr Pagan at work in the field.

Sometimes George imagines a house where he is ploughing. It is a mild and acceptable form of heresy, he supposes. Instead of the field of corn to sustain them, he invents a house, a family home, built in the modern manner, where he, and Mary, and little Georgie, and the future ones, the Pagan tribe, as yet unborn, will grow and thrive in undirected sinlessness.

Tentatively he attempts to report his fantasy to Mary. It is night and he is wretched with the cold, with the dirt of the land, with the dull accumulated efforts of his blind-horse days. They are in bed; outside, the land is dark with night, fruitful for the imagining of his house, *their* house, their future lives free of the doctrinal diligence of Abram Carter. He imagines his wife reading to their children in the parlour, an infinity of playful little Pagan children gathered around her skirts, heeding the soft musical truths of her voice. He imagines the house, its gables, the fires that burn in its grates, the rooms that meet each other across polished wooden corridors; he imagines a love-seat on the porch, a rope-swing suspended from the branches of the sycamore tree. What he fails to imagine, what he is unable to see, is himself in any of these pictures—his family flourishes in the house that he has generously built for them, but he absolutely fails to see himself. Vengefully, he invents a field, a blind, skittish horse, a rusty plough to which he sternly tethers Abram Carter. Returning to the invented house he still fails to find himself inside it.

'Mary?' he says. 'I've been imagining a house.'

At first he supposes his wife to be asleep. Her breathing is light and rapid. She lies perfectly still as does he, even though his limbs ache with the discomfort of the posture he has chosen or fallen into for sleep. It costs him more to shift than to stay as he is.

'Mary?'

He whispers more loudly: something troubles him, her stillness, the quick shallowness of her breathing. She turns away from him. Her voice is muffled by her pillow.

'Oh, George.'

She is weeping. He would like to comfort her but he has never been skilled at that, and anyway his body, tortured by the day, mortified by the plough, refuses him any movement.

'Mary?'

'George,' she finally manages to say, 'I am so happy.'

6

Edgar liked rebel rock 'n' roll and punk rock and primitive heavy metal, loud noises made before he was born by scowling teenagers in leather jackets with snotty attitudes. Edgar liked songs that rocked and then faded out, as if there was no possible ending to them: shut the door, walk away, and the band still plays on: the drummer keeps clattering, despite the awful weight of his arms; the vocalist sings, his futile eyes examining the sealed room for any possibility of escape; the guitarist picks eternally at his guitar, sitting down now, saving his energy, no more wild darts to the microphone stand; the bass guitarist thuds away, fingers bleeding, and the song goes on for ever. All of Edgar's favourite songs faded out. He was suspicious of music that knew how to stop.

Seed-spattering Edgar, singing along to his Walkman, wiped down his grandmother's bathroom surfaces.

Number two. He wondered how old he would be when he could no longer count the number of times he had done this. That would be the end of innocence, he supposed. Edgar worked with flannel and Ajax fluid, cleaning the bathtub with an assiduousness that would have surprised and gratified his mother.

Cheerfully, he gave a second polish to the handrails on the sides of the tub, and enjoyed a pleasant interlude on his hands and knees inspecting the black and white dominoes of the tiled floor, before he banged his head on the brass toilet-roll holder. He returned the flannel to where he had found it, around the stem of the dripping hot tap. He wondered how his stuff might taste. Sickly sweet like breast milk, maybe, which he had sampled at Herman Opoku's house one afternoon after school before their falling-out. Herman had opened the refrigerator door to show the bottles of milk expressed for his baby sister by his mother, whom Edgar had never met and who worked as a hospital nurse when she wasn't expressing breast milk. Like connoisseurs, Herman and Edgar had taken small, considering sips from a bottle, which they topped up with water, scrupulously boiled in the Opoku kettle. Herman Opoku told him that semen tasted salty, like caviar, and Edgar had changed the subject. He did not want to find out how or why Herman Opoku had tasted semen and neither did he want to show how impressed he was that Herman Opoku had tasted caviar. Edgar, or The Edster as he'd been then (pre-Edgar, a previous life), wasn't even supposed to eat the lumpfish that his mother served on blinis with dollops of cream at her vodka parties. 'It's a sophisticated taste,' she said. 'You won't like it. Hands off.'

Caviar and stuff were linking now in his mind. He chose to go with it, imagining a crucial part of the caviar-production process as the smearing of fish eggs with male stuff, an intricate, costly procedure, which was the secret reason why the resulting delicacy was so prized. Perhaps there were men, perhaps there were *boys*, trained, or bred, a family tradition, or *kidnapped* for that very purpose, condemned to a life of senseless erotic drudgery, milked like cows by Ukrainian women in dairy aprons and hats, or connected, in long, dehumanized rows, to machines by rubber hoses and electricity leads wired into the most sensitive places of penis and brain. *Ruuugghghg*. He shivered. He had never liked milk trucks and now he knew why.

A final inspection of the room revealed only one dollop that he'd missed, on the mirror over the sink. Urbanely flicking it away, he rinsed it under the tap and watched it swirl down the plughole. He sniffed his finger, which smelled both salty and sickly, a scent that reminded him of autumn. His mother was calling him, loud enough to be heard over the Walkman.

'Edward!'

'Coming.'

He was happy here and sorry to leave. The bathroom contained but was not cluttered by old person's things, and Edgar found the place delightful. The walls were papered in purple and gold. The ceiling was white. Along the ledge by the side of the bath were medicines and dried sponges and bottles of bubble bath. The window between the bathtub and toilet looked over the garden, where roses climbed over the far trellis as if they were trying to get away, a wooden shed, some plant beds of what looked like salad leaves. Threads of a long-ago rope-swing hung from a venerable sort of tree. In the alcove by the toilet there was an anthology of cat cartoons, a history of the Onyataka Association, and a guide to the flora and fauna of Central New York State. Edgar was unimpressed by the cartoon book, uninterested in natural history; he opened the Onyataka Association book at the place that had been marked. The pages had been much underlined, with pencilled comments in the margins, and a small black-and-white photograph on the page of an unsmiling woman wearing a plain dress over trousers, but Edgar was more, if briefly, interested in the photograph that had been used as a bookmark. It was a snapshot of Warren, with close-cropped hair, standing out of focus on a front lawn with his arm around a white-haired lady who wore a red shawl over her shoulders and, unlike Warren, was smiling. She was, Edgar decided, Warren's widowed grandmother. He saw her as a retired actress, and liked Warren all the better for her.

The sink was deep white. Like the bathtub, it perched on little bronze scaled feet. Edgar switched off his music and looked sternly into the mirror, pressing his chin down against his chest, crinkling his forehead to squash his eyebrows together, and said, most disapprovingly, *'Edgar. Ed-gah! Ed-GAH! I'm surprised at you.'* Then he rolled his eyes and held his breath until he had to let it go.

'Edward!'

'Yes. Yes yes yes.'

Preparing for his return into the social world, the gentleman at his toilet washed his hands, failed to arch a solitary eyebrow, muttered in his fruitiest tone of warm approbation, *'Ed-gaah'*, and vacated the bathroom with his hands demurely in front of his groin, which was when he realized he'd neglected to zip himself back up, and hurriedly did so.

'Did you get lost in there?' Mon said.

'No, I didn't,' said Edgar, with one hand in a trouser pocket discreetly wiping down a damp patch on his thigh.

'Go to the dining room. The guests will be here soon.'

Waiting for their guests, they sat on high-backed chairs. Mon checked the contents of her handbag once and then again while she told Warren that after what had happened on the 747 she didn't know how she would ever be able to fly again, which Edgar thought was a disrespectful way of thinking about the experience. Fay tried to explain to Edgar about how the state governor was doing such a poor job— *The unemployment rate in this region is scandalous!*—and then she and Warren talked about the faucet in the bathroom and time dripped slowly away. Edgar wondered if this was what the prelude to a funeral felt like. He had not been allowed his Walkman. He sat, as slouchily as he could get away with, then got up to read the mottoes and legends in the faded silk tapestries on the walls (*'Braidings*, they're called *braidings*,' Mon corrected him when dutifully he admired them to his grandmother)—*Followed her far and lone/The ways that we have gone* braided in gold below a purple tree, beneath which some kind of Oriental lady seemed to be pursued by a sheep and a lamb, and a town scene, of church streets and high-necked pedestrians following an alarming little black terrier, *See the gay people/Flaunting like flags/Belle in the steeple/Sky all in rags.* When he had tired of that, he invented horrific injuries to the faces in the photographs on the mantelpiece: the square-faced bearded men acquired scything scars, and arrows through their eyes; the still women with their centre partings died horrific deaths with their heads split open by a vengeful woodsman's axe. And time dripped, and Mon told him to come back to the table and Edgar found himself sitting straighter than he would have chosen, and he was far too enervated even to drum.

Fay had said it might be an amusing evening. Edgar doubted this, but the first guests to arrive did seem built for amusement. Company Bob was a vice-president of the Company or a vice-vice-president, rubicund like a clown, loud and aggressively amiable in a checked shirt that clashed madly with his ferocious skin. His wife was a plump woman with red hair who had tented herself inside a white dress. She stood impatiently at the sideboard that held the glasses and wine bottles until Warren poured her a drink, where-upon she sat at the table guarding herself with a quietly angry dignity that seemed there just to be lost.

'We're cousins,' Company Bob told Edgar. 'Through the Pagan side. And I think through the Stone side also. So's Janice.'

'Who's Janice?' Edgar asked.

'*I'm* Janice,' Mrs Company Bob said.

Guthrie, who was the next to arrive, was nicer. She was a spry white-haired woman with brilliant blue eyes that she enjoyed shining on people with an intimately enthusiastic attention. She kissed Fay and told the company that this was *my very best friend*! Guthrie questioned Edgar on the length of his stay and held his wrists to emphasize the *shame* of him not staying longer, and Edgar responded to her touch with a stiffening that indeed shamed him, but which was nothing compared to his response to Marilou Weathers. Marilou Weathers had wide eyes and a prettily thin chapped mouth and pale freckled skin that was redder around her eyes and mouth, and brown hair pulled back into a pony-tail. She entered the room, giggling timidly behind her husband, whom everyone called Coach. Edgar arranged his napkin over his lap and dared to look at her again. Marilou Weathers was tall and wore a big green jumper with the face of a dog embroidered on the front; its eyes protruded by her breasts, its red mouth hanging appealingly open. Edgar had to look away and inadvertently caught the attention of Coach Weathers, who had a tanned skin and sharp features and carried himself like an off-duty soldier, vigilant and coiled. He wore sunglasses and a peaked cap and baggy shorts and a faded college sweatshirt and spoke the fewest words required of him, as if life were a constant test behind enemy lines. His first name was Spiro. Edgar immediately admired and feared him.

'I got to tell you Warren,' Company Bob said, 'we're all totally behind this musical of yours.' The way he said this made Edgar suspect that one of the secrets of adult life was that everyone said the reverse of what they really thought.

'It's an *opera*,' Marilou said.

'That's what I mean. And you've got permission to put it on in the Mansion House?'

'That's the plan.'

'I love history, don't you?' Guthrie said to Mon.

'Just adore it,' Mon said, making Edgar wince, but the sarcasm seemed to pass everyone else by.

'Bob sometimes says that this place has got too much history,' Janice said.

'You can never have too much history,' Mon said.

'That's *exactly* what I say,' said Guthrie.

'Bob doesn't agree,' Janice said.

'It's not that I *dis*agree,' the vice-president said, 'just that you have to separate the business and the personal. All that nineteenth-century lovey-dovey business doesn't sit well with the issues of corporate life.'

'What's the lovey-dovey business?' Edgar asked, getting interested, his imagination providing an orgy of unlikely images that involved office desks on which were mounted bizarre contraptions that screwed into the barrels of telephone receivers.

'What are the issues of corporate life?' Mon annoyingly asked.

'Leadership, responsibility, profitability,' Bob said promptly. He then went through the flatware and silverware on the table, lifting up each knife, fork, spoon, plate and bowl and reporting its provenance. 'Oh, and this is a very nice piece,' he said, weighing a sauce-boat in his hand, which was soon splashed with Warren's béarnaise sauce. 'This is the Commonwealth line, isn't it? Nineteen fifty or 'fifty-one or thereabouts.'

'That's really, really impressive,' Marilou said, licking and then touching her chapped lips, as if she was reminding herself of a secret.

'Oh I don't know,' Bob said modestly.

'That to me is history also,' Janice said.

David Flusfeder

'It's the history of the *Company*, not its *pre*-history. Whenever we have a new employee I send them down to the display room. I say, look at our product lines, memorize them. We make what we sell and we sell what we make. That's how business works. The shareholders are very happy. And that's what I try to explain to Malcolm.'

'The new CEO's an outsider,' Janice said to Edgar, who was wondering if pretending to faint was a viable way out of this occasion.

'That's history for you,' Mon was saying.

'That's what I say,' Company Bob said. 'Took someone like Mac to bring the whole shooting-match into the twentieth century.' He turned to Edgar. 'Your granddad was certainly a character. The stories I could tell you about him!'

'I've had quite enough of Mac stories,' Fay said.

'I know exactly what you mean,' Guthrie said, patting her best friend's hand. 'But it's true that Mac was such a larger than life character. Mike is just like him in some ways. Do you remember that time on Marble Hill—'

'This meat's very good, Warren. It's extremely tender,' Fay said.

'The soup was good also,' Marilou said.

'I'll give you the recipe,' Warren said.

'I think she *knows* how to cook succotash,' said Janice.

Everyone else had finished the main course. Edgar attempted a larger mouthful of meat in an effort to clear his unfinishable plate. But it was far too ambitious a portion and took an eternity to chew through and he was sure his cheeks were bulging like a cartoon squirrel's. Warren and then Fay, kindly, to include him, asked him questions and all he could do was mumble and retch.

'Don't ever lose that accent. It's terrific!' Bob said.

Plates departed and bowls arrived, all identified by Bob with their brand name and year of manufacture. Bob drank more beer. Guthrie drank more wine and became flushed and talkative. Janice drank more wine and grew sober and quiet. Fay was engaged in a political debate with Company Bob. They were arguing about the Mansion House. Bob had suggested that the Mansion House should be sold off and little pinpricks of deep red appeared on Fay's cheeks. Edgar had not seen his grandmother angry before. Her voice became stern. 'If it wasn't for the Mansion House then this could be anywhere else.'

'Market forces. Place got to pay its way. Here's a building where all the guest rooms are empty, a few old fellows living upstairs on peppercorn rent, and no one visits the museum. If we ran the Company like that we'd soon all be in the street. Got to remember who pays the piper. It's the Company that keeps everything else afloat.'

'Not market forces. Absolutely not. Where did the Company come from?'

'Ancient history, Fay.'

'That's not the point. People around here used to live differently. They *chose* to live differently. It may not have lasted for ever and it didn't bring heaven on earth but it was a very decent time, people looked after one other, worked with one other. It doesn't matter so much what they believed but what they did, and what they did is find a new way of living.'

The conversation went on and others joined in and Edgar stopped being able to follow what they were talking about but he was sure that what Fay was saying was decent and right, as Bob's skin became even redder than before and he kept saying, 'That's all very well but who's going to pay for it?' and 'That sounds a lot like Communism to me and we know what happened to *that*!' The debate collapsed under the force of Bob's repetitions and the table returned to its separate groups. Mon flirted with Coach Weathers, who uncoiled a little under her attentions. Every time he looked to check what his wife was doing, Marilou Weathers held a spoon (1920s, Presidential line) defensively in front of her face.

'So has he got you into this musical of his?' Bob said to Fay, reaching for a conciliatory conversation. 'He seems to've corralled half the women in town.'

Fay shook her head and slowly focused on Bob's redness. 'I don't really have the voice for it.'

'That's not true,' Warren said.

'You've got a much better voice than I do!' Guthrie said.

'You're not one of his victims too, are you?' Bob asked, grinning at Warren as if he might be making a joke.

'Harriet Stone at your service.'

'I'm surprised at that,' Bob said. 'I'd've thought your hands would be full with the Blackberry Festival and whatnot. Which seems to be a much better use of your time. That to me is good history.'

'Bob likes to divide things into good and bad,' Janice said.

When a knock came on the front door, Warren sighed. 'We know who that'll be, don't we?' he said.

'You're too hard on Jerry. You shouldn't be,' Fay said.

'Jerry?' said Bob. 'Jerome *Prindle*? Is he *ambulatory*?'

'In a manner of speaking,' Warren said. 'He's wooing Fay.'

'*Warren!*' Fay said, and the blush on her cheek could have signified shyness or embarrassment or pleasure, or just the spreading of the rash that Edgar guiltily associated with the disinfectant-doused flannel he had used to clean the bathroom.

'I'm sorry,' the wreckage of the man in the doorway said. 'I didn't know you had company. I brought a seed-cake. I'll go.'

'You will not. You'll sit down and join us,' Fay said.

The latest guest was an old man, who seemed to have outlived his body and his clothes. His skin was mottled red and white, his trousers and shirt were brown and stained. His face was decorated with patches of stubble. His mouth hung open, showing his tongue, which was the same pale colour as his lips. He watched Fay through blue eyes that were glazed and swimming, while his hands clawed slowly at the tablecloth. He sat between Mon and Coach Spiro, who both angled their chairs away from him.

'Tom's looking well,' Jerome said.

'He's on a new diet,' Fay said. 'Dry food only. It seems to have cleared up some of his catarrh. But he sleeps all of the time. Sometimes I think it would be a mercy—'

Warren interrupted: 'Maybe Ed should be trying out for your soccer team.'

'Are you a player?' Coach asked, to which Edgar could only shake his head for an answer.

'He's very good at it,' Mon brazenly lied, in misjudged loyalty.

'I'm really not,' Edgar managed to say.

'Better to underestimate yourself than the other. Marilou for example thinks she can sing,' Coach said accusingly at Warren.

'I'm sure she's going to make an *adorable* Mary Pagan,' Guthrie said.

'Do we need that stuff, is what I'm asking,' Bob said. 'It's all kind of weird to my way of thinking.'

'She was a fascinating character,' Warren said.

'A little too fascinating, if you know what I mean. I think those dowagers from the forties had the right idea.'

'What they did was awful,' Fay said. 'Pete was so furious.'

'Yeah. Well. Pete,' Bob said, winking at Coach.

'He was a good man,' Jerome said.

'He was a very good man,' Fay said.

'I guess. But I wouldn't have had Spanky Pete be *my* judge of right and wrong. You know what I'm saying? Those ladies were protecting the families *and* the Company. That's not so awful in my book. But tell me, who's playing my wife's most illustrious ancestor?'

'He still can't find a John Prindle Stone,' Fay said. 'Who would have thought it so difficult to find a good baritone?'

'We're running out of time,' Warren said.

'I hope I'll still be around to see it,' Fay said, with a surprising cheerfulness.

'Is it only me or does this cream taste sour?' said Janice.

'It's *crème fraîche*,' Warren said.

'That's what I'm asking and I don't think it is.'

'What I'd absolutely love to know,' Marilou said fascinatingly, leaning towards Warren, the rough shoulder of her sweater scratching Edgar's arm, 'is Mary's motivation. Do you think much of it is religious or does it all come down to love?'

'What on earth has happened to the azalea?' Jerome demanded to know.

Warren was being besieged on all sides. Janice was waving her spoon (Community plate, 1933) of suspicious cream. Marilou had rested her chin on her fist and was nodding encouragingly to pull Warren's required response out of him. Edgar decided to help. 'We saw some Indians yesterday,' he said.

After watching the drip of cream from Janice's spoon on to the table, Warren, in reciprocation, said, helpfully, 'The bingo hall.'

'It's ironic, isn't it?' Fay said. 'They're making these little amounts of money from gambling when they're such an unlucky people. Warren's thinking of donating the profits from the opera to help them.'

'That's a lovely idea. I think the Indians are tragic,' Marilou said. 'In the true sense of the word.'

'Talk of profits is somewhat optimistic,' Warren said, 'but we're going to try to make some kind of donation to their education fund.'

'Yeah right. Wigwam College,' Bob said.

'I don't think that gives entirely the right impression to our visitors,' Guthrie said.

'With all due respect, I don't think our visitors will ever understand this place until they've been here as long as I have. But the Onyatakas have got to face up to things. The trouble with history, it's like everything else, there's winners and losers and the Indians are the losers. It's unfortunate, but if it wasn't for rain you wouldn't have rainbows, you know what I'm saying?'

'Now they're talking about building a casino,' Guthrie said.

'Pie in the sky,' Bob said.

'Bob says it's never going to happen,' Janice said.

'It never is going to happen,' Bob said. 'The Onyatakas think it's going to be a licence to print money, but they'll never get it together. They never do. I remember something really choice that Mac said to me once. There was this Onyataka who worked as a gardener at the Mansion House— do you remember him, Fay? Kind of scruffy fellow, wore a straw hat. Liked his booze.'

'His name was Ronald,' Jerome said.

'That's right, I think it was. He used to drive this beat-up tractor really super slow around the grounds. And I remember Mac saying to me, "There's progress for you, look at Ronald, a hundred years ago his ancestors were eating each other and here he is now, master of the internal combustion engine." You got to laugh.'

Company Bob and Coach were the only ones laughing.

Janice and Mon and Marilou watched them with dissimilar looks of distaste. Warren was carrying things through to the kitchen, stopping to offer Guthrie something for her cough, which she haughtily declined. Fay had closed her eyes and might have been sleeping. Jerome already was.

7

Mon took flight with regretful hugs and repeated sighs of 'Oh Eddie!' She tousled his hair and he had to pull it straight again. She kissed him for the thousandth time and climbed, as if reluctantly, into the station-wagon.

'Okay Eddie, you'll be in charge,' Warren said, patting out a double toot on the horn as the car pulled away.

Edgar stood with Fay on the porch to wave the car off. Maybe because she'd noticed the bereft feeling he was manfully trying to suppress, she gave him a handful of notes and coins. 'Your father asked me to give you these. It's for spending money until he gets here.'

Edgar didn't trust his voice, so he nodded his appreciation.

Fay rubbed the red patch on her throat. 'I need to pick up my John Mills movie from the video store,' she said, as if this was a matter of great delicacy that she might nonetheless trust him with. 'You might want to come with me, if that's not too boring a project.'

On the way down to the store, Edgar adjusting his walk to the slowness of Fay's, sometimes holding out a steadying hand when she seemed about to stumble or stall, Fay told him about someone called Mary, of whom she spoke with such fondness that he assumed she was her dearest friend, now sadly moved away. The way she spoke about Mary made Edgar like her too.

'Her impetuosity sometimes gets her into trouble, but if you don't get into trouble then how can you say you've lived? Don't you agree?'

'Yes, I think I do,' Edgar said.

'Oh look, we're here already. The boys are very nice to me here.'

The boys at the video store wore tight black polo-neck jumpers and old-fashioned glasses and had short hair that was badly dyed yellow. One of them was an Onyataka and the others from long-time families of Creek. Edgar knew this because Fay had told him so but they were indistinguishable to him. The video-store boys liked Fay. They liked the obscure rigour of her choices. As a special favour, they let her take the picture boxes of the movies she rented home with her, instead of the pink and blue store boxes that the customers were usually given.

'We got you your *Rocking Horse Winner*,' one of them said.

'That's terrific,' Fay said. 'I'm very grateful.'

Fay hardly talked on the way home. She was concentrating on the efforts of her walk. When they had reached the Pagan House she exhaled loudly and smiled, in comradeship. 'What would you like to do now? You could watch my movie with me or maybe you'd like to see something more of the neighbourhood? The Mansion House runs some very interesting tours. I know Jerry would love to show you around.'

She raised an arm towards the Mansion House across the rise and the movement ruined her balance; her foot grasped for the porch step but it was crooked there and the foot slipped and she fell, in slow motion, looking surprised and cross. Edgar, frozen in guilty consternation, watched her go down, crumpling against the screen door.

Fay made little movements of her fingers and looked up at him, baffled, until the sun hurt her eyes so she covered them with her arm. Her legs were splayed wide, and her dress had ridden up over her knees. Edgar's first act was to tug down the dress to restore his grandmother's modesty. He squatted beside her and laid a comforting hand on her elbow.

'I'm so sorry. That was ridiculous,' she said.

'I should have caught you.'

'I'm such a fool. If you could just help me to sit up? Warren's going to be very angry with me.'

Edgar managed to manoeuvre Fay to the kitchen. She was much lighter than he expected and he should have been able to catch her, even one-handed, with his free arm held nonchalantly behind his back.

'I'm going to be black and blue tomorrow. Whenever will I learn not to do that kind of thing?'

He fetched a stool for her to rest her feet on. 'Should I call a doctor?'

'I make it a rule never to trouble the doctor three days in a row. I think I'll just regather and then watch my movie. I'm so sorry for causing such a fuss. What do you think you'd like to do?'

'I thought I might just take a walk around. If that's all right?'

'Of course it is, my dear.'

'But I think I'll wait until Warren gets back. Just in case.'

'There's really no need.'

'I know, but I want to,' Edgar said firmly. 'If you don't mind?'

'Of course I don't mind. You're a very sweet boy. You know, it's very nice to have you here.'

'It's very nice to be here,' Edgar said promptly.

All the same, there was an awful silence in the house, as if it was complicit in Fay's fall and was now planning its next assault upon her. Edgar wondered if he should feel afraid of this house, but that was contrary to the instant congeniality he had felt for its spirit and a way of making excuses for himself, and then he realized that the silence was due to the absence of the cat's snores that had supplied a rumbling rhythm to the soundworld of the Pagan House.

The cat basket was empty, apart from a faded purple cushion, a moss of lost ginger hair.

'Where's the cat?' he asked, and Fay didn't quite answer.

'Cats often go somewhere private to do their, when they're ready to, you know.'

'Yes, I know,' said Edgar, who didn't.

When Warren returned, Fay whispered to Edgar, 'You should go now. I don't want you to take the blame. I know what you're like.'

She knew him better than his mother did, better then than he knew himself.

'I think I'll take a walk around,' he said loudly, attempting a wink.

Edgar left behind the sounds of Warren chiding and Fay's birdlike voice making its apologies. Edgar had been left in charge of Fay and had failed.

The boredom of this town, through which Edgar strolled with a look of quiet dignity on his face. He had never felt so lonely. Trees, timbered houses, sports fields, parks, the video store, the bookshop that never opened, all these things felt entirely indifferent to him. He asserted himself by imagining how a cat might get lost in any of them—stuck snoring in a storage cupboard in the Company administration building or too fat to escape from the hole it had found into the Company Community Center, dreaming of plump mice or the kitten it had used to be, but he had never seen the cat awake so adventurousness was an unlikely quality for it to possess. That suggested malice, then, a human agency at work, the sinister hand of the cat-napper. Why should anyone steal a cat? Perhaps it was the secret historical ingredient that went into the glaze coating of the china produced at the Company factory in Creek. The Indians had been cannibals once, or so Company Bob had said. Maybe they had taken the cat for dark ceremony, old practices that required warm flesh, pulsing blood—but the only Indians he had seen were the stolid men outside the bingo hall, and one of the young men in glasses who worked in the video store, but he didn't know which one, and none of them had looked like a blood drinker to Edgar.

Still, he should not rule anyone out. The cat was missing, everywhere in peril, and everyone was a suspect.

Edgar walked across the bridge down to Creek. He looked for signs of the cat—tell-tale ginger hair, a lonesome mew—outside the supermarket and the gas station, the Silver City Diner, the Campanile Family Restaurant and Pizzeria, a dance studio, nail parlour (Luscious Nails), tanning salon (Tan Your Can!) and another pizza parlour, Dino's. He would not have thought a town the size of Creek could support two pizza parlours. He had walked lingeringly past Dino's twice already, attracted by the pinball machine, deterred by the youths who hung out there, who looked just like the two he had seen outside the supermarket, wild-looking, in cut-off jeans and check shirts, who had squeezed themselves into shopping carts, their legs dangling off the front, and were slowly racing each other down the incline of the car-park. Twice he had resolved to go in and his nerve had failed him each time.

But now he would be strong: a cat investigator required recreation, and he would be protected by the jangle of his father's quarters, the secret music of his Walkman. He would just pretend they weren't there, the two shaven-headed hulking boys with little sprouts of beard below their lower lips, lighting matches and flicking them at a third, smaller boy, who wore the same uniform of cut-off shorts and baggy check shirt, but whose face was narrower, more weaselly, acne-pitted and fingernail-picked. Another, the largest one, who was crouched hammering at the rusted corpse of a motorcycle, wore blond hair and a Dino's paper hat and a grey T-shirt with cut-off sleeves that had the home-made slogan *Indian Fighters!* scrawled across the back.

Edgar walked past them as if undeterred, and went to the pinball machine. He put in one of his father's quarters, frowned, slapped the machine with the heel of his hand to let it know who was in charge, pressed the start button, nodded at the display of lights, turned down his music, acknowledged the chorus of beeps and whistles and bells, checked the action of the flippers, pulled the plunger and let it go, and away he played.

Under the glass was a list of instructions, but Edgar liked to learn how these machines worked by playing them, by their responses to him, and his to them. His first ball was a good one, staying under control, keeping in the lanes, until it hit the left bank at an awkward angle, spun back on to his flippers; he tried to catch it, but the flipper was too clumsy, or he was: the ball hopped and fell between the ends of the two flippers and down the middle and was lost. It's okay, Edgar nodded, this was a decent machine, a worthy opponent. You treat me with respect and I'll treat you with respect. It was hard to find these machines any more. Everything was computer and video.

The lounging youths were walking slowly through, and now he could feel the attention of their unfriendly scrutiny. One of them jostled against his shoulder as they passed into a back room, where they drowned the friendly noises of the machine with loud lurching music, guitars and drums, clattering, angry, incompetent sounds that made the back of his neck vulnerable with their bad intent.

The second ball built up his score, and he was unlucky to lose it, just before he was about to hit the drop-down targets again to claim a free ball, but the pressure was on him, the music had stopped as abruptly and pointlessly as it had begun, and the hoodlums were back jostling behind him, so before he plunged the third ball into play he put another quarter on the glass top to reserve his next turn. The third ball was a disaster, swooping through the gate, down the alley, it took an awkward carom off his left flipper, bounced against the grinning monster face in the middle, which he had learned must be avoided, and fell through the impotent rise of his flippers.

Edgar felt sick. He had confirmed whatever low opinion of him these dangerous thugs might have. He had performed badly under pressure, like a boy, and the largest one, the Indian Fighter with the blond hair and the paper cap, reached for Edgar's next quarter and said, 'Unlucky, kid,' and slotted it into the machine and pushed him aside.

'Let's see the master at work.'

'But that's—' said Edgar.

'I need some room here.'

A hard elbow cracked into Edgar's ribs.

'Tough luck, kid,' said the weasel, unsympathetically. 'You gonna order something?'

'No,' said Edgar.

'We'll see you later, kid.'

Edgar stood disconsolate. They were gathered by the machine with their backs to him. The player used his whole body, flicking the flippers double-fast, hips pushing the path of the ball into the desired lane, his hands slapping the sides of the machine. 'Sky is so good,' he said, supplying his own commentary. 'He's got *all* the moves.'

Stubborn Edgar, alarmed at his own impulses, pushed towards the machine. 'I want my quarter back,' he said.

Ignoring him, Sky flipped and shoved and jerked his head to tell the ball where to go, and miraculously it did, and miraculously his paper hat stayed on his head.

'You're gonna lose it,' said the weasel.

'It's *outta* control,' and 'You is *fucked*,' said the other two, simultaneously, then glared at each other so violently that they had to be brothers.

'In your face. Watch me and weep, you suckers.'

'I want my quarter back,' Edgar said.

Someone else had come into the pizza parlour, another enormous boy—they grow them big here—closer in age to the hoodlums than to Edgar. He carried himself awkwardly, as if he was making a perpetual apology for his size, the fluff of his incipient beard, the cleanness of his jeans and the T-shirt he wore over his sweatshirt, the pimples across his broad Scandinavian forehead.

'Now look what you done made me do! Lost the fuckin' ball!'

Edgar wished the gang's inattention back. The sight of them all staring at him was not a comfortable one. He had met their type before, in London, brutalists, torturers of boys and beasts; they immediately went to the top of his list of suspects. He hoped the bulky stranger would intervene. Maybe their attention would turn to him.

'I want my quarter back. You took my quarter. I want it back.'

He had established his position. There was no turning back. So this was how he was destined to die, friendless and forsaken in a pizza parlour in Creek. He supposed even his mother wouldn't be able to recognize his battered remains after they had been dredged out of the river. *No, no. That's not him. That's not my son. It can't be!*

I'm afraid there's no mistake, ma'am. Dental records and DNA and suchlike prove it. That's your boy, or what they left of him. Just for God's sake get that, that thing into the ground quick, the sight of it is making decent men weep.

'What did he say?'

'I didn't hear him. You hear him?'

'I don't think he spoke. Did he speak?'

'You must have heard. He's got a really funny voice.'

'Did you speak, kid?'

'My name's Edgar.'

It was the first time his secret name had been spoken in public, and how he hoped it had the magic it promised.

'What? What he say?'

'He says his name's Edgar.'

'He's got balls.'

'Where you from, Edgar?'

'Are you British, Edgar?'

'Have you got balls, Edgar?'

'He's got balls. Edgar's got balls.'

'I thought the British were famous for having no balls.'

'You got balls, Edgar?'

'He's not talking now.'

'I don't think he talked before.'

'If you've got balls, Edgar, I think you're gonna have to prove you got balls.'

'You going to show us your balls, Edgar?'

'He might be leaving.'

'I think Edgar's leaving. Are you leaving, Edgar? You didn't say anything and now you're leaving and we're not going to see you again? Give Edgar some room. I think he's leaving.'

'I want my quarter back.'

Edgar had gone beyond being astounded by his own behaviour. He was reconciled to it now and fixed to his path and would take it to its inevitable violent end.

'Did Edgar say something?'

'I think he's definitely got balls.'

'Almost definitely.'

'I think Edgar talks too much.'

'I like how he talks, though. I *warnt* my *quharrrrtarr*. It's funny.'

'Edgar's talking is going to get him into trouble one day.'

'He's in trouble now.'

'Let's see his balls,' said the weasel, trying to incite his more powerful friends.

'You took my quarter. I want it back.'

They were about sixteen or seventeen years old and they had muscles that were streaked with motorcycle and pizza grease and they wore tufts of hair on the chins of their hard, unforgiving faces, and he was almost thirteen and light-weight and maybe they'd go easier on him because of that. He wasn't reassured by the affectionate way they were sneering at him. He had seen enough playground massacres to know that the bully loves his victim.

'Give him a quarter, Ray.'

'*Wha*'? Why me?' whined the weasel. 'I don't have a quarter.'

Sky cuffed Ray on the side of the head and kept hitting him until he pulled out a quarter.

'Shit,' said Ray, enviously. He flipped the quarter to Edgar, who predictably dropped it. He didn't suffer the kicks to the head he was expecting as he retrieved it from the grease-spattered red lino floor.

His new name had proved itself, and this was a good transaction, his father's coin exchanged for the currency of the community.

'Okay,' he said.

The pinball machine sparked back into life.

'Goodbye,' he said.

He was ignored. They clustered around the machine again. Sky pulled back the plunger to propel the ball, but was interrupted by the stranger saying, 'Hi,' and Edgar—shocked at his own malice and ignobility of nature—hoped to see the bad intentions going his way.

'Hey Marvin.'

'Husky! What's up.'

'Guys.'

Sky released the plunger and headed for the back room, with the others following, the ball jittering and pinging, it and the machine and Edgar ignored. He braved himself to leap in to play the rest of the game, as the band clattered back into action with the same mistimed vigour of delivery, but they had a vocalist now, Marvin, he guessed, who sang in a beautiful and reckless low voice that Edgar hated him for possessing.

When Edgar returned to the house, hoping to get to his bedroom, to collapse into solitary consolation, Warren called him into the kitchen, where he was emptying the dishwasher. Warren peeled off the black rubber gloves he wore for the performance of domestic tasks. His hands were, Edgar inconsequentially noticed, slightly paler than his arms.

'You missed your dad.'

'Sorry?'

'Your dad called.'

On his way back to the house Edgar had slowed his heart, calmed the wild pumping of adrenaline by throwing sticks at a pine cone and then pine cones at a stick. He had triumphed in a staring contest with a glum red bird. He had paused on the bridge and tossed pine cones into the brownstoned stream until a passing car slowed down and a bald man had snapped at him to stop what he was doing. He had killed time until it became a point of honour to kill more of it, to sicken himself back into boredom. And meanwhile his dad had phoned and he'd missed the call. Edgar scratched at the inside of his arm until he was alerted to the fact he was doing so by Warren's curious, slightly concerned expression.

'Does he want me to call him back?'

'I don't think so. I'm not sure where he is, actually. He says sorry and everything but he's been delayed. Business to take care of. He'll be arriving a bit later than he thought.'

'Tomorrow evening?'

That was Edgar's furthest projection: the morning was unachievable, the evening made sense, his father driving through the day, birthday gifts carelessly scattered in the back seat of his open-top car, to stay overnight in his mother's house, *his* house—they were always saying how much time had passed since his last visit. Edgar and his father wouldn't want to begin their own drive until the morning, after breakfast: it was a long journey they would be making together.

'Not quite, Eddie.'

Warren was very good at breaking bad news. He should have had a job as one of those army men who stand at front doors and aren't allowed to touch or hug the broken women who've just been told that their boys have died.

'He's been delayed. He won't be able to make it tomorrow.'

'The day after?'

'Probably not till the end of the week. But I'm sure we can keep you entertained up till then. He says, sorry. So. I hope you're hungry. Fay will be down just after she's done her exercises.'

At supper, after Warren had checked that Fay had taken her evening medication, he asked Edgar about his walk.

'It was fine,' Edgar said, and Fay, seeing something sad in Edgar's eyes, had the delicacy to prevent Warren enquiring further.

'These mushrooms are delicious,' Fay said. 'Is there garlic in them?'

'I just stir them around from time to time while they're

cooking, with a fork that has a clove of garlic on its, you know, prongs.'

'Tines,' said Fay.

'Excuse me?' said Warren.

'The prongs of a fork. They're called tines.'

'Oh yes, that's right, of course they are.'

Warren seemed to like being corrected by Fay, the passage of wisdom down the generations. Paintings hung on the white walls of the kitchen, most of them Fay's own water-colours of riverside scenes executed when her sight was still largely intact.

'Have you found the cat yet?' Edgar asked.

'How's your ankle?' Warren asked.

'It's a lot better. Edward was terrific looking after me. I didn't miss you at all.'

She dazzled Edgar with her smile.

'That's good to hear,' Warren said. 'How's the rash?'

'I think it's getting better,' Fay said, covering her throat and chin with a hand.

'We should get Newhouse to take a look at it.'

'No more medication. If you shook me I'd rattle. Don't worry, I'm sure I'll make it through till the Festival.'

'May I leave the table?' Edgar said.

'Of course you can, my dear. I love your manners.'

Edgar escaped to the Music Room, where he compiled a list of cat-napping suspects, which did not exclude his mother—was it accidental only that she had left on the day that Tom disappeared? And then he counted his money, which amounted to seven dollars and forty-nine cents, and went through the record albums, sorting them into separate piles according to likely interest. The interesting pile he further subdivided into those he thought belonged to his father and those to his uncle Frank. He imagined Frank to have a taste for flowery illustration and fanciful covers. His father he allowed all those simply designed albums with the group's photograph glowering on the front. On the window-ledge, he arranged the ones with girls he wanted to look at on the covers, blocking out the shallow lights of the Mansion House opposite.

8

We believe that Kingdom now coming is the same that was estab-
lished in heaven at the Second Coming of Christ [70 AD]. Then
God commenced a kingdom in human nature independent of the
laws of this world. We look for its reestablishment here, and this
extension of an existing government into this world is that we
mean by the Kingdom of God. I will put the question. Is not now
the time for us to commence the testimony that the Kingdom of
God has come?

The Spiritual Moralist, John Prindle Stone, 1845

Mary is gone, in zealous spirit, to accompany Captain Carter
on a missionary visit to an infant Perfectionist congregation
in Greencastle. Little Georgie is with Mary's sister in
Rochester. George spends his hermitry in work upon the
land and studies of the Bible. He has never felt quite so
lonely. His spirits and vitality are sinking. He can hardly
rouse himself to go to the general store on Turkey Street.
Even blind Jess grows peevish with lack of use. In compensation he feeds her too many turnips.

He had not realized how dependent his energies are upon
Mary's. In the absence of his wife, he is without initiative,
petulant and doltish. His beard grows. His clothes are dirty.
Each day he resolves anew to abandon this place, to follow
the missionaries to Greencastle, to join his child in Rochester,
to visit John Prindle Stone in Vermont, or else return to New
York City, where he might taunt his sluggish spirits with the
sin he has left behind. Each night he falls sleepless into bed,

David Flusfeder

the day ahead of him stretching out as empty and useless as the previous one. He sets himself small tasks that seem, in their midnight contemplation, manageable. Each morning he fails to accomplish or even begin any one of them. He has become accustomed to rising late, to sit out the lethargic death of the morning at the table in the parlour, still in his night-clothes and sleeping cap.

He can play the violin, that at least he is capable of: the sounds he coaxes from it, the action of the strings beneath his fingers, bring the image of his wife closer.

They had met for the first time on the Bowery. George was walking back to his lodgings from the newspaper office to wash and change before setting out for the weekly meeting of the Moral Reform League at Mr Green's town-house on Fifty-Third Street. An Irish urchin running pell-mell through the crowd collided with George Pagan, who held him, looking for the purse in his pale hand, the pursuing robbed gentleman. The boy's hands were empty and the only pursuer was a young lady, who smiled at George as she took hold of the urchin. The child twisted and struggled and wept and surrendered. George asked if he should fetch an officer. Her amused eyes reached straight into George to a place that he had no prior acquaintance with or even knowledge of. She told him she was the child's teacher, bringing her charge home.

'This happens at the end of every day. He tries to run back to school. It is my task to persuade him home.' She stroked the child's hair and brow. His shoulders relaxed. She wiped the tear tracks off his face. She whispered to him, comforting words to the melody of a Congregationalist hymn, and George was startled by a stab of jealousy for this child, who could so unthinkingly provoke such actions of heart and hand.

'This is surely a novelty,' George said. 'I would have

thought it a unique case, a schoolboy that cannot bear to be absent from school.'

'We fail the ones who love us best. Education affords a glimpse of somewhere else, a preferable place, without always offering a way there.'

And then, with that quality of quickness that would always so enchant George Pagan, she interrupted his considerations of a reply with a curtsy, as if the drab crowded street were a débutante ball. 'Mary Johnson,' she said.

'George Pagan. At your service.'

'Good afternoon, George Pagan,' she said, and, businesslike, she led the spent, unresisting child to his unwelcome door.

Mary lived, as Mr Stone would later remark, in the perpetual now. Everything moved fast with her as if without precedence or consequence: her decisions, her wit, her curiosity. Where George's understanding crabbed from ignorance to knowledge, dimly inching through objections and inconsistencies like a blind man tapping along a night-time street, the speed of her attention annihilated the distance between darkness and light.

Her pastoral task achieved, she seemed unsurprised to be walking in step up Second Avenue with George Pagan, and her consent to accompany him to the meeting at Mr Green's was only slightly more miraculous than his boldness in issuing the invitation.

At Mr Green's townhouse on Fifty-Third Street, the congregants drank tea and lemonade from Mrs Green's pale blue china. Marriage rights were discussed, and the liquor question, and universal suffrage was allowed, and slavery abolished, and faith-healing argued for and against, while Mrs Green poured tea, and the philanthropist Mr Green blinked merrily at the enthusiasm in his parlour, but for Mary this was never going to be quite enough. Speed of progress, if only in talk, had to keep up with the quickness of her heart.

No photograph could picture her. In photographs—taken at the end of the Prince Street school year, three short lines of pupils and staff, or at the penultimate meeting of the Reform League at Mr Green's, or at their wedding, with her preacher father already standing aloof from his unmanageable daughter—her slim face looked pinched and narrow, her chin and brow too mannishly strong, her eyes wide and impatient. George looked at his best in photographs. His strongly carved features became sculptural, implying all the power he knew he lacked in life. Mary's vivacity charmed and beautified everything around her. Later, he would encounter the ferocity of her temper, which—until events gave her greater opportunity for remorse—was the ashamed subject of her largest self-reproach, flaring with a sudden heat, but then, as abruptly, it would dampen, abate, the flames clearing, her true nature revealed again, unscorched, her good fellowship and ardour and sympathy reestablishing themselves as the ruling agents of her passions.

At the final meeting on Fifty-Third Street, the newly married Mrs Pagan was already with child, and Mrs Green was carrying an equivalent secret proudly beating within: she had been converted to Stone's Perfectionism. She was without sin; she had been reborn in Christ. The philanthropist's wife had not yet announced the news of her salvation, out of deference perhaps to her husband, whose perpetual good cheer belied an unpredictable theology, and out of deference too to those members of her husband's circle who had no favour for the liberty views of Mr Stone's group.

'They greet each other with a kiss!' a poetical young Methodist complained, pushing back his dark curls in outrage. 'Loose talk! Wanton behaviour! They announce their opposition to marriage!'

'Paul prophesied that in heaven there'd be neither a giving nor taking in marriage,' Mrs Green said.

'They prophesy an overcoming of death!'

'Is that so impossible?'

The ardent Methodist shook his curls sadly. 'Desire untrammelled and decency forsworn. Can we have confidence in men who claim they need no laws to live by? Is that the sincere protestation of the saint? Or merely the sophistical philosophy of the criminal?'

Breathing heavily, in a rapture of self-adoration, the Methodist sat down and took a draught of Mrs Green's summer lemonade. Replacing the beaker on the table, he looked belligerently around, daring any of the company to oppose him. Opposition he found. In her musical voice, Mary asked: 'Have you read their pamphlets?'

The Methodist had to admit that he had not. Correspondents of impeccable probity had reported their contents to him.

'Have you visited any of their sequestrations?'

Again, the Methodist had to answer in the negative. But witnesses of unimpeachable correctness had delivered to him descriptions of the scandalous home lives of the Perfectionists.

'We ourselves are the subject of ill-informed gossip,' Mary said. 'Should that not teach us forbearance in the case of others?'

George's boundless love for Mary stretched again, infinite. In his love for her he felt at its purest and grandest God's perfect love for his creatures. George would always deny there was anything in the nature of falling about their love; he had not fallen in love with Mary—rather, with him, it was a rising, a leaping.

To the consternation of the company Mrs Green chose this moment to deliver her fresh-born Perfectionist views. The Methodist was silent. And Mr Green, for once, unbenevolent. Mr Green shortly afterwards declared an adherence to

Shakerism, where no such liberty views held sway, and there he was joined by his wife, who would be renamed by gossiping former friends as Chastity Green. But as Mary was leaving the Greens' house that night, Mrs Green slipped several of Mr Stone's tracts to the ardent, dissatisfied Mrs Pagan.

It was an end and it was a beginning. In her reading of Mr Stone's words Mary at last found what she was looking for: a promise that heaven was not a carrot to tempt children into acting well, but a heartfelt possibility, a sincere way to live.

'It is in high seriousness but never solemn. All life is contained in here.'

Whereas, for George, all life was contained in her. The carnal side of their marriage had been a revelation to him. Never had he conceived of physical pleasures as heavenly as these.

'It is Godly,' she assured him, as, without shame or darkness, Mr and Mrs Pagan conjoined in union of fellowship.

She accused him of idolatry and the charge was no doubt true.

'I am here George. It's me.'

After Mary went into confinement with little Georgie—a most painful undertaking—the parlour of the Pagans' apartment on Lower Broadway became the meeting place of the survivors of the wreckage of the Greens' Wednesday nights. The ardent Methodist was a frequent visitor, and even when the group shifted further towards Stonian Perfectionism, the Methodist companioned it on this journey also. Which was the occasion of the first unquiet words issued by Mr to Mrs Pagan.

'I doubt his sincerity,' he said. 'I suspect the motor of his enthusiasm is more carnal than spiritual.'

She suspected this too, and was guiltily aware of her own

response, which came from a place before language and conscience.

Knowing herself deceitful, duplicitous, George's incapacity to see what was in her brought rise to shame and, shamefully, Mary responded to his attentions as if he was the cause of the shame. Meekly, always meekly, he bowed his head and took fellowship with his violin.

They had uprooted to Rondout on the river, in obedience to a rest cure prescribed by her doctor, who was concerned at her feverishness after Georgie's weaning. The invitation was issued by Captain Carter, a recent missionary of Stone's to their group, to live away from the temptations of the city, to work the land, enact the truths of Biblical Communism. Here she might leave her trespasses behind.

Abram Carter, complacent of his spiritual rank, kissed Mary's doubts away. The rightness of what they were doing was self-evident, their alchemical conjoining: it mixed water with earth and air, spirit and body, Eve and Adam, and— this could not be admitted, because it would pass too dangerously close to Manichaeanism, but often, by Mary, it was glimpsed—God and the Devil. If something felt this good, who could say it was wrong?

A letter from Mr Stone charged Captain Carter to travel to Pennsylvania to act as missionary to a group of converts in Greencastle. The commission would require a two-week absence.

'I shall go with him,' Mrs Pagan told Mr Pagan. 'They are sheep without a shepherd surrounded by beasts of prey.'

And how she wanted him to say no, to fight for her, to announce his unsureness, his jealousy, to remind her of her wifely, motherly duties, to reproach her. Instead, his fingers bruised and earthy, he picked up his violin.

When George Pagan practised the violin he heard the

songs of the heart and the spirit most plainly. Performance was not the aim of the practice—he had no desire to impress others with his virtuosity, and in truth he played better when he thought he was playing unheard, but performance was the price he would pay for his talent: in it he perceived the strivings of his heart towards Christly union.

She came close to hating him then. She waited for him to say something more, to *do* something. A hypocrite, a whited sepulchre, she accompanied his music with the plainsong of domestic arrangements.

'If you take Georgie to stay with my sister in Rochester, then you may return to work and study here without interruption.'

'So be it,' he said, shutting his eyes, sliding his bow across the strings, playing a foxtrot as if it were a dirge.

As she made a pile of her clothes to take on the journey, as she packed a suitcase of little Georgie's things, and as she sat with the child, kissing and petting him, promising that she would not be gone longer than two weeks and how he would enjoy life at his cousins'—it would be a holiday, an adventure—and praising his pictures of sailboats on the river, thin little masts, sails decorated with infant attempts to draw stars, how she hated herself for despising her husband, for blaming him for her weakness.

Poor George. Poor Mary. Happy Captain Carter. They did not go to Greencastle to shepherd the flock. Instead of boarding the train at Onyataka Depot they walked down to the Rondout landing, the Captain at ease with the sailors on the jetty, discussing the Eerie Canal, the sturdiness of the crafts coming in to dock, the poundage of their loads. A construction gang of Onyataka Indians waited for embarkation, eyes closed against the speech of the miracle-oil salesman who was dressed as a preacher. Captain Carter made an offer for a handsomely time- and weather-worn little schooner before they climbed on board the steam vessel that would take them to Manhattan. They placed their bags on the aft-deck, went to stand unsheltered on the bow as the steamship pulled away from the jetty. Mary huddled inside her clothes, looking out at the shore, tasting the sweet heaviness of the air, hoping her conscience would not follow her.

Their New York days passed in a sottishness of the senses; they seldom ventured out, their hotel-room curtains drawn against the traffic on Second Avenue. Much of the time they were naked, the Captain's continuing campaign against shame and bashfulness; his body was lightly covered with copper-coloured hair, his chest and right thigh were scarred from a shipping accident in his youth, his shoulders were freckled, his physique was muscular. When she was tracing the lineaments of his body with her hands, with her pilgrim's kiss, she was happy. As the days went by, less and less was she able to look at his face, the Captain's sharp, proud green eyes. She would press a finger to his mouth when he tried to speak. His orator-spirit had to be satisfied by ventures into mission halls and debating chapels.

It is late morning, full summer; the frogs are singing by the river. George Pagan in his night-clothes sits at the table, blind to the unconsoling Bible before him. Doltish, self-abashed, he sits unmoving, unaware, until dimly he perceives the sound of horse hoofs. He does not get visitors. Occasionally an Onyataka woman comes sullenly begging to the back door, to whom he will donate a parcel of his and Jess's surplus turnips. Beggars do not come on horseback. George waits for the sound of the hoofs to pass and diminish in the distance. They do not diminish. They get louder, and stop. A rider dismounts in the yard. A horse is tethered. For an awful, futile moment, George's heart lifts. It is Mary, returned, his idol, his wife, having cut short her mission to Greencastle.

This is what he has been waiting for; she is whom he sits for, drowsily vigilant, perpetually waiting. Is it so unlikely that she might miss him almost as painfully as he misses her?

Urgently, George rushes to the bedroom, rips off his nightshirt, finds his trousers, an almost clean shirt, his boots, struggles into them, hops, runs, stockingless, folding his shirt-cuffs, to the door.

It is not Mary who stands without. It is John Prindle Stone, brushing off the dust of his journey, smiling, reaching out his hand.

'Mr Stone.'

'Mr Pagan.'

John Prindle turns George's handshake into a brotherly embrace. They have met twice before. The first occasion was after a public meeting in Vermont; the second was in Rondout, early in the Pagans' stay here, a banquet of sorts attended by Perfectionists from Vermont and Brooklyn. It was at the latter event that Mr and Mrs Pagan made the decision to throw in their lot with Stone's under-teacher, to make a sortie at Bible Communism, living in fellowship of possession and heart, without sin.

'Captain Carter is not here,' George says.

'I am not here for Captain Carter.'

John Prindle Stone's aspect is stern, humorous, comradely, fatherly, angelic. He has large, capable fingers, like an engineer's, which he strokes through his beard. George hopes he has not shown too much disappointment.

'I had not been expecting guests. I have been solitary for some time and am not used to company. I hope you will excuse me. Things have been on the slide.'

Mr Pagan bids Mr Stone sit at the parlour table. He brings in a pot of coffee and apologizes again for the house's appearance, for his own. His hand, intending to smooth down his uncombed hair, knocks off his sleeping-cap instead. George laughs, as does John Prindle, who picks the cap off the floor as George's laughter is drowned, inex- • orably, by his tears.

When he manages to exert some order over his emotions or, rather, their outward manifestation, he again apologizes and conquers himself sufficiently to pour the coffee without spilling a drop, which, in a very small way, pleases him.

'Where is Captain Carter?' Mr Stone asks.

'In Greencastle. He and my wife are missionaries to a new community there, as decreed by you, I understand.'

Mr Stone brings out two letters. He passes them to George. The first is from a representative of the Greencastle community, a Mordecai Short, who complains of perpetual darkness. When, he asks, is the promised missionary to arrive, the dispenser of light?

George's understanding struggles with this.

'The letter must have been sent shortly before their arrival.'

Mr Stone passes George the second letter. It is from Chastity Green.

A large angry script, full of underlinings and exclamation marks, tows George through the dry canals of jealousy and unrewarded labour (for the true reward of labour is love). Chastity Green declares her surprise at seeing Mrs Pagan and Captain Carter walk entwined into Union Square for a public meeting of Abolitionists: 'Can this be <u>so</u>?! Mr Stone: Is this being done with your <u>knowledge</u> and <u>permission</u>? Is this the <u>cargo</u> that your liberty views <u>carry</u>? I cannot believe <u>that</u>!' George, reading the letter for the third time, making sharp little grunts that at first he takes as a strange animal sound from outside—a wolverine, an injured bear—grips hold of the parlour table as his world topples down.

There is no spurious sanctimony to John Prindle Stone. Were this Abram Carter, George would find his hand clasped, his eyes met by a look of bogus holiness, his ears thundered with dizzying biblical recital. John Prindle is brisk; and, being holy, he has no need to pretend to be so.

'First we shall put this place in order. Are you to sit here for ever in your sleeping-cap, feeling sorry for yourself?'

'Are you staying? I can make up a bed in, in Captain Carter's room.'

'That would be kind.'

'How long can you stay?'

'For as long as you need me.'

George Pagan's heart swells with gratitude. John Prindle is the most energetic, and the busiest, man George has met. He preaches, he writes, he publishes, he proselytizes, and loves. He is doorkeeper to the new dispensation.

'How can you spare the time?'

Abram Carter would respond with something along the lines of all time being eternal in the Lord. John Prindle instead searches for broom and mop. They clean the floors, they sweep the yard. When the house is returned to order, they sit in the kitchen and eat soup.

'I had hoped to protect her. We had thought it our new Eden,' George says, 'and so it was. Together we enacted our own version of the Fall. Woman tempts, man justifies and conceals.'

'We can begin again,' John Prindle says. 'The garden planted anew.'

Silently, George shakes his head.

'And where will you go? What will you do?'

'Return to the city. Find a situation in a newspaper office or counting-room.'

'And that will satisfy? I have a proposition to put to you. Our family is being driven out of Vermont. We are beginning again, up by Turkey Street. A believer has donated to us some land, where we will build our Mansion House. Join us and spend the winter with me in studying the Bible and waiting on the will of God.'

This is more than he could have expected, the individual fellowship of John Prindle Stone, whose spirit and oratory illumine the dark pathways from New York to Boston to Philadelphia. George cannot comprehend the magnitude of this offer. There are congregations, besieged in dark places, starry lights in the empty American sky, that require John Prindle Stone. And yet he is offering to heap his authority and strength on the unworthy soul of George Pagan, so unworthy that George cannot keep from being reminded at this moment of the Bible-studying ministrations of Abram Carter, so unworthy that he cannot keep from wondering what thing unspoken lies behind the offer, what matter politic, or whether it is offered out of some guilt at what has been perpetrated here in his name.

'I cannot accept such a benevolent offer.'

'Do not misunderstand me. I am accustomed to use words to express rather than conceal my thoughts.'

And bows his head. He has found, or, rather, been found by, a man of solid truth, who recognizes no politeness, no human grace or embellishment, however fashionable, except it be of a pure, sincere, truth-loving heart.

'Yes,' George says, like a drowning man reaching for a rope, a sailor on a sinking ship ready to make the plunge into unknown waters. 'I should be glad to leave this place.'

And as he says this, he is not sure how sincere he is; he has grown used to the house, it suits his melancholy, but he is conscious only of the desire to please John Prindle Stone, and a need to tell him everything, to show him the wound he lives with, the ache in his ribs that corresponds to the absent shape of his wife.

'Has it been so unbearable for you here?'

He cannot answer. He weeps, and this time John Prindle

moves to embrace him, and George shudders and spills against John Prindle Stone's shoulder. He had not thought he contained such a reservoir of tears inside him. Giving himself up entirely, yielding his soul to John Prindle Stone, George yet marvels that he had contained so many unshed tears, and then he marvels too at his capacity to marvel while giving himself up so entirely, and so it spins, a doubling and quadrupling and octupling and so on, an infinite progression of split selves, marvelling and weeping and surrendering; and throughout it all John Prindle holds him close. So it stands: the lion with the lamb. The saint and the saved.

Finally, miraculously, there are no more tears to shed. He has reached the bottom of the reservoir, tilled the depths of the ditch. George's heart and throat are as dry as the land that he and Jess ploughed in their ordeal. He lifts his head from John Prindle's damp shoulder. He is able to talk again. The word cracks in the desert of his throat.

'Amen.'

9

On Tuesday mornings, Warren washed Fay's hair. The first time he observed this ceremony, Edgar was wearing soccer shorts and socks. He stood uncertainly in the corridor outside the bathroom, feeling he was watching something entirely private, unable to pull himself away.

Fay was kneeling on the floor, her head lowered over the bathtub. Warren crouching beside her poured water from a jug over Fay's hair.

'How's the temperature?'

'Perfect. Absolutely perfect,' said Fay.

Her eyes were closed. Her breathing was deep and gratified. Warren applied the shampoo and massaged her head before rinsing the shampoo away, paying special care to the brow and temples, which was where she suffered the worst of her headaches.

'My face is still very prickly. So are my hands.'

'We'll speak to Newhouse about that but it looks just like a contact dermatitis to me. As if you've been handling something allergenic.'

'You sound very familiar with this kind of thing. Does the other—'

'Dr X had a lot of cases like this one. I'll put in the conditioner now.'

Dr X! No boy detective ever had a better clue. Edgar moved closer. He had not heard Warren interrupt Fay before, it shocked him, a new tone in their relationship of mistress and companion. She didn't seem to take offence, which was maybe more sinister than if she had, and the slightest tilt of her head was acknowledgement that she was ready for the next stage. Warren rubbed in the conditioner, threading the lotion through the strands of her hair with his finger-tips. He twisted the hot-water faucet further shut but it continued to drip.

'I can hear that sound at night,' Fay said.

'I'll have another go at fixing it,' Warren said.

'It's another reason why I can't get to sleep.'

Warren rinsed the last of the conditioner from Fay's hair. He rubbed her head with a towel roughly and fast, which made watching Edgar gasp. He waited for the violence of the action to crack her pale skull open, egglike. Somehow it survived, and Warren draped the towel around Fay's shoul-ders, which seemed to be shedding the flesh around them. Her shoulder-blades protruded like the sharp stumps of wings.

'Thank you Warren, that was very nice,' said Fay in the tone, restored, of complacent mistress.

'Should I give you a comb now?' he said.

'Please.'

Edgar tiptoed away. He would have to put on the rest of his loathsome soccer uniform and visit Warren and Fay when they were involved in a less intimate activity.

'Let's see you.'

'No,' said Edgar.

'Let's see you.'

'I look ridiculous. Where does this go? And this?' Holding up a semi-circular plastic thing with a greyed foam pad inside and straps hanging down like spider legs, Edgar stepped into the kitchen.

'You look very good,' said his grandmother.

'Sporty,' said Warren.

'Yes,' said Fay.

Warren's expression was stern as if he was forcing himself to pay proper attention to this moment or just trying to keep himself from giggling.

If his mother were here she would be tousling his hair until he made her stop. Then she would go away to find her camera, which would take an age, and force him to pose for her while she adjusted for the light and criticized the expression on his face. If his father were here, as he was meant to be, Edgar wouldn't have to be doing this at all. How Edgar wished his father was here. The car waiting outside, the two guys together, talking about love or sport or gambling as the fat tyres of the Cadillac ate up freeway miles.

'What *is* this?' he asked.

'It's what they call a cup,' said Fay. 'You wear it down your shorts and it's a perfectly respectable piece of apparatus. Now, I suppose I ought to take a picture. Your mother would never forgive me if I didn't.'

'It's what they call a box where I come from,' said Warren.

'That tells us something, doesn't it, about the differences between our two cultures? But I couldn't say what,' said Fay.

'I'm not going to wear it,' said peevish Edgar.

'Stand straight please young man,' Fay said with mock severity while she snapped his photograph with an ancient Instamatic, which she carefully placed on the kitchen table and her energy fell away and she looked at Edgar and then at Warren as if she had no idea who they were.

Edgar was the only person to arrive in his soccer clothes—everyone else carried a sports bag and went into the locker room to change—and he was noticeable for this and therefore risible, but Edgar preferred that to doing the locker-room thing. He had considered wearing his box outside his shorts because the resulting ridicule would have got all his humiliation over straight away and he wouldn't have to come here ever again. Instead he wore his kit in its appropriate way and assumed an expression of wise indifference and a posture that was both casual and alert and which he hoped might imply barely contained power.

He wore a red bib for the first part of the practice, during which he touched the ball six times: the first two were random kicks that went straight to the nearest opposing player, the third an aerial event that smacked into the back of his head. The fourth was so nearly the ignominious moment he had been expecting: his hand slapped a shot clear of his own goal but, despite the ferocious appeals of the opposing players, Coach Spiro was busy refereeing the A-game and didn't notice. Edgar was praised by his goalie and slapped on the rear by a boy he nervously recognized as weaselly Ray from the pizza parlour. Most of the opposing players cursed him. One of their attackers, an olive-skinned girl who had black hair and a lazy eye and a blue *Forza Italia!* shirt and a weird kind of beauty, shook her head sadly at him. He watched her for a while and was impressed by what he saw. She ran very well and very straight with her hair lifting and falling like the flaps in airplane wings, and when she kicked the ball it went where she wanted it to go.

The fifth time he touched the ball he kicked it hard to try to get rid of it and the ball ballooned off his sneaker—Edgar was one of the few here not in soccer boots—and over green-bibbed opponents and into the path of Ray, who was so surprised he fell over. Coach Spiro, red-faced, hard-breathing, ran up to Edgar. 'Good play, Ed.' And ran off back to the A-game, tersely berating Ray along the way. Edgar had received the coach's benediction and even though the next time he tried it, the ball went sailing out of play, the coach was on the other pitch at the time, and Edgar had won, at least with Spiro, the reputation of a skilful long-pass specialist.

At half-time Edgar and Ray, undeservedly, and the Forza Italia girl, deservedly, were promoted into the A-game, whose star was Husky Marvin, who slammed in goals with apologetic power. Edgar was placed on the left wing and told to restrict his running to 'the channels', so, dutifully, he ran up and down the sideline in careful incongruity with the passage of the ball, hoping it would never come to him and it seldom did.

Walking slowly home, he prayed that on the next day it might rain. He glumly inspected the sky, which was desolately blue and clear. Glumly he waved to Warren, who was standing in the porch of Guthrie's house, returning a casserole dish while Guthrie stood with her arms crossed, as if she was blocking the way. Glumly he went up to the music room and listened to some of his father's records and waited for the magic of music to dispel his mood, which, magically, it did.

10

*If we walk in the light, as God is in the light, we have commu-
nism one with another, and the blood of Jesus Christ His Son
cleanseth us from all sin.* (I John, 1:7)

The Perfectionist Bugle, John Prindle Stone and George
Pagan, editors, 1847

Winter passes in chaste ecstasy. The donated land, which lies
either side of Onyataka Creek, is paradisal, woods of beech
and maple and white pine and silver birch, and a hundred
acres of alluvial soil—a revelation of earth raised from the
water, their new new Eden on which George Pagan and John
Prindle Stone plant crops and the future.

Their neighbours are bears and muskrats and racoons and
mink, cardinals and bluebirds and nightjars, and further away
the score or so of Onyataka Indians, who had previously
held title to all this land but have been limited by government deed to their longhouse and surrounding reservation
at Onyataka Castle where they subsist with a few head of
cattle, their ears of corn, a desultory trade in pelts. A wooden
shack, until recently an Indian habitation, becomes a horse
barn into which George tethers blind Jess, a shelter for her
to die in. George and John Prindle work the land, cut timber.
They build themselves a winter cabin on the rise above the
horse barn. Their land stretches out further than they can
see, bounded by the train line to the east, the Indian reservation to the west, past the trading post at Turkey Street to

the blue hills of the south, and Lake Onyataka to the north, to which, on a sabbath after their spring crops have been planted, George and John Prindle make a trek in the company of a local fur-trapper, Seth Newhouse.

John Prindle teaches George the truths of Bible Communism, and Newhouse instructs John Prindle and George in wood-craft and hunting. John Prindle is the better student: George's boots crack twigs hundreds of yards behind his companions on their forest hike, the gun in his hand weighs impossibly heavy—a bluebird startled by his unsubtle approach launches into flight with a rustle of brown leaves; and despite this, George feels stronger, more alive than at any moment since the first days of his marriage. His muscles strengthen, his intellect sharpens. They camp at the lake, Seth Newhouse roasts their catch, they unburden their hearts. George talks about Mary, and John Prindle describes his own path, his capacities early noticed by his seminary teachers, his unorthodoxy, the schism, his exile, his engagement to Hester Lovell, broken upon her rejection of his teachings, the primitive gospel recovered through sorrow and pain and doubt.

On their return, they burn more fields for farming and in the evenings they sit with Newhouse, who, somehow, unspoken, has become the third member of their household. Newhouse has tastes for tobacco and whiskey and silence and doesn't seem to attend to their debates, George's questions, Stone's elucidations. George follows his master along the path of wisdom. Christ returned in 70 AD at the destruction of the Temple. The fallen dispensation ended then but that knowledge has been lost, until now.

Master: 'Private property will be abolished.'

Adept: 'Revelation chapter twenty-one, verse seven: "He that overcometh shall inherit all things."'

Master: 'And the marriage contract will be abolished.'

Adept: 'Matthew twenty-two, thirty: "For in the resurrection they neither marry, nor are given in marriage, but are as the angels of God in heaven."'

Master: 'Death will be banished in the Perfectionist passage from law to grace.'

Adept: 'And so we arrive regularly at the tree of life, as per Genesis three.'

Newhouse doesn't appear to listen to any of this. He sits by the fire, smoking his pipe, drinking from his bottle, worrying over his prototype for a new species of animal trap, spring-driven, because Newhouse has become dissatisfied with the hole made by even a tiny shotgun pellet.

'It's on account of the profit,' he tells them, one of his longer speeches. 'You catch the animal by the foot, makes for a better pelt.'

John Prindle disagrees. He tells him that the issue is an aesthetic one, and moral. 'I might even say *religious*. You are as much in love with the perfect as we.'

Newhouse blinks his suspicious eyes at this and shakes his head. He refills his pipe. His skin is the same colour, and almost the same texture, as the cherrywood of the chair on which he sits. Newhouse is a year or two younger than George but George feels towards him the same deference as to any tree or bear or lake.

'We can count you in the justified one hundred and forty-four thousand,' says George, joining in the game, but Newhouse is not listening: he's at work with the steel mechanism on his lap that he's squeezing apart at the hinge, ready to snap, and John Prindle laughs, and says that Newhouse in his heart is as sincere as the most assiduous worshipper.

And George's heart? He misses his child, he misses Mary, who lodges with her sister in Rochester, disavowed by her parents for her Perfectionist views. Her liaison with Captain Carter is buried, as are her letters to her husband that lie unopened at the bottom of George's valise. His letters to her are written in the periods of John Prindle's absences, when George and Seth Newhouse return to the condition of awkward solitaries in each other's presence. These letters, candle-lit, on which he expends such thought and pains, remain unsent, consigned weekly to the fire that warms them.

John Prindle believes that everyone is capable of every task. Discipline, patience, hearts open to the breath of God's inspiration, books of professional knowledge will build them their Mansion House. He sits at the table, his sleeves rolled up, a green visor worn low on his brow, muttering and coughing, his breath rolling out ghost-clouds into the wintry room, as he steadfastly works, reads, discusses, designs, discusses, rejects, scraps.

'Providence shall make all things clear,' is all he says when George or, more mischievously, Seth Newhouse, enquires of his progress. And George is reminded of that other house without foundations, that he dreamed of, three miles down-river, in his blind-horse days. And he decides that that was a clouded vision of this true one: the family house was earth to heaven, beast to man, man to god, a fore-glimpsing of the task he had been put on earth to achieve.

John Prindle shows his typical energies and a unique indecision. Their cabin has become a forest of paper and blueprints, books everywhere, half-completed plans tacked to the pine walls, paper cities of imagined and demolished buildings pushed by the breeze along the floor. His outlook changes again, colonnades crumble; and John Prindle is not so exalted that he does not recognize the desirability of some professional opinion. The Mansion House is not only unbuilt, it has been undesigned a hundred times, and the first families from Vermont are due to live in it.

These signs of Providence: the fore-party of Perfectionists fleeing the gossip and narrow-minded outrage of its Vermont neighbours arrives in the New Jerusalem by horse-drawn cart; it comprises John Prindle's wife, Mrs Harriet Stone, who is more substantial and yet less corporeal than George had expected, and John Prindle's sister and brother-in-law, the Fletchers, and Mr Fletcher's friend Erasmus Hamilton, grimly holding the sides of the cart, his stove-pipe hat atilt on his whiskered, leonine head. George Pagan tries to conquer in himself an immediate antipathy. Hamilton is the sort of burly, self-assured man to whom Mary would trust her confidence. He is a Yale man from Newhaven, and an architect.

John Prindle is delighted. That first night, he walks the perimeter with his providential architect. They make plans by starlight. A week later, their cabin has been demolished, tents erected by the horse barn, and work has begun. Everyone mixes cement, everyone lays stones and saws wood. The building takes root and grows. When spring comes, the roof goes on with the help of their Indian neighbours and the sons of the owner of the general store on Turkey Street. More Perfectionists arrive, former Congregationalists and Methodists, renegade Baptists and Anabaptists, two Anglicans, one Roman Catholic, children reborn in the primitive church, living without sin, bringing heaven on earth.

It is one of George's tasks to make a list of all the items that each member of their Association has brought. All things are to be held in common—but should any member choose to leave, he may, without notice, and without concern at being economically disadvantaged by the decision. In his first Home Talk, John Prindle says, 'Anyone choosing to leave this family shall be able to take away the goods he brought in with him, or their equivalent value, whichever he so chooses. Common interest shall be paid on their value.'

'But what if our enterprise should not be profitable?' asks

Matthew Fletcher, John Prindle Stone's equanimous brother-in-law.

'It shall be,' says John Prindle Stone.

The Association's first charter announces that they shall live by the fruits of the land, as their precursors as tenants here, the Onyataka Indians, used to do. They shall trade the surplus of their harvest to their neighbours. They might even consider manufacturing Seth Newhouse's new animal trap, should it ever meet his perfect specifications.

Their house is a large one, with room for further communitarians to join. The parlours are larger than the private chambers because the Association is a family, and there is no need for family members to hide in private spaces. Nonetheless, the sleeping room that George has been allocated is one of the larger ones. This goes undiscussed. It is, he supposes, the fruit of his seniority in this enterprise.

On the third day in the Mansion House, George goes to the horse barn to feed Jess for the final time. In their beginning is her end.

In Paradise, the angels dance, and in this fore-Paradise so do the communitarians. And George Pagan, previously remarkable for his dry correctness in all things, amazes his new family, first with his violin and then, even further, when he lays down his instrument to join the family dancing. His consciousness scatters as they move to the music that their boots make dancing on the Mansion House floor.

On the seventh day, a cart comes along the road from Turkey Street. It rattles over the creek, continues along the rutted path, then makes the gentle climb up the incline to the Mansion House. Its passenger dismounts, the cart-driver unloads the luggage: two trunks, a box of linen, a bagatelle game. The boy who had been running the last part of the journey stops shyly at the front door of the Mansion House.

His mother, in a long black dress that clings unwidowlike to her body, shields her eyes against the sun, and George Pagan, sitting by the front parlour window, working on the first week's accounts, looks up at the new arrivals; and his heart leaps, stutters, and seems to fail. He gets up, then makes himself sit down again. Someone else will welcome Mary Pagan, his wife, to their community.

He tries to delay his journey downstairs. He cannot keep himself from her for longer than a few minutes. In the small parlour, Mary, still dressed in all the outerwear of her journey, sits across from Mr and Mrs Stone. Little Georgie pulls away from his mother's side to rush to his father, but then stands uncertainly in the space between them, unparented, bashful. Mr Pagan cannot look at his wife; neither does Mrs Pagan look at her husband. Both gaze upon Mr Stone.

'I am here in repentance,' Mary says.

'And?' says Mr Stone.

'And hope.'

Captain Carter would have pushed her harder. Mr Stone just smiles. He suffers all that is in her heart and he forgives. Mr Stone invites Mary to stay as long as she feels able, if Mr Pagan should consent, which, gruffly, Mr Pagan, does; and Mr and Mrs Pagan make silent simultaneous vows that they will prove themselves worthy of Mr Stone's love, which is God's.

11

It did not rain on the next day. Nor did Edgar go to soccer camp.

'Warren's making me see the doctor,' Fay complained, when she came into the kitchen.

Edgar managed to restrain himself from saying, *Dr X?!* Instead, wiping some of the sugary excess of YooHoo away from his mouth, he announced his intention to find the cat. 'I'll look for him. I should have done it before. I'll start looking for him straight away.'

'No, of course you won't. You have your soccer to go to.'

'I don't mind missing it.'

'That's very dear of you but I wouldn't dream of taking you away from an activity you enjoy so much.'

He cycled down to Stone Park on a girl's bicycle that Warren had borrowed for him and dismounted when he saw the Forza Italia girl coming towards him. She was smiling. He had not seen her smile before: it made her look even more imperiously beautiful, and the smile was directed towards Edgar. Edgar stood on one leg and then the other. He smiled back and arranged his voice to slide out a hello, which fell away as she walked past him to greet Husky Marvin, who was stretching by the wire fence behind him. The Forza Italia girl cradled her fingers around the wire to watch him perform his warm-up routine with his acolytes, Todd and Andy, who both wore the same outfit as Marvin, T-shirts over hooded grey sweaters, except theirs weren't filled out like his by apologetically worn muscles. Edgar, blushing, walked on, leaving them, the girl leaning into the wire, Husky Marvin lifting his tops to show her the bruises on his skin.

Edgar walked on past Stone Park. He lay beside the creek, shadowed by the bridge. Chin cupped in his hands, he eased his groin against the hard earth of the river bank.

The image of Forza blue was still in his head. Embarrassment fading, Edgar was, he was pleasantly surprised to realize, both bored and contented. A day, a lifetime could stretch out of this moment, in the green prickly heat of dry grass, the buzz of mosquitoes and lonely wasps. Edgar drowsily, luxuriantly, *sensually*, he thought, yawned. A dry leaf drifted against his face and he crushed it, crackling, between his forehead and the ground.

To forestall the inevitable implosive inhibition should he ever talk to Forza Girl, Edgar built a new erotic linkage. He invented a tanned girl called Lucy, who wore denim shorts and a white bikini top. He closed his eyes the better to see her, and he was lying on the poop deck of his yacht. Lucy blows him a kiss, she airily waves, and dives off, jack-knifing into the dolphiny blue of the Mediterranean or Caribbean Sea. Edgar follows: they make love in the water, dolphins and starfish, the sun glinting off the telephoto lenses of the newspaper photographers who are Edgar's constant escorts, hungry for every image of Edgar's life and doings.

A car went over the bridge, rumbling the ground, and Edgar opened his eyes, forced himself still, stopped humping the earth, and saw the station-wagon going past, Warren efficient at the wheel, Fay fanning herself with her turquoise sun-hat.

He would resume his cat investigations now and, after the triumph of those, attempt the more sinister task of uncovering Dr X. Perhaps, even, the thought was audacious, the two were connected? Hunched over his bicycle, his penis jauntily squeezed between waistband and belly, Edgar cycled surreptitiously back to the Pagan House, snaking a route away from the soccer pitch through gridded streets, the rain of garden-sprinklers, roller-skating children with blank unen-quiring faces, lazy fat dogs.

Walking up to the porch, Edgar heard a rustle in the bushes by the side of the house. He clasped his hands behind his back and bent double to inspect the undergrowth. He might solve his first case straight away, discover Tom asleep in a grotesque spider's web—already he could hear breathing, harsh and laboured, and that might be the cat or maybe the sound of one of the wild erotic couplings that he was sure the blameless youth of Creek and Vail enjoyed. Pushing through dry leaves he found no Tom, no sex, but Jerome, on hands and knees, wearing gardening gloves and a battered straw hat. Jerome's brown cardigan and trousers were spotted with stains that Edgar squeamishly chose to connect to gardening work.

Jerome looked guilty. He performed a strange ballet of trying to rise and failing. 'I'm sorry, I couldn't resist, but you can't, I know it's not—oh, young Edward. Hello.'

'Hello.'

'I'm glad it's you.'

'Oh.'

'It was a risk, I knew that. Sometimes he stays with her at the doctor's and sometimes he comes back and picks her up later. I took the chance that he'd be with her throughout. You won't tell on me, I hope.'

Edgar nodded, because Jerome's insistence of attention required him to do something.

'The flowers are going to rack and ruin and he won't let me look after them. Says I'm not up to the job any longer. Says he's protecting me, and that's when I really can't stomach the gall of the man, really can't. You won't tell?'

Jerome anxiously wiped his forehead with a gloved hand, rubbing off flakes of dry skin that drifted to the rosebed like snow.

Edgar shook his head, not quite sure what it was he was agreeing to.

'That's enormously decent of you. You wouldn't help me out here, would you? I just need to turn over this earth. Tom has a dreadful habit for urinating on the roses. Plays havoc with the pH levels. The shovel's just there.'

'I'm looking for the cat,' Edgar said.

He had decided to be the sort of detective who solved cases in flashes of inspiration—where others stumbled he would leap, not for him the plodding forensic logic of slow minds, but he supposed that any detective, even the most inspired type, would have a list of suspects. And pushing himself to the top was Jerome, complaining of the cat's destructiveness to flowers, to which he showed a peculiar, perhaps criminal, attachment.

Under Jerome's direction Edgar dug into the earth and scattered it around and wondered if this was what was meant by the dignity of labour.

'You're a very decent boy, Eddie. You like lemonade?'

'I suppose so.'

'Then we should move on. I don't want to run the risk of *him* finding me here. Help me up now, will you?'

Jerome picked up his basket of gardening tools, which was the same basket he used to bring his evening offerings of snacks and pies to Fay. They climbed the rise past the Mansion House, a sprawling red-brick building, with wings and alcoves and chimneys, that looked as if it had been built by a mad god architect with a box of random house parts.

A sour-milk smell clung to Jerome. He was not good at shaving: maybe his eyesight was not so good or he didn't trust the tremors in his hands, but there were bristly clumps of grey hair below his ears and under his nose. Edgar regretted this. Jerome was the sort of man his mother had warned him about. *Don't talk to strangers—Never accept a lift in a strange man's car*—and she would surely have said, *Never ever go to a cemetery with a strange man*. Jerome was clearly a strange man, and Edgar and he were walking through the graveyard.

'Ever since that fellow came to town I haven't seen as much of Fay as I would like. What do you think of him?'

'Of who?'

'Warren, of course.'

'I think he's okay.'

'Do you?' Jerome sounded disappointed. His hands clutched and opened, never fully. He examined them, daring them, Edgar supposed, to make a deadly move. To live that old, Jerome must have incorporated astonishing quantities of vice. Below the cemetery was a golf course. Stout men in brightly coloured clothing ambled after their clumsily shot balls. A boy could die here and no one would ever know.

'Well, if you say he's okay I guess he might be. You wouldn't help me out here now? There's weeding to be done at the monument.'

Edgar, hypnotized by the suspense of Jerome lowering himself to his knees, slowly joined him, hunched down, pulling away at the tight clumps of dandelions that had sprouted from the base of the stone obelisk, which was the one extravagance in an otherwise austere cemetery. All the other graves were marked by identical small headstones, names and dates of birth and death. As Edgar pulled away the weeds the back of his head felt painfully vulnerable to an old man's attack. He had no weapons to protect himself with, except his mission as a cat investigator.

'Guthrie doesn't like him. She won't let him in her house. But Fay seems very fond of him, he's certainly won her over and maybe, I couldn't deny it, there's a *spot* of jealousy in my outlook. I have lemonade in my flask. Would you like some?'

'No. Thank you.'

Perhaps the thing to do would be just to relax, give in to the inevitability of it, the anticipation of horror is always worse than the horror itself—*or is it*? That might be the sort of lie that victims tell, to console their families, to protect themselves, to make it possible to live in the monstrous, damaged aftermath.

'Do you like cats?' Edgar asked.

'Mary Pagan, who's buried here, is our mutual ancestor. I used to be the CEO of the Company, I don't know if you know that. Which to my mind is the same thing as the Association. Until recently, that is. It's an awful shame it's moved out of family hands. Fay's right and Bob's wrong, that's what you've got to remember.'

'Some people kill cats,' Edgar said, 'if they consider them a nuisance.'

'She's a very fine woman, your grandmother.'

Jerome sighed. So did Edgar. And here it came, what he was dreading, or its presage. Jerome's hand clawed towards him. It touched his shoulder, a grisly intimation of what would follow, and then it withdrew, like a greedy animal deferring its feed to derive maximum pleasure, and cruelty.

'I know I'm a nuisance to her but you know, I used to propose marriage to her, twice a year, regular as clockwork, on our birthdays. I don't do that any more, it's no longer charming, she doesn't even enjoy the sentimentality of it, so I've stopped myself.'

'Oh,' Edgar said.

'That's right. That's right.' Jerome shook his head a number of times and his jowls shook and the bones in his neck cracked with the effort. 'All I can do is offer my advice, that's all I can do, isn't it? Offer my advice and hope she takes it, and if she doesn't I'll offer it anyway, because how else am I going to get to see her, Eddie? How else?'

'I don't know.'

Jerome looked at Edgar as if he had said something very profound. 'No. That's right. I don't know either. And believe me I've spent a lot of time thinking about it.'

Down in the scrubs of bushes between the golf course and the graveyard, three of the Indian Fighters picked through the earth. Jerome waved to them and they didn't wave back.

'What are they looking for?' Edgar asked.

'Balls.'

'What?'

'Golf balls. They sell them back to the club house. It's interesting, those boys, the Ashton boys are descendants of workers in the factory, the original residents of Creek. While Newhouse of course is descended from one of the owners of the factory and therefore of course from the Association. He's a cousin of yours. We're cousins too, you know.'

While Edgar knew of the existence of the category of his American cousins, he hadn't thought it would include Company Bob and Janice, and now Ray Newhouse and Jerome.

'It's a while till the Blackberry Festival. Things can change. Except, when you get to my age, seasons go by in less time than it takes to change a colostomy bag. I think I'll go in now. I'm so grateful for your help, and your discretion. You're a bright kid, and a sympathetic one. Are you sure you don't want a lemonade?'

'Yes. I'm sure,' Edgar said.

Edgar had an empty house to explore and assert himself inside. Calling 'Tom!' in a high-pitched maternal voice, he followed a trail of cat hairs through the rooms, where he

121

stamped his ownership in discreet but certain ways—timid graffiti signatures, the carving of his initials with a kitchen knife beneath the window-ledge in his father's old room, where a flap of paper had pulled away from the damp wall. It was good to be a cat investigator. It gave purpose to things.

Bending forward from the waist, Edgar's trail brought him to Warren's room and Warren's things, his T-shirts and sweaters and jeans, his papers—which Edgar thought of half interestedly as his *private* papers—everything neatly piled and folded along the window-ledge. There were no cat hairs in Warren's room. There was nothing extraneous in Warren's room. It showed hardly a trace of being lived in.

There was a photograph on the window-ledge of an old lady, again in a front garden—Warren's photographic eye seemed to have a fetish for gardens—and again her face was out of focus, so Edgar couldn't be sure but he suspected that this was a different old lady from the photograph he had seen before. That was it. Edgar leafed through the private papers and found nothing implicating or even interesting among the bank statements and legal documents. He heard the sound of a car slowing outside and Edgar squared all the papers as neatly as he could and fought to conquer the burn of anxiety and fear. The car passed. Edgar tiptoed out.

In Fay's room, he sat on the foot of the bed and looked at his reflection, bounced and endlessly multiplied in the triptych mirror on his grandmother's dressing-table. He lifted a silver hair away from the bristles of a silver brush, which was part of a matching set, with comb and hand mirror. It was the unguents that interested him most. From the lotions and creams he selected a cocktail of Nivea and something lilac-green from a slender unmarked jar to soothe his penis, which was reddening and rawing from his frequent attentions, which he now renewed. And stopped, his penis high and bobbing, his soccer shorts around his shins, when he saw a handwritten page that was headed Emergency Numbers, and third on the list, between Dr Newhouse and Onyataka Druggists, was written 'Dr X', followed by a telephone number and address.

'Gold dust,' said Edgar. He looked for pen and paper. He was too much of a professional to take the original document because that would alert his powerful enemies—whose identities were as yet unknown, a further testimony to their power and threat—to the progress he was making. He copied the number on the back of a piece of paper taken from Fay's wastepaper bin, and triumphantly renewed his attentions upon his capacity, when the telephone rang.

He answered it, expecting to hear the sound of his enemy's voice or, failing that, his father's. It was neither. The voice was his mother's, quick and excited. She was still in New York. Edgar cursed her witchlike talents for embarrassing him from afar. He protected his modesty with a corner of Fay's bedcover.

'I thought you'd be back in London by now,' Edgar said.

'Oh. Well. Hen, and. It's very nice here. You'd like it. But let me have a word with your father, and then we'll speak again after. Eddie?'

Edgar was silent.

'Eddie?'

'Hello.'

'Could I speak to your father please?'

'How's the weather in New York? It's very nice here. Warren says that it's unseasonably warm. Usually the summers are mild while the winters can be very severe.'

'Can you put your father on, please?'

'The cat's missing. I've been looking for the cat. He's called Tom.'

'He is there isn't he?'

'I haven't found the cat but—' Mon is not the girl assistant Edgar the detective would have chosen but he had to tell someone about Dr X. 'But, there's this—'

Typically she barrelled past what he was trying to tell her. 'Edward. Your father. Please.'

'He stepped out,' Edgar announced decisively, as he lifted the cover to inspect his penis wilted on his thigh. 'He went to visit a cousin of his.'

'A *cousin*. Which one? It's not *Gus* is it?'

'I'm not sure, I think so. Maybe.'

His mother snorted. Or else it was the crackle of interference on the line. *'Gus!'* she said.

'It might not be Gus.'

'Well whoever—'

'Whomever.'

'Yes. Thank you Edward. Whatever. When he gets in tell him I rang and need to speak to him. You can do that, can't you?'

'What's New York like?'

He was seized by self-pity: Edgar in Creek and Vail, his father nowhere, his mother in New York; for some reason his imagination demanded, he saw her wearing a painter's smock and a very silly hat with a feather attached, sitting on a revolving bar stool, opening lipsticky smiles for men who drink martinis and talk in guttural European accents, gold jewellery around thick necks and wrists, dark coarse hair sprouting from tailored suits, shining gold credit cards and gold-capped smiles, while Mon twirled on her bar stool, acting like a swan. And he was here alone, thinly protected by Fay and Warren from the antagonism of high-spirited youths and the neglect of his parents and the world.

'New York's wonderful. You'd love it here, and next time I promise I'll bring you, I promise. I'd come and get you now but if your father's there that's okay. But look, I'd better go. I'm ringing on Hen's phone and it's costing a fortune. I'll speak to you tomorrow. I love you. Edward?'

'Yes, you too,' Edgar said, hoping to imply nothing beyond empty formality.

Returning to the dressing-table mirror, he felt jaded. He pulled up his shorts and secured Dr X's address between stomach and waistband. He sat on the cushioned stool, wondering if this was the item of furniture called a pouffe, and sighed. Enjoying the sensation he performed it again, and then stopped, pinched his nose silent when he heard footsteps and a woman's chirruping voice.

'I always love the windows here. Old windows are the best, wouldn't you say?'

'Yes,' said Warren.

'And where is the lady of the house today?'

'She's with Doctor Newhouse. I'll be picking her up shortly. So if we could just move on with this?'

'She's a very lively lady, isn't she?' said the woman.

'Yes,' said Warren dully. 'Very lively.'

'Probably see us all off.'

'Yes,' said Warren.

Their footsteps advanced. Edgar slipped off the pouffe, rolled on the carpet, lay with his arms outstretched between the bed and the window as if he was holding a revolver. The door opened and he could see their shoes from under the bed.

'Sorry to put you through all this again,' Warren said.

'Not at all. Out there is what I call a very *volatile* market.'

Edgar couldn't resist peeking above the bed. Warren was standing impatiently in the doorway. The woman with him was small, crinkly-old, with yellow skin and alarming crimson hair. She wore a blue nautical blazer with a gold anchor embroidered on the breast pocket. She carried a clipboard and wore a sea captain's hat.

'Yes,' said Warren.

The woman moistened a finger and ran it along the inside frame of the doorway. She glanced meaningfully at Warren both when she was performing and after she had finished executing this peculiar, perhaps technical, manoeuvre.

'We'll get your valuation in the usual way I expect,' said Warren.

'Oh yes,' the woman said, lifting a hand to her face to tap her cheek. Warren was performing the same action on his own, paler cheek and Edgar wondered which of them had initiated it and which was, consciously or unconsciously, mimicking the other.

'I'll leave you to it,' said Warren.

Warren departed. The woman approached the window. She saw Edgar outstretched on the carpet. 'Hello handsome. How are you today?' she said, brightly and unsurprised.

'I'm looking for a cat,' Edgar said, and ran downstairs and fled.

The afternoon was clear and sunny, he had survived an adventure and discovered much and enjoyed the state it had aroused in him, and he had enough money in his shorts to buy pizza at either of the establishments in Creek. He strolled over the bridge and past the silverware factory, which was a rectangular building of dirtied brick, and to Dino's. At the counter Sky was at the controls of a tape machine, which was bellowing out noise, crooked train-track rhythms, the pure unmistakable voice of Husky Marvin riding effortlessly on top.

Edgar didn't have the appetite for a further ordeal. Yes, the Indian Fighters were near the top of his list of cat-napping suspects; yes, he would have to interrogate them—he had had experience of boys their type in London, animal torturers, whose greatest pleasure was strapping a firework to a cat on a rooftop. But first he needed to fortify himself. He would treat himself to the executive pleasure of a restaurant. He retraced his steps along Main Street, past the dance studio and Luscious Nails and Tan Your Can!, and into the Campanile Family Restaurant, where he was led by a bruised-looking matron to a corner table, red-and-white tablecloth, unlit candle in yellow frosted glass, landscapes of Italian holiday destinations on the walls. He gazed at the menu for a long time: there were many pages of it, vellum-style paper, with brown spots dotting the grain, and when the waiter removed the yellow napkin from his water glass, and deposited it on his lap—an over-familiar gesture, Edgar primly thought—Edgar ordered pizza, the largest size, on a thin crust, topped with pepperoni and mushrooms. The waiter asked him when he was expecting the rest of his party and Edgar squirmed in his chair. 'No. Just bring it please.'

He had thought the menu boast that the large pizza was sufficient to feed a 'mob' was just empty bragging, but the thing that arrived, overspilling from its steel tray, was enormous. He started to eat, trying to find a rhythm to work to, keeping his eyes down on his task, away from any pitying glances. The cheese burned the roof of his mouth, then promptly went cold. The mushrooms were hollow and ancient. This was probably how the night tasted in his grandmother's mouth. This was probably how *death* tasted, thin cold mushrooms greased with metallic tomatoey goo. Pushing through subsequent slices—cold chewy slabs of cheese and base, which was cardboard in some places, swampland in others, from where the gloop of it all had soaked through—Edgar imagined himself as his grandmother. He imagined what it must be like to have a body that was failing, what it was like to be in constant pain. He lifted his water glass with a crotchety unsteady hand and sipped from it with pursed lips, and Edgar became angry.

He was angry at his father for not being there; angry at

his mother for enjoying herself in New York; angry at his grandmother for being dependent on Warren; angry at Warren for dominating his grandmother's world; angry at himself for not having any power; angry at his mother for doing whatever it was that she did with Jeffrey; angry at the Forza girl for adoring Husky Marvin; angry at Husky Marvin for being so apologetically competent; angry at the cat who could only snore and moult and flee, which was maybe the sanest response to life in the Pagan House; angry at the Campanile Family Restaurant for allowing him to order this ludicrous surplus of pizza that reminded him of an old woman's death. With a curt shake of his head at a watching waiter, to indicate that, no, he was not finished, no representative of the house may remove this pizza yet, he would come back to it, but meanwhile he had business to attend to, Edgar smoothed out the page he had purloined from Fay's room.

Dr X lived in Onyataka Depot. Edgar's imagination jumped into a dozen pictures of sinister doings in laboratories, hospital sanatoriums, dangerous experiments, unwilling victims, out of human tissue are born grisly perversions of humanity. On the other side of the paper, which Edgar turned to, just so he could grant himself the pleasure of turning the page over again, was a bank statement. Greedy for the sight again of *Dr X*, Edgar deferred it. He chewed on a slab of cold pepperoni.

'Checking your portfolio?'

'No. What? I'm just—Oh, *hi*.'

It was the girl with the blue Italian shirt who played soccer with more gusto than most.

'I'm Electa.'

'What?'

'Electa. Yeah, I know it's weird. It's like a family name.'

There was an ensuing silence that Edgar broke by saying,

'Oh. Right,' and then, seizing the moment, 'And I'm Ed— Edgar.'

'Hey Edgar. Where are your friends?'

'Uh?' he said, maybe less suavely than he'd intended.

She nodded at the pizza carnage on the table.

'Oh. That. I just felt, like a, you know, blow-out. Do you want a piece?'

'Uh, *no*. I get kind of tired of pizza. You can have a soda if you like. On the house.'

'Thanks. I'll have a Kool-Aid.'

'Seven-Up Sprite Coke Diet Coke root beer.'

Edgar asked for a root beer and Electa went behind the counter. He was impressed by the way she treated the restaurant as a receiving room of her house. He was impressed too, how the soda came, with no ice, and with a straw professionally stripped of the wrapper except for the short paper cylinder surrounding the top. She had brought one for herself and sat across from him with her lips pursed around the straw.

'Don't you like ice?'

Electa blew a couple of small bubbles in her glass. 'Sometimes I like ice. Sometimes I just fill a glass with ice and eat the whole thing.'

'Oh. Do you?'

It was a fatuous remark but he was required to make some response and couldn't think of anything else to say.

'But if I want soda, I want soda. Why weren't you at soccer?'

'Is it finished?'

'Sure it's finished. Why weren't you there?'

She didn't sound interested and nor did she act it. She slouched in her chair, leaning away from Edgar who was leaning towards her, keeping his soccer shorts well hidden beneath the tabletop.

Electa yawned quite lavishly. She batted the O her mouth made with the palm of one hand. Her fingers were long. Her skin was sallow, with thin lines of red by the corners of her mouth and eyes. She was, Edgar thought, exotic. Electa reached to remove the hairband twist that tied her ponytail. She shook her head and black hair tumbled down. Behind the bar, a big, bearish boy in a white T-shirt muttered something and laughed, and Electa snapped something angry back. They fought in grunts in this place, bullet shots of consonants, with Electa clearly an unbeatable adversary. The boy, whom Edgar presumed to be an older brother, stomped away into the kitchen, beaten.

She raised one eyebrow. Edgar was further impressed.

'Did anyone notice that I wasn't at soccer?'

'Oh sure, that's all we talked about. In fact, we didn't play any soccer at all. Spiro stopped the play so we could form little discussion groups and talk about you, so we could *speculate* where you were. And then we *pooled* our speculations. I said you were tracking the progress of your portfolio. And I'm pleased to say I got it right. How was it on the markets today?'

'Yeah right,' said Edgar, impressed again by her ability to belittle any male within speaking range.

'You don't live round here, do you? You live up in Vail?'

'Sort've.'

'What's that mean, "sort've"?'

'It's my grandmother's house, where I'm staying. You could come see it if you liked?'

Edgar was pleased at his own craftiness. He liked the image of the two of them arriving at the house together. It would prove to Warren and Fay that he had been at soccer camp, after all. He had no picture of what he and Electa might do once they got there. The prospect panicked him. Might he tell her about Dr X? Would it entice her to kiss him?

'It's a really interesting house,' Edgar said.

'It's a really interesting house,' Electa said, mimicking him.

'That sounds kind of lame, doesn't it?'

'Kinda,' agreed Electa.

'There's something else though. I could do with some help with.'

'What's that?'

'It's a mystery.'

Perhaps it was because she was so at home in the material world that the possibility of mystery seemed to exert fascination. 'What kind of mystery?'

'I can't really tell you here,' Edgar said decisively.

Electa considered. The passing attention of her brother returning and saying something mocking might have swung the situation Edgar's way. She was the sort of girl who could achieve most things, especially if someone stood in her way of attempting them. Edgar was in awe.

'Okay,' she said. 'Let me just go tell my mom.'

He had not expected it to be this easy. He was proud to have her walking beside him but his panic had not died. He tried whistling. He tried walking more slowly. He tried to bring Lucy to his mind but he couldn't remember what she was meant to look like.

'Do you ever think what it must've been like to live here, olden times?'

'All the time,' Edgar lied.

She inspected him for obvious signs of deceit or facetiousness and, finding none, continued.

'Must of been wild. For the white folks at least.'

'I guess,' said Edgar.

He had no idea what she was talking about but he was far too preoccupied with hoping Fay and Warren weren't back yet, but assuming they would be: neither seemed to like to be away from the house for long. How could he possibly manage the introductions? *This is Electa. She's my friend from soccer camp.* Or: *Hi, everybody. This is Electa.* Or:

Hello. Let me make some introductions . . . But he didn't know what Electa's last name was or how to ask her without clumsiness. Nor did he know Warren's last name. A formal introduction was out. *Dr X.*

'Your grandmother descended from them? *You* descended from them? Most everybody of the old people in Vail is.'

'Yes, I think I am. Here we are. This is the house.'

'I like it. It's one of the old ones.'

Hoping he was exuding old-world charm, Edgar held the screen door open for her. Warren was in the kitchen.

'Hey Eddie! How was practice?'

'This is Electa. She's my friend from soccer camp,' Edgar said gruffly.

He tried to take her up to his room but Warren detained them. He mixed up a batch of his famous fruit smoothies in the blender.

The situation felt agreeably sophisticated. Edgar could just sit and smile and worry about what was going to come next and let the conversation about the people who lived in this house, about the community in the Mansion House, glide over him.

Walking uncomfortably slowly into the kitchen, Fay took an age to focus on Electa, and brighten. 'You're the lovely girl from the restaurant.'

Edgar had stood when his grandmother came into the room, and he forgot to sit down again. He was concerned that his grandmother might need protection from Electa's sharpness. But Electa was respectful, almost demure. She had been trained in ancestral respect.

'Why don't you play?'

Yes indeed, why didn't they?

They sat in the music room, and Edgar played some of his father's records at a discreet volume, choosing only the tracks that faded out.

'Was she born here?' Electa asked.

'I don't know. I think so. Probably.'

'What about your grandfather?'

'Uh. I don't know. Probably.'

'You're weird,' Electa amiably said to Edgar. 'Living here—'

'I don't live here. I'm only—'

'Staying. Right. But doesn't it do something? All those people who sat down here, right here, all that time ago. Doesn't that make you feel . . . ?'

'Feel what?'

'I don't know.'

Electa shivered and became businesslike again. 'What's the mystery you wanted to tell me about?'

Edgar began by reporting, and embellishing, the fact of Tom the missing cat. 'Someone's stolen him, no one knows why.'

The subject interested her as he had dared to hope it would. They built a list of suspects together. At the top of the list were Jerome and the Indian Fighters but Edgar insisted they had to be scrupulous about suspecting everyone. He was more tireless in the task than Electa, whose interest waned and she took to looking at the door and the window, so Edgar told her about Dr X.

'Right,' she said.

'No really. It's true. I've got his telephone number.'

She did not kiss him and Edgar could hardly blame her. He had to admit that there was nothing conclusive or even impressive in the sight of a telephone number written in the hand of a nearly thirteen-year-old boy.

'Do you have a girlfriend?'

He used to get asked this quite regularly, but always by men. His father would ask him, and Jeffrey, leering, vulpine, offering bogus fraternity. It was to Warren's credit that he never had. Edgar's answers had always been unsatisfactory,

133

even to him, the apologetic shake of the head, a hunched rise of the shoulders. This time he was equal to it. 'Yes. She's called Lucy. She lives on a Caribbean island. By the sea.'

Electa shrugged. Edgar wondered if he had made a mistake. Maybe a road had offered itself here, a journey into something bewilderingly wanted and grand, that he had carelessly closed again.

'Do you have a boyfriend?'

Electa shrugged again. She lay back on the daybed. 'That's a beautiful ceiling,' she said.

Edgar lay beside her. He tried to look how she was looking, to find the detail or the totality she saw that made her describe it as beautiful.

'I'm glad you have a girlfriend,' she said, as she got back to her feet and went to the door. 'It means we can be friends without any of that other stuff getting in the way.'

'Yes,' said disconsolate Edgar.

Edgar ate dinner with Fay and Warren at the kitchen table. Jerome came from across the way to join them for coffee, and Edgar failed to avoid Jerome's winks and twitches of complicity. Warren, who noticed most things, didn't notice them, but then Warren was distracted.

'You seem jumpy,' Jerome said, not without malice, to Warren.

'Warren always gets nervous the night before an opera rehearsal,' Fay said.

'It's dignifying it, calling it an opera. Company Bob's probably right.'

'Hardly,' said Fay. 'It's a wonderful piece of work. And since when has Bob been right about anything?'

'A lot of people here don't want this thing put on at all. Maybe I should listen to them.'

'No you shouldn't. They're a lot of nervous old ninnies,' Fay said.

'And I still haven't found my John Prindle Stone. Someone with a voice. A proper male voice.'

'There's a boy, I think his name's Marvin,' Edgar said.

'Husky Marvin? We know Marvin,' Warren said.

'He's a cousin of yours,' Jerome said.

'Can he sing?' Warren said.

'He sings very well,' Edgar said vindictively. 'I've heard him.'

'He's very young,' Warren said.

'He's older than me,' Edgar said.

'This coffee's very good,' said Fay, carefully moving away her untouched cup. She reached for her water glass and swallowed her yellow pills and shut her eyes. Her energy levels would suddenly drop, usually in the middle of the afternoon and after she had eaten her evening meal.

Jerome gathered up his bag. 'I'll be making my excuses,' he said.

'Mind how you go,' Warren said.

When the telephone rang, Fay slowly opened her eyes. She looked for a moment as if she had no idea where or who she was.

'Should I leave it?' Warren said.

Edgar, panicking that his father would be ringing unanswered, got out of his chair. Fay shook her head. Warren reached for the phone ahead of Edgar.

'She's a little sleepy right now. Maybe I could ask her to call you back.'

–

Reluctantly, maybe angrily, but it was always hard to tell with Warren—he kept his emotions out of his face—he passed the telephone to Fay.

'Hello, my dear,' said Fay, in a voice that was too

diminished for the comfort of anyone who had the kindness to pay attention. Warren gathered up the tray and tidied the things away and made almost as much noise as he could doing so.

'Yes. We're expecting him by the end of the week.'

–

—

'No. Nobody's shutting you out of anything.'

—

'How is Lucille?'

–

–

'My splendid grandson Edward is here. From London. He—'

—

—

'How are the kids doing? Did Paul get that camp thing he was after?'

–

—

—

——

'Well, that's terrific news. We'd love you to visit—'
Fay hung up the phone.
'Some things are better left unsaid,' Fay said.
'I can't agree. You know I can't,' Warren said.

12

It is evident that no one should attempt to revolutionize sexual morality before settlement with God. Holiness, communism of love, association in labor, and immortality must come in their true order.

We can now see our way to victory over death. First we abolish sin, then shame, then the curse on woman of exhausting childbearing, then the curse on man of exhausting labor, and so we arrive regularly at the tree of life.

from the First Annual Report of the
Onyataka Association, 1849

A session of Free and Mutual Criticism begins with the atmosphere of a family excursion to the circus. Entertainment will be had, and blood might be spilled, and anyone may be picked out, the victim pulling himself into a cautious smile, *Yes, I'm ready for this, it is right practice, we shall all be improved.* And when the show is over the family returns from hall to bed or parlour or workplace, for prayer and further fellowship, the bonds of love all the stronger—and there has been no victim, it is no circus; any pain felt is only the pang of the perpetual rebirth into sinlessness.

Squeaks of chairs attend the first remarks, a hitching of skirts—all the women now wear the uniform of pantalets and overskirts that Mary Pagan devised for work on building the Children's House. It is Mr Hamilton who is the first subject of Criticism, and George Pagan relaxes a little in his chair, listens to Mr Fletcher criticize Mr Hamilton for his want of humility, his Special Love for ornamentation, as displayed in his architecture and verse and costume, and Mrs Pagan lightly remarks it a very wonder that the Mansion House they sit in has not toppled down under the ornate weight of its weathervane. Mr Hamilton blushes, bridles, submits. He bows his head. He takes the remarks in the spirit of humility and sincere desire for self-improvement.

Unusually, Mrs Pagan is criticized, by Mrs Skinner, for excessive vitality, for always *doing* rather than *being*, for raising the temperature of any room, or individual, she visits. Mr Pagan joins in with the criticism of Mrs Pagan before it is required of him. He suggests that she holds herself apart too often—although he does not tell of the occasions he has watched her doing so. Mary's head bows as he talks and her colour rises and she looks at him, not without coquetry, as if to say, '*You* can do better than *that*, George!'

And unusually, Mrs Stone is criticized, for her very tenderness to Criticism. Mr Stone agrees that if he criticizes her it flings her into self-condemnation; he wishes Mrs Pagan would put some of her courage and self-respect into her. Mr Pagan, dissenting, applauds Mrs Stone's courage and self-respect, its quiet, unshowy strength, the true humility of a character that does not look for praise—and the attention of the meeting turns to him.

Mrs Stone and Mr and Mrs Pagan are seldom criticized; John Prindle never (there was an imputation at one of the earliest such meetings, from Mr Hamilton, of the *Moses-Spirit*, but that was met with a general silence that accorded all privilege to the subject rather than the speaker).

It was Mary who first referred to them as a *quartette*. The Mansion House was filling with new-born adherents of the

Primitive Church—each gesture an expression of the new dispensation, every moment a divine service. The community is growing, purses are shared, and labour and hearts, a perfect Bible Communism, with John Prindle its understood head, but all in equal, sincere fellowship; but there was an inner group, Mr Stone, Mrs Stone, Mr Pagan and Mrs Pagan, whom Mary named the quartette.

They have been five months together in the second temple of their marriage. Both have grown immeasurably. It was Mary who adapted from Wesley to produce community hymns. It was George, discovering in himself unexpected capacities of acumen, who had become the community's business manager and has remained so, as has Mary remained at her occupation in this world of constant flux and Stirring-Up, in charge of the Children's House that she had helped build, raising the roof beams sitting high astride, angelic. She is loved by all the children and loves them all, her natural child no less than the others. As John Prindle reminds us, 'All here are cousins.'

When Mary referred to George as being 'A Very Marvel of the Machine Age!' she was not praising his amative technique. The Locomotive George Pagan, steaming ahead with his pregnant wife below, could not change gear, forswear, forestall—abrading on his run, chugging, his corporeal body and eternal soul were never so painfully extwined.

Like the locomotive at Onyataka Depot, his arrival may always be predicted from its signals. We see the steam here, we note the grinding of metal wheel and rail here, we espy the doors opening here, and we wait, here, on the platform in this regular scuffed spot, and know the moment of cessation, of power spent, is now.

'Must it always be done with effort?' she asked him, as if

139

suggesting a text for one of John Prindle's Home Talks, but for one whose ear for heart music is so exquisitely tuned as hers, this was a disappointed chiding.

Not only has he never stopped loving her, not only can he not imagine or remember a time before he loved her, not only does he experience his love for her as being without limits, his love has, it seems to him, and he is not of a poetical burst of mind, so this perception is all the more troublesome yet irresistible to him, continued to grow. The conclusion to be drawn from this is as weird and unfixed as its premise: for how can something that is without limits become larger?

And yet he had found himself more in the company of Mrs Stone. There was, is, a heart's ease in their fellowship. He does not stutter or dote or become foolish with Mrs Stone. Mrs Stone is doughty, solid and wise, promising the comfort of her husband, if not his majesty. George seeks her out, engineers tasks to share in office or kitchen or printing works or storehouse.

He sits beside her now, taking comfort in her presence, as it is his turn to be criticized, as he has been before, for his display of the *Killjoy-Spirit*, his excessive sombreness when not at music-making. 'I feel awkward and judged in your presence,' Mr Hamilton says. Mr Pagan accepts the Criticism and resolves to evince more sincerity and candour. And the attention moves on. Mr Fletcher criticizes Mr Skinner, and Mr Miller criticizes one of their latest arrivals, Mr Carter (no longer a captain, there are no ranks here), for his display of the *Rooster-Spirit*, and is the humility, George wonders, that Mr Carter shows in response a true mark of his sincerity or just the proof of his improved theatrical skills?

Mr Newhouse is criticized for his independence of heart and mind. While praising him for the efficacy of his animal traps, and their economic value for the family, Mr Hamilton suggests that they show a Special Love. Mr Newhouse answers that without his animal traps the Association would have foundered. He then makes some remarks about 'gentleman farmers' tilling unforgiving soil. This is not a ripe subject for Criticism. Mr Stone watches over them all, stroking his beard, seldom intervening except to bring the conversation back to good practice. He draws a close to this session of Criticism with a reminder that all shall produce all. The farmer shall become an actuary, the slaughterman a teacher. 'There must be constant flux,' he says, 'and music.'

George's violin joins in with John Prindle's, more roughly played, and Mary's voice: hymns for the New Jerusalem, borrowed from elsewhere or freshly composed, by Mary Pagan or by Erasmus Hamilton, with his ornamentalist aptitude for rhyme and metaphor. They perform a recital of 'Jeannette and Jeannot'. George Pagan looks over the music stand to see Abram Carter, his one-time rival, dancing.

Afterwards, George submits to family embraces as he makes his way outside. Just down the rise from the Mansion House, beside the horse barn, is an untamed meadow, which is Mary Pagan's favourite spot. He sees his wife, already swelling with child, lying in her place between the cherry trees, flat on the prickly ground, arms stretched out wide, as still as she can make herself, practising not-doing, making herself content just *to be*. And Mr Pagan, watching unobserved, is envious of her solitude. His old fantasy returns, his hidden special love that he can never share, not with Mary, not even with Mrs Stone. On Mary's seclude is where he should choose to build his house.

David Flusfeder

JEANNETTE AND JEANNOT

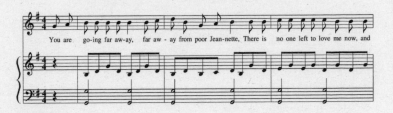

You are going far aw-ay, far aw - ay from poor Jean-nette, There is no one left to love me now, and

you too may for-get; But my heart will be with you, wher - ev-er you may go; Can you

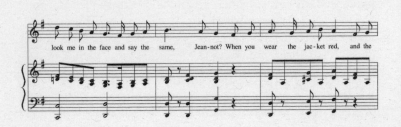

look me in the face and say the same, Jean-not? When you wear the jac-ket red, and the

142

beau - ti - ful cock-ade, Oh, I fear you will for-get all the pro-mis-es you made! With your

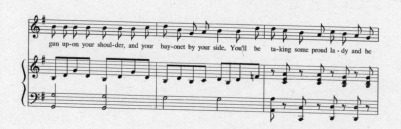

gun up-on your shoul-der, and your bay-onet by your side, You'll be ta-king some proud la-dy and be

ma-king her your bride, You'll be ta-king some proud la - dy and be ma-king her your bride.

Or, when glory leads the way,
You'll be madly rushing on,
Never thinking, if they kill you,
That my happiness is gone!
If you win the day, perhaps
A General you'll be;
Though I'm proud to think of that,
What will become of me?
Oh! if I were Queen of France,
Or, still better, Pope of Rome,
I'd have no fighting men abroad,
No weeping maids at home!
All the world should be at peace;
Or, if kings must show their might,
Why, let them who made the quarrels
Be the only men who fight!
Yes, let them who made, etc.

13

The Wednesday-evening opera rehearsals would always begin in a loose sing-along, the wilder energies of the cast discharged in manic renditions of Motown and Stax and Atlantic, the Supremes, Otis Redding, *Sitting on the dock of the bay, watching the tide ro-o-o-ll awayyyyy!*, with Warren on piano or pedal-steam organ, pumping out the rhythms and the melody, overseeing it all with a thinly indulgent air, hardly ever wincing.

'Now ladies,' he would say, judging the moment when they could start in earnest, 'might we now begin?'

The disappointed women fetched out their sheet-music. Truth is, they liked this first bit the best, the free-form part of the evening, *I was born to love yooooou!* or *Shake it up baby now twist and SHOUT!*, vamping it up, acting to their notions of how showgirls might perform. They liked these communal sing-alongs, even if Marilou Weathers went madly out of tune, unrestrainable and uncontainable, even if two or three of them turned their voices and warmly expressive eyes to Warren, the only man in the room—but not the only male: Husky Marvin was here now, his effortless baritone having proved him a natural for the part of John Prindle Stone. And Edgar was here too, sitting invisibly by the doorway, frozen by the sight and sound of so many passionate unyoked women.

After the disappointment of their conductor bringing them to only slightly rebellious order, after the songsheets (as they persisted in calling Warren's tenderly written transcriptions)

145

were brought out rustling on to music stands, after the gossip and high spirits quailed before their leader's authority, the singers gave enthusiastic, orderly voice.

It was the fact of re-creation that delighted Warren so, of music returning to where there had been silence, and Warren could put up, almost tirelessly, with all the irritations and the tiresomeness; what had once been community hymns and popular songs and Mary Pagan's words, her letters and journal entries, black marks fading on a brittling page, had grown into song and it was he who had made it happen.

Warren had wanted a part for Fay, and that of John Prindle's sister suggested itself, seen always at committee work, so she wouldn't even have to stand, and he had told her that her voice was up to this, as indeed it was. But she had refused all entreaties. She brought in refreshment half-way through the rehearsal, and how Warren argued that she shouldn't—one of only three times Edgar would see them in open disagreement—and not just because of the effort that this cost her. The ensemble disintegrated into chattering neighbourhood hobbyists so readily. And Marvin came unstuck at these interruptions. When he was singing he forgot himself. Standing in a crowded living room with nothing to do, he was stricken, Edgar was pleased to see, by nerves and diffidence. Marvin's voice was special. It outshone all the others, especially Marilou's, whose attempts at the title character would have been embarrassing, had she any capacity for self-reflection.

When they got to the performance—*if* they got to the performance—then a whole other set of problems and anxieties would expose themselves, but for the moment, this was difficult enough, coaching Marilou in her love duet with young Marvin, Warren trying somehow to instil in her some depth, some bottom. The aria was the most difficult one in the opera because, Warren suspected, it was the only one he had written from scratch himself. Mary has died, and John Prindle has a dream-vision in which the lost Magdalene appears to him, pale but vivacious, obliterating any wall between this life and the next. The way that Marvin and Marilou sang it, John Prindle was possessed of a transcendent humanity, invoking the depths and the stars, while Mary was a shrill creature, more annoying in death than Marilou had made her in life. It had taken a great struggle to persuade Marilou not to dance while she sang.

'It makes me feel, you know, more free.'

'This isn't the point about you feeling free.'

'Well, *my* understanding of Mary is that she is a free spirit. And now in death she is, like, released.'

'But it's *his* vision. And in *his* vision she's neither dancing nor free.'

'Oh, okay,' she reluctantly said. But she continued to imply the possibilities of freedom by gaily lifting her arms up and down until Warren ordered her to stop doing so.

Marilou plainly wasn't up to the job. At the auditions Warren had been fooled by her shallow, slightly eczematic beauty and by her quietly self-contained manner into thinking that not only did she look right for the part but that she must also possess the spirit for it.

'I didn't realize that it was all to do with the Prozac or the Calmitol or whatever it was she was prescribed,' he told Fay. 'I blame her husband. Spiro's a thug.'

What Warren had initially taken for character in Marilou was in fact the disembodied slow cloudy panic that the drugs had induced in her. Coming off the medication had done wonders for her, she told him, and any other members of the cast she could get to listen, usually Guthrie. Warren had tried suggesting that maybe she had come off the drugs too quickly. He had even toyed with finding out what drug it was and mickeyfinning it into the sodas she habitually drank, despite the obvious ill-effects on her teeth.

'Or maybe I could get Marvin to sing a bit worse. The disparity between their voices is *horrible*.'

But Marvin didn't know what he was doing any more than Marilou did. He just did it. It was best not to talk to Marvin at all in rehearsals. Once Warren had made an attempt to improve his 'acting' and that had done nothing to lessen his wood-puppet demeanour but for the rest of that rehearsal he had hopped about with his eyes tightly closed. Marvin's was a talent not to be tampered or trifled with.

Except he was still too good. Standing in the living room of the Pagan House, his large face pitted and pocked with acne, blinking as he often did, he released that effortless voice.

I saw you in my dream, Mary
I saw you in my dream.

And Marilou, giggling (how much caffeine was in her perpetual soda bottle, or was this excess of personality the reason she had been prescribed drugs in the first place?), hurled herself at Warren's most delicate melody:

Is this me that you see or just what you want me to be?

Which should be a profound moment, Mary Pagan punished, even in death, by the part she must play in John Prindle's grandiose imagination, and which instead was performed as if she was a shrilly skittish ghost.

Warren lifted his hands away from the piano. The singers turned his way.

'You're windmilling again.'

'I'm what?'

'Doing that flappy thing with your arms. Please don't.'

Marilou licked her lower lip. Her mouth was always damp and chafed from her habit of dipping her tongue over her lips. 'I didn't realize I was.'

'Well you were. It's bogus. Please stop it.'

He had spoken more harshly than he intended. Even Marvin looked hurt on his co-star's behalf.

'Well what do you want me to do with them then?'

'I don't want you to do anything. Just keep them at your sides.'

The cast was splintering, attention turning to Marilou now sobbing: pain and tears in her eyes, a scarecrow lurch from the living room, reproach on the faces of the remainder of the cast.

'Let's do a run-through of "Jeannette and Jeannot". Guthrie, can you take the piano?'

The cumbersome strains of the song that the community had sung on the jetty before Mary Pagan took her final voyage followed Warren out as he went to comfort his star.

Warren was still so off-kilter at suppertime that he over-cooked Edgar's scrambled eggs.

'It's one of the things I usually do well,' he said, pouring a refill of chocolate milk in apology. 'The trick you see is to cook them very slowly, hardly at all, then it all comes together and you take the pan off the stove and the eggs finish cooking in their own heat. But this . . .'

'It looks fine. It's delicious,' Edgar said.

'Yes, well, that's very nice of you.'

'Have you thought,' Fay asked, 'that Marilou might be in love with you?'

'I can't really think about how I appear to my cast. I'm far too busy keeping them vaguely on track and in tune.'

'I think it's the only possible explanation,' Fay said.

'It's a grisly thought,' Warren said, shivering dramatically.

So grisly that it was Edgar rather than Warren who remembered to remind Fay to take her evening medication.

14

Edgar enjoyed vocabulary. In his grandmother's bathroom, his home from home (and Edgar would forever enjoy a sentimental and erotic attachment to bathrooms, particularly those of old ladies, bottles of lavender water on frosted-glass shelves, dark water rings around wash-basins, handles on the sides of tubs for the elderly and infirm to lift themselves away from the slurpy seduction of gravity, squeezed up tubes of denture-kind toothpaste lying belly up and nearly spent on the soap dish), having teased himself with the memory of sixteen female bottoms in denim, thirty-two breasts swaying under slogan T-shirts and knitted sweaters with cute animal faces, having rubbed himself into pleasure, release, and beyond, Edgar inspected his now shrunken, reddened, chafed penis.

'Somewhat scraggy,' he said.

Looking into the mirror, he said,

'Edgar said his penis was somewhat scraggy.'

And,

'Edgar announced his penis was somewhat scraggy.'

And,

'Edgar *averred* that his penis looked somewhat scraggy.'

Which verbal formula he found pleasing, he then went to work on pitch and delivery,

'Edgah averrrrred his penis looked somewhat scraaaaaggy.'

'Ed-gah a-verred his pee-*nus* looked somewhat scraaaaaaaaaGGY!'

His penis did indeed look, as Edgar averred, somewhat scraggy. He'd rubbed it raw on the underside, made the foreskin into a ragged puffball skirt, scrubbed the head swollen. He feared he'd ruined it for ever. He'd done the same with a vintage clockwork tin train that a pre-Jeffrey boyfriend of Mon's called Rufus had given him for his sixth birthday, and in his pleasure at the toy he'd overused it, given it fresh challenges, sent it over higher and higher precipices, until the train was tinny pieces of rubble and his birthday had hardly started yet and his best thing ever was destroyed.

'Ed-gah a-verred his pee-nus looked somewhat scraggy.'

Could it be that delicate? Maybe that accounted for the bad moods and bad manners of men. Teachers, bus drivers, dentists, walking around with a ruined flap of gristle between their legs, hating themselves for not having looked after it better. Who could he ask? Warren? His *father*? Was there a book on penile care and grooming available from the library, from bookshops? Maybe this was the knowledge that Jewish boys were rewarded with on their bar mitzvahs. Were there exercises you could do? He would have to look it up somehow.

'Ed-gah a-verred his pee-nusss looked, somewhat, scraggay.'

He wiped away a final leaking tear of his stuff. Was this it? Over? He hadn't even reached his prime, and in his eagerness, his stupid impetuous eagerness, he'd spoiled it all for ever.

'Ed-gah a-verred his pee-nusssss looked, somewhat, scraggay.'

And yet he did not feel entirely disconsolate. There was the magic of words that lifted him from the mud of feeling bad, but he was nonetheless almost sure that he hadn't ruined it, that everything was all right, temporary malfunction only. Looking into the mirror, a boy imagined himself a man, painted a dark moustache under his nose, gave a sneer to his lips, which, when he was a man, would be like the rest of him, muscular and suave and hard. Briskly, he said,

'Edgar averred his—'

'What are you doing?'

'Oh? What? Sorry. Nothing.'

A girl stood in the doorway of the unlocked bathroom. She was not the kind of girl he would normally think of as beautiful, preferring, he would have thought, slim athletic girls with straight black hair who knew how to sneer, but there was something beautiful about her all the same. Her face was freckled and sort of smudgy and she looked like a sleepy plump squirrel who had been disturbed from hibernation; her hair was reddish and her body was a mystery under her bulky sweater and baggy blue jeans that were, excitingly, dirty.

It was only when she had slipped past him and closed the bathroom door behind her, after allowing him a glimpse of hipbone and baggy elastic of knicker-top as she began pushing her jeans down, that he realized his penis (scraggy) still protruded from his trousers.

Zipping himself up, he did the stairs in a kind of daze. Fay had company, so Edgar would compose himself by practising his catching on the front lawn.

'What's your name?' she said.

She had found him, as he expected her to, as he had in some respect ordered her to. Edgar tossed the ball against the house wall, reached for it rising on the bounce and palmed it one-handed most nonchalantly.

'Edgar,' he said suavely. 'What's yours?'

He made the mistake of attempting the nonchalant catch again, and this time gave the throw too much weight, and the ball hurtled in a heart-stopping moment against a downstairs window, which rejected the ball without being affected by it and sent it bouncing past his hand into the density of an overgrown flowerbed.

'Michelle,' she said.

She laughed, clearly at him. Usually he didn't like it when people laughed at him, but with her there didn't seem to be anything aggressive about the act: it was all an overflow of generous feeling.

Michelle didn't offer to help him. He had hoped she might. Edgar on his knees pushed through heavy heads of flowers, monstrous snaky clumps of leaves. He didn't want to lose this ball. He supposed he would, eventually, because he always did, but it represented London to him and he didn't know where he could find a replacement, and he certainly couldn't ruin the impression he was making in this neighbourhood by asking where the nearest toy shop was.

Maybe though, he thought, scrabbling, cutting his palms on biblical thorns, pricking and burning his knees, everything was different now. Boys lose toys. To be a thing in a boy's life is a precarious short-lived existence. Boyhood things get ruined and smashed. The train he had been given on his birthday changed direction whenever it encountered a solid barrier—a chair leg, a boy's foot, a door—but then he had placed it on top of a table to see if it was as clever with abysses as it was with obstacles, and it had shattered into a hundred tin pieces on the floor and made him cry, and the memory of its fragments still had the sentimental power to arouse in him something stronger than pity. But life now had changed for him, in a qualitative way. A fuzz of hair under his arms, soon the beginning of down on his face. Potency and capacity.

In the undergrowth, the skin memory of Michelle's hand brushing against him as she went into the bathroom and he went out, the way she stood with her hands in the pockets of her jeans, these were all stimuli that he responded to manfully with a twitch of blood, a creak of internal hydraulics, a lengthening and consequent hardening of his penis. He had ruined nothing after all. This was a most perfect resource.

A boy, a *man*, could go missing for lifetimes in here. He wondered how many gardeners had gone to their deaths in his grandmother's garden. As he crawled, hands and knees against sharp stony earth, he became fearful of skeleton bones, empty wellington boots in the shrubbery or, worse, their blind rubbery feel against his hands.

What Edgar found: an unopened packet of birdseed, a crucifix, a tattered leather dog lead and collar, a silk scarf, which the mud brushed off of to reveal as purple, a mulchy cigarette packet that he was disappointed to find empty, because he had contemplated smoking as his next accomplishment, a plastic magnifying-glass, and, penultimately, just past the corpses of two bees curled by each other, something familiar and orange that became more apparent as he dug away at the loose soil. He dug further until Tom the cat lay half disinterred. His glaucomic eyes were open and blanketed with earth. His head lay at a horrible angle showing the wound in his neck that must have killed him, the slash of a kitchen knife, the scythe of a garden trowel. Edgar's list of suspects shrank to two, the cook Warren, the gardener Jerome. He pushed the earth back over the cat again while avoiding touching its dead body.

'It's a stiff,' he said, to regather himself, as he found his ball.

The girl was gone. Squeezing the ball tightly in his hand, which fell in dwindling triumph, he softly said her name, 'Me. Shell.'

'Edward? Come in here. Meet your uncle Frank.'

Uncle Frank had brown-grey hair, which was brushed

back, and he wore glasses, which he probably thought made him look intelligent. Everything he did was done with belligerence and scorn.

'And this is your aunt Lucille, and your cousins Paul and Michelle.'

Frank was dressed in the same sort of clothes as his son, khaki shorts and a grey hooded top, except that the clothes made Paul look like an athlete while Uncle Frank looked like an accountant pretending to be an off-duty policeman. Paul had blond hair and lounged in a chair with the physical ease that Edgar had always longed to possess. Aunt Lucille was painted and voluptuous and made everything she did into an erotic event. She opened her arms to Edgar. 'I haven't seen you since you were a baby. You were adorable. Are you too old now to give your aunt a kiss?'

Edgar, mutely, nodded. He was saved by Warren: 'Eddie's got soccer camp. Maybe Paul is going to want to go with him.'

Edgar wanted to go to soccer camp. He wanted to see Electa. She would be the first to hear about his discovery of the corpse. He did not want Paul to go with him. He hoped very hard that Paul was not going to want to come with him.

'Sure. I don't mind,' Paul said.

'You need kit,' Edgar said.

'What's that?'

'What you wear.'

'Like uniform you mean? I got something I can wear.'

Edgar argued further until he realized that he had gone some way beyond the point of appearing ridiculous. He did not want this blond, goddish boy with him. The ease of Paul in his own skin called everything about Edgar into question. He had thought Husky Marvin was severe competition. He did not want to see Electa's face in that moment of revelation, the eye-widening, heart-quickening moment of seeing Paul for the first time, and everyone else belittled beside him.

'Michelle?' said Warren. He had to say it a few times before she noticed. She had her hands wrapped up inside her jumper and her eyes on the cookie jar.

'Michelle?'

'What?'

'You want to come? I can run the three of you down in the station-wagon.'

Edgar was pleased to see Paul struggling with an equivalently ignoble feeling. Michelle reflected badly on Paul just as much as Paul outshone Edgar. The same genes, a different combination.

'I don't mind,' she said.

Michelle didn't have a kit or a uniform. Nor did she join in. She stood, hands inside tailing jumper sleeves, by the wooden rail that separated the soccer pitch from the running track. There was soon a cluster of boys beside her, led by the scrawniest and pimpliest of his intimidators at Dino's pizza parlour. Sidled beside Michelle, Ray Newhouse made his pitch, talking loudly, purportedly to Edgar.

'I'm a direct descendant of the greatest lover in history. Giacomo fucking Casanova. You know what Casanova means in Italian? "New house", that's what it means. And the expertise, my friend, is in the blood.'

Michelle was unimpressed. She left Ray Newhouse and went to where the other girls were, watching Husky Marvin warming up out on the field, because the girls liked to adore Husky Marvin. Ray Newhouse spat into the dirt. He watched the girls watching Husky Marvin and held on tightly to the fence, disregarding the way the wire cut into his fingers.

'We better go through,' Edgar said.

'I won't be much of a player,' Paul said. 'Soccer is not really my sport.'

But, of course, he excelled. It was not so much the natural skills he showed, the goals he scored, the runs he made into the space that his body (Edgar doubted his intelligence) somehow knew was where the ball was going to ricochet to, although all that was impressive; what really clinched it were Paul's mannerisms, as if he'd spent half a lifetime looking at photographs of footballers and practising how they sat on footballs with a towel around their shoulders listening to the coach, or playing keepie-uppie with a ball, juggling it between instep and thigh. A marvellous narcissism led him to the most elegant, most camera-ready posture.

'He's my cousin,' Edgar admitted to Electa, when she ran over to ask. And he hated her at that moment. He had expected this but all the same had hoped for more, that she at least would put up some resistance to the phenomenal Paul. At the end of practice, Paul detached himself from the admiration of Coach Weathers, and Michelle from the attentions of Todd and Andy and Ray, whose hand tugged at her jumper as she was leaving causing the hem to rise, revealing a flash of skin, white and smooth and less baggy than Edgar had expected—he had supposed her flesh to be the same shapeless texture as the concealing clothes she wore. He was also surprised by Michelle's movement, a controlled spin, a chiding smile, *You leave me alone, you're nasty, you're a nasty boy*, performed with an unlikely grace that was quite powerfully erotic.

Electa seemed to be waiting for Edgar to approach her, so Edgar, to test her, waited with his sneakers laced around his neck, his sports bag in one hand, his ball in the other, for Electa to come to him, but it was a test she failed—with a dismissive wave she made her way back down to Creek.

At supper, Edgar sat angled away from Lucille at all times because she terrified him. Michelle and Paul sat opposite

Edgar. They were going to sleep in the room next to him, their parents in Frank's room, which foolish Edgar had thought was being prepared for his father.

'I tried to take a shower,' Frank announced. 'Can you believe this? They don't have a shower in the house. How can people live like this?'

'Warren persuaded me to change the fittings after he moved in here. We decided the house should look as its makers intended.'

'Oh yes? And what else has he persuaded you to do?'

Uncle Frank questioned Warren throughout the meal, and at first Edgar had been relieved—any new assemblage of company usually meant questions for him, school, girlfriends, favourite subjects, hobbies, the cuteness of his accent, the originality of his hair, what he thought of America, was Britain going to the dogs—but it went on, relentless and dull, with Warren answering every question with courtesy and care. Edgar tried to help. He volunteered unlikely information. 'Soccer camp is fun,' he said.

Michelle giggled. She giggled a lot. Warren nodded gravely, in acknowledgement of Edgar's attempts to shift the focus. Paul stretched, beautifully. He did everything beautifully and there wasn't a thing in his head except the warm glow of self-pleasure.

'The weather here is quite a lot like London, except it's not as damp,' Edgar said.

'Just you wait,' Fay said. 'After the Blackberry Festival, the fall gets awful damp.'

'Please,' said Frank. 'We haven't driven all this way to talk about the weather.'

'I should think not,' said Lucille. 'The traffic on the inter-state was atrocious.'

'Or the traffic. Let's get a grip here.'

Michelle giggled. She slouched back in her chair and her

foot rested, Edgar supposed inadvertently, against his knee. He lifted his leg to allow Michelle to realize her mistake but the pressure of the foot became, if anything, stronger.

'Maybe we should, you know, wait for, more appropriate,' Fay said, wheezing lightly, waving a hand towards the younger family members at the table.

'I hope I'm not embarrassing anybody. I'm not embarrassed,' Frank said. 'Are you embarrassed, kids? You see, Mom? They're not embarrassed. They're family. In fact, that might be the point.'

Lucille nodded sagely. 'Frank's a very good son. He thinks of you all the time. It makes him very sad how neglectful Mike is.'

'But at least he's family,' Frank said, turning his belligerence full on to Warren. 'What are you?'

'Please leave him alone,' Fay said.

'Uh. No.' Frank laughed. His laugh was abrupt and wolfish. 'I'm not going to leave him alone. That's just what I'm not going to do. There are things have to be said. You don't mind, *Warren*, do you? I'm not embarrassing you?'

'No, Frank. You're not embarrassing me.'

Edgar admired Warren for the quiet suggestion in his tone that Frank might be embarrassing himself, and felt guilty for having gone through his room and being suspicious of him and he vowed to make it up. He shifted quickly in his chair and achieved the double success of feeling Michelle's foot drop from his knee while avoiding eye-contact with Lucille.

'That was delicious,' Lucille said, pushing her emptied plate towards the centre of the table.

'Come on Lucille. Not you too now.'

'I'm just saying the meal was delicious. It doesn't hurt to be a little polite. You're a very good cook, Warren.'

'Thank you. I'm glad you enjoyed the meal.'

'Oh I'm sure Warren is a very good cook. No doubt about

it. I'm sure Warren is very good at lots of things. Come on. Let's not beat around the bush any more. Warren, tell me. Enough of all this bullshit. Where do you get your money from? Fay pay you a salary? How much?'

Warren nodded, as if he had been expecting this question. He continued to nod as he answered, 'I have a little income.'

'An income?' Lucille echoed, tasting the word pleasurably in her mouth.

'An *income*? What kind of income?'

'From back home.'

'Yes?'

'The rent, on some property I own.'

Frank and Lucille awarded him a slight, grudging respect. Warren owned property, therefore he couldn't be all bad.

'So you're doing all this for love?'

'In a manner of speaking.'

He looked to Fay, who shook her head.

'Well I'm fucked if I'm going to say sorry,' said Frank, which was the first interesting thing he had said. 'Sorry,' he then said. 'I mean, excuse my French, I'm not apologizing for anything else.'

He fell into a belligerent silence, which Lucille filled. 'Paul is a very talented athlete,' she announced.

Paul, to his credit, looked neither proud nor coy. He took tributes as his due.

'They've got a wonderful sport programme at the high school in Onyataka. And Michelle is really very gifted at art and communications. They have a very good art and communications programme also.'

'The school they go to now is a jungle,' Frank said. 'Metal-detector at the gates, can you believe it? Kids in junior high carrying knives, packing heat.'

'I've really fallen in love with this neighbourhood, it's s-special,' Lucille said.

161

'The landscape is very pretty,' Frank said, without conviction. 'Wherever I've gone I've always taken a part of it with me.'

'But I think it's the *people* that make a place what it is, don't you agree?' Lucille said. 'Where are you from, Warren?'

'Near Dublin. A little place called Mulhuddart. You won't have heard of it.'

'I love Ireland. There's something so magical about the Emerald Isle. But doesn't your mother miss you?—living all that way away?'

'She's not, I'm afraid, with us any more.'

'Oh. I'm sorry.'

'She died. Some while ago.'

'And your father?'

'He keeps himself busy. He has a drinking hobby to sustain.'

'Oh really. I'm sorry. And what about a sweetheart? Have you ever been married?'

'Ha!' said Frank.

'No. I never have.'

Warren was very good at treating questions on their own terms. He was very good at most things. The questioning went on, and Warren gave his scrupulous answers, and Edgar and Paul and Michelle were encouraged to leave the table. Michelle suggested a game to play but Edgar, fearful of her smile and intentions, stretched and yawned and announced his intention to sleep.

In the night, hungry for cookies and chocolate milk, for the possibility of Michelle, Edgar went downstairs. He was expecting to find the kitchen empty, but Warren sat at the table, his shoulders hunched, a ruler beside him, head studiously close to the words he was writing. Edgar stood in the doorway. Bare-chested, the lino cold against his feet, he felt narrow and unsure. Edgar moved closer, his thirst gone: he wanted to see what Warren was writing. He walked making no sound; he reached the refrigerator, inched forward. Warren was drawing single words in block capitals inside neat squares. He had nearly filled the sheet he was working on. There was one sheet already done, on the table to his right. Edgar walked closer. He had read the words 'POTS (MISC.)' and 'BAKING' when he felt the further chill of Warren's attention upon him.

'Anything I can do for you Eddie?'

'Uh. No,' Edgar managed to say. 'I was just thirsty, going to get a glass of water.'

'Sure, help yourself,' said Warren, who was now, perhaps accidentally, covering both sheets with his arms.

Edgar selected a glass, went to the sink.

'You sure you wouldn't fancy a YooHoo instead?'

'Yes. I'm sure,' Edgar said, careful to hide his weakness and his greed.

15

Edgar saw flickerings of the argument on the Mansion House lawn. Across Vail Avenue, between the Mansion House and a copse of beech trees, was a small romantic place, a summer-house made of twisted and entwined branches of nineteenth-century wood that Edgar's imagination filled with midnight trysts with Electa, except, in his susceptible imagination, her face kept getting blurred into Michelle's. Fay was on the gardening rota, because Warren hadn't been able to persuade her to give up much of her volunteer work at the Mansion House. She was leaning against a wheelbarrow, huddled in a man's overcoat, antique and fur-collared, while Warren deadheaded roses with a viciousness that was unusual to him. Edgar, remembering his private-investigator status, crept up the slope to listen and observe.

'If that's what you choose to believe,' Warren said (*thwack! thwack!*), 'then who am I to try to take it away from you?' (*THWACK!*)

'But you . . .' she said sadly.

Warren took a moment away from his brutality to the flowers to wipe his forehead with the sleeve of his sweat-shirt (grey, faded letters, occluded crest) and to shrug. 'Whatever,' he said. 'Thirty-five, fifteen, infant, human, animal, it doesn't make any sense to me. But I guess that's what faith's all about,' he added, straightening his shoulders, making himself agreeable again. 'It's an individual thing, right?'

'What does the other woman believe?'

Warren looked pained. 'Please,' he said. He turned to pat down a fresh mound of earth beside the summer-house and saw Edgar. 'Hey Eddie, how's it going?'

'Good,' Edgar said.

Pleased that his grandmother no longer looked sad, he felt no lingering obligation to stay.

In the Music Room, Edgar listened to his father's record collection through headphones. He drummed along, hoping the sound was muffled by the tea-towel he had smuggled out of the kitchen and laid over the coffee-table. These sounds are raw and thrilling, primal he supposes the word is, but, alarmingly, every single song on the album he was listening to faded out. He used to like fade-outs. Now he didn't. They worried him. Somewhere, thought Edgar, there was a room where the songs that faded out continued to play, muffled, perhaps even hidden from earshot by thick, corklined walls but sustaining, despite the efforts of the musicians to end, but there can be no ending; the engineer's careless fingers damp down the sound for the listeners but not for the players, who are doomed to play this song for ever—and every time the song is played, another doomed identical band joins its brothers in that cursed room; and Edgar was implicated, how can he not be? Each listening cursed another mirror band. So, as the record spun, as the arm holding the needle bobbed along its groove, Edgar quickly lifted the arm away because part of the magic of it was that the curse only began to apply when the engineer's hand lowered, when the volume faded, and Edgar had saved at least one incarnation of the band from playing perpetually in that awful room where the cacophony and the repetition must get too loud to bear.

Although maybe a counter-magic was possible. If you listen very carefully, if you turn the volume right up when the final fadeout begins, then all kinds of things might be happening; what sounds like a stray bum note on the guitar might have been the beginning of something extraordinary, because maybe the musicians are aware of it too: they watch the engineer, they see him look to the clock, yawn, shift forward to the console to fade the song away, and *now they can do what they really want to do*, they can play the *real* music that the rest has been just the necessary, public, prelude to; first comes the job, the ordinary expected song, and now come the occult sounds that only those who know can possibly hear.

Blasting himself back into the now, Edgar put on one of the loudest records of his father's collection and he danced, happy dervish flailing. Warren found him there, finally attracted his attention by waving the spanner in his hand. 'So this is where you hide yourself!' Warren yelled.

Edgar, embarrassed, lifted the headphones away from his ears. 'Not hiding,' he said.

'What's that you're listening to?'

Edgar, to answer, pulled out the headphone lead and enjoyed the effect of the desperate power chords that could shatter anyone's soul. Warren pantomime-cowered with his hands over his ears. 'For God's sake you'll kill us all!'

Edgar, happy, lowered the volume. 'It's the Stooges. It's from my father's collection.'

'Is that right? Well I'm glad you found the headphones. Have you got a moment? Fay would like to see you.'

He was unfamiliar with the ways of an invalid's room. The door was ajar but he knocked anyway.

'Come in.'

Fay was propped on pillows in the centre of the bed. She patted the coverlet beside her for Edgar to sit. Her hair was most magnificently disarrayed. She smiled. A sketchbook was beside her on the bed. She had begun a drawing, in quavery lines, of trees and bushes surrounding an empty field.

Edgar wondered if he should have brought a gift or at least some grapes, but then he hadn't known he was coming.

'It's kind of you to visit me. I know boys are very busy.'

His dread lifted immediately as it always did in her company. He liked Fay. He enjoyed her flattery. 'That's okay. How are you feeling?'

She lifted a hand and it slowly moved, flooded by the bedside lamp, fragile bones lit by angel light, pale rivers of arteries and veins. 'I'm fading away,' she said.

He wanted to protest but he didn't have the words to use or the tone so he imagined he was his uncle Frank and he jutted his chin and stuck out his chest and was about to tell Fay how *robust* she looked, when she asked him, in a heart-breakingly humble voice, if he would brush her hair.

'Of course,' he said.

He used the middle-sized silver hairbrush, which was agreeably cool to his hand, and heavier, he fancied, than Fay's head, which, he horrified himself by imagining, could be batted away from her frail neck with a single confident swing.

'Try to keep your hand steady.'

'Sorry.'

He found a pleasure in the operation. He worked, pulling at the fine white hairs that clung to the brush, gently lifting them away from the tiny red dots on her scalp that reminded him of the spots on eggshells.

'Where's Warren?' she asked.

'He was doing something with a spanner.'

'He must be trying to fix the faucet. I've got used to it. It reminds me of me. Do you like it here? Do you mind being here with us? You must miss all your London friends terribly.'

'That's okay,' Edgar said.

'I'm so sorry your father hasn't come yet. I wish he could be more relied upon. At this rate he won't be with us till the Blackberry Festival and what will be the point of that?'

'Yeah. Well,' Edgar said.

'Don't get old. It's the worst mistake I ever made.'

Edgar snuffled to suggest laughter but he couldn't tell if Fay was making a joke or not.

'Have you been over to the Mansion House yet?'

'Uh. Not yet.'

'The Mansion House is living history. Rather like me. Except it will last a lot longer.'

He managed one jocular, Frankish 'You aren't going anywhere,' but Fay waved that away with her translucent hand, which rested, in exhaustion or benediction, on the side of Edgar's head.

'I think you should try the smaller brush now. You're very good at this. I knew you would be when I saw you grooming Tom.'

Edgar returned to the dressing-table. He put down the medium-sized brush and picked up the smaller one and resumed his task.

'Um. Tom,' he said.

Her eyelids fluttered open and shut again.

'I hope he's not dead.'

He hated himself for even this softened brutality. He waited for his grandmother's tears. She didn't provide them.

'It was time for him to go,' she said.

Fay smiled or it might have been a wince of pain, from Edgar's strokes, or from the loss of her cat, which, although fat and ginger and leaking, might still be, conceivably, an object of love.

Edgar wanted to give her something to make up for her loss but he couldn't think of anything he had to give, other than the facts that he could successfully masturbate, that Jerome gardened illicitly, and that his mother had a boyfriend called Jeffrey. But the first didn't seem appropriate and the other two he had promised not to tell.

'You know, my real name isn't Edward?'

Fay nodded, encouraging him to go on, but that snagged the brush with a clump of hair that he had to twist and roll to remove from the bristles before it tore away from her scalp.

'I've got like a secret name? It's Edgar.'

He had expected to feel ridiculous saying it, but it had worked with Electa and with the Indian Fighters so he assumed it would work here too; the saying of it aloud and bold always made Edgar feel strong and it induced respect in his listeners.

'Why Edgar?'

'It's my real name. It's kind of a secret, but I don't mind if you know.'

'Thank you, Edgar.'

'That's all right. You can call me that, but not in front of, you know, people, my mum, or anyone like that?'

'Warren?'

'No, not Warren either. He doesn't know.'

She seemed pleased by the confidence.

'It's nothing against Warren, you understand.'

'Of course. I'm very glad to have been chosen to know.'

She said this solemnly, and he wondered for a moment if she was laughing at him, but then decided that that was a suspicion born of the moments spent in the derision of Electa.

Warren was in the corridor when Edgar left Fay's room. He looked past Edgar and was about to say one of his pleasant Warrenish things but stopped when he saw Fay sitting up in bed, her hair perfectly straight and brushed, and he looked sharply at Edgar, out of jealousy, Edgar supposed.

16

In the Kingdom of God the intimate union that in the world is limited to the married pair extends through the whole body of communicants; without however excluding special companionships founded on special ability. (John 17: 21)

The System of Complex Marriage, John Prindle Stone and Mary Pagan, editors, 1849

I appeal to the memory of every man who has had good sexual experience to say whether, on the whole, the sweetest and noblest period of intercourse with woman is not that first moment of simple presence and spiritual effusion before the muscular exercise begins.

But we may go farther. Suppose the man chooses for good reasons, as before, to enjoy not only the simple presence but also the reciprocal motion, and yet to stop short of the final crisis. What if a man, knowing his own power and limits, should not even approach the crisis, and yet be able to enjoy the presence and the motion ad libitum? If you say that this is impossible, I answer that I know it is possible—nay, that it is easy.

Paul intimates that some cannot 'contain.' Men of certain temperaments and conditions are afflicted with involuntary emissions on very trivial excitement, and in their sleep. But I insist that these are exceptional, morbid cases that should be disciplined and improved; and that, in the normal condition, men are entirely competent to choose in sexual intercourse whether they will stop at any point in the voluntary stages of it, and so make it simply an act of communion, or go through to the involuntary stage, and make it an act of propagation.

You have now our whole theory of 'male continence.' It consists in analyzing sexual intercourse, recognizing in it two distinct

173

*acts, the amative and the propagative, which can be separated
practically, and affirming that it is best, not only with reference
to prudential considerations, but for immediate pleasure, that a
man should content himself with the amative act, except when he
intends procreation.*

The System of Male Continence, John Prindle Stone, 1850

The communitarians wear the short hair and self-devised
uniform of God's soldiers. In the main hall of the Mansion
House, they listen to their general.

'We wrestle not with flesh and blood,' Mr Stone says, 'but
with principalities and powers. We have abolished marriage.
Soon we may abolish death.'

George Pagan's ardour for his wife, of whom he is
unworthy, will never diminish. Nonetheless, he had realized
that he was in love with Mrs Stone also. And when he
announced the fact—having received permission first from
Mrs Stone, a request made, and granted, in a letter—he was
neither surprised nor happy to discover that his state
mirrored others'.

Charles Skinner and Charlotte Fletcher revealed a similar
amity. So did Miss Glass and Mr Newhouse, and Miss
Markham and Mr Fletcher—and Mr Stone and Mrs Pagan,
the other half of the original quartette.

With the consent of the community, Mr Pagan was joined
in fellowship with Mrs Stone, and with the consent of the
community Mr Stone was joined in fellowship with Mrs
Pagan, and Mr Fletcher with Miss Markham, and Mrs
Fletcher with Mr Skinner, and Mr Newhouse with Mrs Holt
rather than the more skittish Miss Glass, of whom it was
decreed better that she should be united this initial occasion
with Mr Hamilton, and so it went on. Later, it would be
suggested that this was all a manoeuvre of Mr Stone's, that

he and Mrs Pagan had already begun the practice that was once called adultery but in this dispensation is the godly principle of Complex Marriage. In a community of love there can be no fixed objects. In heaven, as Paul said, there is neither a giving nor a taking in marriage. In the supper of the Lamb, every dish is free to every guest.

There are to be no special loves. George Pagan must not show too great a pleasure in his business position, nor may he play the violin as much or as heartfelt as he would choose. And yet Mrs Pagan and Mr Stone are closeted together more than most. This is, of course, because together they are writing editorials for the *Spiritual Moralist*, but there are gossips— and there are gossips, even in this garden of heaven—who call her his consort.

Mr Stone has recently returned to his family. He takes frequent absences, to preach to the unenlightened, to rest his fragile throat, for the purpose of his own investigations and contemplations, and for the benefit of his flock to develop its own principles with no shepherd or star to guide them. Sometimes Mary accompanies him, other times one of the younger women of the family, whom he has been instructing in the tender ascension of Fellowship. Rumours have recently been circulating that John Prindle has made an approach to Hester Lovell, his once-fianced, to join the community. George Pagan has not been above feeling a small measure of happiness at this news.

'To be full of happiness,' John Prindle continues, as he approaches the conclusion of his Home Talk, 'is to be full of liberty, genius, inspiration and everything that makes man fruitful. The true economy of life consists in finding out a way to have abiding communion with God, so that we shall be kept full of life; that is the great victory of our existence.'

The original quartette continues to be. Most of the committees have at least one of the quartette presiding upon them.

And the quartette sustains at night too. Beside Harriet, who had been and is still known as Mrs Stone, the comfort of the bedchamber can be gentle. George has if not mastered at least accomplished, sometimes unsteadily, the doctrine and practice of male continence. And in the absences of John Prindle, it falls upon other senior members of the community—Erasmus Hamilton, Matthew Fletcher, Seth Newhouse, George Pagan—to bring the new converts unblushingly into the light.

These are rare nights, the interviews with the converts, touch reaching down in descending fellowship, and he is gentle, he is careful, there is a distance that the Devil must not be permitted to cross between spiritual sensuality and licentiousness; but these girls, no matter how eager for perfection, are still sometimes not so fluttery as one might expect, not so nervous or unbidden at an older man's hand; but such delicacies do not seem to trouble John Prindle—certainly after time spent in fellowship with him, the girls' ardour and aptitude for perfection, and its chief proponent, is only increased.

George is on the correct path, of that he is sure. He has cast away so much that was bulky. John Prindle Stone is anointed in divine commission, there is indisputable proof of that. He has abolished marriage; he will soon abolish death. But *happy*? George's happiness is dependent, or so he used to imagine and sometimes still does, upon the woman who had been his idol and his wife.

'We each must do all things,' Mr Stone says. 'If we don't know, we will learn from each other. Tomorrow I am going to build a stone wall. I have never built a stone wall before. Mr Miller will show me how.'

The wall shall enclose the southern perimeter of the community graveyard. As the family grows, despite its soon-abolition of death, the cemetery receives. Mr Short lies there, father of the gloomy Mordecai. The headstones are simple, undistinguished, modest: there is no distinction of spiritual rank in life or temporary death. Mr Short's stone is the same as the one that George frequently visits.

Mary's twins, her second and third children, were born eight months after Complex Marriage was adopted: Henrietta survived a few hours; Henry Stone Pagan flourished.

'One twin each,' George murmured to John Prindle, who was holding baby Henry in his arms after the funeral service—the heartbreak of an infant coffin lowered into hard ground, the empty consolation of God's love—and John Prindle had been wise enough not to reply.

On some debased Spanish square . . .

George awakes, pulsing, spurting, appalled, remembering little of the dream place, except that Mary had been there, Spanish lace, Spanish leather, fingers stroke a guitar, sunlit verandas, a mocking duenna.

Other men abide by this regimen so why mayn't he? His incontinence exposes him. His body, his sin, betrays him. In daylight hours he is the very model of the Perfectionist; his energies bring doubtless credit to the community and its endeavours. At night, in storm-tossed disarray, the truths of his incapacity reveal themselves in brute expulsion.

George shivers. His bedclothes are damp with his shame. The only consolation is that he may sleep now without fear of further crisis. But he is not ready for sleep yet. He removes his nightshirt, dabs it against the stains on the sheets. He sits on his bed naked in voluptuous unease. The Mansion House is alive. Floorboards creak as lovers return to private beds. Prayerful cries of ecstasy echo along metal pipes. Seth Newhouse snores. Mary calls John Prindle's name. George calculates. Are the moments of his shame coincident with the visits of John Prindle Stone? In some bitter harmony do his crises occur when John Prindle and Mary renew their Fellowship? Are the moments of his incontinence simultaneous with the highest pitch of their delights? Does one, somehow, *depend upon the other*?

He knows—or at least can be fairly certain he knows— that this is early-hours thinking. A world twists and distorts at night remaking itself in the images of a drowning man's fancy. George Pagan prays. And in some debased Spanish dream square, Abram Carter fingers a guitar, Mary preens and stretches in sensuous gratification, and John Prindle struts amid shafts of suspicious sunlight, shadows and lace.

George, gratefully alone with his figures, tots up the account books. His ploughing days are over. They may one day resume. John Prindle urges a permanent revolution upon the community. One day a farmhand, the next an accountant. Soon a cook, a baker, trap-maker, salesman. The trick is to show no special love for any occupation; one learns how to hide in some favoured spot behind a mask of enthusiastic duty. Here, in the business room, there is little traffic. Ledgers sit on sedate shelves. Dry correspondence waits in pleasant trays. George taps his pen into the inkwell. He hears Mary's voice in the schoolroom. Slyly, he ambushes her when the bell sounds for lunch.

She discerns his embarrassment. Perhaps she might also discern its cause. 'It is a personal matter,' he blusters. She is at first concerned, for his health, for Georgie's.

'No, it is not that,' he says.

'You are unhappy,' she says.

To this he agrees. He has never been able to lie to her. He should not want to have the skill.

'But that is not, what . . .'

She takes his hand, in a gesture he cannot mistake as signifying anything other than sisterly affection. She declares herself always, as ever, willing to be, a confidante of his heart.

'That is not what . . .'

'What then? What?'

Her spirits rise; good humour is ready to take the place of concern. He has always aroused in her an amusement as well as a protectiveness.

'I would ask . . .' He clears his throat. In anticipation of this conversation the request had not been so hard to make.

'Ask what?'

He should like to be looking at her. He should like to be holding her hand with simple, unambiguous pressure. He should like to be playing his violin or dancing. In music he feels his connection to the Lord most freely.

'In fellowship, you, and I.'

His tongue fails him. He is grateful that she is looking neither reproachful nor amused. She does not say, '*Oh George!*' She does not make light of the request or of him. Neither does she reject him. She will give herself to him, if that is what he wishes, and it is what he wishes, beyond anything; but in her demeanour and in her use of the word 'wish' rather than 'desire', it is clear, to both of them, that her acquiescence is unmistakably a duty, an honour owed, and it hurts him all the more.

George puts the request in to the Committee in the usual way. *Yes, the matter has been previously initiated and discussed, yes, both parties are willing for the Fellowship to take place, yes.* And when George looks at the paper, where he has written down his wife's name and his conjoined, is he reminded of their wedding day? Their names have been together on other official forms, most recently on the birth certificates of the twins Henry and Henrietta and on the death certificate of Henrietta. Henry Stone Pagan is a boisterous, lustrous child, fast on the ground, big-boned, his restless spirit pardoned by his sincere heart, but who knows what damage he wreaked in the womb? Henrietta Stone Pagan was frail, sickly; she languished, dead within two weeks, and sentimental George took the lineaments of the dead infant for the embodiment of his once-marriage.

The past is gone. John Prindle Stone laid claims to Mary's future and his own. 'Little' Henry flourished then, he flourishes still, he towers over his playmates in the Children's House, and much as George would like to lay claim to his putative namesake, it is the boy's turbulent heart, no less than his red hair, that marks out his undeniable progenitor.

The committee headed by Harriet Stone turns down his application for a night with Mary. He knows this is the correct decision: there are to be no special loves in the Association. God says no.

17

Edgar liked the light, the sunshine, the smell of hard summer turf. It was his penultimate day as a twelve-year-old and Edgar was playing soccer. He liked running in this world and felt tireless here, indomitable. If it were not for the ball, bouncing between the better players, slung out low by the goalkeeper wearing an orange-yellow cap and wraparound sports shades, his contentment would be thoughtlessly complete. But sometimes the ball did come his way and he had at least to affect to run towards it, attempt one of his scissoring kicks that he might later claim was intended for Husky Marvin or Ray Newhouse or Cousin Paul to run on to. The other players knew how bad he was, but somehow the news kept failing to reach Coach Spiro, whose attention was always elsewhere when Edgar was executing the most shaming of his pratfalls and incompetencies. It had lodged in Coach Spiro's mind that Edgar was a British virtuoso of the sport, and nothing, not his own demurrals, not the other players' anguished, almost tearful protests, could prevent Edgar's name—or, rather, the name he went by in the ordinary world—from being read out on the team sheet for the opening game of the season. Electa had been named only to the substitutes' bench.

'And the captain will be Paul. This represents no judgement on you, Marv.'

How can it not be? How can Marvin not take it as such? The indignity of Edgar was forgotten. Paul had beaten out

Marvin for the captain's armband and this was news. Paul was in his white shorts on the changing-room bench, pulling off his socks, sweat dripping photogenically on his chest, unselfconsciously resting an arm on Todd's shoulder for balance or just to demonstrate his ease and manliness to the world. Todd and Andy used to be Husky Marvin's friends, partners, supporters, apostles. Now they were Paul's. Husky Marvin busied himself with a liniment rub, furiously taking out on his calf muscles the rage he felt at Paul's ascension.

'Settle down now. We've got a treat for you.'

The 'treat' was the arrival of Company Bob with a box of soccer-team uniforms. They were red and green and each had a number on the back and the Onyataka Ltd logo on the front of a dish and spoon hanging from a tree.

'This humbles me,' Company Bob said. 'I know you're going to wear these with pride. When you put on this shirt—and the shorts, of course, and socks—you're representing a lot of things. Not just your team, although I know that Coach Spiro has done a fabulous job with you. No, you're representing a lot more than that. You're representing Creek and Vail and the company and the community, and you know what? You're representing history too. This is how we show who we are!'

He went on, being inspirational, Edgar supposed, but Edgar had stopped listening, because Edgar was making a vow: he had decided to ask Electa out to the cinema and he would do it the first chance he got and Electa would say yes and then he would kiss her. He has promised this to himself.

'Thanks Bob,' Coach said, clapping his hands. 'We meet at ten thirty next Saturday. Training as usual on Wednesday. Stay sharp, men.'

Electa was waiting outside. She might have been waiting for Edgar or she might have been waiting for Husky Marvin,

but the two boys walked out together and neither wanted
to test if he was the less preferred, and maybe that was how
Electa wanted it, as they fell into step, she in the middle,
the three walking so carefully together that none was in
charge of their direction. Edgar practised nonchalant
whistling. Husky Marvin kept clearing his throat as if in
preparation for a speech. Husky Marvin was wearing a
checked shirt over a black polo-neck jumper. He always
seemed to reverse the order of his tops and Edgar would
never find out why.

'How's your cat investigation? Made any breakthroughs?'

This was what he had been waiting for. They walked down
to the creek and he conquered her facetiousness in complicit
whispers with his report of the discovery of the body of the
victim.

'Wow,' she said.

'That's right.'

They lay side by side in the sunshine in the long grass
beside the creek and Edgar offered his theories about the
perpetrators of the crime—the Indian Fighters did it, or
Jerome; he tested the theory and found it wanting that Janice
and Guthrie and Marilou Weathers belonged to a witch cult
that sacrificed animals and might soon be moving on to
bigger game. Midges circled above their heads, a slow swarm
in the heat. Edgar's and Electa's shoulders were touching.
Her face was inches away from his. Edgar stopped talking,
held his breath to listen to Electa's breathing; he tried to shut
out the sounds of birdsong in the trees, the croaking of frogs
by the creek, faraway voices outside the Community Center,
the rumble of traffic on Route 5. He watched the rise and
fall of Electa's azure-blue shirt, the grain of the cotton on
her sports bra beneath.

If he kept his scope of vision narrow, he could pretend
Husky Marvin wasn't here, he could banish him from this

world, where every chosen detail was lovely, the poignancy of the blades of grass that have escaped their feet and bodies, a rogue dandelion that receives a strand of Electa's hair, Electa's skin, dappled with hair and sun. A fly settled on Electa's shirt, worked its legs against the thread of the embroidered crest, and lifted away again.

'No flies on me,' Electa said.

In this charmed moment, Electa's joke was as funny as anything he had ever heard. He laughed, and his delight provoked hers. When their laughter fell away, he wondered if he might kiss her now, if she should like that: her mouth was still open in a smile, and across her lips were tiny lines like the veins in tangerine segments that he longed to press his mouth against, but he could feel Husky Marvin watching them, and greater than the prospect of her anger or Marvin's response if he should assault her was his fear of destroying this moment. He was saddened by its impermanence and he wanted above all to prolong it, keep the two of them like this, touching and delighted. Already her eyes were looking up now through the branches above them, as if for diversion. Her eyes were pale green, almost to grey.

Edgar made the mistake of looking up too and his gaze largened to include Husky Marvin, who was sitting with his arms around his knees. He wasn't watching them any more. His attention was on the softball diamond just up from the creek. The center fielder was standing, hands on hips. The pitcher was whirling her arm. The hitter stood, undersized and unready. On the edge of the field, a woman under a large sun-bonnet sat at an easel.

'Let's watch the game,' Marvin said.

Husky Marvin and Edgar sat either side of Electa on the bleachers. They pretended to be interested in the softball game. Husky Marvin was still nursing the wound of losing his captaincy.

'I gotta go home,' said Electa, showing no signs of moving.

'Sucks,' said Marvin. 'How long you say he's staying? He's not going to be here for football season, is he?'

Dimly Edgar worked out that soccer season and football season were two different time periods. He had no idea when football season was, but he was not above further worrying Husky Marvin. 'I don't know, he might be.'

'Sucks,' said Marvin.

'Big-time,' agreed Edgar, confidently.

'You said it,' said Marvin.

'You like the sister, though,' Electa said.

'Do not,' Marvin said.

'Okay. I was just going to ask why. I don't know who would.'

Electa's capable hands were on her lap. There had been one previous moment when her right hand glanced as if by intention across Edgar's left. Edgar, elaborately, moved his whole body to the side, leading with his shoulder, a gentle bump, delighting in the strength that Electa's tight body had, shoulder to shoulder, and he swivelled slightly, picking, as if interested, in what might lie underneath, worms, worlds, chasms, white flakes of paint from the bleacher seat, so their hips now touched and, discreetly, without looking, he brought his hands further up his thigh, as if to warm them on this breezy, summery evening that fell towards night, and now the side of his hand was touching the side of hers. And, he must be quick here, fear of what his rival might do gave Edgar boldness, he reached, he took, he held her hand in his. Continuing to look away, as if inspecting the clouds for tomorrow's weather, Edgar exulted. He had achieved something grand here. He held the hand tighter and the hand squeezed back. It was daring to be sitting here, out in the open, something being revealed and displayed.

A finger flicked across his hand, an enticing movement that was not quite what Edgar would have expected from Electa, and was therefore all the more exciting. It encouraged him to make the most difficult movement, of slowly moving his head so these secret lovers might meet in vision as well as touch. He hoped taste would be the next sense to match, inextricable with smell—and so it would go until all six were involved, all six of hers and all six of his, combining, which makes thirty-six possible combinations or, no, it must be more than that: her taste, his taste, her touch, his smell, her smell, his touch. 6 x 5 x 4 x 3 x 2. Edgar's head dizzied. Electa, however, stared straight ahead, at the softballers, at the windmill arm of the pitcher, the ball that whizzed through the flail of the batter's swing to the catcher who tossed it back to the pitcher again. The boring thing about sports was their repetition, or maybe that was what people liked about them, doing the same thing over and over until everyone was machine. He would not have thought her interested in this kind of spectacle, or maybe, crafty Electa, she was seeking to distract Husky Marvin from the grand event that was going on here, the statement being made. And Marvin was indeed staring straight ahead, face a little ruddier than usual beneath the beard of his acne. Perhaps he was embarrassed. Probably he was furious at the quiet intimacy that Electa and Edgar were putting on show here today. Electa's arm was still tight against Edgar's. Edgar looked down, his gaze following the line of her blue Italian soccer shirt, the pale yellow of her wrist, the piano-playing fingers that gripped the bench. Which meant, Edgar realized, that it was her other hand he was holding. This delighted him at first, her audacity of reaching across with the arm that was next to Husky Marvin's, that might even be touching it!, but then he became concerned at the effort it must be costing her, the muscular pull across her shoulder. She showed no discomfort but all the same. Edgar leaned back to enable her arm to perform a less unnatural twist. The hand he held, as if in gratitude, clutched his more tightly, fingers resumed their explorations.

Edgar watched the softball players. He would be content to sit here for ever, enjoying the pleasant sounds of birds in the sunset, Husky Marvin's throat performing its nervous manoeuvres. Floodlights flickered on. The softball players continued to do what they were supposed to do. His hand was gripped more tightly. An urgent message of some kind was being squeezed across. Over in the direction of Route 5 a fire gaily burned.

Slowly lowering his head, a reluctant horror growing, Edgar looked down at his hand being held and caressed by Husky Marvin's.

Marvin had been making the same mistake as Edgar, that much was obvious from his face, staring straight ahead, reddened with the blood of arousal rather than embarrassment. Edgar had to end their entanglement before Marvin realized whose hand it was he had trapped, which he held so tightly, stroking with a virtuoso touch. Edgar pulled away. Marvin held him tighter. Edgar didn't know if Electa was aware of the battle that was being fought and he didn't want to know. It must be over. Edgar relaxed his hand, played dead for a moment, an awful moment, in which his maidenly hand lay vulnerable for Marvin's next assault, and just as Marvin was deciding in which direction he should seize his advantage, Edgar's hand had gone, nursed, protected, in his lap.

Marvin finally was looking at Electa, who was still oblivious to the clutch and the struggle, or at least politely appeared to be so. Marvin smiled, deciding that this was all in complicity against Edgar. He does not know and never will. This was a moment that may be unwritten, despite the gaze—prurient, disdainful, comradely?—of the center fielder out on the diamond.

As they left the sports field, there was one last chance. Husky Marvin was already away. They watched him, slouching shoulders, lightly running across lawns, vaulting over playhouses, dog kennels and bicycles. Electa adjusted her sports bag. The instep of her right foot scratched the back of her left calf, the rope strap of her bag sliced a line too tender to bear between her breasts.

'Do you want to come to the cinema with me?'

If he had said movie-house or theatre she'd have said no straight away, he could see that while she was considering the invitation—for once, with this obscure girl, everything she was thinking was apparent to him; and he gave her a further incentive by saying he had another discovery to report to her, and she did say yes: amused, scuffing her foot into the loose pebbles on the road, kicking up a grey cloud of dust, she said she would go to the cinema with him the following night.

'I'll get tickets,' he said and he was about to say more, but some new instinct that he recognized as reliable instructed him to end the conversation now.

Edgar on Vail Avenue exults. The air is pure, the dying sunshine is good, glaring off the silver roofs of cars, and Electa has consented to come to the cinema with him. He wishes he could drive, he would like to drive now, radio on, roof and windows down, steering one-handed with his elbow out. There is an almondy scent to the day, which he breathes in deep; he jumps, attempts to click his heels off to the side while in air, but he doesn't quite make it, he nearly falls, foot scrabbling on impact with the loose stones of the road, he has to put out a hand to stop himself, grazing his palm. But no one sees, Electa is gone over Creek bridge, he is alone in his exultation; he may regather his self-possession, and whistle, and saunter.

When he got back to the house, Paul was outside, lounging with a giggling harem of blonde Vail girls.

'Hey Eddie,' he said. 'Your dad's here.'

TWO

The Inheritors

1

Edgar watched his father driving. Edgar's father's hair was streaked brown and grey and attached itself in damp strands to his neck, which was sunburnt into little cross-hatched diamonds. Edgar had an early childhood memory of sitting in the back seat of an open-topped car like this one, perhaps it was this one, and counting the diamonds in his father's neck, and watching his girlfriend (his stepmother, Edgar supposed he could have called her, except their relationship was never quite formal enough for that), and the way Edgar's father's girlfriend's fingers would walk along the headrest like little men, commuters on a jaunty break from office routine, until they found a place to play in Edgar's father's hair, twisting and coiling and releasing thin brown strands.

'How's Jenna?'

'Who?' His father pursed his lips, flicked at something irritating in the corner of his eye beneath his sunglasses, then patted his empty shirt pocket.

'Jenna. Your, you know, I don't know, girlfriend.'

If his father heard his struggles to say the word 'girlfriend', he didn't remark on it. But then his father seldom remarked on anything Edgar did in the world.

'Jenna? You remember Jenna?'

'Sure I do,' Edgar said, bravely attempting American usage. And it was true: he remembered Jenna very well. She had been very good at menu complicity with him, whispering that she bet he would love the steak and fries and how about a rocky-road sundae to follow? And Edgar, little pre-Edgar, liked to seem as if he was pondering, weighing up his choices, but there was a part of him that was disgusted by these gross American things, these hunks of cow, bleeding and browned; everything to eat in America had seemed brown to him, he had wondered why that might be, and in fact he had once dared to ask the question out loud, but neither adult had heard him.

'What happened to her? Fu— Damned if I know what happened to Jenna. Got married again I heard. That was years ago. Kid now. Moved back to Ohio. Columbus?'

Edgar had admired Jenna while being terrified of her. She had reminded him somehow of a horse, the same pride in her own movements, the warning gleam in her eyes that there might be trouble if she was approached in the wrong way, the same satiny unselfconsciousness about her.

'Do you have, you know, now, have?'

'Have what?' Edgar's father asked.

'You know, like a girlfriend?'

'What's all this interest in my romantic life? Your mother told you to find out?'

There was no getting back from here. Once Edgar's father's suspicions of Monica's stratagems had been aroused, they were locked into place. Edgar's father rolled another stick of chewing-gum into his mouth and again it didn't occur to him to offer one to Edgar, nor did Edgar presume to take one: it seemed too far to reach, to the cubby-hole below the radio, where his father kept his gum and quarters and spectacles case. Edgar's father jabbed the radio from one classic rock station to another and tapped the place over his heart and drove and chewed gum and didn't talk to his son for another forty and some miles.

The part that Edgar had enjoyed best about seeing his father again, better even than the first hug, his cologne smell, the casual 'Hey, how's it going, buddy?', was watching his father deal with Uncle Frank. Edgar's father's presence immediately quickened Frank's already quick temper. Uncle Frank's lips pouted. His face and voice became petulant. Edgar was glad he didn't have any brothers and sisters if this was what happened, the permanent sibling war.

Edgar's father infuriated Uncle Frank by nature. He sat on the sofa—Edgar primly beside him, not quite touching, hoping for his father's arm to fall expansively over his shoulders—while he gently rocked his whisky tumbler making the ice clink and roll.

'Don't know why I'm surprised it took you so long to get here. You've always left it to me to take responsibility,' Uncle Frank said.

'Johnny-on-the-spot,' Edgar's father said.

'What's that supposed to mean?'

Edgar's father turned his attention to his brother's wife. 'You're looking very gorgeous, Lucille. He treating you right?'

Lucille crossed her legs and glared in brief contempt at her husband before smiling again at Edgar's father.

'We got to come to some sort of strategy here,' Uncle Frank said.

Uncle Frank's invitation to conspiracy didn't interest Edgar's father, who took another sip of his whisky, leaned back and blew an invisible smoke-ring. 'Whatever, Frank. You keep me posted. But in the meantime me and my son are hitting the road.'

'He always was an asshole,' Edgar's father confided in him, as they climbed into the car and drove off into freedom.

Edgar had been looking forward so hard to this that maybe the urgency of his hopes had ruined it, he and his father together, two men, Two Guys. Or maybe it was the bad timing of his father's arrival, just when something was due to begin with Electa, just when he was making his first real discoveries, proving himself as an investigator. In the moment of their greeting, reaching out to find his uncomfortable place in his father's arms, he had wished his father had come earlier or later or not at all. Maybe that was the treachery that had ruined it. They had been on the road for half a day and he still didn't know how to instigate its beginning.

They were on Route 79 West, going past a strip mall, satellite dishes and sports shoes, movie-house, computer store, Italian restaurant, McDonald's, Kentucky Fried Chicken, hairdresser's, furniture warehouse, All Your Pet Supplies, a china shop, bathroom store (*Your tush is OUR concern!*), department stores, including Two Guys. Edgar liked Two Guys. When he was younger and they were performing similar car journeys to this one, his father would point at the sign and say, 'Two Guys, just like us,' and Edgar's six-year-old heart would swell with pride.

'Two Guys,' said Edgar.

'Uh?' said Edgar's father.

'The store there, Two Guys.'

Edgar's father was about to flash his indicator stick. 'Do we need something from there?'

'Don't you remember? Two Guys. We used to see it and you used to say . . .'

'Say what?'

'Two Guys . . . I guess you don't remember.'

'Sorry Eddie, I guess I don't.'

Edgar had not found a way to declare or allude to his capacity, and neither had he yet revealed his new, preferable name, and nor had he shared any of his discoveries, and he felt lost. While he recognized that his father was ahead of him, more worldly wise, more experienced, yet he had finally entered the same manly category, but how was he going to announce this? He needed some clubbable moment, the two of them together, dark-panelled walls, dim light, swirling a root beer around a heavy crystal tumbler—and just breaking off from discussing the baseball scores, or a current sensational murder case, or the twilight of some star, and his father would look over his tinted bifocals as if he had heard the first fore-whisper of the son's announcement, a smile already starting on his face as if he knew or could anticipate what Edgar was about to say—but they never did have clubbable moments, not like this, not at all. The best he had done was awkwardly to introduce a conversation point. His father would sometimes permit himself to be captured by conversation points, when he would forget to look doubtfully at his Edgar—*This, he, is my son? How can that be?*—but it was always unpredictable which points or observations or, very occasionally, jokes his father would allow himself to be interested by.

Or maybe it was all going to happen on the following day, Edgar's birthday. The two of them had reached a silent understanding that Edgar's birthday should not be mentioned until it happened, so the surprise that Edgar's father had planned should not be threatened, but all the same Edgar, impetuous, couldn't resist sliding towards the topic.

The car picked up speed after a toll-booth, and Edgar introduced the topic of Judaism. 'You know when I went to Gary's bar mitzvah?'

He saw his father about to repeat the formula he had used so many times over the years, *Who's Gary?* or *Who's Herman?* or *Who's Rufus?*, all of which meant, simply, *Who are you?* but he stopped himself, repressing the question with a thin-lipped nod, either because he sensed that he might be getting something wrong or else because he was genuinely uninterested in the answer.

'What does it mean, the expression, "Today I become a man"? What's all that about? Why thirteen? What *happens*?'

Instead of reaching the suave understanding that his son was announcing something crucial about himself, declaring himself as part now of the propagating world, no longer innocent, no longer a child—or maybe he was just affecting not to understand, not getting it, maybe he was getting it all too well, maybe he was, impossible thought, *embarrassed*? could he be?—Edgar's father waved the whole matter away. 'Who knows?' he said, and the subject dropped, a forgotten stone.

'Dad?'

Dad raised an eyebrow. He had been fiddling with the radio, and the map, which he didn't let Edgar help with, and patting his chest from time to time in a forlorn kind of way.

'Where does wind come from?'

Edgar's father slowly shook his head. 'What do you mean? It's an intestinal thing.'

'No. I mean, wind. You know, the weather, breezes and gusts and so forth. Where does it come from?'

Edgar had an imaginary picture of a cave in the Ural mountains (not that he knew where the Ural mountains were, but the name implied both the Arctic and Valhalla to him) where a young wind was born, blustering out, eager to prove itself, blowing its youthful energies around the world.

His father merely shook his head, so Edgar tried another.

'What were your favourite albums from when you were young?'

'I don't know. I liked the Doobie Brothers.'

'What about the Stooges?'

'A little unsophisticated for my tastes. That was more Frank's territory.'

The day was just getting worse and worse. Maybe the lesson here was not to ask questions. Edgar couldn't help himself. 'Do you believe in the afterlife?'

Edgar's father shook his head again in the same impatient, baffled way and said, 'I don't know what you want from me.'

His father looked close to exasperated. Edgar's company often made his father exasperated. Some knowledge had been all that he had wanted, something passed on from father to son, an inheritance of wisdom. And maybe Edgar's father felt some of this and was guilty about his response, because he smiled and said, 'I can tell you one thing. When you're lighting a cigarette in a wind, the trick is to stand *against* the breeze. You get me? You stand facing the wind, not away from it. Most people don't realize that.'

'I don't smoke,' Edgar said.

His father seemed annoyed by this. 'Well when you do. Just bear it in mind. You hungry?'

'Sure I am,' Edgar said, even though he wasn't, but giving what he hoped was the correct response.

'Let's get ourselves something to eat.'

They sat in a roadside lounge. His father joked around with the waitress and gave Edgar quarters to put in the silvery rainbow jukebox mounted on the wall, and watched him play with the car key-ring, with the little black sensor button that was meant to open the door lock by remote control but didn't work any more. His father drank Heineken. Edgar had a root beer.

Edgar's father rested his elbow on the table and shook his arm so his silver bracelet slid down from his wrist to his forearm, which was tanned from open windows, open roads. 'Your mother has done a great job with you.'

What did this mean? Edgar's father lowered his tinted glasses to beam a look of dreadful sincerity at him.

Something about this look told Edgar to shelve his family-united fantasy as being just that. His father would never be in residence with them at his grandmother's house. They would never drink beers from frosted glasses together at the P-shaped swimming-pool. They would never bat around balls on the snooker table. And, for a reason that he didn't quite understand yet, Edgar was coming to hate Warren because of this. It was as if Warren had stolen somehow the good-son stuff, all the nurturing and caring-for. Every cup of tea Warren made for Fay *in the English style* was another cup of tea that his father had failed to make. Maybe if Warren would just let up for a moment, it would give someone else a chance, someone for whom it was more of a struggle.

'What's the Blackberry Festival? When is it?'

'Blackberry Festival? It's something they celebrate back—' Edgar heard his father very nearly say the word 'home', but correct himself '—up there. It's a little before Labor Day. Kind of marks the end of the summer. Couple of weeks away. Why?'

'I don't know,' Edgar said.

Their food arrived, Edgar's steak, his father's egg-white omelette, brought by the waitress with whom Edgar's father had struck an immediate rapport, a shared way of being that Edgar jealously despaired of his father ever finding with him. Edgar waited for his father to be finished with the ketchup bottle.

'You want the ketchup?'

Edgar nodded.

'Sorry, pal. There's new research shows kids shouldn't eat ketchup. It's carcinogenic.'

Sometimes life was truly desolate. Even the things that Edgar normally took delight in, well-done steaks on large white plates, the metal page mechanism of the tableside jukebox, his father's hands, gnarled and freckled and capable, the sight of his father's car through the window of the diner, top carelessly down, its battered red colour putting to shame all the grey and tan sedans, all these things seemed unkind.

'Hey, I'm kidding you!'

His father reached forward to grab one of Edgar's hands. The bracelet slid down to the wrist and Edgar's father withdrew his hand to shake it up again. He winked at Edgar. Edgar tried to wink back but feared he might have muffed it. Generously though, his father, perhaps alarmed at Edgar's mood—and it was true, Edgar had been close to weeping just now, had felt his throat rawing in preparation for tears, his eyes smarting—didn't draw attention to Edgar's performance of blinks and twitches but, almost courteously, nodded.

'You take things too seriously all the time, that's your problem.'

'Is it?' Edgar considered this. His father seldom made direct personal remarks or observations so each one had a consequently elevated status. Perhaps Edgar did take things too seriously. He would learn to be more carefree. 'That's interesting,' Edgar said.

'You see? You're doing it now.'

Edgar responded with a wry laugh that pleased him with its intimations of mature sophistication, so he performed it again. His father looked at him a little oddly and patted his chest and returned to his omelette. 'How's your steak?' he asked.

'Very good. How's the omelette?' said Edgar.

'Good also. Want to try a taste?'

'No. It's okay.'

Edgar didn't like the taste of his father's omelettes, the tartness of slightly burnt peppers and onion, with the quantity of salt that his father liked to put on all his food, but the fork with some omelette and its grungy filling and a merciful slop of ketchup was coming his way so he reached for the fork but his father wanted to feed him so he dutifully opened his mouth and let it slide in and he hoped his look didn't show too much distaste and he washed it down with a big gulp of root beer.

'You've got to learn to chew. You'll give yourself indigestion. How do you like it?'

'Good, very good,' Edgar said. 'Would you like to try some of my steak? It's also very good.'

Already he was cutting a piece of meat and shovelling some ketchup and sweet mustard on top, but his father made a sour expression and shook his head and said, 'No. Enjoy it.'

Which made Edgar feel slighted. He was sure that if he were a grown-up then his father would be honour-bound to take a taste of his meat. That somehow it was an expression of relative power inequality of who got to offer food and who had to taste it. He presumed business power lunches were a desperate duel of offered forks and submissive mouths and triumphantly shaken heads as stronger, better men made their inferiors accept, swallow, and praise.

'I'm going to have a coffee. You want something? A milkshake or something?'

Edgar indeed wanted a milkshake and his father let him order for himself and Edgar, renewed in companionship, effortlessly dealt with the waitress's enthusiasm at his accent, and when the milkshake came he used two straws and sucked merrily away at it, and used a long spoon to dig away some of the gloop that had collected along the side of the glass, but the concern hit him, as they walked back into the diner car-park, his father's hand steering him somewhat uncomfortably by the neck, that maybe he should have ordered a coffee too.

'We're making good time,' his father said.

'Good,' said Edgar.

'We're in Connecticut now.'

'Oh. Good,' said Edgar.

He was losing all conception of place. Everything looked the same to him, the neat, well-mannered towns, the long stretches of highway cut through forest and rock.

It was good to be in the potential of his father's fellowship, yet Edgar's mind kept turning Vailwards; he was needed at the house; he worried for his grandmother in the dangerous air that Frank and Lucille made everyone breathe; he worried for Fay without him there to keep an eye on things. And—a lurch to the belly that brought his forehead into contact with the glove compartment—this was the day he was due to be going to the cinema with Electa. The glamour of his father's company had pushed that away. She would be standing outside the movie-house, her scorn rising, pretending to be interested in the pictures and names on the film posters as Paul and Husky Marvin gathered themselves to intercede.

'That house is a goldmine,' his father said.

'What house?' Edgar looked out of the window, hoping to see a building with miners surrounding it, a campfire, an old man playing a harmonica, everything glimmering and glistening with fresh-dug gold.

'Fay's house of course. The old spread. The family manse. What I could do with the cash from that, I couldn't begin to tell you.'

'You'd *sell* it?'

'What do you expect me to do with it? Live there?'

It had never occurred to Edgar that anyone might want the house sold. Even in the selfish nakedness of Frank and Lucille's hunger for it, the house was still occupied by family.

Images collided in Edgar's head: Electa outside the cinema—gold-miners occupying the Pagan House—his father and Lucille counting out attaché cases filled with money. He wanted to argue, he wanted to introduce his father to his favourite game. Instead he hiccuped.

'You're a little weird but you're a great kid. Your mother's done a terrific job with you. Want a stick of gum?'

'No. No thank you.'

Edgar was still hiccuping and in shock and brooding when they pulled off the highway towards the resort.

It was a gambling place, of course it was. Edgar would have known to expect this if he had allowed himself to expect anything, if he had not deliberately emptied his mind of the future, tried to find a weighty comfort in the immediacy of his father's presence. Gambling was what made his father come alive.

'I think you'll like it here. It's got plenty of facilities for kids,' his father said.

An illuminated totem pole stood outside the main entrance. The hotel was set off from the casino, a glass tunnel connecting the two. At the side of the hotel was the children's so-called fun area, which they passed on their way to the guests' elevator—two narrow rooms, one with video games, the other with ping-pong and pool tables. A scrawny feral child, wearing multiple rows of braces on his teeth, was playing a basketball video game. He looked at Edgar and warned him away with an unmistakable snarl.

'You see? You're making friends here already,' his father said.

The room was good. Two double beds were separated by a bedside table. A large television set was on the chest of drawers with a remote control and cable guide. The curtains were operated by a push button. Black-and-white pastoral scenes of Indians at idyllic work and play decorated the walls.

On Edgar's last night as a twelve-year-old he and his father ate room-service dinner companionably together, sitting on their twin beds.

'You grab some shut-eye. I'll take a little stroll around the place, get acquainted,' his father said.

Edgar piled up the plates and aluminium lids of their dinner. Rebelling against an invisible, perhaps non-existent authority, he neither brushed his teeth nor washed his hands and face. He felt desolate. He called his mother.

'I was going to phone you tomorrow, but I didn't know where you're staying. Are you having a great time with your father?'

'Terrific,' Edgar said. He invented a different kind of hotel that he was staying at, with all kinds of friends and activities. He told his mother about the medal he'd won in a fathers-and-sons archery competition but his triumph dissolved when he could hear in her silence the reminder, and self-reproach, that tomorrow was the first of his birthdays that they had spent apart.

'I've got to go now. There's a barbecue dinner by the swimming-pool.'

'Isn't it rather late for that? Well I suppose it's your birthday. And your father . . . Anyway, what's the telephone number there? I'll call you tomorrow.'

Edgar impressed himself by twice reciting the same random string of digits. He told his mother he loved her too and hung up the phone and lay in his bed waiting anxiously for sleep while watching TV with the sound turned down.

2

'You don't want breakfast straight away, do you?'

Hungry Edgar shook his head.

'Let's go find the fun room.'

It was only when Edgar and his father parted at the entrance to the glass tunnel, under the sign that announced that no minors were permitted beyond, that Edgar finally realized that there was no birthday surprise; the only question was whether his father had forgotten his birthday or if he had never known it.

'I'll find you in the kids' room. Be about twenty minutes, just get a little pre-breakfast action, you know what I'm saying?'

The room with the pool and ping-pong tables was occupied by three sandy-haired youths and the most beautiful girl Edgar had ever seen, whose proximity made it difficult to breathe. Edgar took sanctuary in the video-games room. He was carrying no money so he took on the role of a connoisseur, examining each machine in turn as if he was finding disappointing reasons not to play. He carried on his performance long after it was exhausted, but his father had yet to show.

'What's your name?'

'Edgar. What's yours?'

This was the fifth time he had revealed his new name, and how he hoped it would guide him through this extraordinary moment.

'Lisa.'

Lisa was even more beautiful than the Lucy that his imagination had invented as her precursor. She was a perfectly tanned girl of, he would guess, about fourteen, in a white halter-top and cut-off blue jeans and sneakers.

'Do you play ping-pong, Edgar?'

'Yeah. Sure I do,' he said expansively, to indicate that ping-pong was just one of his many talents, one he probably played to a championship standard, but not one he was going to be bragging about, because there were all those other things that he could do miraculously well also, including the sexual pleasuring of extraordinary beauties called Lisa.

'Do you want to play ping-pong with us?'

'I'm supposed to—'

He had been about to say, *supposed to be meeting my dad*, but that, Edgar decided, would reduce him, establish his status of dependent child rather than the independently minded, and acting, man of the world he had chosen to project, so, instead, lightly, he said, 'Sure,' and followed Lisa to the games room, watching the movement of her buttocks beneath worn denim, the pinpricks of goosebumps at the top of her waist, and he was glad that he was wearing his baggy jeans today, they gave him room, with just an adroit flick of hand inside pocket, to move his erection safely, more or less invisibly, vertical.

They required a fourth for their game. Edgar's predecessor, a glowering boy named Jackie, had hurt his knee and his ankle and his pride and was sitting on the pool table, viciously caroming the white ball around the cushions while staring lustfully at Lisa and balefully at her three companions, of whom Edgar was nervous to find himself the youngest and, at ping-pong, the worst. Lisa didn't seem to care. In his desire to impress, Edgar would try to command too much of the table, and once their bats clashed, and once he nearly hit her, and several times the physical confusion that he pushed them into of waving arms and Lisa's long hair flying and her breasts rising in laughter and exertion meant that the ball went past or sometimes even through. The boys they were playing were brothers, perhaps twins, who wore identical frowns and Red Sox T-shirts and baggy shorts. They called Edgar Junior, even though Lisa told them what his name was, twice, and Jackie latched on to the nickname as something worthy of derision and kept up a bantering sardonic commentary: '. . . and Lisa to Mickey who whips in a backhand and Junior—Oh, *big* surprise, ladies and gentlemen—Junior hits the net!'

When the game was over the victorious Red Sox twins invited Lisa to join them for a milkshake. Jackie was already heading for the door to the ice-cream stand, walking in a monkey lope that he exaggerated for unfunny comic purpose.

'Do you want to come?' Lisa asked Edgar, whose stomach was desperate for any kind of substance.

'I'm supposed to be meeting someone.'

'You met me,' Lisa said.

Her hair was long and brown and streaked with sun. There was grandeur about her, in the way she stood and carried herself: she knew perfectly well how beautiful she was and it didn't intimidate her. Jackie was gone, the Red Sox twins were waiting at the door, and Edgar was familiar enough with the wiles of women, in imagination at least, if not experience, to realize that Lisa's attentiveness towards him probably lay more in her lack of interest in the twins than in any attraction to Edgar.

'How old are you?' Edgar asked.

'I'm thirteen.'

He managed not to say the *wow!* that he was thinking. 'I'm fourteen,' he said. 'It's my birthday.'

'Happy birthday.'

Which was when his father appeared. Edgar would never

lose the image of Lisa in his mind and, in some super-
stitious way, he came to associate it with the moral qualities
of honesty and integrity. 'I got to go, that's my dad.'

He knew Lisa was looking at him as he left, and he walked
stiffly, envying for a moment the joker Jackie with his monkey
repertoire of ludicrous gestures to mask his embarrassments.
And he knew Lisa would be looking at his father's face and
admiring it, because women did, and he hoped her admiration of it would reflect well on him. He turned to wave to
her as he left and he knew she had just been looking at him,
waiting for the farewell, and he waved to her departing back
instead, noticing how her left sneaker was more worn on its
inside, because of the way her ankles tended slightly towards
each other. He waved goodbye to her and surreptitiously
blew her a kiss, and she looked back at him a fraction after
he had done that, and said, 'I'll be in the Chinese restaurant
for supper.'

'Cute girl. You've been making out like a bandit,' his father
said.

Edgar followed his father out of the games room towards
the elevators, searing light through Plexiglas windows. Edgar
presumed his father had lost money, because Mon said he
usually did, but it was difficult to tell, especially when he
was wearing sunglasses.

'Could you wait for me a moment? I got to . . .' Edgar
said, pointing to the sign for the rest rooms.

Edgar's father snapped his fingers three times, to register
disapproval, impatience, reluctant assent. Then something
in him softened; Edgar wondered if it had been the sight
of Lisa that had changed his mind about who Edgar might
be.

'Yeah. Sure. I'll call Fay. Promised I would.'

He leaned into the bubble of a pay-phone and patted his
shirt.

Edgar went into the men's room and had to take the nearest cubicle because the other two were occupied. He locked the door, and unlocked it, to make sure that it had been locked, then locked it again. The panting coming from the neighbours on his right was at first scary and then unmistakable. Modestly keeping himself, and his breathing, quiet, Edgar masturbated. There was a brisk efficiency to the image of Lisa, the squeeze of her breasts beneath white halter-top nylon, the curve of her shoulder when she executed a smash, her laugh, the matching gold-flecked brownness of her skin and hair and eyes.

When he was done, he efficiently wiped away the traces and flushed the toilet and zipped himself up. He worried that he had cheapened Lisa, debased her, even, that he should have kept her image separate from the cruel urgency of his body's needs. As he came out of his cubicle the Red Sox twins came out of theirs. That he and the Red Sox twins had been cubicled beside each other to the same purpose, performing the same function, with the same white halter-top image in their heads, did not bring them closer together. Edgar nodded curtly at each boy in turn but neither acknowledged the greeting as they went to simultaneous sinks to wash their hands and do watery things to their hair. Edgar felt their mirror eyes watching him as he left the men's room.

When they got back to their room, his father convivially cracked open two Diet Cokes from the minibar. 'I made the mistake of calling home,' he said, in the tone of someone comfortable in the knowledge that the person he was talking to was as equally amused and irked by the exigencies of duty as he.

Edgar was zapping through the remote control. He was wondering how much authority he could bring to selection of TV programme. Should he politely give his father first choice or would that set an unassailable precedent? Deciding to be bold, he left the channel on a Three Stooges movie and compromised by turning the sound down. Moe fell over. Moe got up again. Larry and Curly fell over. Edgar laughed.

'I called for Fay and that over-age Playboy bunny of Frank's is who I got. Fay's in the hospital. I don't think it's serious, but the Irish guy isn't around and Lucille is hysterical. I said sit tight, we'd check in with her tomorrow. Monitor the situation. I told her we want our time together.'

Even if his father was lying, even if it was only a charming alibi to account for his need to be at the casino, the claim filled Edgar with pride. He wanted nothing to change this day, or threaten the forthcoming evening. The two hotel pencils that he had used as drumsticks before were now the chopsticks he was practising with in preparation to impress Lisa at supper.

His father was approaching with a packet of very desirable chocolate-chip biscuits. 'Want a cookie?' his father said. Edgar shook his head decisively. No matter how hungry he was, he had put away childish things. He would breakfast on the bunch of grapes on the side-table.

'I think we should go back,' Edgar said, breaking his own heart. 'We might be needed.'

It was as much the raw fact of Edgar's exertion of moral authority as what the authority dictated that influenced his father, who grumbled as he threw hotel writing-pads and complimentary jars of hair products into a gift-shop bag. Edgar ate grapes and watched the Three Stooges with the sound turned down and waited for his father to be finished.

'You know they're going to stiff us for the whole stay? You know that?'

In the car going back his father chewed gum and didn't talk. Edgar switched the radio on and his father stabbed it off again. He would never see how Lisa dressed for dinner—

he had supposed a variation on her daytime wear, tailored designer jeans, open-toe high-heel shoes, diamanté spangle on her evening-wear halter-top. Edgar mourned the passing of everything glimpsed, half tasted.

3

The marriage supper of the Lamb is a feast at which every dish is free to every guest. I call this woman my wife—she is yours, she is Christ's, and in him she is bride of all the saints.

from the Second Annual Report of the Onyataka Association,
John Prindle Stone, January 1851

The church on earth rises to meet the approaching kingdom in the heavens and, correspondingly, its representative Mary Pagan is to travel into New Haven darkness to bring light to a woman whose part in the pre-history of the Association had been, so might have been supposed, so might have been hoped, fixed, and finished. George Pagan is to travel with her. He has volunteered for this mission and refused all dissuasions. He stands awkward in a corner of the room as Harriet Stone helps Mary dress for her journey. Harriet comments upon how easily Mary slips inside her old clothes.

'I could not do that,' Mrs Stone says, without spite or envy. 'My body is not so docile an instrument.'

'These are like a chap-book of former days,' Mrs Pagan says.

From the fallen dispensation, these taints of a sinful past: in this dress she had sat in a New York parlour where an ardent Methodist had pressed his kisses and his lust upon her; and here, beneath, a bloodstain on her bodice from where she had pricked her finger in self-mortification at her duplicity; and here, above, a burn mark on her collar, a

215

smudge memento of ash from the fire of the old stone house at Rondout, where Abram Carter, that imperfect instrument of grace, had led her, through passion, to John Prindle Stone and the promise of perfection.

Harriet remarks on the pallor of Mary's face, the tremors of her limbs. 'Are you anxious?'

Mary does not reply. It is unclear whose feelings she is protecting, Mrs Stone's, Mr Pagan's, or her own.

Harriet, the original Mrs Stone, pulls straight the lacy collar of former times and her capable fingers provide the rough soothing touch of a mother or a nurse.

George carries the luggage into the hall and Mary waits for John Prindle Stone to make his appraisal. His speech is humorous, if not quite mocking. 'We had thought you were embarking on an expedition to New Haven, not a journey through time.'

'My clothes? I—we—had judged these more suitable.'

'You are an ambassadress from the Association. When dignitaries visit foreign lands they wear their own clothes. Soldiers do not put off their uniforms for battle.'

'I feel far from being a dignitary or a soldier.'

'Nonetheless.'

He smiles and so does she, and George can taste the longing now, as she waits for John Prindle's touch to guard her, the warmth of his breath on her skin to serve as armour for the soldier that she feels herself far from ready to be.

The only words John Prindle says as he leads her back to her room are, 'Mary, you know that we will always be in perfect fellowship, no matter where the success of your mission may lead.'

George waits in the hallway. It is a long wait, but he could wait for ever if need be. When Mary returns she is dressed, perhaps by her consort's own hands, in her customary black blouse and pantalets and overskirt, the court uniform of the

216

dignitary, the soldier's garb, which she epaulettes with tears as they leave the Mansion House.

George and Mary Pagan, the ambassadors, travel by post-coach, railroad, hackney carriage and on foot to sit opposite Mary's rival in a chilly New Haven parlour whose walls are papered a dull green that has no correspondence to anything in nature. A wintry fire dies in the grate. George wants this mission to succeed. Mary is desperate for it to fail.

George wonders if Mrs Duckworth, the former Hester Lovell, is so haughty that she will not lower herself to place more wood on the shivering flames, or if it is some kind of challenge, to test the softness and submissiveness of her female visitor. George Pagan knows that Mary will not complain of the cold or comment on it either by word or physical inflection. He introduces himself and his once-wife, then hardly talks at all. He listens to the women duel, as they talk of Mr Stone, and of Christ their mutual Saviour, and Mrs Duckworth is as fluent in tongue as Mr Stone had warned (and how Mary had striven to ignore the admiration almost amounting to pride in his warning), and Mrs Pagan must be on her guard. She has come here—why has she come here?—because Mr Stone had asked her to and because she had been curious, more than curious, *frantic*; this is from need, she has been giddy with it, to see the woman who still commands Mr Stone's heart. Part of her, almost an absent part, conducts the theological discussion, which is, in truth, a skirmish, a battle for betterment that requires all her energies and intelligence, while the worldly, womanly part of her examines her rival, her frame, her complexion, her manners—and who is to say, heresy though this doubtless is, which part of her is more authentically her own?

'You are his ambassadress,' remarks Mrs Duckworth.

'Perhaps,' says Mrs Pagan. 'Tho' I would say that our places are distinct and appointed us by God.'

'The chapels and meeting-houses are filled with God's messengers. Or so they claim.'

'And mistakenly so.'

'But who is to be so sure of another's mistake? These false prophets are as sincere in their mission as you no doubt are in yours.'

'Mr Stone tells us that these mistaken messengers tap from the same currents. Things are at hand. The rappings in Rochester, the Shakers in New Lebanon, even the silly Millerites waiting for the world to end on their lonely hilltop. They are not so insensitive, the age rings through them also. Mr Stone says they are like tuning-forks that sound the wrong key.'

'Mr Stone was always fond of musical metaphors,' says Mrs Duckworth, reminding Mary of their order of precedence in John Prindle's affections. 'But Mrs Pagan, what precisely is your mission? I had not heard of you before today.'

'But we have heard of you.'

If it had not been for Mrs Duckworth then her own life would have been so different, and so unutterably unenriched. It had been Mrs Duckworth's rejection of Mr Stone's wedding proposal that had led to the banishment of marriage from the earthly dispensation. So many lives have been altered by Hester's disavowal. And so infinitely for the better. Is she then, in some way, a sacrifice? Those lines by her eyes have been cut by sorrow, not joy. Mary Pagan is somewhat ashamed of the pleasure she gains in her reading of her rival's skin and soul. But she is not sufficiently without egotism not to exult in these signs and not sufficiently without sin not to paint an envying picture of twelve years previous, a room not unalike this one, where John Prindle Stone and

Hester Lovell would have sat with a Testament and tracts, his ardour no doubt quickening her own—how could it not?

'Mr Stone has often spoken of you. More recently, more so.'

'Since he learned of the death of my husband.'

Mrs Duckworth has the grey eyes and pale papery skin of an English gentlewoman, which is flushed now with a becoming indignation. There is something of the girl about her, high-spirited, self-conscious, proud, untouched, maybe untouchable. Mr Stone has mentioned her skill with horses.

'He describes you as the prodigal son.'

'He is not my father, nor yours.'

Said more tartly than her conversation thus far, which indicates that her passion is aroused as much as her temper.

'The Association to which I belong considers itself a family, and Mr Stone is at its head,' remarks Mary Pagan, as lightly as she is able, pursuing the high ground of her advantage in this struggle.

And continues: 'Fourteen years ago you publicly confessed the doctrine of holiness in this city, and it was through your influence that Mr Stone gained admission to the Free Church; and it was through your withdrawal that the testimony of salvation from sin has been repressed here. Christ has many people in this city who are captives, and you are holding the door shut which would liberate them.'

'I cannot believe the power of my influence is as great as you say. Let me assure you, and whoever might be interested in your report, I have not altered my position. Christ is in me, a present saviour. I am not perfect in every word or thought, but Christ gives me the power to overcome.'

'And when you deserted Mr Stone? Did Christ give you the power then? Was it Christ who made you deny *him*? This was not proper treatment, giving him no chance for explanation, whatever you may have thought of him.'

Mrs Duckworth smiles at the transparency of her old suitor speaking through his current consort. Yet she makes no response. Her husband has been buried one year since; she continues to wear widow's clothes. His portrait hangs over the mantelpiece and George Pagan doubts his competencies were a match for his widow's. Weakness is betokened in the softness of his jaw, the wary lassitude in his eyes.

Mrs Duckworth, the Hester Lovell of jealous myth, bows her head in this New Haven boarding-house parlour and shivers as if against the cold. Mary shivers too, in sympathy.

'I shall call Sammy and ask him to build up the fire.'

'Let us do it ourselves,' says Mary Pagan, brightly.

On her hands and knees, watched by Mrs Duckworth and Mr Pagan, she covers the embers with wood from the basket and blows life into the dying flames with her own breath. She is glad to be doing this, glad to be doing something beyond the duel of conversation. She must be doing something now, and if she were not repairing the fire, whose capacities she doubts to warm this chilly, dully green room, she feels she might be compelled to embrace Hester Lovell, to comfort her in her sadness and confusion and pride; and it is quite beyond Mary Pagan to predict the effect of an embrace upon her rival, whether it would coax her into intimacy or drive her further away; and it is quite beyond her too to understand which in her heart she would choose.

'Please, do not misunderstand me. I am here merely to issue an invitation, in Mr Stone's name and that of the Association, to visit us, in Onyataka.'

It pains her to pronounce the name of her home to a perhaps enemy and Mrs Duckworth notices the weakness; and even if mistaking its source, it gives her the energy to resume the conflict.

'Mr Stone is a married man, and if he has any such love

for me as has been represented, then it is a sin in his heart. I had a dear, good husband and do not wish to extend my acquaintance in the direction of any gentleman, named or otherwise. I do not want a husband or a . . .'

George looks away from the fire to see his wife's adversary waving a hand towards the word that she will not say.

Mary has no such compunction or shame. 'The point is, not to help you to a husband or a lover, but to have you do the right thing by Christ and his gospel.'

'I shall speak plainly too: I do not believe the Kingdom of God has come, and furthermore I do not believe in the abolition of marriage, no matter how suitable or congenial some might find it to live otherwise.'

'Have you read our Annual Report?'

'I have not, but I have heard it spoken disapprovingly of as at war with the Bible.'

'Oh no. It is in the very spirit of it! Nothing can be more so. If you came to live with us at Onyataka'—here she steels herself to pronounce its name as casually as she may, without any motherly restraint or protectiveness—'you would soon find out that we are at the beginning of the day when the secrets of all hearts are to be revealed.'

Her own heart keeps no such secrets, not from Mr Stone, nor even from Mr Pagan, and not, it seems, from Mrs Duckworth, whose grey eyes steadily follow her from fireplace to chair.

'And would you raise the dead also? Is there no end to Mr Stone's miraculous accomplishments?'

In truth, they have tried but, unsure of her ground, wary of the superciliousness of her rival, Mrs Pagan does not mention the Perfectionists' attempts to push aside the veil that separates the inhabitants of the visible and invisible realms. They have had more success in healing the sick than quickening the dead.

221

'We live in both the material and immaterial worlds,' is how Mary contents herself with a response.

'I am curious. This interview cannot be any more agreeable to you than to me. I would even suppose that it is less agreeable. Why did not Mr Stone come here himself? Why did he send you in his place?'

It is a question that George has asked Mary. And they both know the answer even if they have left it unspoken: she is paying the price of free love, forcibly made to disentangle herself from the ties of special affection.

'I don't think,' she slowly says, 'that even if I could answer your questions you would be able to comprehend my answer. Our place is far away from yours.'

'And I don't believe that I am ready to make the journey.'

'We are greater than we believe ourselves to be.'

The ensuing silence is broken by a knock on the door, a voice from the stairs—*Mrs Duckworth!* The interview is over.

'You will pardon me,' Mrs Duckworth says, in the manner of someone unused to asking forgiveness.

'I hope only that I have not offended you.'

'You have not offended me.'

'And perhaps you will read our Report. And visit us.'

'Perhaps so.'

They bid each other good day and George follows Mary Pagan out into a coldly sunlit New Haven afternoon.

Perhaps it is the sunshine, or more likely the efforts of her intercourse with Hester Lovell, but Mrs Pagan is dazzled on the street. She walks in some kind of daze, allows herself to be supported by her erstwhile husband, unsure of direction, unsure of herself, unmoored, a rudderless boat on difficult seas.

When their return journey is done, Mrs Pagan leaves Mr Pagan to make the report at the Mansion House. Postponing the greetings and embraces, she walks down the rise and sits in her favourite place, the copse by the horse barn where blind Jess died, between young cherry trees where cardinals busy themselves by day and nightjars at night, where the seniors in their enterprise had camped while building the Mansion House, where once Seth Newhouse had caught a bear. Which is where she sits, unable to eliminate the image of her rival from her mind. Plainly God does not mean Mrs Duckworth to rest in her present situation, but stirs her up from time to time. Plainly the visit has not been a success, for any of them. Mary Pagan has tried to wash out the claiming spirit but it resists, this most stubborn stain, which persists in identifying happiness with place and person rather than with meekness of spirit before God.

She should rest, learn meekness to God's will. She should subside, as she does now, leaning back against a pillow of heather, spreading her arms wide, the joyful thistles scratching against her wrists, the sun beating against her closed eyelids.

Mr Pagan could watch her for ever; he might build a house on that very spot to contain her, and she could lie here for ever, wait for the vines to entangle her limbs, the birds to peck her flesh, the dead woman of the copse, wide awake.

4

The Pagan House had been subtitled. It was like a movie for the stupid. Every drawer and cupboard in the kitchen and bathroom had been labelled with the sticky white tags that Warren had written out and applied: POTS AND PANS, TEA AND COFFEE, BAKING SUPPLIES, HAIR CARE (MALE), HAIR CARE (FEMALE), SOUVENIRS, FLATWARE (EVERYDAY), FLATWARE (BEST), SILVERWARE (EVERYDAY), SILVERWARE (BEST), PHOTOGRAPHS, BILLS (CURRENT), BILLS (ARCHIVE), RESTAURANT MENUS, IMPORTANT TELEPHONE NUMBERS. He had put up a chart in the kitchen that showed the meals and doctors' appointments and committee meetings of Fay's usual day, and another in the bathroom that he'd colour-coded with the times and quantities and names of Fay's medications (generic and company-branded); all this was to fill the absence of the presiding wisdom of Warren, who had gone.

Despite his preparations, the household was in rackety consternation. Paul was absent, being splendid somewhere. Michelle was curled on an armchair, picking at damp loose threads on her sweater sleeve. Lucille, who wore a lower-cut cleavage for times of emergency, was mixing drinks and sneering at Frank, who railed and shouted, while Edgar's father patted his chest and drank.

'This wouldn't have happened if you hadn't spoken to him like that!' Lucille said.

'How was I to know he was so fucking sensitive? She's better off without him, if this is how he acts.'

Edgar's father said, 'Uh. Excuse me. She wasn't in hospital when he was here.'

'Yeah, and excuse *me*, I didn't see you around to help.'

'We figured everything was under control.'

'Well, it is. Everything is perfectly under control. Mom was taken to hospital last night. How much more under control do you want?'

'Where is Warren?' Edgar asked, and when no one responded, Edgar's father repeated the question.

'We don't know where Warren is!' Frank shouted. 'We had an argument—'

'*You* had the argument,' Lucille said.

'Takes two to tango, baby,' Frank said. 'He left and Mom had her attack and we took her to Onyataka General. That's all we know. Fucking fag.'

'I'm sure he'll be coming back. He's got his opera,' Edgar said to his father.

'What about his opera?' Edgar's father asked.

'Don't get me started,' Frank said.

'Is that what they call it?' Lucille said.

For a moment Frank and Lucille were united: eyes rolled, fingers gripped noses, invisible toilets were flushed.

'What kind of attack did she have?' Edgar said.

'Do we know where he's gone?' Edgar's father said. 'Has he taken the car?'

'He wouldn't have,' Edgar said.

This was the first thing he had said that gained the attention of his uncle and his aunt.

'*Waddyamin?*' Frank and Lucille said together, which confused Edgar, who was silent.

'What do you mean?' his father asked.

Edgar said, 'He wouldn't take anything that didn't belong to him. He's scrupulous.'

'*Scrupulous*. That's a big word, that's a ten-dollar word,' Frank said.

Edgar didn't like his uncle, he didn't like his bigness, the chummy violence of his company, he didn't like the way he wore shorts all the time and called Fay 'Mom', and Edgar didn't like being talked about in the third person when present. How could someone who liked the sort of music Frank did when he was young turn into the sort of man he was now? The passageways to adulthood must be even more treacherous than Edgar had supposed.

'He's a bright kid,' Frank said, with contempt. '*Scrupulous.*'

'Maybe we should visit the hospital?' Edgar said, and in the absence of any better idea, Paul was retrieved from his glittering world and the family loaded itself into two cars and drove the five miles to Onyataka General.

The doctor, a man of Asian origin, diagnosed anxiety and stress and mistakes in her medication schedule.

'Well I don't see how that could have happened,' Frank said.

'Oh don't you?' Lucille jeered.

'Well thank *you*, *very* much,' Frank said. 'How long do you want my mother here?'

The doctor looked to the double doors that swung into the emergency room. 'Under normal circumstances, I would like to keep her in one, two days.'

A golf swing sent an imaginary ball, which represented Fay, towards the car-park.

'Waddyamin?'

'We are backed up. All beds full. Your mother is not at risk. She is in competent care, I understand?'

'Oh yes,' Lucille said. 'Super-competent. More than.'

Frank stared disbelievingly at his wife. Her mockery of him was not usually exercised in front of strangers. Paul studied the reflection he made in the polished side of a crash cart. Michelle, empty-eyed, chewed on a sleeve of her sweater.

'You sure she shouldn't stay in longer?' Frank said. 'You did say you'd like to keep her a few days.'

'In normal circumstances. These are not normal circumstances. The fire means that we are rushed off our feet.'

'What fire?'

'At the bingo hall. We're overloaded with burns cases of varying severity.'

The doctor fired a second imaginary golf ball, adjusted his watch and nodded in leave-taking.

'What happened at the bingo hall?'

'I couldn't tell you. That's not in our purview.'

'*Purview,*' scoffed Frank.

Edgar stood on tiptoe to look through the circular windows into the emergency room where all the beds were filled by stout dark-skinned women and the air resounded with the plaints of their relations.

'Can we see my mother?' Edgar's father asked, patting his heart.

'She has already been discharged. And has been waiting, I think for some time, in the family room.'

'Well, congratulations, you've made it,' Jerome said, when they arrived at the beige low-ceilinged room decorated with posters advertising the dangers of substance abuse. Fay had a small suitcase, neatly, squarely, at her feet. The state of her hair indicated her ordeal. It looked as if she had been struck by lightning.

'She won't let me take her home,' Jerome said.

'I'm waiting for Warren,' Fay said.

'Warren's gone, Mom.' Frank puffed out his cheeks and slowly released air. He offered his arm, and Fay stared at it as if it were an animal in whose dangerous presence she had to remain perfectly still.

'I want Warren.'

Edgar held out his hand and Fay smiled slowly and accepted it. 'Edgar,' she said.

'*Edgar,*' Frank repeated, with a roll of his eyes and a screwball gesture at his own temple. 'Sticky fucking wicket.'

'We should go home,' Edgar said.

His grandmother stood, supported by Edgar. She was even lighter than the last time they had done this. Fay leaned on him for the walk to the car-park and wouldn't settle in the car until he was beside her.

In the living room there began what Frank was pleased to call a family conference. 'Okay. Let's set up some kind of schedule here,' he said.

'There already is a schedule,' Fay said.

'I think it's time we did things properly. Mike?'

Edgar's father kicked off his loafers. He lay on the sofa, holding a braided cushion over his eyes. 'Absolutely Frank. You're the boss.'

'And that's exactly the kind of attitude we don't need.'

'Excuse us,' said Edgar, which wasn't necessary because no one heard and no one paid attention to their leaving.

Edgar took Fay upstairs. She climbed into bed and Edgar managed to persuade her to remove her overcoat. He didn't dare attempt encouraging her out of her clothes and into her pyjamas. She looked to the dressing-table and Edgar understood. He fetched the smallest silver brush and worked at her hair until it passed her mirror inspection. 'Perfect,' she said, and fell asleep.

Edgar went down to the parlour to make his phone call to his mother.

'Eddie! Happy, happy birthday! Tell me about your day.'

He was inspired. He had never talked so long and so freely. Oh, the evening before—barbecue by the swimming-pool, a Cuban band playing, fireworks in the moonlight, waltzes and salsa, the man who had fallen into the pool, the whiskey sours that Edgar's father had let the birthday boy taste—

'That's entirely irresponsible. There's *bourbon* in those.'

'I only tasted a little. It was my birthday.'

—but all this was as nothing to the excitements and glamour of the day. A fashionable restaurant commandeered for the occasion, the immense cake, the photographs, a girl called Lisa, the presents heaped upon him—

'I don't know how I'm going to get them all home, it's so many.'

'I've got you something too. I was waiting to give it in person.'

'That's okay, don't worry about it,' Edgar said grandly, proceeding to itemize a bicycle and a drum kit and various arcane books—

'What do you mean, *arcane* books?'

'Oh, you know. Arcane books.'

—and he was about to add a computer but decided not to in case that taxed her gullibility. He and his father had gone fishing together and were about to climb a mountain—

'A *mountain*? Where *are* you? This doesn't sound like Connecticut.'

'Oh yes. It's old Indian territory. Well, maybe it's more of a hill. But it's a pretty big hill.'

'Give me the number again of your hotel. I haven't been able to get through. I must have taken it down wrong last night.'

'We're leaving in the morning. I'll call you from the next place.'

They argued to and fro about that until Mon relented and supposed that would be all right. 'Could I have a word with your father now, please? I do love you so much, you can't know how awful it is not to be with you today.'

'What have you been doing?'

'Oh, you know, the usual kinds of things, but could you put your father on now, please?'

'Uh. He's talking to his brother.'

'To *Frank*? What's Frank doing with you? Mike can't stand Frank.'

'No. I know. But.' Edgar considered turning the scene downstairs into a family party in his honour but rejected that as being both too unlikely and far too unattractive. He would keep his preferred life entirely separate. 'He's talking to him on the phone. Dad's got a mobile phone. They call them cellphones here.'

'Oh good. You can give me that number then, and I'll be able to reach you whenever. Eddie?'

'I don't know the number.'

Edgar was resolute on that point and on his refusal to interrupt his father's telephone call, which was happening on the croquet lawn, quite far away. He agreed that his father would call Mon back straight away.

'I promise,' Edgar said. 'I love you too.'

Reluctantly he went to rejoin the people he supposed he had to call his family.

5

Under Uncle Frank's regime the house disintegrated further. Pills went untaken, Fay's dermatitis grew worse. 'It's an anxiety thing, clearly,' Lucille said, sitting on the sofa with Edgar's father, who refreshed her glass with whisky. Lucille and Edgar's father spent most of their time on the sofa; her complaints about Frank grew in volume, and cheerfulness, the more whisky she drank. At unpredictable moments she would violently put together a tray of water and fruit and medicines and go up to the invalid room. Edgar from the corridor watched Lucille sitting on the bed, holding Fay's hand, cooing insistent soft things that Fay pretended to sleep through. When Lucille had gone, her thighs in white canvas jeans brushing together as she walked, her scent of ripe fruit and spices, which Edgar decided was Levantine, hanging in the bedroom air, Edgar brought the middle hairbrush over to the bed, for which thoughtfulness he was rewarded with the saddest of smiles.

Jerome arrived in the mornings, usually with a burnt offering from the Mansion House kitchen. He was not allowed to stay long with Fay. 'You'll tire her out,' Frank and Lucille said. He brought his own sandwiches and flask of coffee, and would happily see out the day gardening until the family was sitting down to supper, when he would walk slowly back across the road, carrying his folding chair, newspaper and picnic bag.

'How you making out, Eddie?'

'Like a bandit, Jerome.'

Interactions were not so cordial between Jerome and the rest of Fay's family. Edgar's father was blatantly and sometimes unkindly amused by Fay's suitor. Frank and Lucille found no amusement. They fought against his presumption but Jerome was unshiftable. Neither could they give full vent to their loathing of him. He was the executor of Fay's will and therefore had power. But on Sunday, the third night of the new regime, they attempted what Edgar's father called their charm offensive.

'You should invite him in,' said Edgar's father.

'Go invite him in,' Frank said to Lucille, as they were about to sit down to a supper of Lucille's tuna Bolognese. Through the window, Fay's suitor could be seen packing away the small quantity of garbage he had generated in the course of the day. His folding chair had already been folded.

'You invite him in,' Lucille said.

Jerome joined them at the table. He would not eat any of the offered food, calling up for excuses his health, his diet, his digestion. 'I can only eat from two very specific food groups at a time,' he said.

He poured himself a glass of spring water from a bottle in his picnic bag. He did consent to drink the Scotch that Frank offered him.

'I know that Fay is very grateful for . . .' Lucille waved a hand to indicate the unlikely things that old people could do for each other.

'I'm caring for a dear, dear friend,' Jerome said.

'Of course you are,' said Lucille.

'We understand that,' said Frank. 'We all want what's best for her.'

'I hope that we do,' said Jerome. 'That spaghetti looks very interesting.'

'Please say you'll try some,' Lucille said.

'My proctologist would never forgive me.'

'Oh ho ho,' Edgar's father said.

Jerome looked down at his whisky glass, which Frank refilled. Paul asked if he might be excused from the table. Lucille smiled at her son and encouraged him to stay a while longer. 'Paul is a very talented athlete,' she announced.

Paul looked neither bored nor surprised to hear this.

'They've got a wonderful sport programme at the high school in Onyataka. And Michelle is really very gifted at art and communications. They have a very good art and communications programme also.'

'The school they go to is a jungle,' Frank said. 'Metal detector at the gates, can you believe it? Kids in junior high carrying knives, packing heat.'

'I've really fallen in love with this neighbourhood, it's s-special,' Lucille said.

'The landscape is very pretty,' Frank said wearily. 'Wherever I've gone I've always taken a part of it with me.'

'But I think it's the *people* that make a place what it is, don't you agree?' Lucille said.

'You planning on moving here?' Jerome said.

Lucille made fluttery motions with her hands, like a child signifying snowflakes. 'Oh we'd love to. But, you know, that's dependent on so many *factors*. The children love it here.'

Michelle giggled behind the damp sleeve of her sweater. Paul amiably spun the salt cellar on its side. Edgar, suddenly furious, wanted something bad to happen to all of them.

'Frank would love us to be closer to his mother.'

'His mother might have other ideas,' Edgar's father said.

Frank scowled. Lucille pretended to find this very funny. 'Mike's got a terrific sense of humour.'

'Yeah, he's a really funny guy,' Frank said. 'We need an incentive to come here though. Difficult to ask a family just to up sticks.'

'I guess it is,' Jerome said.

Lucille looked admiringly at her surroundings. She gazed out of the window in order to sigh at the beauty on display.

'Blackberry Festival's coming up soon,' Jerome said, winking inexplicably at Edgar.

'Want to ask you something, Jerry,' Frank said.

'Um-hmn?'

'You're Mom's friend.'

'*Confidant,*' Lucille murmured.

'What do you think might be going to happen to the house, this house, in the event—'

'In the *sad, awful* event.'

'In the sad, awful event of, you know, when it happens, and God-I-hope-it-doesn't-and-I'm-sure-it-won't-for-many-many-years, uh, my mom's passing?'

'You might want to speak to your mother about that,' Jerome said.

'Yes,' Frank said, nodding carefully. 'That's right. That's absolutely right. But—freshen up Jerry's glass, Mike—you know, I have to say, even before this whole hospital deal, I was worried for Mom, not just, you know what I'm saying, but her mind, or her *morale* might be the right way of putting it, there's a kind of morbidity at work, which I don't want to, to do anything to encourage, if you know what I'm saying.'

'I think I do,' Jerome said.

'And then this Warren character. It all seems pretty fucked up to me. Excuse my French. I'm glad he's out of the picture.'

'We can agree on that,' Jerome said.

Edgar wondered how Lucille kept her lipstick and mascara intact, no matter what she did with her mouth and eyes. When his mother wore makeup it smeared immediately. Lucille cradled her precious chin on her hand and leaned towards Jerome, resting her breasts on the lip of the table. Her cleavage was low, freckled and lined, and Edgar was seized by the fear that someone, perhaps himself, was about to stick his hand down it.

'We're talking as friends here. Just friends,' she said.

'Okay,' Jerome said. He narrowed his eyes, then widened them, looking for some way to focus his vision. 'Well what we're hoping for of course is that the house is donated to the Mansion House Corporation.'

'Right,' said Frank.

'Yes,' said Lucille.

'It's a site of tremendous historical importance, and there are things, *exciting* things, educationally speaking, that can be done here that can't be done over at the Mansion House. We could even get some actors in place and turn it into a kind of living museum. Wouldn't that be a peach of a thing?'

'A peach,' Lucille said.

Frank put away the bottle of whisky, which Jerome recognized as his signal to leave.

'You're a good man, Jerome,' said Frank.

'We're so glad she's got you for a friend,' said Lucille, her hand on Jerome's worn sleeve; her radiant eyes, the inviting posture of her body, beamed out admiration and respect and perhaps even love.

'Want you to know,' Frank said gruffly, his voice cracking with emotion and fellow-feeling, 'that you should come by whenever you like. We consider you family, isn't that right, Lucille?'

'Family,' Lucille said.

When Jerome had gone, Lucille asked Frank, 'You don't think she'd actually leave it to the Mansion House?'

'He's her executor, he should know.'

'But he said *hoping for*, so I guess her will must say something else.'

'And he's trying to persuade her different. Miserable sly fucker.'

'Unlike anyone else, for example.'

'What's that supposed to mean?'

'Whatever you want it to mean. I'm not that tremendously concerned.'

Lucille sighed and stretched and her blouse lifted away from the waistband of her slacks showing a band of tanned, rounded flesh, and she looked at her husband as if she was daring him to hit her, which was probably what he wanted to do.

6

Warren had been keeping her alive; Frank and Lucille were killing her. Fay grew thinner and frailer. Most of the time she slept. Sometimes she sat up in bed to draw the same tentative picture of an empty field. When Edgar visited Fay, and she leaned forward for him to brush her hair down towards the nape of her neck, the sharp stumps of her shoulder-blades looked ready to chrysalize into wings.

'Do they know who burned down the bingo hall?' she asked.

'I don't think so.'

Frank claimed to believe that Warren was the arsonist. 'It's kind of a coincidence, don't you think?' he asked, with tremendous self-satisfaction. 'Bingo hall burns down. Outsider skips town. Why'd else he go? Tell me he didn't do it and I'll call you a liar.' Frank had gone to the police to report his suspicions, filled out three forms, spoken to two police officers, one of them a detective from Syracuse. Edgar didn't believe Warren had burned down the bingo hall. He suspected the Indian Fighters: in his imagination he could see them, wearing paper pizza-parlour caps blackened for camouflage, carrying canisters of gasoline from which deadly wet rags protruded for a wick, a trail of fire stretching behind them. His father didn't care. 'Shit happens,' was all he said on the subject.

'Is Warren back yet? Brush my hair some more, please.'

Edgar brushed her hair. His right arm ached so he used his left, which he feared would become risibly thin by comparison with the over-employed right. 'Do you think Warren's coming back?'

'Of course he is,' she said, in a tone as close to snappish as she had ever used with him. 'Pass me the mirror please.' He passed her the hand mirror and she remembered to smile at him in appreciation, before examining her hair from different angles. 'He's with his other woman,' she said, and she looked how Edgar had felt when he first saw Electa with Husky Marvin.

Edgar's father was in the living room. He was watching a baseball game on the TV, drinking beer, his feet on the coffee-table. Edgar's father favoured thin socks, almost transparent where they stretched over the toes and heel. The heels were on a scattered stack of Fay's *Smithsonian* magazines, which his father used as coasters, and Edgar was disappointed that neither of his father's heels was quite inside the rings that his beer cans and whisky glasses had made as targets.

'Hey, come and watch the game with me, buddy!' his father said awkwardly. He patted the sofa seat beside him, and Edgar sat down and dutifully tried to find some meaning or grace in the game. Occasionally his father would try to point something out to him but his explanations further obscured an already incomprehensible event.

'You see there. Runner's taking a bigger lead now, pitcher can't afford to go into the wind-up. First baseman on the bag. Big space to hit into.'

'I've just been with Fay.'

'Is that right? And I'd say the hit and run is on as well.'

Edgar looked optimistically to the screen for some monster truck chewing up the turf as it crushed these bored-looking Latino men in tight breeches, churning up mud as it sped away aiming for the next. Instead, the hitter patted the ball back to the pitcher, who blew gum as he stepped off his mound, turned around and threw the ball to someone else, who caught it and threw it to someone else.

'Or you get a double play. Inning over.'

'Right,' Edgar said, more emphatically than was appropriate, which made his father give him an odd irked look.

'You want a nut?'

'No, thank you.'

His father yawned, which he always did when the commercial break came on, then sat forward ready for action.

'We're nearly at the end of the bag,' he said, turning it upside down over a magazine and picking through the dust for the last whole cashews.

'Maybe we should take a run down to the supermarket,' Edgar said.

Edgar liked to go to the supermarket with his father. They had been twice so far. They would drive down in the Cadillac, park the car near to where Doug and Rocky were racing each other inside supermarket carts, and it was Edgar's job to put the fruit and vegetables into plastic bags and weigh and sticker them. His father had shown him how to twirl the bags into a half-knot and Edgar took to the job with meticulous consideration, until his father would get bored and take over the task himself.

His father yawned. 'No. Supplies are good.'

Their conversation resumed at the next commercial break.

'I've just been with Fay,' Edgar said, although it seemed like hours ago.

'Yeah? I'll be going up to take a look at her after the game.'

'She said an odd thing.'

'Yeah, well, she does that. She always did, in fact. Kind of out of kilter. Used to embarrass the hell out of the old man. But he was busy elsewhere, if you know what I mean.' A fatherly primness overcame him and he leaned back and tried to look sentimental. 'Always the oddest things. I kind of liked them. You know, it's my contention that when you get old all these things drop away and what you're left with is the person who was there all the time.'

'Oh.'

This was as close to philosophy as he had heard his father speak and Edgar wanted to think about it, partly because it sounded like parental wisdom and also because if it meant what he thought it meant then he completely disagreed with it. He intended to make and remake himself over and over again, and when Edgar was old there would be no trace of any of the previous Edgars at all.

'What she say?' his father asked.

'Who?'

His father shook his head. 'When they made you they threw away the mould.'

Edgar concentrated hard and recollected himself. 'Oh. Right. Yes. I don't mean odd in that way. She said she thought Warren was with his other woman.'

The sight of his father laughing was alarming. His father hooted and he jerked his legs up and down, and when it was over he took off his glasses and wiped his eyes. 'Oh that's priceless. Priceless. Warren the fag with his other woman. I love it. Wait till Lucille hears that one.'

He turned his attention to the game. Edgar tried to entice it back again. He was hoping to invite his father to the Campanile, where he might enlist his father's charm in the battle to reinstate himself in Electa's world. At soccer practice she had ignored him in a way that was colder than scorn.

'I thought maybe I'd go get some pizza.'

His father held out a ten-dollar bill for him to take. 'Why don't you do that?' he said, not unkindly.

Edgar prepared himself in the bathroom: he was going through the jars of unguents and oils, enjoying the slow selection, the pleasure he was deferring, when Michelle came in, chewing gum noisily, popping it and making it snap. He grabbed a dollop of his uncle's hair grease and shoved it on top of his head for an alibi.

'What you doing?'

'Nothing,' he said.

'You fixing your hair? I can do that for you.'

She was an agreeable girl and kind-hearted, and it would have been rude to say no. He sat docilely on the edge of the tub. She stood over him, careless of the contact her body made with his. 'You've put a lot of this stuff in.'

'Maybe too much.'

'It's okay.'

Her hands were strong. He liked the feel of her fingers on his scalp.

'I do this with my friends all the time. Drink beer and fix each other's hair till morning. Kind of dumb, I guess. Where you going out to?'

'Nowhere. For a pizza maybe. Nowhere.'

'I like pizza,' she said, as if this was a rare coincidence. She rubbed his hair vigorously and laughed. 'The geek look, it suits you. Super-dweeby-nerdo-geek.'

He was annoyed at this, and because there was none of the formality with Michelle that attended his dealings with other girls, he could just grab for her hair and twist it all around until the results were equally laughable. She shoved against him and giggled and he reached for the tube of gel, which he squeezed out in dollops and rubbed it around and pulled her hair into two high spiky towers.

'I like it,' she said. 'I should come for a pizza like this.'

For a moment he considered allowing her to come with him. He imagined arriving at the Campanile, wild-haired, with this smudgy, carefree girl beside him. He could picture Electa's haughtiness turning to disdain. She didn't like

Michelle; she disapproved of anyone who chose to be in Michelle's company. Michelle would be oblivious, saying the wrong thing, doing, *being* the wrong thing. The prospect filled him with consternation. He pulled at his hair to make it more normal and so did she to hers.

'Okay. We ready?' she said.

To delay their progress, he pushed through the undergrowth in the garden.

'What you doing?'

'I'll show you.'

Except, he couldn't. The dead bees were still curled together. The body of the cat was gone.

'There used to be a cat here.'

'Why would there be a cat there? Come on, Dweeby, let's go.'

On the walk down to Creek, Michelle chattered away. She was telling him about how much she liked it here, and what a nice place it was and how cool it would be to live here, and Edgar dimly heard her mother speaking through her. They were past Stone Park, about to cross the bridge, wet leaves on the sidewalk. Could he faint?—crumple consumptively to the ground, fling out an arm, send her for help before consciousness dripped away and then, when she was gone, run away? He could hide out in the cemetery, sit by the Mary Pagan monument, which was his favourite place in this town. Might he kill her? Roll her body into the creek and bury it beneath stones and silt? Experimentally he lifted his hands towards Michelle's throat as if in play and she knocked away his arms and bounced on the balls of her feet and asked him if he wanted to wrestle and Edgar said no.

'Okay, then. I'm hungry. Let's eat.'

He walked very slowly but they still covered ground until, despite all his efforts, they were in the car-park of the Campanile.

'What we doing in this place? I thought we were going to get pizza?'

She walked purposefully across the road to Dino's. Edgar followed.

7

*We confess Christ within us a risen Savior, and fully believe that
by yielding ourselves to the inspiration of his spirit we can do all
things. So far from finding ourselves cramped and fettered, we
are realizing that 'where the spirit of the Lord is there is liberty'
of speech and action. Had we no Christ within, a mere display of
ourselves might with propriety be called arrogance; but the confidence and freedom which it is our privilege to exercise toward
him, will in due time characterize our intercourse with each other,
and the simplicity and absence of affectation which distinguish
childhood will also be the distinguishing traits of children of God.*

'Notes on Shame and Bashfulness', *The Spiritual Moralist*,
Mary Pagan, March 1851

At the Home Talk, when John Prindle Stone, newly returned
to the family from his missionary travels to the west, extends
the Operations against Shame and Bashfulness, George Pagan
experiences a heaviness in his belly, a dryness in his throat.

'The purpose,' John Prindle says, sitting in a chair like any
other, 'is neither to embarrass nor to ridicule. Neither is there
the intent to orgy. Babylon is where our neighbours choose
to live.'

Gathered in the Hall, the communitarians nod, as if com-
prehending their leader's words when, rather, they are
confounded by them. Mary sits a few rows away from George,
a faint smile on her face indicating her pre-initiation in
John Prindle's newest plan. The Association has grown settled
in its routines, become complacent in the quotidian, this

establishment of a new, ordinary kingdom, which, for those familiar with the workings of John Prindle's spirit, should have alerted them to the likelihood of an imminent Stirring-Up.

'Tomorrow,' says John Prindle Stone, 'we extend the Operations against Shame and Bashfulness.'

John Prindle Stone, stroking his beard, an action that in a lesser man might connote self-love, announces the formation of a Committee to supervise the running of the Operations. These, our spiritual engineers, the list of whom, George Pagan is at first relieved, then irked, not to hear his name among. Drily, like a foreman of works, John Prindle outlines the procedures for the next Operations: removal of all water-closet doors from hinges (hardware and parts to be stored in the workshop); fearless Sincerity to be the keynote of all communication, physical, verbal and amative; and a state of Edenic nakedness to be enacted in daylight hours, to be performed free of shame or vain display, for a limited time of perhaps a week, the exact duration to be decided by the Committee members, excepting, of course, protective clothing to be worn by those working in the trap shop, at the printing press, at the kiln, and most likely the laundry, although the Committee would rule upon that also.

'In case of inclement weather,' he says, forestalling the easier questions he sees rising to the lips of his audience, 'good sense shall guide us.'

A moment or two of almost silence passes between the last echo of text and the first murmur of commentary. A chair squeaks, Seth Newhouse fills his pipe—he has not yet conquered the Tobacco Principality—John Prindle asks if there are any questions.

There are none: no one wishes to appear ashamed of shame. Chairs are pushed aside, members of the band take up their instruments (for there is a programme to be followed:

this is a Thursday and there is always music and dancing on Thursday), and George Pagan is pleased to have a violin to tune, a bow to tap against his trouser leg. Before the dancing can begin, a useful denouncement issues from the visiting mother of one of the members, who had enjoyed a pleasant probationary stay thus far. The widow Mrs Short, newly born into the Association, remembers the manners and prejudices of her former existence and, red-faced, with dowager jowls ashake, bemoans the sin that declares itself so brazenly to be sinless, the crimes that her hosts and, she had thought, redeemers are committing against common decency, the scales that have fallen from her eyes, the satanic monster apparent, the creature made bare, undisguised, shameless. It is at these confrontations that John Prindle excels, although, in this unequal encounter, so enraged and foolish is his adversary that even Abram Carter would hold sway, and as he enlarges upon the terms 'common' and 'decency', with gentle irony and godly sincerity, his un-redoubtable opponent is left disarmed, weeping, astonished, and almost convinced of the falsity of anything she had ever believed to be true.

George Pagan awakes the following morning in trepidation, dreading the extended Operations Against Shame and Bashfulness. Shadow shapes pass across the sheet separating his sleeping area from Harriet's, unclothed silhouettes stretched into monstrous distortions by the morning breeze. George Pagan removes his nightshirt. He sits on his bed as he has on any day, so why should this one feel so very different? Solemnly, George Pagan, the wooden floor cool against his toes, pushes aside the dividing sheet to join his community on its new morning.

Elaborate courtesies preside at the breakfast table, *May I ask you to pass the gravy, sister?* and *Yes, indeed, the day is clement*. George Pagan wills his attention to rise from the buckwheat pancakes and baked potato in front of him. The Operations against Shame and Bashfulness must not founder in bashfulness renewed. He smiles at his companions beside him, whose answering smiles demonstrate their concord, the collective resolve not to fail this latest challenge. It is the sheer variety of physical types that he notices first. He is not surprised by Seth Newhouse's muscular frame—and Newhouse, efficient in nakedness as he is in every project, sits compactly, lightly haired (although George Pagan had expected a more bearish physique). Brother Carter, of course, takes to the expedition with vigour and flair, finding frequent reasons to display himself on the walk from dining hall to kitchen, ever eager to fetch more maple syrup for his brothers and sisters.

George had expected to be timid, blushing, newly virginal, crouching bashful beneath the reminder of sin in the Garden, but, in this bright spring light, to his, and, he suspects, others' surprise, he takes to the state of sinless nakedness whole-heartedly, showing neither an excess of modesty nor its animalistic opposite, which John Prindle calls the Babylonian Spirit—and for which Brother Carter is punished by the penalty of having to wear his clothes for a day. Indeed, it is a positive exultation that George Pagan feels, as if his skin is stronger following its casting-away of clothes. Even the act of evacuation is a source of gratification. In the benevolent proximity of the public eye he feels the generous gaze of God most warmly.

The widow Short, too: her pink, creamy folds, her large arms folded beneath her immense breasts, the zany grin on her suddenly beautiful face. She, too, has given of herself, yielded to the Association in its operations. Her son Mordecai, though, is, as ever, aloof, sallow, bashful. He works in the pea garden with his harvesting bag held bashfully over his groin.

When the week of extended Operations is over, and the Association returns to the polite state that the unenlightened call civilized, George is sorry. He has avoided the pitfall of vainglorious display and conversely the selfish withdrawal that calls itself modesty. Yes, there are scratches on his skin from careless walks through the woods, and it was he who, on the perimeter of the cornfield, was seen by a Lutheran neighbour who crossed himself and spat three times, but in this week of the extended Operations he has felt as close to the celestial music of the senses and thus to heaven and perpetual life as on few occasions besides.

8

The Indian Fighters clattered to some kind of stop, after-shock thuds of Rocky's drums, dirty trailing chords. Husky Marvin, head bowed, stepped back, one hand loosely holding on to the microphone stand. Edgar applauded.

Edgar was sitting in the doorway to the back room of Dino's, tolerated because he had arrived with Michelle, who was as easy and knowledgeable in this world as her brother was in Coach Spiro's. She sat against Doug Ashton's bass amplifier, rolling a joint that she twisted at the end and pulled through her dampened lips. Edgar had last seen a joint in an era before Jeffrey, when Mon's boyfriend was Rufus, who had curly black hair and pale brown skin and wild slovenly ways that Edgar (pre-history, BE, Before Edgar) had admired. He had liked being with Rufus, had enjoyed the weight of his company and mourned his passing, after Monica had ended things, citing his impossible geniality, his lack of ambition.

Michelle passed the joint to Sky, who lit it up. It was much smaller than the joints that Rufus rolled. Rufus billowed smoke from the sofa in a slow act of letting-go. Sky sucked in three, four, five quick, hard drags, holding the smoke down before breathing it all out in one explosion. By the time the joint had come around to Edgar, it was a third of its original size, damp and blackened along the seam. He tried sucking on it as Sky had done and his lungs filled with dark horror, twisting him double, coughing, hacking, needing to inhale and having to exhale at the same time, locked into an airless evil place that echoed with the sound of his own choking and the others' laughter; he was inside that hellish room where the band was doomed perpetually to play.

'Way to go, Edgar,' Sky said.

'One two three four!' Rocky yelled, and the band started up again. Husky Marvin shut his eyes and gripped the microphone stand tighter and released his voice, which rose above the ugly swamp that his bandmates made out of metal.

Edgar subsided. He sat beside Michelle against the vibrating amplifier. He watched from a distance his damaged world.

Proud of his putative ancestor's prowess in love, Ray Newhouse was no less proud of his own expertise on the electric guitar. He played twiddly anaemic lead, with whiny trebly little shrieks and intricate work on the high strings, sitting cross-legged on the wooden floor, his small head bent over his instrument, oblivious to everything but the intricate movements of his fingers, not noticing the others' changes in rhythm or key, or even that Doug Ashton had kicked the guitar-lead out of the amplifier and that all his gorgeous trills and frills were unhearable except in Ray Newhouse's own head.

Edgar doubted he could ever move again. But what if he had to go to the toilet? He worried, worse than he had ever worried about anything before, how he could make that horror-journey. Then he worried harder about the repercussions if he failed. What if he pissed himself? What if he already *had*?

The band fell to a lumbering stop. Rocky and Doug complained about each other's time-keeping. Sky shook his shag of blond hair, examined his fingers, used his guitar pick to lever away some of the grease beneath his nails.

'Was that a customer?'

It had been designated Edgar's job to look out for customers.

'I don't think so,' he managed to say, and his voice came out of some faraway place, which was maybe where wind came from too, he would have to investigate this perception when his thoughts and breathing and blood had become more reliable, if they ever did.

Ray unfurled the banner he had made, red background, with a pale limp cylinder cracked in two under some sort of black object.

'What *is* that?' Michelle said.

'What do you think it is?'

'She don't know, asshole. Why do you think she asked?' Doug said.

'It's a flag. Band needs a flag. Hang it behind us on stage.'

'What stage? We ain't never played yet, and with you in the band we ain't never going to.'

'We know it's a *flag*,' Sky said. 'But what's that on it, that black kind of thing thing?'

'And what's that white thing?'

'It's a tomahawk,' Ray said, wide-eyed at everyone else's stupidity.

'And that black thing? What's that?'

'Horse's head?' Rocky said.

'I'm betting it's one of those doofusses they have in Australia,' Sky said. 'What do you call them? Like a Frisbee? You throw it except it comes back?'

'Boomerang,' Edgar quavered out.

'It's a gun,' Ray said.

'Looks more like some kind of musical notation,' Marvin said.

'Exactly,' Ray said in triumph. 'It's both.'

''Cept it don't look like neither,' Sky said.

'Well you should fucking do it then. Took me hour and a half to make that.'

'Is it supposed to mean something?'

'Well, duh. It's symbolic. The power of the Indians crushed under the might of the gun and rock 'n' roll.'

'What power of the Indians?' Michelle asked.

'They haven't even got their bingo hall.'

'I hear they're getting these gas and cigarette franchises.'

'And a casino. Word is bingo hall's going to become a casino.'

'Not happening,' Doug said. 'Firewater and falling over is all they can do.'

'Happening right now. Construction already starting.'

'I hear they got some like major investor from Thailand?'

'I heard the Philippines.'

'Jack Diamond in the liquor store? He told me it was the Mob.'

'Since when did they let you in the liquor store?'

'Redskins and half-breeds going to be *printing* money up there. Governor's given his say-so.'

'Governor's a faggot.'

'Fuckin'-A.'

'You see?' Ray said. 'All this is in the flag. And *more*. People going to know we're the Indian Fighters.'

'Uh, excuse me?' said Marvin. 'I thought it was Indian Fighters in, like, *Indian* Fighters. You know, spirit of the noble warrior, Indian brave? That's what I thought it meant.'

'Oh. Did you?' Doug said.

'I thought so too,' Rocky said.

Doug glared at his brother.

Ray jeered at Marvin, 'You some kind of faggot, Marvin? I heard you were in Warren the Fag's faggotty opera.'

'You in an *opera*, Marvin?' said Sky.

Marvin shrugged. The shame of it was written on him.

'I don't want to be in the band if the singer's some Indian-lover opera guy.'

'And we don't want you in the band anyhow so that's

not a problem, is it?' said Sky, who threw the first pizza box at Ray's head. Doug and Rocky threw the most. Ray kept ducking and looked as if he was going to cry and reached to Michelle for consolation, but Michelle recognized where the power was, and wasn't, in this room and threw several boxes at him herself.

Rocky sat at his drums and beat out time on the snare. 'Come on! Let's play some rock 'n' roll. One, three four!'

The Indian Fighters started up again. Ray plugged in his guitar lead and Doug kicked it out again. Sky turned his back. Ray, as if performing a burial, packed away his guitar case and walked out. Edgar, seeing this as maybe his only chance to get away, followed him. At the corner of Route 5 and Prindle, outside the Onyataka Silverware factory, Edgar managed to say, 'Do you know anything about dead cats, Ray?' and the guitarist sprayed him with imaginary bullets from his guitar case and walked away, hunched.

Edgar felt as unready and incapable of action as he had ever been in his life. Walking was a trial. Breathing was an issue. He needed to lie down. He was outside the Campanile. Edgar performed the bravest act he could attempt. He pushed open the door of the Campanile, where all the tables were empty and mauve prints of Italian piazzas and gilt mirrors hung on the lavender-striped walls, and Electa was at the maître d' station with a stack of menus and a dust of flour on her cheek.

'Table for one?' she asked him.

'No. Uh, yeah. No. Please,' Edgar said.

She put him in a seat by the window, which was exposed to stares from passers-by and was blindingly sunny.

'Can I sit over there?' he managed to ask, pointing to one of the tables in the shadows towards the back.

'Those are reserved. Did Sir make a booking?' she said.

'No. He, I, didn't.'

257

'Our specials today are home-made New England clam chowder, *amatriciana* sauce on the pasta of your choosing and a seafood gumbo *à la casa*.'

'I just need. Want—'

'I'll take your order now. We're rushed off our feet.'

Electa looked around at the gloomily deserted room, which the air-conditioner worked noisily hard to freeze.

'Uh, okay. I'll take a pizza. Margarita.'

'Small?' sneered Electa.

'Large,' Edgar said defiantly.

He promised himself to begin his apologies—for breaking their date, for himself, for everything—when she came back with his glass of water, but she brought him a root beer instead, which silenced him, so he resolved that he would speak to her while she was lighting the candle in its plump orange glass, but he could only watch her doing that, the steady sureness of her hand, the delicacy of her wrist, the dark hairs lying transverse across her yellow skin, and when he had discovered a kind of calmness in closing his eyes, the pizza arrived in its immensity of steel-trayed horror.

Edgar chewed endlessly at unswallowable bulges of grease and gloop, and she stood there, openly laughing at him.

But he was Edgar, who had taken drugs, and nothing should be beyond his capacity. So when Electa spoke to him just when he was at his most defenceless, with the most intractable lump of sludge in his mouth, Edgar rose to the challenge.

'How was it on the markets today? Portfolio going strong?'

'Bootde szerimina.'

'Excuse me?'

Edgar forced himself to swallow; the bolus of gloop rose back up, and he could see it as a little doughy cheesy monster with grinning evil mouth and tenacious hands, and he made himself not think about it and forced it down again. 'About the cinema.'

'Please. Don't mention it. I know how busy you are. Have you found your darling little cat-killer yet?'

'Well, no, not yet. I'm still conducting investigations.'

'Yeah right. Oh, I *see*. That accounts for you being so busy all the time. You're *investigating*.'

'Look. I'm sorry.'

To cover his embarrassment and shame he made the awful mistake of biting into the slice again.

'No, no. Please. A man of your responsibilities. How's your pizza?'

'Zzhumsztug.'

'I guess it is top secret. You must lead a really thrilling life.'

'Zzhumsztaszh.'

'Really? You don't say? Well, it would be nice to stay here and talk about old times and all but I've got other tables to wait on.'

'Zhsnngyay.'

'Sergei? Uh no. I don't think he's come in today.'

He had achieved it. He'd swallowed. 'I don't think he's gay.'

'I'm sorry?'

'You know, Warren, who lives at my grandmother's? He's not gay. He's got a woman. My grandmother said so.'

This statement intrigued her. Enough to keep her at his table. 'So?'

Edgar looked shrewdly around. He implied the invisible presence of dangerous individuals, the immanence of evil machinery. 'So, everyone thinks he is. Some people call him Warren the Fag.'

'Um. Yes?'

'So.' Edgar wildly, wet slice of pizza drooping in his hand.

'He's not what he seems. If there's one thing bogus, then maybe everything else could be too. You see what I mean? Maybe he killed the cat.'

Edgar felt guilty impugning Warren, because he liked Warren, who was scrupulous in all his dealings, but Warren was gone and he had always been obliging, so maybe he wouldn't mind being used like this.

'Right. I get it. That's really sinister. There's a cat that's dead and Warren pretends to be gay but he's not. Is the FBI involved? I think they should be.'

'But that's not all—' He went on before she could interrupt or leave, and in his stoned inspiration he reverted to London-speak. 'He did these labels right, so everyone would know where everything was when he was gone, so nothing really bad would happen to her, and he left because my uncle's an arsehole but he did these labels *before* they had their argument so maybe he engineered the whole thing because he wanted them out, and the best way to get them out was to show everybody including them how bad they are when they're *in*, you know what I'm saying?'

If she followed what he was saying she believed in it as little as he did.

'Which means,' he persisted, 'he'll be back soon to show everybody how needed he is.'

'I don't know what you're talking about but in the meantime you'll have to excuse me, I must attend to my other customers.'

He resumed his ordeal, she folded napkins at the maître d' station. She looked his way at least twice.

Having eaten way beyond his capacity and further, his body blocked with food, his soul utterly contaminated and impure with food, and leaving only about a third of the damp horror remaining, Edgar dropped the ten-dollar bill on the table and vomit-coughed out a goodbye and exited the restaurant without too inept a performance at the door. His body is weighed down with fat and gloop, he can feel cheese throughout, sluggish cheese slowing his blood, his vision has turned yellow, he's sweating cheese.

9

The real stockholders in our institution are the men and women of the invisible world.

Home Talk, John Prindle Stone, June 1851

In the official history of the Onyataka Association, written in 1891 and republished in 1919, 1943, 1985 and 2001, there is no mention of the Operations Against Shame and Bashfulness. These were classified as belonging to the 'class of heavenly things' that was fit only for the saints. In the official history, relations between the Mansion House and its neighbours, as between the Perfectionist satellite communities and their neighbours in Brooklyn and Niagara, were untroubled. (In the official history, Complex Marriage was begun by George Pagan and Harriet Stone; there was never any jealousy or reproach; there was no breeding programme; few attempts were made to push aside the veil between the material and immaterial worlds; and all was easy and unanimous in the new dispensation.) In the official history, the inspiration for the Blackberry Festival was entirely hospitable: there was nothing tactical or strategic about it.

In truth, word of George's naked appearance spread through the vicinity. He was the beast of the undergrowth, the devil in the thicket, denounced at town meetings, at trading posts, from church pulpits. And yet—or, as Mary Pagan suggested, *because*—there has been a consequent increase in willing converts to the Perfectionist cause. And

263

how disappointed some of them are when they see the family so modestly and unorgiastically at work and at play, every moment a prayer, salvation to be found in newspaper work, in farming, building and selling an animal trap, shelling peas, manufacturing plates and dishes, whose first designs are made by a committee of children led by Mary Pagan. Most are turned away. A few are invited to stay, as probationers. Free love, John Prindle tells the curious and the prurient, has its price, to be paid in God's coin.

On the balance sheet of the world, the Association prospers; its neighbours prosper accordingly. Local merchants, traders, farmers, all profit. Every worker employed, on most enlightened terms, at the new tableware factory in Turkey Street, which is now renamed Creek, is another potential enemy recruited, another soldier for the march to Paradise. Each dish and plate produced from Mary's, and the children's, designs is a charming artefact of the war being won. But still, as in Vermont before, gossip ferments and threatens. At a Home Talk John Prindle announces his army's latest initiative: 'We shall use the weapons of charm and diligence and sincerity, lower our drawbridges, open our gates, let the neighbours see us as we are, in all our virtue that does so much outshine theirs.' At the end of the summer the Blackberry Festival shall take place, a grand occasion of Christian hospitality.

10

Edgar, exhausted, returned to the house. It was an exertion to pull open the screen door. He leaned against the doorpost, forehead to the wood. On the wooden radiator cover inside the hallway were several knick-knacks—a brass hand-bell, a ceramic shepherdess, two silver spoons. Edgar looked at these with the utmost gravity. All he wanted was a quick efficient visit to the bathroom, drain himself to the furthest reach, and then to sleep. He couldn't stop looking at the knick-knacks. The missing lines of blue paint on the shepherdess's skirt hurt him. He wondered if he should break the figurine, put her out of her agony. Soon he would have to contemplate the stairs.

'Eddie? Is that you?'

It wasn't. He didn't know at this moment who he was. Slowly though, he, or someone vaguely occupying his shape, walked to the living room and burst out laughing when he got there.

It wasn't his father he was laughing at, sitting on the sofa, looking down at the glass in his hand, making the whisky wash around like a drunken tide; and it wasn't Frank, standing by the bureau, his lips pouting like a teenager's; and it wasn't Lucille, who was dressed for some reason for Warren's opera, full in the dark pantalets and skirt and blouse that the women of the Association used to wear, her voluptuousness revealed more emphatically when buttoned and pinned; and it wasn't Jerome, wearing his windcheater and holding his picnic bag, either on the point of arrival or departure; and it wasn't Fay, who was sitting on the hard chair, hands demure on her lap. He was laughing, he finally decided, because the room was so empty of the slightest reason to laugh.

Faces soured towards him, except Fay's. 'Hello dear. You might want to help Warren in the kitchen,' she said.

Edgar stopped laughing. He wanted this day over. He was thirteen years old and everything was mildly horrible. He looked for help from his father, his uncle, his aunt. None provided any. No one met Edgar's gaze, considerate maybe of Fay's delusion, annoyed probably at his ability to find humour in a mirthless room. Edgar had not seen his grandmother out of her bed since her return from hospital. Her hair was wild but she looked happy.

'In the kitchen?' he said.

'That's right. He's putting a tray together.'

Edgar moonwalked through to the kitchen, pitying Fay for her fantasy. Should he be supporting it or, gently, destroying it? Should he put together a tray himself? What sort of things would Warren put on a tray? Olives and cashews, crackers and cheese. He could get Michelle to help him. Issue stoned, black-lunged, pizza-engorged instructions while she performed the intricate skills of opening cupboards and lifting things on to a tray. Everything was easy to find in there, because everything had been labelled by Warren before he went away.

'Hey Eddie. How's it going?'

Warren was at the dishwasher, unshaven, gloveless, in unpressed jeans and wrinkled T-shirt. This was more surprising to Edgar even than his return, because Warren was always most fastidious in matters of hygiene and appearance.

'Warren. You're back.'

'So it seems. You might want to carry this through.' Warren held out a tray that contained a bowl of olives, plates of crackers and cheese.

Edgar stared at it with great dignity and poise. 'Maybe we should put out some cashews too,' Edgar said.

'Why not?' Warren said gaily.

Fay was exultant, the rest of the household in consternation. Warren took brisk command of everything, reminding everybody how integral he was to the life of the Pagan House, suffering Lucille and Frank to acknowledge his triumph without any need for him to draw attention to it. Edgar helped Fay carry her easel out to the back lawn, where she sat draped in cotton and muslin against the evening breeze, drawing trees and bushes and an empty blue field.

Edgar was so tired that he wanted to defer sleep as long as possible. He lay on his bed, floating on time, listening to it stretch out all around him. Edgar adored his theory about Warren. This must be how Jeffrey felt about his opinions. That he didn't believe it to be true made it beautiful.

There was a knock on his door. Warren, newly washed and shaved, restored to creased jeans and freshly pressed T-shirt, held out a package wrapped in gold paper. 'Happy birthday. I know it's a bit late but we got you something,' he said.

'That's really nice of you. Thank you,' Edgar was able to say. Tears of gratitude were frighteningly close.

Warren noticed his discomfort without, Edgar hoped, discerning its self-pitying cause. 'I'll leave you to it. Hope you like it.'

This was his only birthday present. Edgar sat on the bed, picking at Scotch tape, tapping his fingernails against the wrapping paper. He felt guilty. He had said bad things about Warren, who was the only one who had thought to give him a birthday present. Edgar assumed it would be a good choice, because everything Warren did was good, except running away for a weekend.

The present was a book, *A History of the Onyataka Association*. On the flyleaf was an inscription: *To Edgar, a souvenir of his time in Vail*. The tears of his self-pity dried as he failed to work out how Warren could possibly know his secret name.

11

In the morning Frank, truculent, muttering, defeated, threw family belongings into the Lexus. Lucille fixed her lipstick in the rear-view mirror. Michelle sat in the back seat, chewing on a sleeve of her sweater. Paul lounged beside her, spinning a basketball on his finger, breathtakingly casual. The weeping virgins of Vail mourned at the kerbside as the Lexus drove away.

And then his father was going too. Edgar's father tossed his suitcase into the trunk of the Cadillac and climbed into the car. Jerome, despite Warren's reappearance, was still defiantly gardening. Wearing his straw hat, he slowly pushed a wheelbarrow towards the compost pile.

'How you making out, Eddie?'

'Like a bandit, Jerome.'

Edgar's father hit two quick stabs at the horn and sat forward with his arms draped over the steering-wheel. 'Okay, Eddie. Let's hit the road. Time waits for no man.'

Edgar composed his bravest, cruellest face.

'What's the matter? You got wind? Come on. Climb aboard.'

'You don't think? Maybe we should stay a bit longer?'

'No Eddie, I don't. You know how it is.'

Edgar was afraid that he did not know how it is, nor that he would ever know what *it* was.

'Let's be making tracks. Nothing more for us to do here. Where's your stuff?'

'I think we ought to stay,' Edgar said. 'Bad things happen when I'm not here.'

'Hey come on. No kidding around.'

'No,' Edgar said.

He has never said no to his father before. The novelty of the act provides its strength.

Edgar's father frowned. He lowered his glasses to inspect his son.

'Is it Fay you're concerned with? Don't you worry about your grandma, she's a tough old bird. She'll outlive us all.'

'I guess so.'

'It's a sure thing. Everything's copasetic. Let's make a move.'

Edgar shook his head. 'I'm going to stay.'

He rested one arm inside the car to make it impossible, just yet, for his father to leave.

'*I'm* not staying,' his father said.

'You don't have to,' Edgar said.

He has given his permission and it makes him fearful and vulnerable. No one had ever told him that adulthood would feel so cold.

'You're a great kid, Eddie,' his father said, and applied his mouth to where Edgar's cheek could have been. He pushed Edgar's ear the wrong way with a bristly rub of his chin.

Warren came out of the house to say his goodbyes. He looked surprised and, Edgar thought, disappointed when Edgar told him he was going to be staying. 'If that's okay?'

'Sure it is. Of course. No problem. Just thought it was all a little dull for you here.'

They watched Edgar's father leave. The Cadillac turned, its front left tyre mounted a Vail sidewalk, squeezed over it and, with a bump, the car was facing the right way, it picked up speed as it approached the bridge, and was gone.

Warren dispatched Jerome later that day.

'I'd like to pick your brains,' Warren said.

'Gladly,' Jerome said, blinking suspiciously.

'I wonder if you'd know someone who could do a little research for me? It's a number of historical details I'm missing for the opera. Maybe it's not important but I like to be a stickler for accuracy.'

'What kinds of details?'

'George and Mary Pagan mostly. The service held at their wedding. Hymns. Their address in New York City before they fell in with the Perfectionists. Anything more that can be dug up of Mary's letters and journals. *Is* there anything that survived the burning of the forties? And Mordecai Short, I know he came from Pittsburgh but—'

Jerome had been nodding, interested but impatient, going *Yep yep yep*. Finally he interrupted: 'I think actually you'll find he was born in Vermont, he may well have spent some time in Pittsburgh, but he was a New Englander, that's for certain.'

'There. You see? I'm all adrift with this. There's a number of other things also, a whole slew of them, I've made a list. It's for the programme notes, historical outline. But you know how it is—between Fay, rehearsals, there isn't the time . . .'

'You've looked through the library at the Mansion House?'

'I have.'

'You've picked Janice's brains? She knows everything there is to know about the Association.'

'And drawn a blank. *She* didn't know Short was from Vermont. I need to get to the collection in Syracuse. Probably a day there is all that's required . . . If there's anyone you can think of who could do this, I'd be very grateful.'

'And you really think it's necessary?'

'I don't want to make any mistakes. You know, if you get one or two facts wrong then the whole edifice crumbles.'

Jerome considered. 'I'll do it,' he said.

'You? But—'

'There's no one else who can be trusted to get these sort of things right. I would have said Janice, but if she didn't know where Mordecai Short was born . . .' He shook his head sadly.

'Come on, Jerome. I can't put you through the trouble. It's visits to Syracuse. Days in the library.'

'You said just one day.'

'Well, I hope that's what it is. It could stretch to longer, I don't know. You know how slow they are in there, I really couldn't guarantee . . .'

'I'll do it.'

'If you're sure?'

'I even think I might enjoy it.'

'Well you're a life-saver, Jerome, you really are. And there'll be a dedication in the programme for you.'

A more confident boy could leave his crumpled tissues where they lay, to dry and crisp by the morning. Edgar went to dispose of them in the bathroom. On his way back he nearly ran into Warren going into Fay's bedroom. Edgar froze in shadows as Warren stepped into the corridor, tying the cord of his dressing-gown and securing it in a double knot. He wiped his hair down and entered Fay's room, pushing the door softly open. Edgar crawled down the corridor because for some peculiar night-time reason that seemed easier, and more appropriate, than walking.

Edgar scuttled into his bed. After he had closed his bedroom door and covered himself with the bedclothes safely over his shoulders, his imagination failed him when he tried to guess what Warren might be doing in Fay's room at night.

12

Warren was returned, his enemies scattered, except for Edgar, who had no allies. He called his mother.

'You still haven't given me your father's cellphone number.'

'Uh. It's not working. That's why.'

Mon asked him for the number where he and his father were staying, and Edgar said it didn't accept incoming calls.

'I thought you were in a motel.'

'We were. There was a swimming-pool, and a restaurant, and a games room for the kids.'

'You're already sounding American. *Kids.* Where are you now?'

He invented a friend of his father who was a reclusive inventor of some kind and was putting them up in a large, curious house where the electricity was always blowing and the communications were usually down. 'I think that's why the cellphone isn't working. Interference from all the power supplies.'

'It sounds very strange to me. Where is it?'

'Uh, I'm not sure. It's near a highway.'

'What state are you in?'

'I'm quite relaxed, actually. It's all been very easy-going.'

'Very funny, ha ha. Where *are* you?'

'Um. Pennsylvania somewhere. There's these Amish nearby, got beards and horse-buggies and stuff. It's really interesting. Historical.'

Edgar added this detail from a TV documentary he had

caught the end of with Fay while she was waiting for a John Mills movie to come on for the afternoon matinée.

'I bet you haven't sent your grandmother a thank-you card?'

'What? Sorry. This line's not very good.'

'The line's perfectly good. Have you sent Fay a card?'

Edgar found it curious that he was able to lie so fluently about some things yet not about others. Considering this anomaly, he decided that while he was perfectly adept at lying to protect others, he hadn't developed the skill when it was himself at threat.

'Eddie?'

'I'll do it first thing.'

'I'd better call her.'

'I'll send it first thing, I promise. I've got some postcards with stamps on already. I'll do it, believe me.'

'There's such a thing as elementary courtesy, you know.'

'Yes, I know,' he said feelingly.

'So who is this inventor?'

'He's called Dave. He's got a swimming-pool in the shape of his monogram, and servants.'

'How does your father know this Dave?'

'It's a business thing, I think. But they're friends too. They play chess together.'

'I thought he was a recluse?'

'He likes to play chess. I've even played against him. I beat him once.'

And Edgar wasn't bragging here, he was seeing it all, the evenings spent in a green velvet library, the atlases and rare books open on lecterns, sporting prints on the walls, and Dave, the millionaire, sitting at the chessboard, his chin in his hands, an expression in his eyes of the infinite weariness that infinite knowledge brings, pushing back his grey hair and nodding. *Well played, Edgar.*

'Maybe he let me win,' he admitted.

'I don't think it's healthy, how you're spending your holiday with your father.'

'We eat muesli every morning, with fruit.'

'You should be with people your own age. It's not right to be cooped up with a recluse called Dave. You're thirteen not fifty. There used to be a poet in the family. Maybe that's where you get these funny things from.'

'How do you know about a poet?' Edgar said, aggrieved that she was presuming knowledge about the history of the house.

'Someone must have told me.'

'Jeffrey, I suppose.'

'It could have been. He's very interested in transgression.'

'What's that?'

'It's all a bit technical and grown-up for you. I'll tell you when you're older. But I'll tell you something about Jeffrey.'

'Please don't.'

'He's the only man who ever admired my feet. He says I have pretty feet. It's true. I do have pretty feet, but no one else has ever said anything nice about them.'

Edgar, gruesomely fascinated, wondered if Mon just spoke out of her own pathology here, or was in fact representative of her sex.

He hoped that music could lift him from this mood, but it failed him. The magic was gone, nothing in the guitar, the singer's voice; the ability to soothe, to cure, had been spent, squandered, when he hadn't really needed it. The record spun, one of Uncle Frank's records that he had mistakenly supposed to be his father's. Edgar occupied himself for the rest of the evening by scratching geometric shapes across the groove.

13

Jerome was not a disciplined researcher: every day he uncovered more information that led him into further investigations. He went each morning to Syracuse, returning around dusk. They'd see him at the start and end of his day, his anxious battered car, reckless and slow on the descent and ascent of the rise into Vail.

'What sort of car is that?' Warren asked him one evening.

'It's Japanese,' Jerome confidently said.

He'd visit Fay briefly at the end of his day, eager to keep the household up to date with his discoveries, impatient to get to bed for an early start the following morning.

'It would take a lifetime to go through it all properly,' Jerome said. 'It's captivating, absolutely fascinating. Every day I turn up new stuff that I didn't know before. You know that crazy guy, Guiteau? The one who assassinated McKinley? "I am a Stalwart of the Stalwarts! Now Arthur will be president!" That's what he said when he fired the shots. Well I knew he'd spent a little time in the Association but it turns out he was here for five years, off and on. It's fascinating, isn't it?'

'Fascinating,' Warren said.

'Now in this context, of course, "Stalwart" doesn't mean what you might expect it to mean, Eddie'—because Jerome, for purposes of his own, perhaps purely rhetorical, laid the burden of his discoveries on Edgar—'you've got to look at it in terms of US reconstruction politics. There were the Stalwarts on one side against—now *what* was the other side called? Was it Niggers? Half-Breeds? Or am I getting them muddled with something else?'

'I'm not sure,' Edgar said.

'And Guiteau switched from one side to the other quite a few times. It was the struggle that interested him, like a holy war—it might be a heresy this, but he had his own messiah complex quite as much as John Prindle. The difference between them, of course, was that people wanted to follow John Prindle.'

Jerome smiled at Edgar. Pieces of his face moved in unlikely directions.

'Which raises some very interesting questions, I'd say, into the whole nature of religious leadership and divine commission. Is something true if enough people want to believe it to be true? I don't know the answer. It's deep waters. And all this is a long-winded way of saying I haven't uncovered yet all of the rather basic information Warren is looking for. But it will come, it will come. So. How's our convalescent?'

'I'm not a convalescent. I'm fine, Jerry, really I am.'

'And you look it! You're looking tremendous,' Jerome said.

'It's such a relief to have Warren back.'

'Yes,' Jerome said doubtfully. 'I suppose it might be.' Finally Jerome allowed Warren his attention. 'That smells very good.'

'Lamb chop and beans on the menu today. You're more than welcome to stay. Plenty for everybody.'

'No. Thank you. As a matter of fact I'm keen to get to my bed. I'm aiming to get through boxes five to eleven tomorrow.'

'Don't let us keep you,' Warren said.

The researcher hoisted his picnic bag on his shoulder and went back across the road. Fay made her way slowly towards her easel in the garden.

Watching Edgar clung to shadows as Warren went into Fay's bedroom.

He waited and watched as Warren, like a hairdresser gone silently amok, an anti-hairdresser, gently pulled and twisted and tangled Fay's previously neat white hair. Edgar went back to his room, keeping close to the corridor walls, where the floorboards seldom creaked. After hearing Warren's footsteps return to his own room, Edgar went back to Fay's. The door was ajar, his grandmother slept, her hair criminally wild on the pillow. In time to the rattle of the nightjars outside the window he brushed. Fay stirred. A sleeping hand rose to stroke her own cheek. Grateful shadows slid across the walls of the Pagan House.

He brushed. He kept brushing until her hair was smooth and straight and he continued to brush until the muscles ached in his forearm and wrist. He returned to his room exhilarated, sleepless, heroic.

In the morning, Fay's hair was messy again. There was no sign of Edgar's handiwork. It was as he was pouring himself a bowl of cereal (Doctor Chox, 'It's Chocolaty!') that Edgar glanced up and saw Warren looking at him. There was an unmistakable challenge in Warren's expression, an incipient triumph.

Edgar took all his meals with Fay and Warren. Daytime was cordial, with no references ever made to the battles that went on, with brush and comb, at night. Fay went up to bed at about eight thirty, after watching a John Mills movie. Jerome didn't come by in the evenings any longer; he was too busy with his researches. Edgar set the alarm for midnight. Usually her hair was undisturbed then, but Edgar would perform a little touching-up. Then again at six in the morning, when her hair would always be mussed, far more maliciously than could be accounted for by Fay's innocent movements in sleep. He was finding the days wearing, and had taken to after-lunch naps, or siestas, as he thought of them. He was considering eliminating the midnight visit but worried that might be a dereliction of duty. Most people died between three and four in the morning.

'Sometimes I experience air as oppression. I can almost detect the colours of all the layers of stuff that press down on me. It's a spectrum, from orange to blue,' Fay said.

'Oh,' Edgar said. He was in her bedroom, combing her hair that Warren would later disturb and Edgar would later set right.

'I've forgotten to do my homework,' she said. 'Do you think they'll mind?'

'No. I don't think so.'

Fay was sometimes lucid, sometimes inexplicable.

'Do you like Mary?' she said. Her voice remained that of an apprehensive schoolchild so Edgar assumed Mary was a controversial girl whose friendship she was hoping for or else a playground bully against whom she was shyly trying to gather support.

'Um,' Edgar said.

'You can be honest with me.'

'Yes. I think I do like Mary. Very much.'

His guess was rewarded with a sunlit smile. 'I'm so glad. I knew you would. She was the best of them. This is her house. No one who's lived here has been worthy of the privilege. Maybe you could be.'

She closed her eyes and her stillness alarmed Edgar. He brought her back with talk of the cat. 'Tom's dead. Your cat. He's dead.'

'Oh I know *that*,' she said, a little impatiently. 'Warren killed him.'

The battle for Fay's life will be fought with combs and brushes, tortoiseshell, ivory, silver and plastic, stroking through her fine white hair.

Except, now, she has had enough. She is done; she longs for oblivion, obliteration, extinction—a boat casting off from shore, a balloon let go by a child's hand, to drift. But a rope keeps pulling her back; a pale hand holds tight.

14

Whenever Edgar left the Pagan House something, usually bad, happened there. But Edgar had been picked for the first soccer game of the season and neither Warren nor Fay would hear of him missing his opportunity, as they called it. Before the game began, Coach Spiro called Edgar over to walk with him to his pickup truck where Marilou was sitting, looking skittish and wild-eyed. Edgar took the opportunity to protest the unfairness of Electa's exclusion from the team.

'Your loyalty does you credit,' said Spiro.

'I'm not being loyal,' said Edgar.

'If there's one thing missing from your game, it's self-belief.'

'Maybe,' Edgar conceded, because Coach Spiro's scrutiny was an uncomfortable form of attention.

'No maybes or ifs or buts about it. The men will realize how good you are and then *you* will too.'

For a moment Edgar could almost believe in the coach's hopelessly mistaken judgement of him.

'You'll be taking the corners from the left side. And the attacking free kicks from the right.'

Edgar's moment of near self-belief collapsed under the weight of inevitable shaming exposure. He was happy to wear team colours. He was happy to run around on the wing, regardless of the weather. But *corners*, and *free kicks*.

'Oh. But. I think—'

'And *that*'s your problem. You think too much. Free the

body and it will do what it needs to do. The best golfers can play blindfold.'

'Really?'

'I know you won't let me down,' Coach said. 'Oh, Eddie?'

'Yes?' said Edgar, interested in the way Spiro's fingers dug into the skin of his wife's arm making little red shadow fingers. 'You might want to give a message to Warren. Isn't that right, Marilou?'

Marilou Weathers licked her lips and smiled and looked terribly sad.

'Marilou isn't going to make rehearsals tonight. In fact, she finds that she's unable to take part in the *opera* at all. Isn't that right, Marilou?'

'Tell Warren I'm sorry.'

'Yeah. Tell Warren she's sorry.'

To dismiss Edgar, Coach Spiro tipped the peak of his cap in a military salute. He was more intimate but equally soldierly in his leavetaking of his wife, who licked her chapped laps after he was finished with them.

The game began, and Edgar tried Coach Spiro's advice and shut his eyes. He stumbled into one of his own teammates and took a hefty blow to the nose that brought tears to his eyes and made him reconsider his tactic. For the rest of the half he trotted up and down the wing, relieved that no one passed to him. His team at least knew his insufficiency. He touched the ball twice in the first half. The first, a miscued return pass to Husky Marvin, spun wildly into the opposition penalty area where Ray Newhouse, surprised, failed to run on to it. The second time, the ball bounced off his shins, ricocheting to Husky Marvin who gathered it in his stride and cracked a shot from outside the area that powered into the net before the goalkeeper had even registered the need to save it. (Although, to his credit, the dive he

executed after the goal had already been scored, was sump-
tuously balletic.)

At half-time the score was 1–1. The players sat on their
bench, eating slices of banana and swilling their mouths with
water, which their regimen did not allow them to swallow,
while Coach Spiro hectored them on their need to get the
ball out to the wing, to Edgar, who was, Spiro declared, the
one true playmaker on the team.

The second half was torture to Edgar. The group mind
of the team had decided to follow the coach's instructions
in the interest of showing him just how bad Edgar was.
He had to chase after unreachable balls that were skilfully
overhit by just a fraction. He endured the injury of fast-
hit passes that skipped on the turf to sting his thighs. But
he drew a crowd. Opposition defenders and midfielders,
anticipating where the ball was going, gathered around
hapless Edgar to retrieve the inevitably uncontrolled pass.
This had the effect of leaving unoccupied space in the
middle and when Edgar, with tears stinging his eyes, frustration and rage firing his muscles, saw another humili-
ating pass coming towards him, he made no attempt to
control it, just kicked it as hard as he could; the ball bounced
against the hip-bone of the nearest defender and lolloped
over his teammates into the space for Husky Marvin to
gather, run, and dribble past the goalkeeper for the winning
goal. The goalkeeper beat the grass with his fist. Edgar
was impressed by the gesture, the shiny dazzle of braces
on his teeth.

In the dressing room, drinking Gatorade, strutting, slapping
backs and tousling hair, kicking plastic bottles away, hands on
hips, in, as ever, sunglasses and shorts, the vindicated coach
permitted himself some lordly self-congratulation. 'Good play
men. Now in future when I issue an instruction I expect it
executed in the moment!'

'Well played,' Electa said, as they left the club room.

'Thanks,' Edgar said. He assumed she was being sarcastic. He didn't mind if she was being sarcastic, he was just glad she was talking to him, that the possibility existed that he might be renewed in her world.

She permitted him to walk down with her to Creek and he justified himself with a summary of Warren's tactics. She wasn't convinced.

'He drove everybody away.'

'Except for you.'

'Except for me. It's so he could have the coast clear.'

'Clear for what?'

'He does things. At night.'

'What kindsa things? I'm *agog.*'

'And he killed the cat.'

'Really.'

'And something's going to happen at the Blackberry Festival.'

'Like what? A party? That's really interesting. You're outdoing yourself,' she said.

'There's something else.'

Edgar was saved temporarily from Electa's scorn by the drama of a police siren, a patrol car spinning up dirt from the side of the road as it slowed to take the corner, and Ray Newhouse, looking triumphant and silly, held up his manacled hands high from the back of the car for them to see. He hooked his thumbs together and made the shape of an eagle dropping from the sky until the cop sitting next to him cracked his elbow against his head and Ray Newhouse fell out of sight.

After a pause, Electa said, 'Wow.'

'There's something else.'

'I really have to tear myself away from this and go to work.'

'You've got very pretty feet,' Edgar said.

Her reaction to this compliment, which was colder and more impressive than fury, was a further reproach that he could hold against his mother.

15

Warren was on the porch wiping his hands.

'I'd like to ask you a few questions,' said Edgar, filling his voice with knowledge and dread.

'First things first, Edgar,' Warren said, brazenly using his secret name. 'Come into the living room.'

Fresh luggage was stacked higgledy-piggledy in the hallway. Edgar slid behind Warren into the living room, where his mother was standing by the sideboard, wearing white-rimmed sunglasses and a headscarf.

'You look so glamorous,' Fay said.

'Oh, really, no. I got you this,' Mon said.

'Thank you very much, Monica. You really shouldn't have,' Fay said, looking doubtfully at a red and silver box of chocolates.

'And these. But be careful with the little one, it's quite fragile, I had a nightmare bringing it over and—EDDIE!'

He had thought to make his appearance quietly, as background. Imprint his presence on his mother's consciousness without any fuss or show; he had almost managed to persuade himself that she had known he was here all along, that the imaginary travels with his father he had reported on the telephone had been just a game they were playing, understood by both of them without needing to refer to its facticity, like the perfect house they used to invent for themselves to live in in an impossible preferred future. Clearly, though, despite the wildness of his reports, she had believed them all, Dave the inventor and the Amish,

289

the motel forecourts, the episode with the hoodlums and the nun, the monogrammed swimming-pool, all the unlikely hotels and motels and mansions and friends. She lifted her sunglasses to stare at her son.

'Hello,' Edgar said, with, he thought, an appropriate simplicity.

He smiled wisely, hoping to imply the peculiar workings of the world, the unlikely events that transpire, the way Providence spins things in unpredictable, perhaps delightful ways—this the joy of being alive, of being a human in the world. It was not a joy that Mon could immediately grasp.

'Excuse us, I just need to have a word with my son.'

'I'll carry your bags up to your room,' Warren said.

'That's so kind of you. Edward, come with me. We need to talk.'

'It's very nice to see you too,' Edgar said.

They sat by the landing window.

'Well?'

How to go about it?—the mood she was in made her unreceptive to narrative. He would try. 'I've made some discoveries.'

'Edward. Listen. I want to get to the bottom of all this.'

'Do you remember the cat they used to have here?'

Mon puffed herself up to be her most pompous. 'I haven't come all this way to talk about cats.'

Edgar's pride shrank beneath his mother's intransigence. He shook his head.

'Look. Where *is* your father? It's very noble of you to try to protect him with your blather but it's just one of his typical derelictions of duty. Do you even know where he is?'

'I think he might be—'

'Exactly. That's what I thought.'

'He did come. And we did go off together. You can ask. But we had to come back. Fay got ill. She was in the hospital. Warren was away. And Uncle Frank couldn't cope. Lucille drinks too much, I'd say, and have you ever seen her in winter? Does she wear the same kinds of things? Doesn't her cleavage get cold? Fay's a little better now. I brush her hair. She likes that.'

'Look,' Mon said. 'All I know is that it's awfully inconsiderate to foist yourself on your grandmother like this and we'll go into that another time, but you're here and if I'd known that, I'd have—'

'You'd've what?' Edgar coldly asked, furious at the unfairness of his mother's remarks, *foisting* himself on his grandmother, when in fact he'd been heroically defending her. The worst thing about unspoken heroism is that you can't tell anyone about it and if you try to they don't understand anyway. He felt like crying. He hadn't felt so alone since, he reflected, the last time he'd seen his mother, which meant that the two of them just did not go together well, in some chemical elemental way.

'Never mind what I'd've done. That's hardly the point. I'm just glad I'm here now. Eddie, this just isn't funny, you know, and I only hope that when Jeffrey gets here—'

He had instructed himself not to speak another word. Dumb nobility was the only decent option. But he couldn't help himself. *'Jeffrey!'*

The small consolation was that his mother was on the defensive now. She pretended she wasn't, with little exasperated waves of her hand and a worried crinkling of her brow, but he could see through that.

'Jeffrey!' he said. 'Jeffrey. *Jeffrey*. Jeffrey—'

'I'd really appreciate it if you'd stop saying that.'

'Jeffrey. Jeffrey Jeffrey Jeffrey.'

'Look. I know he brings out the worst in you but when

291

Jeffrey comes I'd like it if you were on best behaviour. I really would. For my sake. Oh Eddie. I've missed you I really have.'

He consented to be hugged by her and tried not to show the pleasure he found in her arms. Warren, wiping his hands, announced that all Mon's bags were in her room and winked at Edgar as he went down the stairs, elegantly taking them two at a time. Mon went into the room that Frank and Lucille had recently occupied. Edgar followed her in. As he sat on the bed, wondering if this was Lucille's side, and Mon unpacked her bags, he heard what she called her *news*. Bashful, blushing, she showed him the silver ring she wore. 'It's an engagement ring.'

He had been making his calls in order, he thought, to protect his father and instead had just given licence to his mother. It was unthinkable and vulgar and obscene and there was no way he was going to tell her anything of what he knew. She was going to marry Jeffrey and that was horrible and it was Edgar's fault.

'There'll be some changes of course, at home, but there's plenty of time to work those out. Where we're going to live and so forth.'

To Edgar that felt like the wrong question: it wasn't where to live, but *how*.

'And we'll have a big party. You can be a page boy or something like that.'

Edgar stared at her. He had lost his mother. He was an orphan.

'So be nice. Jeffrey likes you, he really does, all he wants is to be friends with you. And you know,' she added, as if this was going to be the clincher, 'if you knew half the things about him, you'd have a lot more sympathy. He had a very difficult childhood.'

Edgar blinked at the mad unfairness of this. As Mon broke

their embrace to return downstairs to resume her gift-giving, he couldn't stop himself calling after her, 'But I'm having *my* childhood right here and now! And IT'S VERY DIFFI-CULT INDEED!'

16

Jeffrey arrived wearing open-toed sandals, a tartan cap and a yellow Fred Perry shirt under a blue linen suit. He looked even worse in the hairy-toed flesh than he did in Edgar's memory, which was therefore proved to be generous and charitable.

'Geezah!' said Jeffrey, blinking in sunlight, adjusting his cap.

It was reassuring in a grisly sort of way to hear the first London-accented twinge of Jeffrey's affectation. Edgar hoped he wasn't becoming sentimental. 'Jeffrey,' said Edgar, as coldly as he might.

Edgar was reassured in the solidity of his feelings to Jeffrey when Mon offered his tour-guide services to show the new arrival around the house and he felt the instant rise of his own proprietorial irritation. He would have hated to think that in this new place and in their new supposed attachment, he and Jeffrey might find a more relaxed footing.

'And that's one of Bridie Stone's braidings. The colours have faded of course but they still have a certain sharpness.'

'How's it all going?' Jeffrey asked, trying to deflect Edgar from unrelentingly pointing out uninteresting detail after detail.

'I'm making out like a bandit,' Edgar said. 'And over there you'll see some examples of early Association plate. The Commonwealth line, I think you'll find.'

'And your father? How's he doing?'

'He's well. Copasetic. On a clear day if you look out you

can see all the way to Onyataka Depot. And that's the downstairs toilet. It's got the original plumbing, that's what Warren
says.'

'Does he indeed? And your grandmother? How *is* she?'

Here Jeffrey performed the manoeuvre with his voice that
most adults used when enquiring after Fay: it went solemn
and whispery, with intimations of hospital and graveyard.

'She's okay. She gets by. She'll outlive us all,' Edgar said,
quoting his father and hoping his less versatile voice could
connote the same obvious world-weariness, a readiness to
be surprised by the twists and turns of human events, and
a lightly displayed love.

It might not have worked, not all is connoted: Jeffrey
looked at him curiously and told him he'd grown a lot in
the time he'd been away.

'Yes, I do that. Maybe it's the sunshine,' Edgar said, and
was pleased to note that his voice at least was becoming reliable, and indisputably male.

That night they went in so-called celebration to the
Campanile, despite the protests of Edgar and the less frenzied ones of Warren, who claimed Fay wasn't up to a restaurant outing. But Jeffrey and Mon insisted (*It's our treat. It's the
least we can do, you having had Eddie here all this time*) and
Jerome and Guthrie were invited to join them and Edgar
helped Fay to creak herself into the station-wagon.

They arrived early and they were the only diners, and
Mon was the first person he'd heard to pronounce the name
of the restaurant in an Italian way. Did she do these things
just to embarrass him? Why couldn't she be content just like
everybody else to call it the Camper-Nile, like an Egyptian
minibus? It got worse. Mon entertained the table with early
anecdotes about Edgar that he could only escape by
pretending to go to the toilet but in fact throwing himself
on Electa's mercies.

'Is that your dad?' Electa said to him, arching an eyebrow towards Jeffrey, which was the single most malicious question she could have asked.

Edgar had not ordered a first course. He couldn't afford to. The rest ate pasta and garlic bread and salads with blue-cheese dressing, and Jeffrey treated them to a lecture on Edgar's ancestor, the poet Pagan Stone.

'He was a great poet,' Jerome said. 'His stuff is way too deep for me but that's what I understand.'

Jeffrey looked at him with some measure of scorn. Guthrie coughed, and Warren shifted his attention from Fay to her friend, and Edgar watched his grandmother grab it back by wincing with pain, real or affected. Jeffrey lectured, oblivious.

'No he was not a great poet. He was a very *mediocre* poet, that's one of the points about him. He was the *archetypal* mediocre poet of the twentieth century. Which is why he is such a rewarding case to study. He was capable, I grant you, of some startling lines. "The bread is kind." What's that about?'

'I like that. It's nice. I like the idea of kind bread,' said Fay.

'Yes. I do too,' said Edgar, pleased to have an opportunity to ally himself with Fay against Jeffrey.

Warren shook his head. 'I'm sorry. I might be a little slow on the uptake but what does that mean? How can bread be kind?'

'I know what he means by it,' Fay said.

'And it does you credit,' said Jeffrey. 'But all the same Warr's right, it's nonsense, reaching for some sort of high demotic diction that he didn't have the linguistic apparatus to express or even—and here of course we lurch danger-ously close to romanticism—the heart to feel. But Stone lived the life of the exemplary twentieth-century poet. He did all the right things, Montparnasse in the thirties, knew the right people, *Drunk On Life*, that memoir which I'm sure you're all familiar with . . . No? Huh. And he was queer of course, but no one knew about that at the time, or hardly anyone, least of all himself. Then, later, back here, he just kept at it, there wasn't much competition, he became a minor regional figure, churning out his pastoral lyrics. And why do people study him today?'

Innocent audience that they were, most at the table didn't realize that this was a rhetorical question. Warren shook his head. Fay looked at Jeffrey in a strange combination of benevolent and alarmed. Guthrie coughed. Jerome tried to answer: 'Because he was a great—'

Jeffrey brushed him away with a stuttery imperious wave. 'I'll tell you why. Because of his pornography. *The Governess's Rod*, it's on everyone's list of the major erotic texts. He wrote it—and the later one, *Squire Rodman*—anonymously, for money, a Parisian lark, Victorian pastiche. But in their own terms they're certainly more satisfactory aesthetic documents than his so-called serious work. And of course they revealed more of his self than his poetry did, if you're the kind of reader who looks to touch and shake hands with the author through his words, then the porn's the stuff for you— although of course he'd prefer you to be touching him with a cane or the bare palm of your hand, and him crouching, the sissy-boy punished for his desires, naked rump in the air, knees hurting on the nursery floor—'

'Jeffrey!' warned Mon.

'Of course the irony now is that the only reason he's studied is for his marginal activities. His life's work, kind bread and all, those interminable lyric cycles, his monumental *Syracuse Songs*, which, let me tell you, is even more turgid than it sounds, all that's been pushed to the margins, and the only reason any of us would have heard of him is through his pornography. Well I'm going to change that. Everyone I've spoken to in departments is in love with the idea. And you live in his house. It's wonderful. I'm going to rehabilitate him, reappropriate him. *My* work is to bring the centre back in from the margins.'

'Why?' Warren asked doggedly.

'In an act of recusal of course!' said Jeffrey triumphantly.

No one dared ask what recusal meant. They gratefully watched Electa advancing with the main courses.

'Pizza sir?' Electa said.

'Yes, that's for me,' Edgar said, trying to sound jaunty and matter-of-fact as the giant steel tray was placed hideously in front of him.

Eventually they talked of the house again. Jeffrey showed his enthusiasm for the Pagan House, with his swimmy blue eyes blinking behind his glasses and his pale tongue wriggling and his lips splashed red from tomato sauce. Edgar took no part in the conversation and ignored the questions pushed his way, as he sank beneath the pity and astonishment directed at him for his ordeal of pizza.

Dimly, through endless threads of cheese and glut of dough, Edgar heard Warren observe that recusal was an anagram of secular. Jeffrey, with some spite in his voice, said that was a clever thing to have noticed.

'Warren is very clever,' Fay said. 'He's producing an opera. *And* writing it.'

'It's small-potatoes stuff,' Warren said. 'Amateur production with all that that implies. It's not serious, like your work.'

'Oh it's very serious. It's really quite beautiful,' Fay said.

'I'd like to hear about it,' Jeffrey said reluctantly.

'It's in disarray,' Warren said.

'Nonsense,' Fay said. 'All the best productions have difficult rehearsals. That's well known.'

'I wish that's all it is. Marvin has been taken in for questioning by the police. He's been released but his confidence is fragile at the best of times. Seems a friend of his confessed to burning down the bingo hall. And that's not all. I don't have a Mary any more. Marilou has just stopped turning up. Although that might be more good than bad, I don't know.'

'I know we can find you another Mary,' Fay said, 'who I'm sure will be better than Marilou.'

'She could hardly be worse,' Warren said. 'But it goes on. I've just been told that the Mansion House is double-booked and I've got to find another venue.'

'But Warren that's terrible!' Fay said.

'Without even a word of warning.'

'Jerry will make sure you get your hall. Won't you?'

'Will I?' Jerome asked.

'Of course you will.'

Jeffrey took back the conversation. He had been listening to other people for longer than made him comfortable. Jeffrey was on a triumphant (he hoped) interview tour of East Coast campuses. Fast-track academic appointments, tenure guaranteed, a research budget. So far, the University of Ottawa was the only one to have offered him a job, but he expected better than that, and this house was the perfect stage for his academic performances—*perfect*, echoed Mon, catlike—he'd maintain an apartment on campus, he supposed, at Brown or Columbia or Cornell, but this would be his residence, where he would compose his intertextual metatextual polysexual groundbreaking gravity-defying performance of a book. Here he would retreat to write, to think, to create, sitting in the garden, in a pair of shorts, Birkenstocks, a hat of some kind, possibly straw, bare chest, tanned; and here he would throw the house open for wild transgressive parties. Jeffrey liked this house.

Edgar chose to walk back from the Campanile. He had wildly hoped for further discussion with Electa, but Electa was unavailable to him, viciously filling baskets with rolls. He tried to go to Dino's, but Dino's was closed. A home-made poster filled the door. It pictured a saintly, spotty teenager, half naked, clearly based on Ray Newhouse, who was strapped to an iron cross, while a dark house that might have been intended to be the bingo hall burned beneath his ennobled, tormented body.

The evening pulled around the house. It was the sort of evening where ghost stories should be told, or confessions made. Edgar sat in his room, staring into the night outside, shadow images on the glass, the consolation of stars.

He went through his gallery of erotic images. Lisa was there, with her halter-top and ping-pong bat. Marilou Weathers was always a reliable provocation. Electa he had always kept separate, and pure. But he did not always have control over the gallery: one awful night, he had been unable to obliterate the image of his aunt Lucille and cousin Michelle, speculatively naked, playing football. In desperation he had turned to *The History of the Onyataka Association* that Warren had given him. On a black-and-white page he had found a photograph of a woman who had given him hope. He found qualities of life and possibility in her unsmiling narrow face, her short hair with its sleek centre parting. He had saved an airplane with his capacity. Is it so unlikely that he can keep one woman alive?

He stepped silently along the corridor. Someone seemed to be drumming in the guest bedroom. The glimpse he caught of Jeffrey's feet twitching by the bed made Edgar shiver. Fay's door was ajar. There had been a change in the odour of his grandmother's room over the past week or so; something bitter-sickly and new rose above the airless scent of ancient unguents. It was like the smell of violet creams melting in the sun.

Tenderly, soothing himself, Edgar brushed his grand-mother's hair as moon- and starlight made warning patterns on the coverlet.

17

Jeffrey sauntered through the hall in his East Coast summer wear.

'Geezer,' he said.

Jeffrey's summer wear was comprised of blue linen shorts, his Birkenstock sandals, a vintage *I Like Ike* T-shirt, and the new snake tattoo on his back, which he took every opportunity to display with a bend or stretch.

'I've had enough!'

They heard Fay say this to Mon from the bedroom upstairs and there was only a murmur of Mon's voice in reply, and Edgar was sure he knew what Fay had had enough of—it must be Warren, his cruelty with hair, the control he exerted over all the operations of the Pagan House. Fay required Edgar to rescue her as she had never needed him before. Mon's plaintive murmurings went on, interrupted only by another harsh bird-cry of '*I've had enough!*' followed by the unmistakable sound of two women weeping.

'They're arguing again,' Edgar said.

'It's what women do. Hey. While I'm here. Maybe we could make an expedition.'

'What kind of expedition?'

'I don't know, what would you like? We could go to a sporting event, a baseball match maybe.'

'They're called games.'

'Excuse me?'

'They're called baseball games.'

'Well a baseball game then, or one of those NASCAR races,

303

or, something, I don't know, take a visit to Indian country or check out the sailing on one of those lakes.'

'Do you know how to sail?'

'I know how to do lots of things, geezer.'

Edgar studied the offer for what it was rather than what it pretended to be. Clearly it was an effort to move Edgar off-site, to manoeuvre him out of the battle. Was Jeffrey in league with Warren? Was *Mon* in league with Warren? Had the three of them reached some secret accord? Or maybe it was Jeffrey, just Jeffrey, whom Fay had had enough of, and how could she be blamed for that? No one, especially the frail and sick, could be expected to tolerate Jeffrey and all the Jeffrey-related crimes that Mon had committed in this house as elsewhere.

'I'm kind of busy right now,' Edgar said.

Jeffrey was used to rebuffs from Edgar and liked to pretend that they amused him.

'Well okay. It's your funeral. Hey babe. What's up?'

Mon clattered down the stairs, swept past the pair of them in the hall and went out, weeping, into the garden.

Edgar and Jeffrey looked at each other, waiting, hoping, to stand aside while the other went to comfort one or both of the women.

'I'll go see Fay,' Edgar said, authoritatively taking charge of the situation.

His grandmother lay in bed, painting one of her fieldscapes. Little splashes of brown and green dotted the counterpane around her. One frail arm lifted to his shoulder as he leaned to kiss her river-bed cheek.

'Hi, Fay,' Edgar said, as cheerily as he might. Her pale eyes blinked at him. They reminded him of the eyes of the horse that she had started to draw, to populate her empty blue fields.

'You're looking well,' he said.

'You're getting older,' Fay said, and he couldn't decide if this was the simplicity of wisdom or decay.

'Yes, I think I am,' Edgar said, not without a certain amount of pride.

In the next, awful, moment, something went from her face, from her eyes. She was looking at him without recognition, without consciousness, even. Then it, she, slowly returned and she smiled.

'Have you seen Warren?' she said.

'He said he was going to Guthrie's. He had something to give her for her cough.'

'Mary is never ill,' she said.

Edgar had intended to badmouth Jeffrey to her, to enlist Fay in a campaign against Mon's loathsome fiancé, but this seems inappropriate now. Instead he asks her if she would like him to brush her hair, and she gravely nods and says yes she would. Tears roll down the channels of her cheeks and she makes little kittenish sobs, but the combing seems to soothe her. She raises her head against the pillow to aid him, and the weeping softens and dies.

Proudly, his aching arm a testament to his capacities, Edgar told Warren in the kitchen that Fay would be coming downstairs shortly.

'I've been brushing her hair,' he said.

'Oh. Have you?' Warren said.

Warren was putting supper together when Fay made her way into the kitchen. Her colour was heightened. She walked slowly, statelily in, went, without stopping for rest, to the window and looked out over the garden. When she turned her head, her hair lifts and settles again into its perfect brushed shape.

'I think I'll be downstairs for supper tonight,' she said.

Warren didn't say anything. Perhaps he banged the plates slightly louder than necessary.

'If you don't mind,' she said.

'Why do you think I'd mind?' he said.

At supper Fay was lavish in her praise of the food. 'That smells very good. Is it shrimp?'

'Cooked Cajun-style,' Warren said.

'It's delicious!' Fay said.

'It's what I'll be cooking for the Blackberry Festival,' Warren said.

Fay smiles. She looks happier than Edgar has ever seen her.

'Your appetite seems to be coming back,' Mon said.

'Yes I think it is,' Fay said. 'But this is so good. It's like a curtain has been pulled away. I can even taste the celery seed. There is celery seed in here isn't there?'

'Yes,' Warren said. 'There is.'

After Fay, in gustatory triumph, had returned to her room, this latest version of the household gathered in the living room to outdo one another in sombreness.

'I'm worried about her, I really am. She's in decline,' Mon said.

Edgar protested. 'She said she could smell the food. *And* how good it tasted.'

'She was pretending, anyone could see that,' Jeffrey said.

'It breaks my heart,' Mon said.

'What about the celery seed? How could she know there was celery seed in it?'

'It was one of her favourites. Is,' Warren said, correcting himself.

Arms are busy at night in the Pagan House. Edgar combs, his mother's hand beats.

18

If printing is the most important art as the medium for uttering truth, navigation properly stands next in importance, as the means of transporting it. With these two arms, a competent and organized Press and a suitable Marine, truth is furnished for the conquest of the world.

Letter from Niagara, John Prindle Stone, July 1851

Is George Pagan ever stabbed by envy when watching John Prindle and Mary together? And if so, of whom was he more envious? The modern saint answering his special call from God, or the woman he had chosen as handmaid, help-meet, and answering heart—in lieu of Mrs Lovell, that is, who remains resolute in Newhaven, resisting? In truth George Pagan is jealous of them both, a jealousy that increases when they are separated, the Pagans at the satellite community in Brooklyn, John Prindle in retreat at Niagara, but George has little time for jealousy; he has been printer, editor, business manager, trap salesman, kitchen hand, and he is newspaper publisher now, allowed an office of his own, whose door he craftily pushes near-shut, and a congenial set of tasks to which he is careful not to display any special love.

His office door swings open.

'They are here!'

Mary adores jamborees. Pleasure animates her face in a way that no photograph can ever catch, proving the Israelites right about graven images. It is a mockery of God's work to represent appearance without essence.

'Who is here? Who is here, Mary?'

But she is already gone, quicksilver, and she knows and he knows perfectly well who it is who has arrived: the captain and crew of the vessel that will take them home from Brooklyn, where the winters are always snowy and the summers stultifying.

The travellers are seated together in the dining room. They have been afforded time for rest, reflection, prayer, sanctification, ablution, and now they sit, in the glamour of recent arrival and imminent departure: Franklin and Glass good-naturedly mock each other's seamanship; Abram Carter is a captain again, with a rough trim of beard, a blue sailor's cap (it was he who bought the sloop *Rebecca Ford* with his own funds and presented it to the community—and how does he have these funds, when private property no longer exists?); and gloomy Mordecai Short, Mary's latest mission and charge, stares sullenly at his food, his melancholy face typically lean and bitter.

Some who do not love Mary so much say that there is a deficiency in her spiritual self, but George Pagan, still the idolater, loves Mary (this his own error, his cleaving to untranscendental stuff) best of all. Perhaps she is not so shrewd at others' motives—her gift is for the instinctual grasp, not the analytical. But Mary Pagan is without sin and she still bears his name, and shows no desire to slough it off; as a result, his own standing has always been higher than it might otherwise be.

Onyataka is the sacred ground of the new covenant. It is the manufacturing headquarters and sincere heart. Brooklyn is for publishing and trade, Niagara is where the salesmen are trained and where John Prindle makes his retreat, often companioned in fellowship by a recent female convert to the Perfectionist cause. It is where he goes to catch his breath

and rest and mend his throat, and consider. They have a
fresh letter from him, outlining the content of the Home Talk
he will deliver when they are all soon reunited in time for
the Blackberry Festival at Onyataka, where the family has
outgrown its parlours and barns. Erasmus Hamilton is
already at work on his designs for a new, larger Mansion
House. Bible Communism flourishes; the new order of things
is only a corner or two away.

'Happiness is the natural element of man,' Mary reads,
smiling, stroking the words on the oilskin page. George sits
perfectly still, hands smothered between thighs and chair.
The *Rebecca Ford* carries a load of limestone for the new
Mansion House. It will also carry Mary and George. Mary's
purpose is known to George Pagan, perhaps not to the men
of the boat. She is to lift gloomy Mordecai Short, a frequent
dissenter, a victim of choleric moods and petulant doubts,
higher into the world of the heart. Images of some of the
acts that can be consequent upon descending fellowship
scorch George Pagan's unholy imagination. He winces, a
gesture that Abram Carter does not fail to catch.

'Brother George?'

'It is nothing.'

If this were John Prindle as his interlocutor George Pagan
would feel less easy. He has never been able to escape the
superstition or truth that John Prindle's clear blue eyes see
all the way into souls, most particularly his own.

'Indigestion only,' he says, and Abram Carter nods super-
ciliously, and all at the Willow Street table know what is
signified by the nod. Everyone knows that suffering of the
flesh has a purely spiritual cause. 'A cold in the stomach,'
says George Pagan.

Well, not everyone: 'Sometimes a cold is just a cold,'
mutters Mordecai Short, defiant and shy, face colouring,
sullenly looking down.

'Oh Mordecai,' says Mary, and this attention of hers makes him even shyer, even more bashfully stubborn, and he draws an invisible line with the toe of his boot on the floor as if to mark out a fortification.

George clears his throat. He reminds gloomy Mordecai Short of the fundamental truth: 'Christ is the physician of the body as well as the soul.'

Abram Carter, always ready to demonstrate his own spiritual acuity and wisdom (and how many times has he been criticized, justly, for pride and the Prophet-Spirit?) says, in his hateful confidence-man's voice, 'Redemption of the body is twin to redemption of the soul and both may be obtained through sweet communion with God. Brother Mordecai suffers because he is unable to grasp this simple truth.'

By smiling at George, Carter reminds the room that the announcement of indigestion is hardly less revealing than the display of spiritual canker. And he is about to go on, in his own Moses-Spirit, but Mary silences him, defending both Mordecai and George, and George, in his gratitude, detects inside himself nonetheless a resentment at being classed alongside Mordecai Short.

'The new man's birth pangs are the death throes of the old,' says Mary.

Mordecai Short seems both ungrateful and unconvinced. He can't, though, keep from looking at Mary, sly life-seeking glances that remind George most of all of the false attentions of Abram Carter in those days of trial at the old stone house. And yet, is not Abram Carter also an agent of redemption? Were it not for that episode would George have found his place at Onyataka, or in this house, 'Hope Springs', as their less respectful neighbours call the Brooklyn community, in this spiritual dispensation? That episode is long past, a finished shame that served as a stepping-stone to freedom. He will not though acknowledge Captain Carter's subtle look of complicity.

And later, in bed, George paints the lineaments of his once-wife on to the sincere willing body of the printworker Martha Ashton, while in the room next door he can hear the unmistakable bed-scrapings, gasps and pleasures of continent love.

In the morning, after breakfast, inner reflection, group prayers, the Brooklyn family gathers on the dock and Mary is urged to sing. In turn she coaxes George to fetch his violin. Together they perform 'Jeannette and Jeannot', George's unpractised fingers surprisingly agile, her voice more beautiful than ever.

She has never sung so well. In the intervals of her voice are the unapprehendable truths that George Pagan so effortfully strives towards. In her performance she still has a moment for everyone, the look of mock-surprise she sends him (*Oh, if I were Queen of France . . .*), eyes widened, shyly smiling, as if to say, *Who would have thought it, George?* and George sends back, he hopes, a blithely appreciative smile, when all he wants to do is to build a house to lock her inside. The printworkers from the basement, blue-capped apparitions, have silently joined the audience for the recital. When Mary finishes (. . . *let them who made the quarrels be the only men to fight!*) the applause is huge. George Pagan bows. He takes Mary's hand and shapes her into a curtsy and he tucks his violin into the crook of his arm and pounds his own hands together in applause so hard that surely they must soon feel the refreshment of pain, and how could he ever have hoped to claim this woman for his own?

They all walk down to the wharf. A breeze disturbs the skirts of Mary Pagan as Abram Carter offers her a hand to board the boat. George Pagan stands on the foredeck, crossing his arms and stroking his beard as John Prindle would do, emulating his master's manner if not his substance. Franklin tosses the bowline to Glass as Mordecai Short, his manners unimproved, his vitality wretched and sluggish, desultorily watches. Abram Carter at the helm raises his skipper's cap to wave to the watchers on the shore as the sloop, heavy in the water from the limestone cargo she carries, gathers up speed to the north.

'Happiness,' says George Pagan, holding his balance on the deck, squinting into the sun, his words carried on the wind, 'is the natural element of man.'

19

At the Blackberry Festival, trestle tables laid with Association plate and tableware almost covered the south lawn of the Mansion House. Most of Creek and Vail was here, receiving the Company's annual festival of hospitality and charity, eating blackberry pancakes and drinking late-summer lemonade. Electa was with her family at a table of merchants and restaurateurs. Edgar had been placed at the dignitaries' table between Janice and Guthrie. There was an empty place at the high-school sports-hero table because Husky Marvin, blushing and awkward, was sitting with the cast and crew of the opera. Even the Indian Fighters were here, at a table of unskilled Company employees, almost all of whom, Guthrie pointed out, were descended from the Association's factory hands of Creek. The Indian Fighters had been placed discreetly away from the tables of Onyataka Indians.

'Those are the good Onyatakas,' Guthrie says. 'None of the bad Onyatakas are here.'

'What's a bad Onyataka?' Edgar asks, unanswered. Shiverily, he imagines men in loincloths and scars, reeling from whiskey, stringing more poisoned arrows into their unerring bows.

The Company glee club sings Association hymns and the good Onyatakas answer with traditional chants and the Company-sponsored Fun Run circles past. Edgar sees Company Bob puffing along, red-T-shirted, red-faced, white sweatbands on his wrists, insect trills from his headphones. A looping contingent of Down's syndrome children wobbles

313

up through the trees from the golf course. Coach Spiro shepherds them on, barking a clumsily walking boy back into a trot.

All the town's Prindles and Stones and Pagans are at the dignitaries' table, apart from Jerome and Fay. They are of varying ages and occupations and shapes, but all, even Edgar, no less than the doctor or lawyer or university professor or newspaper editor, have the same square chin that Edgar has always disliked in himself, preferring slimness and neurasthenia. Fay is across the road in bed, pleading weakness. Jerome is absent, pursuing his researches. He has tracked down a path to a cache of letters and journals that Spanky Pete saved from the dowagers' flames. And Mon had been sitting at the opera table, which is already empty as Warren's show is soon to start.

There are posters outside the Mansion House, clucks of neighbours on the rise, the warm-up sounds of the opera band drifting out from the Big Hall. Except there is nothing airy or watery about this music, which moves around like mechanical sound blocks produced by a grim machine, one of Seth Newhouse's traps made into music, or maybe it is water after all, water and metal and wood, the sounds of crashing waves and a splintering boat. The posters show the same black-and-white photograph—Marilou Weathers, in pantalets and plain dress and slicked-down hair, smiles madly at the camera while Husky Marvin, with stuck-on beard and whiskers, his acne buried beneath mounds of foundation cream, stares baffled at his ghost-consort siren.

But Marilou is not in the opera; she's at a lower table with school husbands and wives. (*The Blackberry Festival Welcomes the Educators of Creek and Vail!* is the placard on the centre of their table.) Mon is to sing the part of Mary Pagan, despite Edgar's advice and protestations.

'But you won't know the words!'

'Warren's written them all out for me.'

'Or the movements.'

'Warren says that's a good thing. When in doubt I'll just keep still.'

'But,' said Edgar, 'but but but but.'

'You sound just like a speedboat. Don't worry, it'll be a laugh.'

A *laugh*! Edgar likes the sound of Mon's singing voice, it is very tuneful and pure. He always liked to hear her doing chores in the flat in their pre-Jeffrey days, singing the country-reggae songs that Rufus's band used to play, but that was a private, intimate pleasure that he would pretend not to be listening to and which she would pretend was something for herself alone.

'Would you like to come up to the dressing rooms?' Guthrie asks, and Edgar says that he would, even though there are few things he would like less.

In the frantic waves of activity before the performance, last-minute costume alterations, Guthrie coughing through the pins in her mouth as she stitches and sews, Husky Marvin stoically waiting his turn in frock coat and underpants and glued-on whiskers, his trousers folded over his arm, Mon's nerves show themselves in a rising flush in her cheeks as she recites the first few words of each of her speeches and lyrics in soft cradle-song, and Warren is everywhere, trying to summon up the Association past in this unruly, unmanageable present—at the piano; checking the tape-player; lightly clasping Mon's shoulder saying, 'Yes, yes, that's right'; adjusting Marvin's chin-beard; with a paintbrush in his hand touching up the backdrop on the stage, the first, wooden, Mansion House executed in a smeary shade of brown that even children would avoid.

The audience gathers, not quite filling the Big Hall. They sit on wooden benches, dark with the weight of generations of Association members and descendants. Photographs hang on the wood-panelled walls, men in frock coats and trim little chin-beards, women in dark blouses and pantalets and overskirts. Dew-drop electric lights that might once have been modern jerkily dim.

The curtain rises to show the cast in frozen tableau on the stage and it all instantly feels interminable. Warren conducts from the piano. Jeffrey has been put in charge of the scenery. It might have seemed like a good idea to have so many back-drops—a nineteenth-century Bowery scene for George and Mary's first meeting, a rugged farmscape with a glimpse of the river for the old stone house at Rondout, and the bare wooden walls of the Big Hall for all the Mansion House scenes; but it hadn't been properly considered how the scene changes were going to be made. The curtain drops and rises often to show Jeffrey, in desperate exertion, moving off one painted wooden board and, puffing, sweating, pushing on another. Seldom do the backdrops stand quite straight, which gives, Edgar thinks, trying to be charitable, a becoming weird-ness to the show. But Jeffrey's scene changes are, by far, the most entertaining thing about the whole enterprise, and no one laughs louder than Edgar when the curtain rises too abruptly, finding Jeffrey trying to move off the harbourside scene whose casters have become lodged between floor-boards on the stage, the spotlights gleaming on his bald head, his toe-hairs made golden.

The singers, in ensemble, don't notice that the harbour-side scene is stuck, askew on the stage. Already, and they haven't even reached the interval yet, they want this event over no less than the audience does. Headlong, at double-triple-time, despite Warren trying to wave them slower, they sing the first big number: Mon waves her arms just as Marilou Weathers would have done, Husky Marvin whirls an imag-inary microphone lead, the chorus jumps and hops as they race through the words towards an envied, seemingly unreachable peace and silence.

The Soldier's Wedding

*Give me your hand, my own Jeannette, the wars at length are
    over;*
*And welcome are the wedding bells that welcome back the
    rover.*
The Song of Peace is on our hills, and all is cheerful labor,
*Where late we heard the din of strife, the war-pipe and the
    tabor.*
*Good omens bless this happy day, the sun's bright rays are
    shedding*
Their loving light of Hope and Joy upon the soldier's wedding.
*Rich fields of waving corn are seen where hostile flags were
    streaming,*
*And where the sword was flashing, now the sickle bright is
    gleaming.*
*Lie still, ye brawling hounds of war. Let peace our hearts
    enlighten.*
*Rest sword, and rust within your sheath, but let the plow-
    share brighten.*
*Good omens bless this happy day! The sun's bright rays are
    shedding*
Their loving light of Hope and Joy upon the soldier's wedding!
*The loving light of Hope and Joy uh-pon! The—SOLDIER'S
    WEDDING!!!*

And Edgar ducks out. He slips past the Indian Fighters taking suck of reefer and beer, and walks across to the Pagan House, drinks two glasses of milk, eats three cookies, and carries a fourth upstairs. He knocks softly on his grandmother's door.

Fay is wearing her best clothes and lies perfectly straight on the bed.

'I've finished my picture,' she says.

Edgar praises the painting of a large horse in a small field. The horse pulls a black instrument behind it that Edgar guesses might be a plough. The horse is brown and the field is blue. The picture has been done on several sheets of crispy old paper Scotch-taped together.

'I want you to have it,' she says.

'That's very nice of you. Thank you. I'll brush your hair.'

'Oh, but I don't want you to miss out on all the fun!'

'That's okay,' Edgar says, in fake magnanimity.

'It's the Blackberry Festival today.'

'Yes. I know.'

20

On the *Rebecca Ford*, there is an air of excursion. The sloop skids swiftly up-river, the passengers interrupt their Bible readings and songs to wave to pleasure boats and cargo vessels and tugs. The wind has been kind to them and they should arrive home in good time for the Blackberry Festival. They have paused along the way for picnics and rambles through the woods, and picked several quarts of blackberries that sit pleasantly stowed beside the cargo of limestone on the deck. Mary, in keeping with her mission, has stayed close to Mordecai Short. But now, as they pass the old stone house at Rondout, she is alone below deck, laying out the supper. Short is at the helm, Franklin and Glass share a pipe on the aft-deck. Abram Carter is plotting their course on an old navy map, and George stands at the bow, watching Short, listening to water and wind.

Mordecai Short, without the awakening presence of Mary, is gloomy as before, mistrustful, his sense of unworthiness perhaps worsened by the touch-memory of her, the brush of her overskirt against his hand when she sat to read to him; perhaps he is thinking of that as he stands absent-mindedly at the helm; perhaps he is seeing the two of them in fellowship, the things that she might allow him to do, the transcendence he could find in her, because all men sense in Mary the glory of infinite possibility. Maybe this so-called Perfectionism is unutterably futile and all that she wants is a man, stripped of Biblical metaphor—except she has such a man: he has built stone walls with John Prindle

Stone, and John Prindle worked harder and happier than all of them.

Whatever he is thinking he is not paying attention to the boat, or to the river, when the sudden squall hits them, a breath of God, punishing Mordecai Short for all his failures and impieties, a reminder, as if he needed reminding, of his powerlessness, God's discarded toy, so when George staggers towards Short, yelling for him to steer, for the love of God, to the starboard, Short does nothing at all: he is shivering with fear and doubt, he cannot control this boat, how can he, when he has no mastery over himself?—and Carter rushes to take the helm but it is too late: the boat is deep to its side in the water, the weight of the limestone on deck inexorably pushing the sloop further beneath the rough waves, and the five men must swim for it, they have no choice, sliding, tossed into the turbulent river.

George catches hold of a snap of wood that is floating towards the shore, Providence here has lent him a helping hand, he is gasping with the cold wet fury of the waves and the struggle to hold on, when the awful realization hits him that none of the heads bobbing around him in the river is his wife's.

He lets the driftwood drift away, the weight of his boots and soaked clothes pulls him beneath the water, he exerts himself to swim beneath the tide towards the smashed sinking sloop, to the cabin porthole to see Mary being tossed and broken by the consuming waves that fill the cabin, her spirit returned to the harsh arms of her Creator; George bumps with hands and head against the porthole but he is nothing here in this abysmal wet emptiness, there is no power in his movements, and the weight of the water is no longer to be feared, it blankets him and he wants only to join her.

This shall be his destiny too, so why does Captain Carter presume to intervene?

George is dragged by Carter's merciless boat-hook to the shore, the water in his lungs is squeezed out of him and life stuffed back in raw into the water-vacated space—but he does not want this life, he has no appetite for it, he wants only to be back in the deadening water beside his bride; but arms more powerful than he, the arms of Captain Carter and gloomy Mordecai Short, hold him so hard, when all he wants is obliteration, the final impeccability.

He is overcome, he is made, against his will, to lie on the riverbank, to stare at the gorse bushes, at the sky, to the rooftop of the old stone house at Rondout that some accident of weather or history or God's mockery or unfathomable love has brought them to.

George could not make her happy. He could not keep her alive. He is not even to be permitted to die with her.

Who may doubt Him in His infinite wisdom and justice? All the haughtiness of man shall be brought low, and the Lord alone shall be exalted.

21

Having soothed his grandmother into sleep, Edgar walked through Creek and Vail, which was filling up again because most of the Blackberry Festival guests have not stayed for Warren's opera. At the Silver City Diner customers hunch at the counter drinking coffee. A Toyota and a Chevrolet are parked outside Tan Your Can! But Dino's is still shut. Edgar stands by the pinball machine on the sidewalk outside. The table glass is cracked, the plug lies shattered by a careless passing skateboard, there's Indian Fighter graffiti on the boarded windows of the pizza parlour. Edgar stands with hips braced against the machine, his fingers poised on the dead flipper buttons.

Time sickens and dies. The sun sets slowly in Creek and Vail. Edgar scuffs through stones by the side of the creek, while a funereal procession walks down the Mansion House rise, the men in frock coats and plain black trousers and sturdy boots, the women in pantalets and overskirts, their hair cut short. He sees Husky Marvin, but then he also thinks he sees John Prindle Stone, so maybe in historical costume everyone looks possible, and he decides not to wave.

The men are heavy and sweating in their black worsted suits and stove-pipe hats, the women walking more freely in skirts and pantalets. The grass is parched, the sun is low and heavy, shining on all ages. The body of the community martyr has been recovered by dredger. Brought home by river, Mary completed the journey she had failed to make in life. A sad

323

procession carries her, or what is left of her, unreasonably light, up to the cemetery. Her father, the Reverend Mr Johnson, paid a stonemason in Onyataka Depot for a monument, a single tower in this burial ground of small unadorned stones. The mourners prefer to look at the waiting earth rather than the pitiable summer sky.

Company Bob carries a bottle of champagne in each hand. Members of the cast, still costumed for the show, stand uncertainly on the lawn. The performance is over and it must have been awful but all the same Edgar had expected an unpinning, drunkenness, post-performance carousing, adults feeling justified by having endured stress to behave at their worst. Candle flames are attracting mosquitoes, so the slow conversations are punctuated by jerking heads and waving arms. Jeffrey is talking solemnly to a square-chinned member of the dignitaries' table who might be the doctor or the newspaper editor. He blinks, sort of forlornly, at Edgar. Mon and Warren are sitting together at a table, talking softly, foreheads almost touching. Edgar's heart lifts. The only explanation that he can find for all this mood is that the passion and intimacy of the production, no matter how inept, have pushed his mother and Warren together.

Happy Edgar, wondering whether he might treat himself to a glass of champagne, is accosted by Jeffrey. Jeffrey's hand presses against Edgar's back. Edgar jerks away.

'I'm sorry geezer.'

Mon looks down, up, down. She opens her arms in the way she used to do when she was picking him up from nursery school and he feels compelled to enter them. She pushes his hair around the wrong way but Edgar, stricken by solemnity, may not wriggle out.

'What's happened?'

'I expect you'll see your father soon. Frank and Lucille are already on their way.'

They are all acting as if someone has just died and, he realizes, someone has. He knows who it is.

His grandmother died just before the final-act curtain. Dr Newhouse is with her now, signing the death certificate.

'Can I look at her?'

Warren says yes. Mon overrules him.

'No. I don't think he should. He's too young.'

Mon and Warren and Guthrie return to the house. Edgar watches his mother walk down the Mansion House lawn, pools of light, fireflies and moonlight shining on her pantalets and skirt.

22

George vows that the next time he visits this place it shall be for his own funeral. He can count more loved ones in the cemetery than the Mansion House.

So this is the consummation of the first annual Blackberry Festival. And now a different kind of ceremony is taking place. The baskets of blackberries that Mary picked remain untouched by the side of her grave.

'We are marching into public notice under cover of a funeral,' Stone says at the graveside, in the exultance born of sleeplessness and grief. A late summer breeze catches at his hat. 'It is a curious stratagem of God's to bring about this death and excite sympathy for us. As the world looks on the funeral procession, they little think that they are looking at an army, that underneath are concealed guns and pistols.'

Amens are muttered, these grieving soldiers accord, for whom every transaction with the world is a battleground, and every forest is a garden.

'This is a woman's dispensation, and I am thinking it possible that Mrs Pagan's death is what the death of Christ was in the Jewish dispensation.'

He pauses, wipes his eyes, looks around, as if daring his listeners, his followers, to guess where this encomium is leading.

'Look at the history and character of Mrs Pagan. It is central and national beyond that of any other woman we have had among us. She was a child of the cities, educated in the metropolis, born spiritually in the focus of the Church. I can clearly see that the Church now being formed is coming out of material that is stored both in Hades and this world. God's mind is on the invisible as well as the visible material. Mrs Pagan, instead of being thrown out of her position as mother of the Church, is now put into it. We have a father of our Church, we are sure now of its mother.'

The breathless purified egoism of the man enchants George Pagan all over again. All truths, all history, cohere in the body and the will of John Prindle Stone. It is a magnificent responsibility even if he is wrong, and George, bowing his head, waits for his faith to be renewed.

Afterwards, the senior members of the enterprise closet themselves in the parlour for the final wake.

Stone says, looking into George, 'In the flesh, the tendency of Mrs Pagan's position has been to produce chafing between you and me and Mr Carter, but now that she has passed into the spiritual world, I can see how her position may be the occasion of a splendid condensation. The women seem to be the heroes and martyrs in this dispensation.'

George can bear it no more. An ecstasy of grief pulses through him, like the paroxysm of the sexual crisis. A world jerks out of him. He is emptying. 'My flesh is suffering and dying out!' is all he can say.

He feels flayed, waterless, martyred, beyond pity. Mr and Mrs Stone hold him each by an arm. Are they trying to regather him to himself? He has no self. All is lost. His body cracks in the heat. The tears, though, once started, seem unlikely ever to stop, tapping to a perpetual reservoir.

'I will behave as well as I can through the process,' he promises.

'I suffer with you,' Stone says, and it is clear that he does. His eyes are wild, sweat sickly on his brow, his voice whispers, rasps with his old bronchial complaint. 'I count this a token of God's love, He chastens those whom He loves.'

And they can accept this? These nodding acolytes, who sob and mourn, who loved her, can they celebrate this too, this abysmal event, as an indication of God's peculiar love? Can George? *Will* he? Is it possible that he too may come round to seeing Mary's drowning as a way-station on heaven's road? What alarms him most of all is that one day, in a month's time, two months', three, a year, he might stop feeling this acute passion of loss, this flagellant pain, and when he does, what will he have left? He had little to begin with. All good things came from Mary.

'I was thinking she had a fifteen-hundred-pound monument to go down with her,' Charlotte Miller says.

Stone says, 'She had the river for a grave, the sloop for a coffin, and her short dress for uniform; enough for any soldier.'

For the first time George Pagan is not convinced by John Prindle's military analogies. Maybe they have always been rhetoric to convince himself with, but his display of suffering might at least suffice to calm George's own.

'There is so much connection between us and her that it is not possible for us to be separated from her or lose sight of her.'

Stone's voice fails him; it was a miracle it endured this far, splintering in a caw of coughing into silence. He looks to Mrs Stone for intervention and she provides it: 'I have never felt to acknowledge her position as I have today. I never felt so much fellowship with her spirit.'

The children rush in, stop. Impressed by the grief, they modulate their movements, smirk nervously at one another as they fail to look appropriately solemn. They want to show the picture that little Bridie has drawn. A steamship on a river, two spindly smokestacks, a flag at the aft with stripes and as many stars as she can scrupulously place in the square at the top corner, another flag at the bow of a single lopsided blue star, the round faces of passengers at the windows, a single sailboat trailing in the wake, and the words 'Mary E. Pagan' neatly printed for perpetuity across the side above the paddle wheel.

But that time has gone, the communitarians fade, death is not overcome, George and Mary Pagan, John Prindle Stone, loyal Harriet, George E. Pagan, Henry Stone Pagan, Aunt Bridie, Wilber and 'Pete' and Tara, Mac Pagan, Fay Pagan, her white hair wild, her young face unlined, the overgrown roses planted by Mary Pagan.

23

In the parlour, Warren laid out wine and crackers and cream cheese and scallions. He brought in chairs for the family to sit on and it only became evident after the will had been read that he performed these acts in the role of host rather than servant.

'We've been fucking disinherited,' Frank said.

'I don't think that's right. There're the clear bequests to Paul and Michelle,' Jerome said.

'What's Paul going to do at a debating society? She's laughing at us. We'll contest it.'

Warren had unobtrusively removed the wine glasses and replaced them with coffee cups. Hardly anyone had been drinking—only Lucille's was drained, with scarlet, un-Association lipstick kissed to its rim—but now was probably the time to start. Edgar went into the kitchen and took a few nauseous slugs of wine from glasses standing by the sink. He returned to the parlour, giddy and vigilant.

'The Mansion House does better out of this than we do!'

Jerome preferred to square off the sides of his papers than be provoked to answer.

'And what's the deal with this Eddie clause?! That's a clear sign she'd gone la-la. It's not even worth paying any attention to this. Come on, Lucille. Kids. We're getting out of here. All this phoney language, "unto perpetuity" and "save the case of", it's self-evident, building in contact between a minor and a faggot. It's not just mad, it's fucking immoral. No court will allow it.'

Frank stood up and sat down and stood up again and turned in a circle, knocking over a side-table, which Paul caught reflexively with an outstretched foot, nudging it back into position.

'Come on. We're going.'

Michelle giggled. Paul stretched. Lucille looked lavishly the other way.

'I'm not sure I understand any of this,' Mon said, which was a good thing to say. It was what Fay would have said had she been in the room, had she been alive.

'It's very clear,' Jerome said. 'Fay and Warren had a legal arrangement. He cared for her and in return she bequeathed him the house.'

'It's robbery!' Frank said.

'I'd love to agree with you but I don't think so. Fay needed constant care, none of her family was able to do the job. She would have had to sell the house to pay for a place in a residential home. Nothing has been lost.'

Edgar examines his enemy. Fay has bequeathed Warren the house. They had an arrangement that came into effect once his amount of care-hours equalled the value of the house. Edgar does not think it a coincidence that the Arrangement came into effect the day she died, the day of the Blackberry Festival.

Edgar is allowed free access to the place throughout his lifetime. Access but not control. His snooker room shall never be built.

'Hey Eddie, how you feeling?' Warren says.

'I'm okay,' Edgar says.

Michelle, cow-eyed, chews her sleeve. Jeffrey stretches, showing the line of hair that disappears from navel to below waistband. His house has gone, all their houses have gone, except Warren's.

'I'm sorry. Excuse me,' Warren says, 'but if everyone's had enough I'll clear the things away?'

'So what are you going to do about this?' Frank says to Jerome. 'I'm going to contest it even if you're not.'

'Well be that as it may I've got some news to share. My researches have borne fruit and then some. I've discovered absolutely the most fascinating things! You won't believe this but I've unearthed a complete record of the breeding-for-holiness programme! And there's more! I think there's a stash of papers that 'Pete' Stone saved right here in this very house!'

'Really. Is that so?' Lucille says.

Edgar adjusts his walk to match that of Fay's grievers, slow steps, hands clasped behind his back, chin respectfully lowered, body leaning to the ground as he climbs the rise past the golf course, where portly men with baseball caps shout to each other on the breeze and blister hard low drives careening through the cherry trees over the heads of the mourners, perhaps by chance.

Mon leans on Edgar's shoulder. One trestle table has been left on the Mansion House lawn from the Blackberry Festival. Flies and wasps buzz around a forgotten jug of lemonade.

'I expect you'll have to call off the wedding,' Edgar said, carefully keeping the triumph out of his voice.

'I wouldn't hear of it! That's not what Fay would have wanted!'

How could his mother presume to know what Fay wanted? Fay wanted people to be kind to one another, for the people she loved to look after each other.

At the graveside, a square-chinned Reverend Mr Prindle made the funeral address and Edgar moved from the family mourners past the Company mourners to the pockets of Creek mourners.

'I'm sorry about your grandmother,' Electa said.

'Thank you,' Edgar said.

Edgar—hard Edgar, pretending to be the soft, unprotected boy he used to be—took hold of Electa's waist as if for consolation.

'If there's anything I can do . . . ?' she said.

He gulped bravely and pretended to consider. Death confers privileges. He may ask favours of her now, and she will perform them. 'Maybe you can come over this evening? It gets kind of creepy there at night.'

'I was going to be busy tonight. How about tomorrow?'

'I'm going back home tomorrow. To London.'

She inspected him and made her decision. 'Okay. I can bring food over. Pizza, maybe.'

'No no no. Really no. No. Please don't. We've got enough food. Come over later. Thank you.'

It is night-time in the Pagan House, and the house is emptying again, and his father hasn't come, and won't, and Electa and Edgar are lying close together, listening to the noises that the house makes, Warren's footsteps, the low undercurrents of murmur, the sound of Frank and Lucille's car as it leaves. On the back of Fay's final picture are hundreds of lines of squiggles, faint blue ink spidering and stuttering across the paper.

'It looks like code,' Edgar says.

'Let me see.'

Electa examines the document. She sits on the bed with her hands supporting her head. She pushes back the flap of hair that has fallen in front of her face.

'Yeah it is a code. It's called English. Look. There's names here, and birthdates I think and suchlike.'

They look at the backs of Fay's other pictures, which all have the same kind of writing. Edgar touches a page—one long piece of writing, perhaps impassioned, with no paragraph breaks—where the impressions of the author's pen have made a stronger mark through time than the thin blue ink.

'This must be the stuff that Jerome's been looking for. Do you think they're important?'

'What's important?' Electa says, as if she actually wants to know and hopes, despite herself, that Edgar might have the answer.

He makes a pile of them for Jerome, except the final painting that Fay gave him, which he looks at before sliding it away between the headboard and the wall. The blue field is occupied at last, by a heavy brown horse that strains sightlessly against the plough it pulls, and sex seems possible now and equally far away.

'What's going to happen to the house?' Electa asks. She had always been inscrutable to him. He is fearful now that the mask is going to slip and reveal her greed.

'Why? Do you want it too?' Edgar says.

'I hope I never own property as long as I live.'

'Why's that?' Edgar asks.

'It keeps everything fixed. I don't want my life to be fixed.'

'No. Me neither. And mine isn't going to be. Italy though? Wouldn't you like to have somewhere in Italy?'

'Why would I want to live in Italy?'

He switches off the bedside light and Edgar and Electa lie in the dark, listening to the sounds, and Edgar wonders if she has fallen asleep, her breathing is so regular. His eyes have adjusted to the shadows now, and he sees the rise of her shoulders, the curve of her brow; he could put a hand out to touch her now, trace the contours of her face. Edgar's hand moves to just above Electa; gently he disturbs the air over her shoulder; lovingly, tensely, he follows the shape of her body with the flat of his hand a fraction of an inch away.

'Quit that,' Electa says.

How Edgar wants only to stay here, like this, with Electa;

he would be content not to touch her, just to look is sufficient, in the shadows and moonglow, the soft sound of the breeze in the trees, the nightjars singing, in the brief world they're making.

24

Warren drove Mon and Jeffrey and Edgar to Syracuse airport in the station-wagon that belonged to him now. They were forced to slow down and halt on the approach to the thruway.

'What's going on here? I don't want to miss our plane!' Mon said.

Edgar did. Edgar wanted to defer their return as long as he could.

'I don't know, some kind of commotion,' Warren said. 'I guess we just have to wait it out.'

Warren switched off the ignition and opened his door and squinted to see what was holding up the line of cars waiting to get on to the thruway.

'I'll take a look,' Edgar said.

'No. Stay here. I don't want to have to come looking for you when the traffic moves,' Mon said, but Edgar was gone.

The Indians were building again on the scorched earth of the bingo hall. A banner made from a sheet was hung on sticks across a yellow dredger. *An Onyataka Nation Enterprise.*

The traffic was being held up by two of the Indian Fighters doing what they did best, lounging on the approach road to the site, drinking beer decanted into Tropicana cartons. Doug Ashton was blocking the path of a cement-mixer trying to get to the site and Sky was haranguing the driver. Edgar's arrival coincided with the county police sheriff's car. The sheriff scuffed out a line in the earth to show them where county jurisdiction stopped and Indian land began.

'We're going to hit them where it hurts, their wallet,' Sky said.

'Just keep it quiet boys, stay docile. We're not unsympathetic to your cause.'

The cement-mixer trundled through. The traffic started to move again. Warren, always a considerate driver, beeped his horn lightly to bring Edgar back to the car.

THREE

Edgar in Creek and Vail, 2005

1

In a market place in Calcutta a traveler met a talking dog. The world is full of wonder, of glimpses of the infinite, the secret words that Moses was told on Sinai, the occult knowledge that Jesus kept from his disciples.

Notes from Niagara, John Prindle Stone, 1879

On the last day of Complex Marriage, John Prindle Stone was at his cottage in Niagara. The day had been spent proofreading his latest, his last, collection of Home Talks, and drinking the soup and tea that Mrs Stone had prepared to ease his again troubled throat. The affair is over, the grand event, the new dispensation. He walked with ghosts, Mary Pagan, Erasmus Hamilton, even the huckster Abram Carter, whose oily super-abundance of posture and rhetoric had served only to scorn itself and further strengthen John Prindle's own authority. Of the founding fathers, and mothers, only the Fletchers and Mr and Mrs Stone and Seth Newhouse and poor silently aggrieved George Pagan were left.

The affair is over, worldly principalities have won, the Money-Spirit and the Property-Spirit and the Marriage-Spirit. Manifestations of Special Love have killed the sinless garden, which has been dying for some time, unwatered, unsunned in the waning of his own light, the diminution of his capacity, that had necessitated longer absences from the Association. Once, it was his body that pulled others into the fellowship

341

of the spirit. For too long now, the blessings of the spirit had cloaked, imperfectly, the dissolution of his flesh.

Harriet had waited, attended, throughout, and her vigilance had grown hateful to him. He knew he was in danger of becoming peevish and querulous, an old man yearning for past conquests. Here, on the Canadian border, an Arctic wind drifts in and John Prindle Stone sits in the garden and looks at what grows and wraps a blanket around himself. Meanwhile, at the Mansion House, in summer warmth, members of the Association in its last days make assignations.

Old passions inflame, former loves, lost opportunities and half-forgotten flirtations—eyes across the communal table, the brush of cotton to silk; a hand rests upon a sleeve while picking apples in the orchard or binding copies of the *Moralist* in the print room. It is the twenty-seventh day of August 1879. On the twenty-ninth, they shall enter a new realm of chastity and marriage, the new Pauline dispensation (I Corinthians 7). John Prindle Stone abolished marriage thirty years ago. Now it will return. He never did abolish death. But for these last days, before couples settle into matrimony, before Babylon inherits the garden that the saints planted, all is banquet. Even leathery old Seth Newhouse, whose ingenious animal traps laid the foundations of the Association's first prosperity, is the surprising object of several young women's desires.

Assignations are made and executed, in the garden, the summer-house, in private bedchambers. Discretion, future domestic arrangements are, for these last days, forgotten. They finish early in the factory, in the fields, from which girls return with flowers in their hair, in the workshops and studios. Sam Fletcher, sunny open face, tousled yellow hair, whose muscles have grown hard in his enthusiasm for labour, walks with Libby Stone. George E. Pagan sits in a corner of the library with Abigail Prindle. Henry Pagan Stone walks to the summer-house arm in arm with Mary Newhouse.

On this last marriage supper of the Lamb every dish is free to every guest.

But George Pagan is not occupied with matters amative. In the company of a somewhat dandified architect from Syracuse he walks across recently levelled land that once held an Onyataka shack and after that a horse barn. The architect has his own fancies and designs, which George fails quite to follow. He reiterates his own scheme for the plot, which is where, more than a generation before, the builders of the first Mansion House pitched their tents, where Mary Pagan used to come to lie in long grass, or hold summer lessons with the very children whose own children are now turning away from the light.

'I do not want these things, Mr Ward Jackson.'

George Pagan's aged voice appals him, its quavery croak of disability, the dry froggish sound of decay. There are to be no looking-glasses in the Pagan House; instead, portraits of Mary shall reflect to him and his descendants a preferable, if unlived, aspect.

Jackson Ward Jackson is of a type familiar from pre-Association days. George Pagan had met representatives of the tribe in New York and Boston. Lean, well-born and well-educated, with drawling vowels, the softening touches he employs do not soften him; the French-style cravat, his wistfully drooping moustache, the padded jacket do nothing to smooth out the sharp angles of nose or neck or shoulders. He has been designed with a set-square. Even his brow and jaw seem to obey the perpendicular rather than the curve.

The architect is young and prolific, and establishing an enviable reputation for being a man who gets things done, with some measure of style. But George Pagan does not require turrets or gargoyles or indeed any trappings of the neo-Gothic that Jackson Ward Jackson outlines with such languid enthusiasm on his sketch-pad. Perhaps the house that George Pagan first dreamed of in his blind-horse days is a dull steady house, but that is the house he has chosen to dream of.

Jackson Ward Jackson holds a bony fist to his mouth and coughs in boredom. George Pagan is interested to discover inside himself a mounting irritation that he has not felt since Abram Carter's funeral. George has been Old Uncle Pagan for the past ten years or so. The name was awarded, in amiable mockery, by younger bloods of the Association, and he has grown into it. His peevishness, which John Prindle unkindly termed the Old-Granny-Spirit, has fallen away. It has taken nearly a lifetime but he has learned humility and quietude.

'You need not take this commission, Mr Ward Jackson.'

'No, I need not,' the architect says.

The day is beautiful. Roses, red, white, yellow, are in full bloom. Frogs croak by the creek. A puppy barks, scattering to wing bluebirds and cardinals. Up the hill, lovers meet in the summer-house; there is nothing unseemly about these last days of Complex Marriage. In innocent hearts the greater innocence that George and Mary and John Prindle built is being passionately demolished.

The architect smiles, bloodlessly, humourlessly. George Pagan is reminded of the cold fanaticism of Methodists from former days and he is reminded too of an earlier architect, Erasmus Hamilton, who drew up the plans for the Mansion House from, of course, John Prindle Stone's designs. He and Hamilton had never got along either. George Pagan wonders if there is an inevitable distemper between the sort of man who makes houses and the sort of man he is. There is no one left to ask or confirm what sort of man he is. John Prindle Stone has taken refuge at Niagara, and Mrs Stone has followed him there, and the only person who has ever truly known him drowned nearly thirty years ago.

They had tried to reach her, in those first months, year, after her death; they had called to her, kept calling to her, to touch her answering heart, to push back the veil to the immaterial world. And they had failed. They had found only silence or, worse, deception in the spirit world. For the final attempt, the Association had employed a pair of mediums, sisters from Rochester: communications were produced that were so unlike Mary in sentiment or grammar that even John Prindle had realized that the enterprise should be abandoned. 'We are not yet holy enough,' he had sadly decreed. And now, for the first time, as he is finally negotiating her long-deferred monument, George Pagan doubts the need to build this house.

'I wish the house to be built quickly,' he says.

The architect shrugs. George Pagan is, in a sense, rich. Not as rich as Seth Newhouse, whose settlement at the dissolution of the Association took into the reckoning the benefits of his animal traps. But George has cash and he has shares in the silver- and tableware company that has grown, with God's guidance, large and profitable, and this architect is not so grand that he is above performing work for rich clients.

'Who are all these people?' the architect asks.

'They are celebrating the marriage supper of the Lamb.'

Slowly walking up the rise past the summer-house, where lovers entwine within the twisted wood, is an Onyataka Indian woman; the brown shawl that covers her upper body might once have been woven of red or orange. She is making for the kitchen door at the side of the Mansion House, walking uncomfortably with the pains of decrepitude or the rage of dependency, but she will be rewarded: it is likely that this day shall be a good one for receiving alms.

2

Older, dirtier, ten years later, Edgar was on his way back to Creek and Vail. He hadn't been Edgar for seven or eight years, but at JFK airport, in a mirrored interview room, as his fingers trembled stupidly to remove the steel chain from around his neck, his old name reasserts itself.

He had been Edward again, and Eddie, and Metal Eddie and Mental Eddie. His hair had been long and now it was shaved, and there were the nicks of scars across his inner arms and on the top of his head, which was maybe why these aggressively polite men, whose bellies swell out their blue uniforms, have stopped him; or maybe it was because of his piercings and face studs that they have already made him remove, or maybe it was because he was who he was and bad things happened around him; and now, as he struggled to take off the chain, this moment had become emblematic of the whole journey—it was all going to go wrong if the clasp broke, if the chain spilled into a useless line of rusted links.

'Take your time, Edward,' the nicest one said.

'Edgar,' Edgar said, and a wave of sentimentality for the boy he used to be nearly drowned him.

'What is the purpose of your visit, Edgar?'

'You don't carry many bags, do you, Edgar?'

'How long are you intending to stay in the United States, Edgar?'

'I'm not sure.'

'What aren't you sure about, Edgar?'

347

'What's the purpose of your visit, Edgar?'

'Are you carrying anything you might want to tell us about, Edgar?' the nicest one said sympathetically.

'No, I'm not,' Edgar apologized. 'I'm here, I don't know . . .' A stubborn reflex or instinct to honesty made Edgar stumble, searching for the words that would satisfy them and not compromise himself.

'Family duty,' was the best he could come up with and it seemed to pass; the clasp released, he could feel it scratched and bending between his awkward fingers, but not broken. He offered the chain for their inspection and the largest-bellied of them fastidiously held out a green plastic bucket to drop it into along with his facial metalwear and coins.

His father was right: Edgar smokes cigarettes and knows to light them against the wind. He rolls his own cigarettes, which the US Customs men affected never to have come across before, and the nastiest one was picking through his pouch of tobacco as if it were contraband.

'It would be more comfortable if you stood up,' the nicest one said, and Edgar knew what was meant by this, he'd been through this procedure before—they put on rubber gloves, he took off his clothes, intimate scrutiny, welcome to America.

3

It was a crowded bus that set off from the airport into the city, romantically entwined European couples with jangling rucksacks, briskly organized Nordic families, who talked in icy cracks of consonants, small Asian men carrying large boxes wrapped with duct tape, Latina girls whose legs bulged inside skintight jeans, a couple of solitary men who stared out of the windows and longed for beer, and, typically, Edgar was the only passenger on the bus with an unoccupied seat beside him. Even the bulkiest of the black ladies with the bulkiest assemblage of supermarket bags that she has refused to allow the driver to stow in the luggage hatch, who muttered and sang and gave off the sweaty odour of her accumulation of disappointed years, preferred to sit next to a dangerous-looking Puerto Rican whose wicked moustache implied he carried many knives. Once this would have pleased Edgar, this proof of his antisocial aura, aversion force-field, unspoken declaration of outlaw status, and now it made him want to cry. He couldn't look normal if he tried.

In New York City, Edgar took long subway rides to nowhere, walking through the carriages, carelessly letting the connecting doors swing behind him. He had the address of a DJ whom he knew from London and who lived here now and was expecting to put him up, but this was a mission Edgar needed to do alone. So, as he waited for his jetlag to subside, he wasted almost all of his trip-money on a Lower West Side hotel where he watched pornography trailers for three seconds at a time and the black-coated doormen always tried to stop him coming in, until he showed his room key, and then they became bitterly polite until the next time.

He bought no drugs, he stayed away from computers. He wasted more money on movies that he watched half of, as if he were a child, paying attention to the colours rather than the words, and on large breakfasts that were intended to keep him full until night-time but instead enlarged his stomach and made him ache with hunger for the rest of the day until he allowed himself his dinner slices of pizza and Hershey bar earlier and earlier each evening. He discovered a bar near to the hotel that was decorated with the sort of brightly incompetent computer-generated art that he would have despised at home but where they considered his appearance modern so didn't mind him sitting glumly through the night drinking one or two small glasses of beer.

Edgar had intended to stay in Manhattan for at least a week, arrive for his duel with Warren with his wits attuned, but he couldn't bear it in this city. He had expected wildness, Bohemians, excess, danger vixen women, men declaiming mad poetry, but everyone here just seemed unnecessarily rich. They belligerently jutted out their chins when they made their orders in coffee shops and bars. They walked slowly along the sidewalks as if staking claim to every moment of time as well as every inch of space. New Yorkers were, he decided, swollen with entitlement. Edgar liked this phrase and repeated it to himself like a mantra, and to the pleasant-faced girl with impressively hairy arms who was waiting by herself on a neighbouring bar-stool at the place where they tolerated him.

'That's interesting, what does it mean?' she said, in an accent he couldn't place.

'I don't know,' he said. 'Are you Italian?'

'Greek.'

Her name was Maria, which was, he decided, a good coincidence, perhaps providential. She was carrying a book of
poems by Rilke, which was exactly the sort of thing he had
expected to find in New York but hadn't yet. Edgar had
never read Rilke but that didn't stop him pursuing aggressively fanciful objections to his work that Maria good-
naturedly allowed him to make, and she went outside with
him when he smoked, and the evening ended with Edgar
walking back to Maria's apartment on the Lower East Side
with her and her friend, who was also studying film at NYU.
Matthias was a boy from Denmark who had the most friendly
and guileless manner that Edgar had ever encountered. It
made him feel sophisticated and bold. As they reached the
front door to Maria's apartment block, Edgar told Matthias
to keep walking and he nodded determinedly and did so.

'Where's Matthias?' Maria asked as they went into her
apartment, whose walls were decorated with film posters
and laminated restaurant menus.

'I don't know. He must have gone home,' Edgar said.

'That's strange.'

'Why's that?'

'Because he lives here.'

This was very funny to her and she was still laughing
when she poured them each a glass of grappa.

Maria lay on her bed and Edgar sat on the floor and went
through the playlists on her iPod. He wanted a song pure
and peaceful, something from an uncomplicated past.

Edgar interrupted Maria telling him about her father, who
was a general in the Greek army. 'Do you have any Kinks?'

She sat upright on the bed and stared at him. 'No one's
ever said that to me before.'

'I'm only asking.'

She looked very serious and excited. 'I've been waiting I
don't know how long for someone to ask me that.'

'"Waterloo Sunset", maybe.'

'I've never heard of that but I know people are much more advanced in London than here. Do you think being a lesbian is *passé*?'

'Are you a lesbian?'

'I don't think so. I think about spanking sometimes and I like to read about it. You could spank me? Or maybe I could spank you. Or is that too 101? I don't want to be boring to you. Doctors. Nothing surgical, you understand, but I have these pictures inside me, like trailers for a movie I've never seen. I don't know how to begin. Maybe you should tell me your kinks.'

Edgar had the presence of mind to smile as if suavely and say, 'No no, this should be about you.'

And she unburdened herself. They spent the night acting out some of the pictures inside her: Edgar was a cruel doctor, a severe teacher, he was an army officer and Maria the disobedient new recruit. And when she demanded that he supply a narrative for their games he told her about 'Pete' Pagan Stone.

Edgar had become something of an expert in the stories of the Pagan House. Before Edgar dropped out of sight of his family and the post office, he used to receive regular instalments of Jerome's transcriptions and commentaries that Warren bundled up inside white envelopes crested with a picture of the Mansion House. When Edgar was at university he spent more time reading about the Perfectionists and their joint-stock Onyataka Ltd aftermath than he did his set philosophy books.

'Who's Pagan Stone?'

'Born 1913, died 1977. Lived for a while in Paris before and after the war. Came home and inherited the house and a position in the company when his brother died. He was a Company man and wrote poetry. People knew him as Spanky Pete.'

'Oh?' she said, as if innocently. 'Why was he called that?'

'Pete was his nickname. You know, sort of regular-guy name suitable for business. Pagan was a bit out-there for corporate life.'

'You know what I'm asking.'

Maria sat cross-legged on the bed. She was naked apart from the blue fisherman's hat she had put on for a reason he could no longer remember. Her breasts were goose-bumped, and around her left nipple were the three strands of hair that she had at first been embarrassed to reveal.

'He had this thing with his housemaid. She was an Indian girl called Tara. There were these rumours that he used to beat her, for sexual reasons. But actually it was the other way around.'

Tara had returned home from her boarding-school, a model of Christian education and humility. A handful of families was left on the Onyataka Reservation, thirty-five inhabitants in all, which grew briefly to thirty-six, then shrank again to thirty-five when Tara took up her place at the Pagan House. She was polished in a small-gem kind of way, and was sincere, and efficient in all her tasks and movements. How did she respond when 'Pete' Pagan Stone made his suggestion? She thought it at first some kind of complicated joke. They were in the parlour, he sitting with a volume of French verse, she dusting down clean surfaces for want of anything else to do. He made his suggestion and she laughed nervously, one dainty hand in front of her mouth. Nothing in her experience or her passions allowed her any conception of what her master was asking her, needing her, to do.

After a difficult beginning, clouds of embarrassment on both sides, awkward negotiations, irritated instructions—*Yes, yes, like that, only* harder—they worked out between them a routine as efficient as any housekeeping rota, and she satisfied his requirements with a brisk diligence that he only wished contained more passion and less duty on her part ('And in the lonely starless night, waiting to be chastized/I attend my cold apt mistress').

'Pete' Pagan Stone entered 'the fire realm of pain' in the small parlour of the Pagan House, his trousers pulled down to his knees, his stomach pressed to the arm of a horsehair chair, looking first out of the window to the rise up to the Mansion House, and then to one of Aunt Bridie's braidings on the wall, on whose brightly coloured innocent pastoral scene his imagination painted darker worlds of pleasure.

He was his accustomed courteously reserved self at Company events, at all the picnics and barbecues and soft-ball games and fishing weekends at the Company lodge on Finger Lake, tall in an old English suit, his handsome, sorrowful face deeply lined down the cheeks, prematurely silver hair combed back, watchful green eyes slightly blood-shot, because Spanky Pete silenced any sense of ridicule he might feel with regular infusions of Scotch and soda.

'Pete' Pagan Stone trouserless on his haunches his thickening Indian servant behind him wields the paddle against his naked rump. She is bored, her arm is tiring, there is cleaning to be done, he is insatiable. There are any number of activities she would prefer to be undertaking than this. She finds the noises he makes loathsome, the yelps and infantile cries. But then, she considers, swinging her arm, raising welts, sometimes, for variety's sake, using her hand, red against red, her hand against the rosy blush of his sagging rear, rather his need to command her to do this than for their positions to be reversed, she on hands and knees, he administering the punishment, there are such men, and she might respect him more if he were one of them—but then again, she reflects, his must be the preferable place for why else is it the servant's and not the master's job to swing the cherry-wood paddle?

This is a separate realm from the rest of their days, never a mention made of it, hardly an allusion. He is not especially strict with her, or over-gentle. She has her tasks to do and he will chide her if she fails in any of them. (And, with her man on the reservation, she has tried this, both ways, to mutual indifference, bafflement and pain.) But here, in the dim parlour light, her master rocks forward driven by the power of her stroke, rocks back eager for the next.

Eventually Tara moved away to join her cousins in Wisconsin. She had grown stout and middle-aged, and 'Pete' wasn't sad to see her go. He would write poetry again (it has been argued that 'Letter to T—, Who Has Gone Away' is the first decent poem he ever wrote), he liked to live alone, and there was an establishment in Syracuse where strong-armed farmers' girls were delighted and relieved to cater for custom like his.

Edgar swung his arm and clapped Maria's right buttock.

'That hurts,' she said.

'Sorry.'

Contrite, he spanked her more softly but achieved a more pleasing percussion of skin.

'I don't mind. It's all right.'

Except this is wrong—if they are being 'Pete' and Tara, then it should be he who is on elbows and knees, swaying with each blow. But that would bring him closer to Jeffrey and he won't let that happen.

In the morning he realized he couldn't put it off any longer. He stepped over Matthias asleep on the floor by the TV and walked across town to the Port Authority building, where he bought a ticket to Syracuse and spent the last of his money on two slices of pizza as he waited for his bus. It could have been the same bus he came in on from the airport: it made the same dry noises, engine grinding against itself, the screech of worn brake-pads, and while it carried a whiter, more demure cargo, Edgar was again the only passenger to have a spare seat beside him.

4

He had not warned Warren of his arrival. The avenging angel would make his own way to the Pagan House. Edgar intended to surprise Warren, his bucket of poisons, the dry, quivery lips of an old lady submissively tasting death. But it was harder than he had expected to hitch-hike out of Syracuse. He stood beneath an overpass in the rain, hungry and sorry, as cars and buses skidded obliviously past. He could be thirteen years old again, he could will himself into a hundred and fifty years ago and the overpass would be gone, but it would still be raining and he would still be hungry and damp and nowhere. Finally though he did get a ride towards Onyataka, high in the cab of a dairy truck.

'People not likely to pick you up the way you look,' the truck driver said.

'So why did you?'

'Bible preaches hospitality to strangers. This'll be my good deed for the day, make up for some of the other stuff.'

'What other stuff?'

But conversation was over. Edgar watched the half-forgotten journey in silence until they pulled off the thruway and Edgar pointed to the huge grey concrete complex that was sucking off most of the traffic.

'The casino? Belongs to the Onyatakas. Biggest thing in the four counties.'

'There used to be a bingo hall there I think.'

The driver shrugged and the truck wobbled at speed. 'Used to be, should be, could be, makes no matter to my

357

way of thinking, nothing changes what is and what is is
usually shit. I'll drop you off here, young feller. Careful how
you go.'

Edgar tried to get a ride by standing with his thumb out by
the fountain at the casino entrance but no cars seemed to be
leaving: all the traffic was one-way—busloads of old people,
contractors' vans crammed with men in blue overalls, coming
to gamble in the casino or build more of it, beaten-up sedans
that reminded him of his father. The casino was a collection
of grey concrete blocks, surrounded by parked cars baking
in the sun and grassland and construction areas. He watched
a casino cart slaloming wildly around pyramids of silt along
a half-laid Tarmac road and then he recognized the driver
and called out his name.

The cart veered around and stopped by the fountain. Sky's
hair was still long but thinner, the scalp visible through the
yellow hard-rocker strands. He wore the short-sleeved purple
and yellow shirt of casino employees, and held a crackling
walkie-talkie to his ear.

'Hey, Sky.'

Sky stared at him with the old dreamy incomprehension
that carried reserves of implied threat.

'Edgar,' Edgar said.

'Edgar? That weird British kid? Is that you?'

Edgar admitted that it was. The way that Sky was looking
at Edgar was probably the same way Edgar was looking at
Sky, as if neither could quite believe the changes that time,
or decay, had exerted in the other.

'Way to go, Edgar.'

'You work here.'

'So long as they ain't fired me yet.'

'Do you still play music?'

'Not really. Now and again. For my own pleasure.'

'What's happened to the others?'

'Doug and Rocky they both work in the oil industry.'

Edgar was impressed. He said so. He asked after Ray Newhouse. If biology was destiny Ray would have been using his jail time to construct ingenious mechanical models or else acquiring professional qualifications. Most of the doctors and lawyers in this town had been called Stone or Prindle or Newhouse.

'Sells pot and elephant tranquillizers to college kids from Syracuse. The pot he buys from Onyatakas on the reservation. He gets the chemicals from an English guy, actually, fellow named Pete, maybe you know him?'

'I don't think I do.'

'You live in London? I think he's from London also.'

'London's a pretty big place.'

'Guess so. Been meaning to make it out there one of these days.'

'And Marvin?'

'College guy. He's like doing a doctorate in the history of science or the science of history or something. Husky Marvin. He could sing, couldn't he? Joined up with the video boys, they had a couple of hits, can you believe it, on the college circuit? Then they got rid of him, it's all machines, and *guest* vocalists, chicks with that kinda breathy voice that the kids like. Not sure where he lives now. Maybe Syracuse. Ithaca? I don't really see him around. You should see Ray, though. He's even more of a case than he used to be. He's got all these medical problems. Last time I saw him was at Onyataka Depot, dripping piss from a plastic bag across the platform, his urine sample was leaking.'

'Maybe that's his punishment.'

'Punishment for what?'

'You know, karma or whatever the Indians would call it. For burning down the bingo hall.'

'You believed that? Probably the only one who did. Ray never burned down the bingo hall. It was another bunch of Onyatakas, from Wisconsin or Canada or somewhere, trying to muscle in on the action. Everyone knew that but they let Ray take the credit because it made him feel good. Hey. I've got a number in my pocket. You want to drive out on the golf course and get high?'

The golf course was a notional place, clods of earth, mounds of turf. They sat on some hard rubble, which Sky referred to as the seventeenth green, and smoked a thin wet joint. Sky's walkie-talkie crackled away.

'I get a pretty easy ride here. They have this quota policy, got to hire sufficient locals, in the interests of public relations and keeping the Governor in office. I'm lucky to have this job, there's a lot of unemployment around. But I tell you, Indians are fucking made here. This place prints money. But though this has been nice, I got to pretend to do some work. You should take a look around. Something for everybody.'

Sky dropped him back at the fountain and Edgar went into the casino. The crowds of gamblers made the place look as if it had been triple-booked by a fat people's convention, a senior citizens' stool-sitting holiday, and a get-together of all the remaining cigarette smokers in America. Walking through the nightmare lights and ching-ching-ching of the casino floor, Edgar had no money in his pocket, and felt therefore, for maybe the first time in his life, free. He wondered if he would see his father here. He thought he recognized Coach Spiro, sitting coiled and vigilant in his shades and shorts and letter jersey, in a corner of the poker room. He did find Jerome, in a wheelchair, with oxygen tank and drip tubes attached, at a slot machine feeding in coins from a bucket.

'Hey Jerome.'

No response, mechanical movements, coin into slot, handle

pulled, coin into slot, handle pulled, as if the wheelchair was making love to the machine, and the wreckage of the man who mediated between them was wasting away with the passion of it. Edgar repeated Jerome's name in a variety of intonations and finally brought himself to touch him on the shoulder. Jerome turned slowly around and when he focused on him he was the first person Edgar had met on this American trip who seemed indifferent to Edgar's appearance, and unsurprised.

'Hello, Eddie. How you making out?'

'Like a bandit, Jerome.'

'Haven't seen you for a while. You been sick?'

'No. I was in London.'

'Well that explains it.'

Jerome turned his attention back to the machine. He inspected each wheel in turn, then put in another coin.

'Do you ever see my father?'

'What's that?' Jerome's fingers twitched. His eyes flicked nervously to the slot machine. 'Mike? No. I haven't seen Mike.'

'Do you still do your researches? Into the Association?'

Edgar had to repeat his question several times before he managed to get Jerome to, irritably, shake his head.

'So what else do you do with yourself? Apart from this, I mean.'

'Sometimes I play blackjack. They're very thoughtful here. They have a special table which is extra-wide for wheel-chairs. But mostly I play the slots. I like the slots best. Last week I hit a jackpot.'

'That's great Jerome. Congratulations.'

'That's right. That's right.'

In a philosophical frame of mind, Edgar walked to Creek and Vail along a sun-dazzled road that had no sidewalk or

verge to protect him from the complacent brutality of afternoon cars. Route 5 took him through Onyataka and on to
Creek and there was the factory building, except the factory
building was boarded up and closed down now, and the
Silver City Diner, and Georgie's Dance Studio (containing
also Luscious Nails and Tan Your Can!) and the Campanile,
and a second gas station, set at a diagonal from the original
one, and an Indian gift store and cultural centre, where Dino's
pizza parlour used to be.

Most of the houses in Creek had American flags outside.
There's the book store that never opens, the video store,
there's the softball pitch and the Stone Park bleachers where
he held hands with Husky Marvin, and the memory of that
had the power to make Edgar blush, which inspired him,
maybe things weren't so irretrievable and faraway after all.
Over the bridge he goes, past the Company building, and
there's the Mansion House and the Pagan House opposite
it, better cared for than its neighbours, and sterner with it.

Warren's house had no doorbell any more, and no television aerial to spoil the antique lines of chimney and gable.
The old station-wagon parked on the grassed-over drive was
the only modernity that would have baffled George Pagan.
The screen door had been removed.

Edgar knocked. This should have been his house: he was
in direct line, from George Pagan to George E. Pagan to Wilber
to Spanky to Mac to Fay to Edgar. He had been bred to it.

He could invent himself anew, in holiness, a mendicant,
honouring houses with his presence. Edgar blessed the lawn.
He blessed Vail and Creek. He blessed the bluebird in the
hedge. He blessed the girl swooshing past on a skateboard
even as she changed direction and crossed to the opposite
sidewalk.

Warren, in his old uniform of pressed jeans and blue T-shirt,
opened the door. There were lines of silver in his black hair.

'Hello?' Warren said.

'Hello,' Edgar said.

'Can I help you?'

He hadn't envisaged this. He hadn't thought he would need to announce himself. Edgar clasped his hands together in holiness. 'I'm looking for somewhere to stay.'

'Oh. Okay. You can find rooms to rent in the Mansion House across the way. But they're quite pricey. Otherwise there's a hostel in Onyataka. That's probably the nearest place.'

'I've just come from there.'

Warren screwed up his eyes and tilted his head to the side and looked at Edgar and slowly he saw him. 'Eddie? Is that you?'

'I didn't know if you'd still be here,' Edgar said.

'Most of the time I'm not,' Warren said.

Edgar looked at Warren with what he hoped was the sharp scrutiny of the implacable detective. Warren did not flinch.

'It's great to see you,' Warren said.

'I thought I'd stay a few days, if that's okay.'

'For as long as you like, Eddie. It's what Fay wanted.'

'Edgar,' Edgar says.

'Say what?'

'It's what I call myself these days.'

'Edgar.'

'Edgar.'

There were more mementoes of Mary Pagan than of Fay in the house. In the kitchen, having turned down the invitation to bathe, Edgar sat below a poster advertising Warren's opera, Husky Marvin as the most shyly diffident Stone with stuck-on beard, Marilou Weathers in her wild-eyed incarnation of Mary Pagan. On the sideboard stood a row of Onyataka Ltd dinner plates. One of them, pale bone, with a faded yellow ring just inside the rim and a child's sketch of a steamship at its centre, was from the very first production line.

Warren sat across from him; both were holding mugs of tea, blowing on the steam.

'Are you hungry? I can fix you a sandwich, or something more substantial if you like.'

Edgar was very hungry. He hadn't eaten anything since New York except for half a peppermint patty that a child had dropped on the concourse at Syracuse bus station and which his mother had forbade him to pick up. He accepted a sandwich and refused anything more substantial, hoping that this compromise did not put him too much in Warren's debt.

'It's really terrific to see you,' Warren said, perhaps more doubtfully than he intended. 'I like your, uh, look. So what are you doing with yourself these days? You were at college last I heard.'

'That didn't exactly work out.'

'Uh-huh. Okay. Your mother? How's Monica doing?'

Warren was ruthless. His questions would persist, leaving no space for Edgar to aim his own investigations at, and they all seemed designed to remind Edgar of his boyish, and therefore powerless, status.

'She's good,' Edgar said, falling easily into the local language. 'She went back to university, did another degree.'

'Your mum's terrific. She's got a lot of life.'

Edgar pondered this remark, inspecting it for meanings both hidden and apparent.

'And how's Jeffrey?'

'He died,' Edgar said. 'On his stag night, he had some kind of cocaine binge, and his brain and heart sort of exploded.'

This was not true. Jeffrey was Professor of Popular Culture

at Huddersfield University. His brain and heart were intact, or functioning at least. But Edgar invented a different Jeffrey, who had lingered on in a wheelchair at a nursing-home, looking at the world through hate-filled damaged eyes until a bout of pneumonia provided a merciful release. Even in fantasy he was a disappointment. He should have been a saintly Jeffrey, performing holy works with the reckless innocence of a simpleton, lying down with lepers and lambs, opinion-free. Or a monkey man, gibbering and drooling, devouring peanuts and bananas while muttering imprecations in a strange original language. Edgar examined himself for feelings of sympathy for Jeffrey, alive or dead, and was a little annoyed to find some.

'Oh that's awful. I'm so sorry. I know how fond you were of him.'

'Sometimes my mother thinks we should have, you know, let him go earlier.'

Warren didn't respond in the way that he was meant to. Gravely he nodded and asked Edgar if he had seen his father yet.

'I don't even know where he lives to be honest.'

'He's in Rome last I heard.'

'But he hates Europe. Don't say he's discovered religion.'

'Not Rome, Italy, Rome. It's a town near here, other side of the casino. I have his address around here somewhere. You can use the station-wagon to visit him if you like. I keep the keys in the ignition.'

'Where else do you spend your time? When you're not here?'

'And how about Frank and Lucille? You ever hear from them?'

It was easier to answer Warren's questions than to persist with his own. 'No, but I saw Michelle and Paul last summer.'

They had been backpacking around Europe and stopped

off in London, expecting Edgar's cousinly hospitality. But Edgar had been Mental Eddie then and he lived in a derelict town hall in Limehouse, sharing a room that had once been some kind of clerk's office and now, like the rest of the building, had sleeping-bags on the floor and piles of books and clothes and sound systems, some of which worked, and many computer terminals and screens. 'We just like to take heavy drugs and mess about with programming,' Edgar had explained, in a lucid moment. 'If you fit in you can stay.' He had seen Michelle around the place now and again, smudgy and sleepy, usually curled inside someone's sleeping-bag, but Paul had gone off on his own and suffered some inelegant mishap. Mon had had furious communication from Lucille and berated Mental Eddie with it, who hadn't listened or cared. He had just achieved his greatest triumph, of hacking into the House of Commons computer so that 'is a cunt' was added every time someone in the system typed in the words 'The Prime Minister'. But he was Edgar now, again. He was drug- and computer-free, and in their absence he had adopted his old Edgar habit of making rhythms on any available surface.

'I expect you'll be wanting to see your old friends here.'

'The house looks good!' Edgar yelled, pounding his mug of tea hard down on the table-top signifying that it was his turn to take the interrogator's chair. 'You've done a lot with it! Haven't you?!'

'Why don't I take you on the tour?'

The house looked very good. A kind of formal dining room was where the snooker room was meant to be. The record-player and albums were gone from the Music Room, replaced by a harmonium and sheet music on stands, and a line of Association clothes hanging on a rail, like in a vintage clothing shop, all the hangers neatly facing the same way. There was no swimming-pool in the back garden, but the pond had been widened and now had a fountain in the middle where frogs played. The place looked as George Pagan might have wanted it, except for the absence of children. There had been few children in this house and Edgar had never believed in his father as one of them.

'You'd probably like to stay in the sun porch. You must be tired after your journey.'

Teens walked giggling past the house, the younger sisters of Paul's admirers, wearing sports tops pulled down by fists, blonde hair reddish-gold in the streetlights. He could just about make out the sign on the Mansion House lawn advertising the Blackberry Festival.

'Nothing changes,' Edgar said.

'Things change,' Warren said. 'Why don't you freshen up and then we'll have a chat in the parlour?'

The parlour accorded with Mon's old vision of what should be more than Edgar's. Fay's wallpaper had been stripped away from the wood panels, which Warren had varnished and hung with Grandma Bridie's silk braidings (*See the gay people/Flaunting like flags/Belle in the steeple/Sky all in rags*). The room was dimly lit as if electricity was a new and possibly dangerous resource that should not be squandered or challenged. The furniture was all comfortably venerable. There was nothing here to surprise George Pagan, except for the colour photographs of women and houses on the mantelpiece. Edgar sat in the horsehair chair that had been Spanky Pete's favourite whipping post.

Warren looked at his hands. He looked at them as a quietly proud technician would look at his tools. 'I'm glad you're here, Edgar.'

'Why's that?'

'Maybe I can persuade you to stay longer. The house needs someone in it and I'm pretty busy elsewhere these days. I've tried lodgers but that hasn't really worked out.'

This was not the conversation they were meant to be having. Warren should be reeling under the blasts of Edgar's questioning. Warren should have his hands up to his face in impotent protection as Edgar relentlessly forced him to admit his guilt.

'Syracuse has some good programmes, I understand. You could enrol there if you fancied starting college again. Get some bartending work or something, live here, you've got the station-wagon. See how it grabs you. You know, start again.'

To start again was just what Edgar wanted. He was infuriated that Warren saw this in him. 'What keeps you busy elsewhere?'

Warren frowned, disappointed. He had thought Edgar a creature of greater tact. 'It's what Fay would have wanted. She wanted you here. She liked you. And you're the next in line, so to speak. You know, she was a great believer in the afterlife. She was sure that she would be up there, down, wherever, reunited with everything she loved, looking down on us.'

'It's a nice thought,' Edgar admitted.

'Do you know what you want?'

Edgar wanted to confirm the truth of his grandmother's death, get Warren to admit his guilt, but after that, what? He hadn't thought past that one. He had expected courtesy from him, justifications and alibis to push through, and then finally, under the focus and weight of Edgar's relentless questioning, he'd break down, admit it all, probably weep, *Yes, yes, I intended to kill her from the beginning, I knew I was getting the house when the arrangement was consummated, the formula come into play, X would occur when Y was equal to or greater than Z*, the market value of the house equalled or exceeded by the value of his care hours.

'I'm surprised,' Edgar said.

The formula came into effect and I took the first chance I could get and I killed her. What are you going to do?

And what would Edgar do? Tie him up and take him to the police? Forgive him? Was that why Warren was so glad Edgar was here? Had he been waiting all these years for Edgar, or someone like him, to come? Did he require confession, absolution? He had been born a Catholic, after all.

'Sleep on it. You don't have to decide anything now. I don't want to push you.'

He wasn't sure. To take possession of the house would be one possibility. Banish Warren from it, and where would he go? Skulk back to Ireland, Mulhuddart, but there were those photographs, some of which Edgar had seen long ago, a succession of old women, and they were not hidden now, they were in full display, in antique silver frames, foxed glass over incongruous colour that would have dazzled George Pagan, in gallery along the mantelpiece.

'You know where everything is. There's towels and so forth in the bathroom. We'll talk more tomorrow. I'm very glad you're here, Eddie. Edgar.'

5

The Perfectionists saw the workings of Providence every-where. The arrival of Erasmus Hamilton, just when they were looking for an architect to build the Mansion House, that was a miracle; the conquest of the Tobacco Principality, the Operations against Shame and Bashfulness, these were miracles; the success of Seth Newhouse's animal traps was a mark of special Providence; so, too, a grander, sadder miracle, containing within it a perpetual loss, was the Association's manufacture of tableware—but that loss too was a sign of God's special favour.

Edgar went into the bathroom, where he reminisced about old-lady unguents and potions. Warren has fixed the leaking tap in the time intervening. Edgar turned it slightly, for a nostalgic drip, then performed the act that he had been accustomed to perform here.

He had expected the process to bring him back into the boy he had been and, therefore, to the possibilities of the men he might have become. Instead, it was like a school physics lesson, a demonstration of the transformation of energy: far better than anything with model trolleys on rickety ramps that balding men used to explain kinetic energy with harried frustration. Just put masturbating Edgar in front of the class. *And you see here, look at the work of his arm, the dulled expression in the eyes, overall the energy put in is less than the pleasure gained. Now remember, boys and girls, energy can never be lost, only transformed. And if the masturbator puts more into the act than he gets out, where does that missing energy go?*

Anyone? Come on, you should all know this. Friction, yes. Good. Wind resistance? I don't know about that. Negligible, I'd say. Any more? Build-up of lactic acid in the arm muscle, yes, I suppose so. The ejaculate. Of course. But I'm still thinking of something else. Anyone? Yes. Edgar? I'm sorry, you're going to have to speak up, I can't hear you.

Afterwards, Edgar poured himself a glass of orange juice in the kitchen, then one of YooHoo. He smeared jam on bread and ate breakfast and read the note that Warren had left on the kitchen table and wondered if this was a sign of special Providence. *Errands to be run. Sorry not to be around. Back either later or tomorrow for the Blackberry Festival. Help yourself to food etc. So glad you're here. W.*

Edgar inspected the photographs in the parlour. A capable-looking woman in gardening gloves is in the first; next to her is the retired actress with the lavender shawl; there's a trim woman in a hippieish peasant smock and jeans; a sad-faced woman with a sheepdog beside her; a woman stands by a bicycle that she looks too small and fragile to ride; and Fay is in the centre one, standing in front of the porch of the Pagan House. There's a new one, not yet framed, at the end. This woman is dressed for summer on a chilly day. Her face is round and strong, with handsome features and a high fore-head. Her head is cocked slightly to the side and she gazes, quizzical or shy, through owl-rimmed spectacles, but it's hard to tell which because she's slightly out of focus. The house, though, is perfectly shot, white and wooden with green-shuttered windows, roses twining by the door. Had Warren never learned to focus his camera? But Warren silently registered most things. Edgar looked at the other photographs and they were all the same, and he finally realized it was the houses, not their owners, that were the true subjects of the portraits.

Slipping the new, unframed house portrait into his pocket,

Edgar took a walk through Vail and Creek, stopping for a while to sit in the bleachers at Stone Park, where an impatient father in shorts and red T-shirt was tossing balls for his daughter to swing at with her oversized bat. Two policemen approached to ask if they could help him.

'I'm Edgar Pagan, staying in the Pagan House.'

'Is that right? I'm Joe Short asking you to move along.'

His name and place of residence used to have more sway in the community than this.

At the Onyataka Indian gift store and cultural centre, where Dino's used to be, instead of the clatter of the Indian Fighters, two roseate women in brightly woven shawls performed slow actions of selling and display. Rocky Ashton, with far less hair, but unmistakably, muscularly, himself, was working at the new gas station. Edgar watched him rolling a tyre across the forecourt, then went back along Route 5 and into the Campanile Family Restaurant, which was as long-lasting and insubstantial as ever.

Apart from two sleek men in blue suits, Edgar was the only customer. He waited at the Please Wait To Be Seated sign and a young dark woman, showing only a tiny smack of distaste, hid him at the smallest corner table.

She told him the specials, but Edgar could order here without looking at the menu. 'I'll take a pizza, margarita, extra large, please.'

Something happened in her eyes when she heard him speak. 'Are you waiting for the rest of your party?'

'Uh. It's just me thanks. And a beer.'

'Heineken Grolsch Bud.'

'Whichever. I don't mind. Heineken.'

The waitress's skin was yellow-brown, there were dark hairs criss-crossing her arms; she was pretty, in a sturdy, overworked way, but what he remembered best about Electa was her pride and this waitress didn't seem especially proud.

He had been expecting the arrival of his order to be an ironical jeer at history, but the sheer gooey expanse of the stuff was an unironical jeer at him.

'Good luck with it. The beer's on the house.'

So would the food have to be. It was unmistakably her. She leaned against a column and watched him pull away the first slice of pizza. Did he have to eat it? Wasn't the gesture of sitting here with it enough? But this was a task that could be achieved or at least grimly attempted.

Electa came by to refresh his beer glass. 'The years haven't done you any favours,' she said.

'I guess not,' Edgar said, through a mouthful of warm sludge that was even more horrible than he'd remembered. 'How are you?'

'Just terrific. Couldn't be better. This is all I ever wanted from life. How long are you here for?'

'A few days. I don't know. Maybe longer. There's some things I want to find out.'

'That's right, the boy detective.'

'Do you want—? Maybe we could go out some time?'

'The movie-house? Sure. There's a film I want to miss there.'

She still bore him the grudge and that was reassuring too. He laughed, she winced.

'Jeez. What happened to you?'

She went back to her station, where she filled wicker baskets with bread rolls and watched him eat.

Together they examined the messy disgrace of his pizza.

'One day I'll finish one,' Edgar vowed.

'More to the point is how you're going to pay for this one. That's eighteen dollars you owe me.'

'Prices have gone up.'

'They don't usually go down.'

'I could pay it off by working. How about I do the washing-up?'

'Got a machine does that.'

'I could work the bar?'

'Excuse me but you don't really have the look that will encourage our many customers to the bar.'

The two sleek men had left. Edgar was the only so-called customer left.

'I know where I can get some money. I'll take you for a drive and we can go there. If you're not too busy. Would you like to come for a drive with me?'

'Not really, no,' she said, but went with him to the station-wagon anyway.

'Hey, nice wheels,' Electa said scornfully.

Edgar asked if he could borrow some money to pay for gasoline, because he would rather be beholden to Electa than Warren.

'Sure,' Electa said. 'We'll put it on the tab.'

Heading for the new gas station, where the prices were lower, he had to make an abrupt, life-threatening, life-enhancing U-turn across lanes of traffic because Electa twisted the wheel and told him to go to the other one.

'How come—' Edgar began, and then corrected himself, she always liked him best as a courtly Englishman. 'Why are the prices so low at the new petrol station?'

She flickered an amusement, then remembered to look severe. 'It's Onyataka. They don't have to pay taxes. It's the same with the cigarettes and the property they own.'

'Then why didn't we go there?'

'Not everyone thinks it's right. It's kind of a principle. Concerns like ours, we've got to pay property taxes every year, we support one another.'

He half filled the tank and Electa went in to pay. He thought that was Doug Ashton working there, sitting with his feet up on the desk, gazing as if in hope at the ceiling.

They waited at the crossroads of Prindle and Main for one of the new Indian police jeeps to make its turn in front of them. The driver waved amiably to Electa. She didn't trouble herself to respond.

'Where are we going anyway? And who's this?' Electa says, pointing to the photograph Scotch-taped to the glove compartment.

'I'm not sure,' Edgar said.

'There's an address on the back.'

'I know.'

Electa jabbed on the radio. It was tuned to a golden-oldies station, which was playing a song that she claimed to like. It didn't have the courage to finish. The song faded out, as Edgar knew it would.

6

Edgar's father's girlfriend used to play piano in the bar of the casino hotel. The customers were usually too sad or boisterous or drunk to listen to what Crystal was playing so she'd get drunk too, sit with a glass and a cigarette at the table of whichever drinker she could find some sympathy with. She had recently been fired for this practice.

'She used to tell these great stories,' said Edgar's father.

'You never listened when I was telling them, sweetheart.'

'Now she just drinks. She doesn't play the piano any more. She doesn't have any great stories.'

'Fuck you too, darling.'

Edgar liked his father's girlfriend. She had a degree of style. She managed to look good in clothes that were too young and too tight for her. She had been disappointed by life, and by Edgar's father, but then most people were.

Edgar's father had shrunk in the years between. His hair and skin used to be brown. Now they were shades of grey. He still dressed the same way, in whatever an enterprising salesman might wear on his day off. Khaki chinos and a long-sleeved T-shirt, whose sleeves were a different colour from its body, did not suit him.

'I'd like to hear you play,' Electa said.

'Would you? That's sweet of you. Come over to the keyboard. Let's leave the gentlemen to have some quality time.'

Edgar's father's girlfriend carried her beer and ashtray over to the piano. She gave Edgar a wink as she hit the first note. She played softly, a slow, rolling rhythm, murmuring words on top like sleepily buttered toast.

'She's good,' Edgar said to his father.

'Yeah. Terrific. Carnegie Hall keeps calling, you wouldn't believe how much the telephone rings.'

'"*I done got over . . . You at last.*" You gentlemen having some quality time over there?'

Electa, with a cigarette inexpertly in the centre of her mouth, turned over the sheet music for Crystal. Edgar and his father sat far away from each other on the sofa. Edgar's father fiddled with the nearest objects to hand. His girlfriend's apartment contained many things. She seemed to be an indiscriminate collector of anything that could be described as cute. Edgar drummed his hands on the silvery face of a cat overlaid on a red satin cushion.

His father made the effort to wrench himself into becoming agreeable. 'So how is everybody? Your mother good?'

'Yes. She's good,' Edgar said.

'And what's his name? Jeff?'

'It's Martin now. Jeffrey was the one before.'

'That's right. Martin. How's Martin?'

'I don't really see them much.'

In truth, Edgar didn't see them at all. He couldn't face the prospect of his mother's disappointment; this at least was something he shared with his father.

'So. What are your plans? What's the deal here?'

'Tell me something.'

'Tell you what?'

'I don't mind. Anything. Tell me about my grandfather.'

'Mac? What do you want to know about Mac?'

'I don't know. Anything.'

Edgar's father did his best to look wistful. 'Mac was elsewhere. He was the straying kind. He had these girlfriends and he was always kind of AWOL so far as the family were concerned. Did a good job at the Company, though. They thought a lot of him at the Company. Which was why I was never going to join it. I made my decisions early on. The secret of life seemed to me to get laid as much as I could and work as little as possible. I've kind of stuck to that.'

'So you're half a Mac.'

The intimacy was gone. The gentlemen had stopped enjoying their quality time.

'So what does that make you?'

It was a good question. The Perfectionists had bred for holiness, sometimes between cousins, sometimes uncle and niece, in the interests of propagating saints, and he was the culmination.

'When someone's damaged, they lose a foot say, are they still the same person? I don't think they are. What do you think?'

'I don't know what the fuck you're talking about.'

'It's like the question about the wooden ship. If you replace all the planks is it still the same ship? The thing it does, of course, is presuppose some essence of identity that is separate from the physical. I can't go along with this, can you?'

'I'll tell you one thing,' his father said. 'Stay away from magnets.'

Edgar was annoyed to find himself touching the iron piercing above his left eyebrow. In retaliation, he asked his father to lend him some money.

'He's a deep kid,' Edgar's father called over to his girlfriend. 'You want money? Things are a little tight right now but I'm sure I could rustle something up.'

The transaction was a good one. Edgar's father could spare him sixty dollars, which made him feel good about himself as a father, and bought him renewed credit in his girlfriend's eyes. Electa was paid, Edgar had money in his pocket, and they drove, in small triumph, to Onyataka Depot where Warren's new woman lived.

She kept them company for the journey, smiling blurry eyes beneath owl-framed spectacles.

'Is this what you came back for?'

'I guess so. And to see my father.'

'Do you think he'll come to the Blackberry Festival?'

'Doubt it. But I came back, also . . .'

'Also what?'

A better father would have given him advice about what to do in this situation; one of the alternative Edgars, a better one, would know how to woo Electa, eradicate the distance between them with a kiss.

'Where does wind come from?' he asked.

'I've always wondered that. I guess it's kind of an atmospheric thing. Let me know when you find out. But I'll tell you something. You know what you should do?'

'What?' he asked, in gratitude.

'Keep your eyes on the road. You're not the most confident driver I've ever encountered.'

7

How do you warn someone of their approaching, encroaching death? It had been hard enough to make the journey, that effort had required all of his energies and tact, steeling his courage to pass big eighteen-wheeler trucks, negotiating the arcana of toll-booths and turnpike exits, and Edgar had just trusted to his future self to be more adroit than any of his previous ones. He stood, still sweating from the exertions of the drive, by the rose-twined porch of a house that was larger than it appeared in the photograph, on a pleasant avenue in Ephrata. He looked to Electa for assurance, but she had taken refuge from his driving in sleep. Hair had fallen in front of her face. Her head rested in the crook of window and headrest. The sun-visor was pulled down, her feet in sneakers pointed away from each other.

This was not quite as affluent a neighbourhood as Vail. The houses stood closer together, on their own little rises, with American flags fluttering in the breeze. Edgar has no plan of approach, he has no idea what he is going to say. He looks at the birdbath on the lawn. He knocks on the door. He trusts, uncertainly, to his ability to improvise when the conversation begins.

The woman from the photograph, their companion on the journey, stood behind a half-opened door. She lifted owl-rimmed spectacles, which hung from a chain around her fragile neck, to peer at him through cloudy blue eyes. 'Can I help you?'

'Well, really no. It's how I can help you.'

The door closed somewhat further.

'I'm not selling anything.'

The door was about to close.

'I'm a friend of Warren's.'

The door opened again a little.

'Warren's not here.'

For a moment Edgar saw himself as she saw him and he shared her distrust and fear. He should be above designing an appearance to frighten old ladies with.

'Can I come in?' Edgar composed his face into a smile and she backed further away. 'I'm a friend of Warren's. I've got something very important to talk to you about. My name's Edgar.'

Again, the alluvial magic of his resurrected name. 'I know that name,' she said, as if she didn't know many. 'Are you the boy from Vail? The grandson?'

'Fay's grandson. Edgar,' he said, and she let him in.

Her name was Hester and she lived in a very pretty house that showed Warrenish touches. They sat in the kitchen and drank weak bitter tea from a cracked service that Edgar suspected was Onyataka plate.

'Warren's on his way back,' Hester said. 'I'm sorry the tea's so wretched. I'm hopeless without him.'

'How long has he been with you?'

'I couldn't say.' Hester's smile was without apology or guile.

'When do you think he'll be back?'

Hester didn't answer that one, but poured Edgar more tea with a confidently shaking hand. 'Your appearance is very original,' she said.

'Thank you. How long have you lived here?'

She gave him the same pleasant smile that registered total lack of comprehension.

'Do you like John Mills?'

'I'm not sure I know him. Is he another of Warren's friends?'

'Not really, no.

'Your clock's stopped,' he said, desperate to produce a conversational fact that they can agree on.

She looked at the grandfather clock by the wall. 'Has it? I think I knew that,' she said agreeably.

Edgar had the disagreeable sensation that they could sit here for ever, taking it in turns to make pleasantries that the other doesn't quite understand. Perhaps they already have. Perhaps this was his fate, for perpetuity, his punishment.

He started again. He asked her questions from which he tried to eliminate the content of time, but it kept flooding in through his words.

'You have family but you don't see them very often,' Edgar said.

'They're very busy,' Hester agreed.

'You don't know where you'd be if Warren hadn't come along.'

'Oh I do. I know that perfectly well. I'd have been in a nursing-home.'

'And you'd have had to sell the house to pay for it.'

'I like my house,' Hester said.

'It's a very nice house,' Edgar said.

'Warren says it's the prettiest house he's ever known.'

'I can understand that. You have an arrangement.'

'Yes we do. That's right,' she said, proudly.

He's got it now, he understood, he swallowed with a horrified gulp, what Warren did. Edgar was here, alone with Warren's latest 'friend', whom he tried, passionately and incoherently, to warn. She interrupted. 'Warren's very good at what he does,' she said. 'He's very tidy and he cleans up after himself.'

'Of course he is! He's done it before. I don't know how many times!'

'Well then he knows what he's doing and he won't bungle anything. Would you like some more tea? Or a bath maybe?'

Edgar always forgot that he smelled kind of grungy. Warren hadn't been entirely able to hide his shock at his appearance, and scent. Edgar had thought it an operation of guilt when it was just concern, and disappointment. Here he has been sucked into a world where time does not exist. Like Mary Pagan, or Fay towards the end, this woman lives in a perpetual now. The past is finished. The future is comfortably taken care of.

'I think I better go.'

'Aren't you going to wait for Warren?'

'Thank you for the tea. I should get back.'

Edgar stood forlorn by the station-wagon, realizing he'd left his keys in the house, dreading to go back in. But he was an adult now and adults do not shirk any challenges, even the greatest. He knocked again on Warren's new house. The door opened a fraction.

'Can I help you?'

'I left my keys behind.'

She stared at him, prettily and blankly.

'It's Edgar,' he said.

'Who?'

'Edgar. Warren's friend.'

'Oh, you must be the boy from Vail. The grandson.'

'That's right. Fay's grandson. Edgar.'

'Warren's not here at the moment. Why don't you come in and wait for him? I'll make some tea.'

Edgar wondered if there was any way out of this except through violence. He sat again at Hester's kitchen table and told her her clock had stopped and she told him that she thought she knew that. They drank tea and took turns to say things that did not meet or match, and when he picked up the keys and told her he had to go she showed no sign of disappointment or even interest. The tea had performed terrible things to his bladder but he couldn't bear to stay in the house any longer without the consolation of time. He went to the station-wagon and urinated behind it, his piss sizzling in the uncomprehending heat. He zipped himself up and gazed at Electa until he could bear it no longer, and kissed her.

Sleepily she opened her eyes.

'Those piercings of yours, they kind of tickle.'

He took that as an invitation to kiss her again.

That night Edgar dreamed of Mary Pagan, and when he awoke he wondered if that was a sign of wonder. Mary was naked below the waist and she carried her skirt and pantalets neatly folded across her outstretched arm. She sang the old song that had been one of his mother's favourites, played most often in her intervals between boyfriends, *We are fam-ileee! I got all my sisters and me*, and her features blurred first into Mon's and then quickly, as if Edgar the dreamer had become abashed by his dream, into Marilou Weathers's, the protuberant eyes, the dizzy caffeine smile, and Mary's white blouse turned into Marilou's knitted sweater with the goofy face of a dog embroidered on it, tongue lapping down, which then became a waitress's outfit, and the face finally settled into Electa's, which was, as he opened his eyes, beside him, miraculous.

8

On the day of the Blackberry Festival Mary Pagan drowned. On the day of the Blackberry Festival Edgar brushed his grandmother's hair. On the day of the Blackberry Festival Edgar dressed himself in Association clothes from the display in the Music Room. He doubted they were original, probably all left over from Warren's opera ten years before, when Guthrie had helped to dress the cast for Utopia, taking the pins out of her mouth whenever she had to cough. Edgar wore the boots he had travelled in; paint-spattered and worn, they fitted in with the baggy trousers and heavy frock coat and cravat and hat. He went back into the sun-porch to pull the covers over Electa's shoulders. Electa sleeping smelled of cloves.

Edgar, bred for holiness, sweating, funereal, hands clasped, walked through Creek and Vail. It had rained in the night. The morning sun burned off moisture on the lawns, raindrops from parasols and bicycles, and from the trestle tables that had been laid out on the south lawn of the Mansion House.

Could he live in this town? He doubted it. He had come to make an end of what had happened here, not a beginning. Edgar, hat atilt, sat by the creek and threw stones into the water.

The Campanile was catering the Blackberry Festival. Electa and her brother and a few straggly volunteers piled food on the trestle tables. Pizzas cooled, untouched, in the sun.

387

The Mansion House bought most of its blackberries from the supermarket but it still produced its own small harvest, which were in bowls on the top table, which was where most of the Festival attendants were sitting, with places for the patrons' committee, the museum director and his partner, and Edgar himself, who represents the unbroken line of descent from John Prindle Stone and Mary Pagan.

'One day your kids will be sitting here,' Guthrie said.

Edgar thought he recognized Marilou Weathers, giddy and become beautiful, sitting with a couple of other women at the faculty table. Company Bob sat by himself, his face flushed by liquor and sun.

'I doubt it,' Edgar said. He could not imagine ever siring children, and he had as little faith in the continuity of this tradition as the reassuringly surly museum director—who was serving out his time in this backwater, and already the better jobs were becoming elusive: he'd applied to Washington and New York, and been turned down, and there comes a time when you've been in a place too long, when no one even considers you for preferment any more.

'There was a time,' Guthrie said, 'when this would all have been full. I think people should realize that. And be . . .'

'Grateful?' said the museum director's partner.

'Well not grateful exactly, but you know what I mean. This whole place is because of the Association, and the Company.'

'Was, you mean,' corrected the museum director.

'No. I don't think I do,' Guthrie said, coughing gracefully, which attracted the attention of Warren, bringing through jugs of lemonade.

Edgar went to join Company Bob.

'Call me just plain Bob, 's what everyone else calls me.'

Just Plain Bob was drinking beer. He had a cooler bag at his feet, and a tower of empty cans on the table in front of him.

'You're not at the Company any more.'

'No one's at the Company any more. Company's not the Company any more. Crying shame. Built this town and look what happened.'

'What happened?'

'Company went belly-up. But I was let go before that. That's what they called it, letting go. We got to let you go. We're letting a few people go, Bob. We have to let you go, Bob. We've let Bob go. Bob? Oh, we let him go. Well Bob ain't going nowhere. Bob stays right here.'

'Good for you,' Edgar said.

'And how large do you think my pension is?'

'I couldn't say.'

'Company town, Company man, Company Bob, gave the best years of my life and what's my reward?'

'I don't know, Company Bob.'

'Just plain Bob.'

'I don't know, Just Plain Bob.'

'Well I'll tell you. Zilch. *Nada.* That's how much. Company folded and the pension fund was empty. Directors'd been dipping into it for years trying to keep things afloat. What do you think of that?'

'I'm sorry to hear it.'

'Don't be. I'll tell you something really choice. There's a few of us just plain types who are fighting that. We're taking the Company through the courts.'

'But the Company doesn't exist any more.'

'You'd think so. But for legal purposes it does, just because of us. Company dead, town dying, and it's our efforts that are keeping the past alive. So long as we fight our case the Company still exists. I'm very proud of that. Hey. Who you come as? I didn't realize it was fancy dress.'

'Maybe we should sit with the others? There's room.'

'Don't mind me. I got drinking to do.'

There were few other tables with any Festival guests. Marilou Weathers sat with faculty wives (*The Blackberry Festival Welcomes the Educators of Creek and Vail!*). The Blackberry Festival also welcomed its restaurateurs, which meant the staff of the Campanile and the Silver City Diner. The other tables were empty, including the one that *Welcomes Its Onyataka Friends!* Edgar went back to the dignitaries.

'I thought my father might be here,' he said to Guthrie.

'He's probably at the casino. Most everybody is.'

'The Onyatakas don't seem to be coming,' the museum director said.

'The casino's having its own festival. Reclaiming the past, so they say.'

'It's a fair deal,' the museum director's partner said. 'We stole their land and gave them smallpox and alcohol. They're selling retribution back to us with gambling and cheap cigarettes and gasoline.'

'You know, it's really horrible to say this, but I liked them better when they were poor,' Guthrie said.

Warren unnecessarily smoothed down his hair and sat beside Edgar. 'So? Do you want the house?' And then, as if to forestall Edgar's objection, Warren said, 'It's not a gift. It's not me who's giving it to you. It's Fay. It's what she wanted.'

'I thought you loved this house.'

'I do love this house. Which is why I want it to go to somebody who appreciates it as much as I do.'

'But . . .'

'It's what she wanted.'

'I'm sorry. I still don't understand why you want to leave.'

'It's not a question of *want to*. I'm needed elsewhere. And there are all kinds of little wars being fought around here. Land claims and legal battles with the Onyatakas over who owns what. I haven't got the energy for all that.'

'Who is it that needs you?'

'A couple of friends.'

Edgar was expecting this. He had met Hester, but he had suspected there were others. Another graceful, elegant lady, whose family had lost interest in her decline, and who lived in a desirable house. How, he wondered, did Warren find these *friends*? Does he advertise? Do they? Or was it all word-of-mouth, *I have to tell you, Marjorie/Fay/Hester, I've found the best man at this kind of thing, the most wonderful man, he's very tidy and he cleans up after himself. I simply have to pass him on to you. After I'm gone, of course . . .*

'If I could find a reliable lodger then I would. But this town is changing. It's not like it used to be. You remember when I did that opera?'

This isn't what he has come for, to reminisce about old times with Warren.

'There was a lot of opposition to the opera, you may have noticed. But Fay supported me throughout. It was an awful endeavour I suppose, but at least it stirred things up. Fay liked that. She had that Stonian thing about her.'

'And what do I have of the Stonian thing?' Edgar couldn't stop himself asking.

'Does it matter? I hope that whole breeding-for-holiness business that got Jerome so exercised hasn't gone to your head. You know what breeding for holiness meant? It meant that only the ones John Prindle decreed were the most holy were permitted to breed, and by definition holiness meant following John Prindle most assiduously. The guy was a despot. It was a decent sort of despotism and people's lives were enriched and all, but despotism was what it was. Anyone looking for a despot can always find one. Decency might be rarer but that's not the point.'

'You still haven't answered my question.'

'Which one?'

Edgar tried another. 'You never told me how you met Fay.'

'Didn't I? We had a mutual friend. A doctor.'

'Doctor X?'

'That's right. How do you know about that? It's a silly name, isn't it?'

'It's a sinister one.'

'I guess so. That's sort of the joke of it. We used to go out with each other. He was my ex, so that's what we used to call him.'

'And did he . . .'

'Did he what?'

'I don't know. Did he know, what, your arrangement would be?'

'Roughly I suppose he did. He knew that Fay required daily care and that there was no one else who could or would provide it. If I hadn't come along, she'd have had to sell the house back then, use the money to pay for a nursing-home. It's what old people do these days.'

'But—'

'Look. Fay didn't want to move. I'm good at looking after old people. I *like* looking after old people. Fay wanted to stay in the house for as long as she lived, and you know the arrangement we had. I didn't get any pay, it was all deferred, to the value of the house. After I'd worked here for two and a half years, I would get the house when she died. There was nothing sinister about it.'

'But it was assisted! That's the point! The arrangement I can understand, but you got greedy didn't you Warren? You had to help her on her way.'

'I'm not a murderer, Eddie. Is that what you think I am? I don't just *kill* people. That's not what I do. Hired killer. I'm offended, Eddie. *Edgar.* Really offended.'

Despite his indignation, Warren was still the generous host, except everything is suspicious now: the pizza slices he tried to pass to the museum director, the dollops of cream he

offered for Guthrie's blackberries, the beer he brought out
from the Mansion House kitchen—his back turned when he
was pouring it, so any number of sinister ingredients might
have been added between can and glass—the knife that could
have been smeared with odourless poison, even the water
jug that sat on the trestle table, refracting the same sunshine
that the Perfectionists must have loved, a light film of dust
on the surface, or maybe what passes for dust . . .

Coach Spiro and a pair of Down's syndrome twins in
shorts and T-shirts stumbled past between the lawn and the
golf course. Warren initiated a conversation between Guthrie
and the museum director and his boyfriend so he could
continue with Edgar unattended.

Warren said, 'There are a couple of points here. Number
one, there's a lot of old people who don't want to carry on
living when their quality of life gets poor. You'll find some
doctors are sympathetic to this, some not. One will intervene
if the client catches pneumonia, another will not, just stand
back from it. It was a disease that used to be called the old
person's friend.'

'But this is nothing like that. Fay didn't have pneumonia.'

'Put it this way then. I know there's doctors who will give
the patient an extra dose of morphine to help her on her
way, there's others that won't. What would you do? Say
you're a doctor and your patient is in awful pain, there's not
long to go, the dying lady wants this over, the family is
desperate for the loved one's suffering to come to an end. If
you were a doctor, would you withhold it? I don't think you
would. Not if all hope had gone. I think you're too kind not
to.'

Edgar brushed aside the flattery. 'It's not that simple.'

'Isn't it?'

'It can't be. Not if the doctor's going to be rewarded when
the patient dies.'

'I know there are people who see it like that. I didn't think you would. I'm not a saint. I like doing what I do, my life is very congenial, but I couldn't do it unless I was being paid.'

'How many houses do you own?' Edgar asked.

'I have six.'

One for each framed photograph on the mantelpiece. For a moment Edgar was silent. He hadn't been expecting Warren to answer so simply.

'Look. I understand what you've been saying. The theory of it makes sense. But let's talk about the real thing. Fay wasn't ready to go yet.'

'That's debatable.'

'Exactly. That's my point. It's debatable. You can't know for certain. Maybe she was feeling awful one day, maybe she was feeling like she wanted it over the day she died, but what if she had improved the next day, found pleasure in things again, was glad to be alive? It would be wrong to deny her that chance.'

'Yes. I can see that.'

'So that's it, isn't it? Your time was reached, your two and a half years or whatever, and—*pop, bang*—she's gone and you've got the house. Don't tell me that the profit motive isn't involved. You can't.'

'I take your point. There may always be doubt. So I make sure that there's as little doubt as possible. If it's time to move on, we can talk about that, but you'd never take matters into your own hands.'

'But that's just what you did! You went ahead and did it. Did you promise Fay she would join her cat and all the saints in the afterlife? She'd get to pick blackberries in heaven with Mary Pagan?'

'The Perfectionists didn't think that Mary Pagan was in heaven. They had her in Hades, which is the next one along.

It was a kind of second martyrdom for her. She had to wait for John Prindle to abolish death on earth before she could move on.'

'How did you do it, Warren? Did Doctor X pass over the morphine?'

'That's not exactly how it happened.'

'Then tell me. How did it happen?'

'I don't think you really want to hear.'

'Of course I want to hear! I've come all this way just to hear it!'

'And what are you going to do with the information when you have it? Have you thought about that?'

The Campanile staff had finished their work. The last pizzas and jugs of lemonade had been served. Electa's brother joined the other restaurateurs. Electa removed her apron and lit a cigarette and sat down at the empty table that had been reserved for the Onyatakas.

'Just tell me, please. How did you kill her?'

'I don't think in this case I'd use the word "kill".' To express the quotation marks around 'kill', Warren crooked his fingers in the air and made a double clicking sound. It was the sort of thing that Jeffrey might have done and Edgar hated him for it.

'Well I would. I'm using it now. How did you [*click click*] "kill" her? Was it morphine?'

'It wasn't morphine. And it wasn't me who killed her, if you have to use that word.'

'Well who did then?'

A very gentle, tender look appeared on Warren's face. It must be the sort of look that his old ladies adore, registering infinite patience, infinite understanding; it's the sort of look that saints and redeemers wear in religious paintings: Christ stands at a crossroads and he gazes upon his onlookers with Warrenish love. John Prindle Stone, in infinite loving wisdom, with Warrenish love, gathers his family for a session of Mutual Criticism in the big hall.

'You did, Edgar.'

Edgar's hands held still in the disturbed air, mid-drum. He wished he could say something beyond *'Whaaat?'*

'I'm sorry,' Warren said.

Slowly, Edgar made his hands lie flat upon the table. He did not have to accept this. The killer blames the victim. The killer blames the witness. The killer blames everyone but himself.

'I don't think so,' Edgar said.

'I'm sorry.'

Edgar laughed to show he was in control of this situation, that he was unfazed by Warren's madness—although if he could make this kind of accusation, then what else might he be capable of? The museum director's boyfriend, startled by Edgar's laugh, tried to find a way into their conversation, but Guthrie ruthlessly pulled him back with her explanation of the concept of good and bad Onyatakas. The bad Onyatakas are the ones who run the casino, who send their children to private schools, who sit on the board of the Onyataka Nation Enterprise, who make money out of the contracts to build the new villages, the extensions to the casino, the ONE schools and ONE hospitals. The bad Onyatakas have law degrees and Italian suits and PR smiles, protected by foreign money and their lackeys in government. The good Onyatakas live in unimproved trailers, they sing traditional hymns and laments. Guthrie liked the good Onyatakas.

Was she next? In the old days she had never allowed Warren into her house, probably worried that he would like it too much. Janice wasn't here. Edgar had assumed that she had let Bob go too, but maybe there was another, darker explanation.

'Go ahead. Tell me how,' Edgar said, hoping he'd found the right tone of sceptical good humour.

'It was her hair.'

'Uh?'

'You brushing her hair.'

'*What?*'

'Fay had this, I don't know, you could call it superstition I suppose, but I'm not sure if that's quite the right word. I've come across this sort of thing before. It's got a little bit of vanity to it and a sense of what is right and proper. I don't know if elderly men have it, I couldn't say, I don't have the experience—but when they're, you know, approaching their end, there's a lot of these ladies they want to look just right. And Fay had this thing about her hair, you know.'

Heart sinking, feeling his face blushing, Edgar mumbled, 'Yes. I know.'

'It wasn't so much to do with God, although that may have been part of it. But she was concerned with how she would look when she was found. There was a solicitation about it, and a propriety. A little vanity too. And she did believe in an afterlife, it was one of the only things we ever argued about.'

'What else did you argue about?'

'Telling the family about our arrangement. I wanted everything to be known and above board. But Fay, I don't know, I think she was trying to give her family a chance to behave differently, she didn't want people to know. I thought that was wrong. Where was I? I've lost my train of thought.'

Edgar shook his head. He wasn't going to help him.

'Oh that's right. She wanted to look her best. When she met Death she wanted Death to see her as she saw herself. Do you understand what I'm saying?'

'I think so,' Edgar said, choking back a bitter, raw taste

in his throat and wondering, pointlessly, if these were the longest speeches he had heard Warren make.

'So when she died it was important that her hair was right, all neatly brushed and combed, the way she liked it. I've seen this with other ladies, with clothes usually, Sunday best. But it got with Fay, this was so important to her, that in some weird way she couldn't die or wouldn't die if her hair wasn't right. Do you follow me?'

Edgar nodded. He wished he wasn't, but he was following.

'So I used to do this thing in the night. I'd go into her room while she was sleeping and mess up her hair. It was just a precaution at first, which developed into a sort of game. I thought at first it was Fay who was waking up to comb her hair, making it all neat again, that she was playing the same game too, but then it began to feel more important than a game. She was making herself more imminent than she needed to be, brushing her hair, brushing it all neat again, which made it possible for her to pass on, as she would say. So I thought it was a game and I was wrong and I thought it was Fay who was doing it and I was wrong, and usually I'd be able to go in later to mess it up again, but that last night, with the opera and everything, I was distracted, I didn't check on her like I usually did. But how were you to know? That's why I wouldn't say "kill". That's why I wouldn't use that word.'

Warren's victory complete, he had the solicitation, as he would call it, not to say anything more. With the same tenderness with which he had been talking, he stacked up the dishes from the table and carried them to the Mansion House kitchen as the rain came.

9

A perpetually smiling Onyataka, who is one of the casino managers, has bought the Pagan House.

Edgar and Electa helped him carry his possessions from where the moving truck had dumped them on the drive. They brought in thrift-store furniture, green plastic sofas with rips in their backs, stacks of tables with chipped wood veneer. They toted boxes of books bought by the yard, laminated posters, smeared with grime and pizza grease, advertising Italian holiday resorts, which used to be on the walls of the Campanile.

'I'll put these boxes down here, shall I?'

'That'll be fine. Thank you very much. I appreciate it.'

'Could you give us a couple of hours? I want to sort through a few things.'

'Of course.'

'You might enjoy a meal at the Mansion House some night,' Edgar said, trying to offer a Warrenish kind of hospitality. 'The food's not very good, but it's got some of the history of the place, and it'll give you a chance to meet your new neighbours.'

'I'm not intending to live here,' the Onyataka said. 'I only bought the house out of spite.'

Still smiling, he gripped Edgar's and then Electa's hand warmly.

McGwire stood on the lawn looking at his new house with his hands in the trouser pockets of his suit. His grandmother had been a maid at this house, or at one like it, his great-aunt Tara used to keep house here. He had grown up nearby, been allowed to work in construction because Indians are famously good at heights, and even if that were true—which he doubted—he was as much Irish or Scottish as Onyataka, but that didn't seem to enter the locals' reckoning: he had been constantly reminded of the Perfectionists' kindness to his people, the jobs they had given, the alms distributed. And *You know, your grandmother used to clean for my mother!* As if that was a good thing, something to bring them together, he born into servitude and they into power.

Jeffrey could argue, and Jeffrey has argued, that 'Pete' Pagan Stone was ahead of his time as well as behind it. Every beat of his housemaid's hand against his reddening quivering rump was a reparation to history. No one believes this, least of all Jeffrey, but the symbol is a powerful one and therefore valid.

10

On Edgar's last day in the Pagan House, Electa helped him to sort through the piles of documents and remnants that Jerome had collected and then abandoned. Warren was gone, back to his friend's house, and Edgar was looking for at least one souvenir that he would take away with him to London.

'What about this?' she asked, holding up a photograph of the Perfectionists enjoying their leisure on the south lawn of the Mansion House. They're playing croquet in straw hats and summer suits. John Prindle Stone stands in profile at the centre of the lawn, holding a mallet ready to address the ball. The other men are looking down at the grass or up at the sky, while all the women are gazing, in passion or hope, at John Prindle Stone.

'Chuck it.'

Everything rejected was going back into Jerome's old archive boxes that Edgar would donate to the Mansion House library. Accounts of séances were there, the Perfectionists' attempts at conference with the immaterial dead; and letters from Mary confessing to doubts and joys; and the record of the breeding programme, almost in its entirety, the carefully tabulated details of the parents' features and faculties, the children's physical and spiritual dispositions.

Dusty from the past, they took a break, sitting on the sun-porch bed that the new owner had consented to keep.

Electa had always been interested in history. He told her about the breeding programme, which the Perfectionists called stirpiculture.

'You know they did this burning in the 1940s. A respectable little group of Company widows decided to redo the past. We found copies of some of what they burned, and Jerome transcribed them. The dowagers didn't mind about the breeding programme. There was no shame in it for them. They liked it, it made them feel special, sort of aristocratic, like pedigree dogs. But what they didn't like was all the sexual stuff. It was a flaw, which they needed to protect John Prindle's memory from, all the fucking, the ascent in fellowship. They even rewrote things so that George Pagan started Complex Marriage, not John Prindle.'

He was telling her this in courtship. John Prindle's sexual energies were his own. He had been bred to them. But she did not take the opportunity to yield to him, to invite him to penetrate her with his spirit. Instead, she told him finally about her history. How her grandparents, tired of social-security food stamps and domestic labour and construction work, had left the reservation and opened the 'Italian' restaurant, and somewhere along the way it was chosen to forget that they were Onyataka.

'Wow,' he said.

'Yeah. Isn't it terrific? We can play Perfectionists and Indians together.'

He is 'Pete' Pagan Stone's descendant, she might be Tara's, and this compels them naught. She does not need to beat him, he does not need to beat her. The secret is not in the soil. That's not what grew them. And the water tap continues to drip.

'You can come to London with me.'

'I can go to a lot of places. I'm just not sure how.'

'You buy a ticket.'

'That's right,' she said. 'That's almost wise, I mean it. But I know one thing, I'm not going anywhere because someone wants me to.'

The Pagan House

'Okay. I don't want you to.'

'Good then. You won't be disappointed.'

By the bed, between the headboard and the wall, Edgar pulls out Fay's last painting, which has been waiting for him, for this unforgetting, ever since she died.

In a blue field, a horse slowly pulls a plough. Except it is not moving, because movement is impossible in a picture. This is what Edgar will take as his memento of Creek and Vail. Out of all of it, this is what endures: Mary Pagan died, George Pagan died, the Association is gone; the Company, except in Bob's court case, is finished; the house is sold; and the spirit of Blind Jess is what sustains.

In a painting, time is abolished. Christ and his disciples stand on a roadside. A horse stands in a field. A ploughman trudges his endless progress. The artist's mother stares in wonder at her son; even there a miracle is in endless progress, the sunset a perpetual slash of red.

Edgar didn't return for the final sessions of the summer school. The last two days went by in the usual delirium of falsely induced hope (most of the students) and the longing to get away (me, and some of the students). He had left a lot of material, or his 'stuff', as he had called it, with me. I had no compunction about using it, although that would come later, but I did about keeping it: much of it was hand- or typewritten and I felt fairly sure that what I had was his only copy.

After reading it and talking with him, I'd become more than interested in his work and—and this seldom necessarily follows—in Edgar. I repackaged it in its padded brown enve-lope and called my family to tell them I'd be late coming home and waited for him in the pub on the corner. I had decided that his Warrenish tact would enable him to under-stand that this would be our meeting-point. It grew dark. The place became full of office workers, then empty of them. The envelope had an address on it, of a street not far away from the college. I went to it.

The house was part of an Edwardian crescent that, in its solemnity and size, was out of keeping with the rest of that part of Waterloo, which is mostly made up of blocks of flats built to replace tenements and houses that had been flat-tened by bombs in the war or by the county council in the 1960s. It was on a terrace that curved around a small private park, an enclave that implied gas-lights, mists, a London that has gone. I walked up the stairs to the front door and rang the bell. There was only one bell but all the same I assumed the building was divided into flats because most buildings of this size are. I pictured Edgar living in the basement or on the ground floor in high-ceilinged, weirdly partitioned, brown-carpeted rooms with his 'friend', whom I hoped was Electa, having made her escape from Creek and Vail to be with him.

An elderly lady answered the door and I realized I'd mispictured the whole thing. Just because someone gives you an envelope with an address on it doesn't mean that he lives at that address.

– I'm sorry, I said. I think I've got the wrong house.

The lady seemed amused by me. She carried herself very still and very straight. She wore a red knitted cardigan over a pale dress and her eyes and voice were very youthful.

– Are you looking for someone? she asked.

– A friend of mine, a sort of friend. He's called Edgar.

– You don't have the wrong house at all. I didn't think you had. Edgar lives here. Won't you come in?

She invited me into what she called the small sitting room, which was an immense room wallpapered in a Liberty pattern and quietly, unobtrusively filled with delicate silver objects. On the wall over the fireplace hung a painting of a ploughman and a horse in a small blue field.

– Edgar isn't here at the moment but you could wait for him? He's with a friend.

This wasn't what I had expected. This was no Electa, she was too old to be Mon. She offered me a drink, which I turned down and not just because I had drunk too many beers while waiting for Edgar at the pub. There was something about this house, about this supremely genteel lady, that made me not want to stay.

– Excuse me. I'm going to have to get back. Perhaps I could leave this here with you? It belongs to Edgar.

I put his envelope on a side-table that had a silver tea service on it that I wondered might be Onyataka plate.

– I'm sorry you have to rush off. I like to take people on a tour of the house.

– It's a very pretty house, I said.

– Edgar says it's the nicest house he's ever seen.

– I can imagine.

And, in that moment, I could imagine much more besides.

– How long has Edgar been with you? I asked.

– Oh quite a few months now. I don't know where I'd be without him.

Except she did know: we both did. She would be in a nursing-home, the house gone. They had an Arrangement: everything about her and the house proclaimed it, the display of silver brushes and combs in the glass and lacquer cabinet by the mantelpiece, his client's wild, untouched hair.

Author's note

Anyone familiar with the history of the Oneida Community, which flourished in Central New York State between the years 1848 and 1881, and its founder John Humphrey Noyes will recognize John Prindle Stone and his Onyataka Association. Some of the language might also be recognizable—I've drawn from letters, essays and journal entries of Noyes, Mary Cragin and George Cragin (the sources for Mary and George Pagan). However, I've bent events, chronology, characters and setting.

The Oneida Community was formed on 160 acres of land in Madison County that had previously been occupied by the Oneida Indians, one of the six tribes of the Iroquois League. The Community followed the charisma and energies of Noyes (1811–1886) along the path of 'Perfectionism' or 'Bible Communism'. This theology decreed that there was no need to wait for Christ's second coming, because that had already happened, in 70 AD, so it was possible to be spiritually reborn without sin, to make heaven on earth. Noyes abolished marriage and private property; he thought he would also abolish death. The Oneida Community was one of the many Christian communities that thrived in that part of New York State known as the 'Burnt-Over District'; nearby were Mormons, Shakers, Spiritualists and Seventh Day Adventists, and many, shorter-lived, others.

Readers who would like to know more about the history of the Oneida Community could usefully start with the volume of documents compiled by George Wallingford

Noyes that is published by the University of Illinois Press as *Free Love in Utopia*. Maren Lockwood Carden's *Oneida: Utopian Community to Modern Corporation* is the definitive account of the transition from Utopia to capitalism, but, as it was published in 1969, it is happily ignorant of the decline of Oneida Ltd in recent years.

The song 'Jeannette and Jeannot' was written by Charles Jefferys, with music by Charles Williams Glover.

There are many people and institutions who have helped me along the way of writing this book, especially my family, Susan, Julius and Grace; my most sympathetic and patient agents, Felicity Rubinstein and Sarah Lutyens; my editor, Nicholas Pearson; Matthew Gibson; Glen-in-the-kitchen for his reading skills; the University of East Anglia for a writing fellowship that bought me valuable time; and the Authors' Foundation for a bursary that enabled me to carry out some of the necessary research. But I would like to thank above all Nini, Lang and Joe Hatcher for their generosity and hospitality, which I've poorly repaid with my version of their town's history.